Flowers by Moonlight

LYNN BAILEY

JOVE BOOKS, NEW YORK

MAGICAL LOVE is a trademark of Berkley Publishing Corporation.

FLOWERS BY MOONLIGHT

A Jove Book / published by arrangement with
the author

PRINTING HISTORY
Jove edition / February 1999

The Penguin Putnam Inc. World Wide Web site address is
http://www.penguinputnam.com

ISBN: 0-515-12448-6

A JOVE BOOK®
Jove Books are published by The Berkley Publishing Group,
a member of Penguin Putnam Inc.,
375 Hudson Street, New York, New York 10014.
JOVE and the "J" design
are trademarks belonging to Jove Publications, Inc.

PRINTED IN THE UNITED STATES OF AMERICA

10 9 8 7 6 5 4 3 2 1

Flowers by Moonlight

One

~

"I have already written to the monastery at Closebeck. The abbot there is an old friend. I'm sure he'll find a place for you." The Lord of Hamdry laid his hand over his son's. Conn flinched, surprised by the touch of his father's hot and dry hand.

"A monastery? Do you expect me to wall myself up alive?" he demanded with a bitter laugh.

They'd been arguing for what seemed hours, Conn refusing to listen to any of his father's reasoned grounds for passing over his eldest son in favor of the younger. He knew that all around him the ears of lackeys and liegemen pricked as they found excuses to pass through the great hall. He acknowledged that they had a right to listen. It was their future as well as his own that would be decided here.

"I don't expect you to become a monk, unless you decide it's best. But there you can perhaps be of some use. Here . . ."

For the thousandth time, Conn declared, "I will never give up my rights to Hamdry, Father. Never."

For the first time, Lord Robert allowed his frustration to show. "If you are wise, you'll go willingly, but if not . . . I can write to the empress to ask *her* to attaint you. She'd do it fast enough. A knight of King Stephen is no friend to her.''

"That—that would be treason. Writing to that woman for a favor . . . We've always stood for the king!'' Conn put his hand to his throbbing left temple, his fingers trembling at the memory of all he'd sacrificed for the king.

Robert stated the cold facts in a hard voice. "The king's imprisoned. They'll never let him out. Matilda's queen now. And you are nothing to her. I, however, am not without influence.''

If he had not been blind already, his anger would have darkened his eyes. Conn broke from his father's clasp, afraid that in another moment his rage would overwhelm him and he'd strike wildly at that stubborn old man.

His stumbling run brought him only to a crashing fall against the cold stone floor of the great hall. He lay there a moment, the meaningless black of his vision as bitter as when he'd first realized his sightlessness.

With a wordless cry of fury, he beat aside the kindly hands that would have raised him up. The sound echoed back from the bare walls, except from on the right. That way lay the open door and freedom. Conn scrambled to his feet and ran for it. He crashed his shoulder into the stone jamb, numbing his arm, but he fell over the threshold into the open air.

His great horse, Arundel, whickered at the sight of him. Following the sound, Conn, his heart beating so wildly that it hurt in his chest, fumbled for the stirrup. Easily, he rose to swing his leg over the broad back. Not even in four months had his years of training failed. Whatever else he had lost, he would always keep the bearing of a knight; he'd sworn it to every saint in heaven.

Conn heard his father call his name, a note of pleading breaking in his voice. Savagely, Conn ripped the reins from the hands of his servant. Today of all days, he'd see himself damned before he'd be led like a woman before his father's eyes. Clapping his heels down, he gave a sharp command. "On, boy. Get on!''

The huge horse, his muscles all the more eager for the

dreary days behind them, leaped forward. Conn heard Gandy's curse as the servant leaped back to avoid being run down. Arundel charged for the open portcullis in the manor wall as he once thundered down the list, his master's lance at the ready.

Conn dropped the reins and rose in his curved saddle, laughing madly as the clean wind blew through him. He heard the hollow booms as Arundel pounded over the moat bridge and smelled the dust rising when they reached the track. The voices calling his name were fainter than crying birds, soon lost behind him as the horse bore him into the woods. He paid no heed to the branches that thrashed his face and body. It was too glorious to be riding free again to mind the pain. At least this was a clean, understandable pain. Not the slow, dark agony of betrayal.

Wrenching his mind away from the memory of his father's threat, Conn urged his destrier on to still greater speed. They would come to look for him; he'd already learned that. Then again, there'd be maudlin kindness and mawkish pity—the taste of which made him long for the sharp bite of mockery.

In a few moments, he came upon a fork in the road: To the left, the estate of his father's oldest friend, Walter de Burke; to the right, a long road that led, sooner or later, to the sea. But there was a third way, screened by trees, straight between the two. It led to the high moor, fertile lands lying at peaceful ease under a vast sky. Up there, where all seemed as open as an honest face but where a misstep meant death in the sucking green mire, he'd find his own peace.

Ever since early boyhood first taught him grief, he'd found his way there when his burdens grew too heavy. He knew every hillock, every trickling rill, learning them in all weathers, by day and by night. For this journey, he didn't need the sight he'd lost. The relentless yearning to *see*, which tormented him, died for a moment. Conn had no hope that it would not soon return, all the stronger for a respite.

When he reached the end of the woods, the sun beat

down like a blacksmith's hammer on the back of his head. Silence lay over all, except for the panting breaths of horse and man. "Not much farther," Conn said, visualizing the dun-colored ears twitching back to catch his voice. "We'll have a good rest soon."

Those of Norman blood feared the moor, disliking the barrenness that made it an ill place for defense. It seemed treacherous to them, and so it was to all who did not love it. Being only half Norman, Conn was not afraid. The tumbled black stones that created rings around the tops of naked hillsides told him that his mother's ancestors had found this an unfriendly land too, but they had made it their own.

In truth, nothing could be less barren. In every corner, birdsong and bee hum rose, busy with the gathering of foodstuffs to feed their hatchlings. Briar rose and bramble, nameless flowers and those found in every herbal, filled the dancing air with intoxicating scent. When a breeze brought a whiff of corruption, he drew back on the reins, shocked by the remembrance of that nightmare amid so much that was lovely.

Slowly, Conn dismounted. The ground felt soft beneath his booted feet, but it was the softness of spring rain, not the boggy deep of the mire. Sniffing the foul sweetness of decay, Conn led the horse, pausing often to catch a whispered sound or a change in the breeze.

Judging by the heat, the sun stood at noon. Conn knew that even if he removed the bandage from his eyes, he would never again see so much as a red glow through his lids. Not the hottest sun nor the brightest light would ever mean anything to him again. Yet he left the bandage in place. So long as he didn't remove it, hope could still be his plaything. Besides, the sight of his blank eyes and fiery scar troubled people. He could still hear the scream of a young maidservant when she'd entered his rooms unannounced.

Busy with his thoughts, Conn tripped over a hummock, falling to his hands and knees. He hadn't time to utter a curse. His hand slipped into sticky ooze that reeked to heaven the instant its surface was disturbed. Instinctively, Conn drew back, his throat closing against the gagging vileness.

An easy matter, some would say, to forget pain and sorrow in the warm clasp of a bog. Men had been swallowed alive here before, countless sheep and cows, and mercy knew how many smaller creatures. The old men said such places were bottomless, and the bodies never came up, falling through all eternity.

Conn felt around for a pebble and found a stick. He slung it into the mire and heard a slurp like a dog devouring meat. His memories told him that it would look like a green velvet cloak laid on the ground, so smooth and thick. The sunlight would glitter and gleam on its surface, dazzling and fascinating the eyes. Easy indeed, to slip into its deadly embrace. Two steps would do it. Then his father would be free to do what he liked with Hamdry. Ross would make a good lord, kinder than his brother, less the soldier but perhaps the better man.

Behind him, Arundel munched unconcernedly on sweet, lank grass.

Conn made a sudden decision and stood up. Hands outstretched, he started toward his horse. When his fingertips brushed the coarse hair, he fumbled for the stirrup. He paused after he gathered up the reins. "I've never done the easy thing," he said aloud. "I won't make it easy for them."

Hours later, worn out from the strain of senses constantly on the prick, Conn put his back against one of the rough-hewn black stones that lay like a crumbled crown around the top of Beldry Tor. Warmed by untold days of sun, the heat seeped into his bones. The valleys of the moor were soft and alive; the hillsides were scoured to the bare rock by the wind that always blew.

Easing the hilt of his dagger so it did not dig into his side, Conn felt at ease for the first time since he'd come home at the end of a winter that had held only defeat. He sighed, feeling the clenched muscles of his body relax along with the tightness around his brow. He slept, slip-

ping from a world of darkness into a world of remembered
sight.

"Oh, come on!" Sira called to the others. "It'll be moon-
rise before we're ready!"

She tried out a few steps of the dance, her arms above
her head, the loose sleeves of her gown fluttering. Crystal
and stone bracelets sparkled and rang on her bare arms,
from wrist to elbow, while the rings on her fingers glittered
in the twilight like the first emerging stars. She broke off
to call again, "Oh, hurry!"

Sira felt her father's smile and turned to him, her hands
held out. "Tell them to hurry, Father. I want everything
perfect before the moon rises."

"Calm yourself, my daughter. One would think this
your first festival."

"Every festival is the first, judging by the way I feel!"
She took his hands and tried to make him dance with her.
When he only gave her the support of his outstretched
arms, she broke away and danced in light, gliding steps
around a circle all her own. Stopping with an exclamation
of impatience, she chose a braided strand of her hair at
random and swiftly wrapped all the rest around with it,
restraining the floating fair cloud.

"That's better."

Changing her mind, she gave up dancing to investigate
the long tables loaded with the evening's refreshments.
Taking a sweet from this table, a morsel of fruit from another, she tossed compliments to the gaily dressed men and
women who worked there. One offered her a foaming
wooden mug, and she drank down the sweet ale. "Deli-
cious, Buskin. Your best yet!"

" 'Twas brewed on your last birthday, lady," the brewer
replied. "In your honor."

"Save me a barrel. Such a brew would get even my
lady Anat drunk enough to look the other way!"

No sooner had Sira incautiously spoken the name when
her nurse appeared. The Wyrcan brewer found business at
the other end of the table. The owner of the only perma-

nently frowning face Sira had ever seen, Anat seemed to have come into the world both suspicious and censorious. "Here you are, and just look at your feet! Filthy already. Where have you left your slippers?"

"I can't dance in shoes, so I took them off. Somewhere . . ." Sira glanced around, half-expecting to find them under her gaze. "Oh, somewhere around."

"And if they're not found when the festival is over— hmmm? Suppose someone finds them who isn't supposed to find them?"

"Anat, you worry too much. They'll be found. Nothing is ever left behind. You know how careful the king is."

"More than can be said for his daughter. We'll just go look for them."

"But Anat—the moon."

"The moon will have to wait. Go."

Sira patted each of the worn black stones as she went widdershins around the circle. When the pipers started up with a few preliminary tweets and twirls, Anat glanced in their direction. No other music appealed to her so much, not even the gliding harp. Taking advantage of her nurse-maid's distraction, Sira slipped off between two stones and scurried along out of Anat's line of sight.

She stopped to catch a breath, stifling a giggle. Humming along with the half-begun tune, she danced a few steps within the circle of stone. She could see for miles here. The sky glowed to the west with the hidden sun's last rays as the blue mantle of the twilight spread out from the east. The first stars spangled as Sira's blood quickened with the excitement of the spring festival, Beltane, the first of May.

"Sira!" Anat sounded peeved, to say the least.

Casting up the hood of her dark blue cloak to cover her all-too-noticeable hair, Sira eased a way under two stones that had slumped together with a shifting of the hill. She could remember when they all stood straight and tall, taller than the men who'd made them, dragged them here over long miles. With a sad smile, Sira recalled watching them work, peering through the strands of the long grass. But that had been before her father had forbidden The People to go out in the daytime. She did not need daylight to see clearly, and yet she missed the sun. To be honest with herself, she missed the Sons of Men.

In homage to them, she busied herself with their memory. They'd been short and dark, for the most part. Once in a while, a head red as copper would appear among them. They'd kept slaves who were no different than their children, living in their simple huts along with their elders and their small horde of livestock.

She'd seen them marry, have children, and die. Then, long after it had been created, the hill fort had been abandoned, and no more humans came. She had tried to write one of their songs down to remember, the better, once upon a time, but her friends had held their hands over their ears, calling the tune uncouth and the words vile. Sira had rather liked it.

She hummed it now, under her breath, as she strolled along. The pipers had fallen silent. She could not hear her people chattering nor the clatter of bowls and plates. They must be gathering on the far side in silent expectation, hand in hand. The Lady's pale face would soon peer above the horizon to begin her ancient journey. The eastern sky had already begun to silver with Her first rays. She should be there, at her father's side, instead of wandering about by herself, dreaming of things long since turned to dust.

Then Sira paused between one step and the next, her sharp ears catching a sound that did not belong on this high hill. She could not fool herself into believing that a sheep or a cow made that soft moan, nor did any breeze ever sigh so sadly. Swiftly now, a huntress on the prowl, she hurried along the ring of stones, her cape sweeping over the thin scattering of dirt.

She saw his legs first, sprawling out from the base of a rock. Standing over him, she took him in at a glance. So this was what the Sons of Men were like now!

Tall and broad, he had boldly muscled arms and a deep chest, shown all too clearly in his flaxen shirt, tight to his body. The shirt was unlaced, his throat a strong column where the pulse beat indomitably. She could not see his face well, for his head had fallen forward in sleep, toward his right shoulder, long, dark hair covered his cheek. His hands were palm up, open on his broad thighs.

Without thought, Sira put her hand out to push back the concealing curtain but she paused, her fingers only an inch from his face. She pushed against the force that held her back, without asking why. Then she realized that somewhere on his person he must be carrying cold steel. She drew back her tingling hand, wondering at her own impulse to touch the human male, knowing how dangerous such a touch could be.

"Sira!" Anat said in a voice like a whip crack.

"Hush! You'll wake him."

"Wake who?"

Her nursemaid, not a whit less spry for her five thousand years, came hurrying up and stopped a few feet off, aghast. "Oh, this is intolerable! What are things coming to when the guards miss something like this!"

"Everyone's entitled to make a mistake."

"Not one that puts us all in danger. Come away, Sira, do! He'll awaken in a moment, and if you were to be caught . . . Come away!" The nurse caught her charge's arm, but Sira stood steady. "Oh, I'll call your father! He'll see to it that this . . . this . . ."

"No."

She had no need to raise her voice. Though she tolerated much from Anat through affection and long habit, she was not a child but sole daughter of the house of Boadach the Eternal, King of Mag Mell, ruler of the Lands of the Living. A great lady and a power in her own right, Sira could command obedience even from her dearest protector.

"But . . . my lady . . . you don't know what the Sons of Men are like. Their greedy, grasping, *wicked* ways! How do we know he's not set some trap for us? Let the king do his worst. What is it to us? It's too bad when we're not even safe at our own revels!"

"The revels have not yet begun. And if this were a trap, would he lie here, helpless at our feet?"

"He bears steel," the companion replied. "I can feel it even from here." Anat had withdrawn to a safer distance, holding up the full skirt of her gown so even it would not be contaminated by contact with a mortal.

"Yes, he carries a dagger at his waist," Sira confirmed. "I wonder where he left his horse. If we could find it . . . entice it to return . . ."

"Don't you dare include me in any such foolhardy enterprise! The man is here, let him stay and face the consequences of his folly. The king will show no mercy to a thieving spy."

Sira tried to stop the pictures from forming in her memory of the last time some poor mortal had spied on The People and their revels. The king's anger had been like lightning out of the sky. Though all The People had vanished on the instant, his wrath had left the poor old man maimed and blinded. Sira hadn't been able to stop her father's retribution, though she'd done her best to soften it with gifts from time to time until the poor man had died, his span of life no more than a twinkling.

Sira looked down on this mortal, still sleeping. His pose told of his utter exhaustion, yet there were lines of strong tension in every limb. On his feet, he must be a formidable presence indeed. Sira wrapped her cloak about her more closely, prey to a sudden chill.

"Wake up," she said. Then, more commandingly, she said, "Awaken, thou!"

"Hush," Anat hissed, raising her hands imploringly. "Someone will hear you."

"You are right, all too right. But he can't stay here to be benighted. Look at him. That's a warrior, I'll be sworn. A man like that needs his eyes."

Suddenly, the drooping head lifted while one large fist wrapped around the hilt of his dagger. Sira found herself looking into the face of a captive falcon, the bandage around his eyes only adding to the likeness.

"You are right, lady," he said, his voice as harsh as stones grinding together. "But alas, too late."

•   •   •

When Conn awoke to the sound of her voice, it was to believe himself finally driven mad by his sorrows. His long years of training had stood him in good stead, however, for he did not cringe or quail, even when he heard the women discuss his dark future. This king of theirs sounded brutal, but Conn was used to that. All kings were given to sudden wrath, even Stephen, who many said was too soft and mild to hold a fragmented England together.

Their talk was strange, full of things he did not understand, their speech oddly accented. It seemed all of a piece with madness that two women should appear on a vacant hillside in the twilight and discuss him.

"Who are you?" he asked. "Egyptians?" When they did not answer, he essayed again. "Wandering folk? Conjurors?"

"Aye, sir, that we be." Her voice had lost all note of command, softening and slurring into simple country speech. Yet even so, it thrilled through him like a carillon in a cathedral.

How long had it been since he'd last smiled? The morning before the battle that took his sight? He controlled the smile that threatened to break through now, forcing his lips to stay stern lest she think him an easy gull. "Now tell me the truth."

"How dare you! Do you think we need lie to the likes of you?" demanded the other one, the one marked in his mind as her mother. He could almost hear her feathers ruffling as she charged in to defend her chick.

"Never mind, Anat." Her voice was closer suddenly, as though she knelt before him. "Yes, you are right. I— we are not wanderers. We belong here."

"The hell you do. This is Hamdry land, and you are trespassers. If you leave now, I won't summon my father's men to drive you off."

Her laughter at his threat was soft, like a whisper against his cheek. Conn began to wonder anew if he'd lost his mind as her scent reached him. Like the essence of a thousand flowers, yet milder and somehow fresher than perfume, it entwined around him like an enchantment. No one he knew smelled like that. Most people stank to heaven. Even he stank, with the slime smell still clinging to his fingers. Even the noblest in the land only used their rich perfumes to cover the stench of an unwashed body. This woman, whoever she was, smelled like the first morning of the first spring, before the stain had come into Eden. Conn inhaled more deeply and felt the talons of the devil in his head relax a moment.

She said, "By the time your father's men arrive, we will have done our business and be gone. You have nothing to fear from us."

"I may be blind, lady, but I'm no coward." Conn rose to his feet, feeling the muscles in his thighs twinge from his gallop of the morning. He stood straight and proud, knowing she must be gazing at him. "I've given you your chance to go. Take it. My father isn't as mild a man as I."

Did she still crouch at his feet? He had not heard her move, though the whisper of her gown had given her away before. With all the speed he could command, he reached out to grab her shoulder. Was his judgment off so badly? His hand closed only on empty air and yet he could have all but sworn he'd felt for only an instant some kind of fabric, soft and cool.

The other one said sharply, "Call your father and have this brute driven away or I will! He offers you nothing but insults."

"No."

Conn heard the curiosity in her voice as she stepped nearer to him. "He may be something of a fool, but he is a brave fool."

"Your kindness is boundless," Conn said bitingly. "Call your father, and you shall see how I can fight."

"You see!" the other one countered. "Not even grateful for his life. It's just as I've told you and told you. They're all the same."

"Nevertheless, he may leave here in peace and safety, Anat. I will lead him off the tor."

"Absolutely not! Have you lost your mind? It's not safe. I refuse to allow it."

"I don't need your help," Conn said, addressing himself sternly to the young lady. "I know this land by heart." Then, belatedly, he added, "Thank you, all the same. I know every stone up here since my boyhood."

"You may find that things have changed somewhat, even since your arrival today. We sometimes alter things for our own purposes."

"Alter? How can you do that?"

She ignored his question. "Besides, Anat is quite right. It's not safe for you to go alone."

"That's not what I meant!"

"I ask only one thing," the girl said.

"What's that?"

"Drop your dagger. I cannot help you if you carry it."

Conn could not recall the last time he'd gone completely unarmed. Even as a boy, he'd always carried a sharp, bright blade for peeling apples or for cutting through a leather strap if he should be dragged by a runaway horse. A knife was as much a part of him as a finger.

"Your price is too high," Conn said, drawing the blade. He showed it to them, moving it back and forth so they could see it flash. "This steel came from Damascus, and the hilt is bound with silver. King Stephen himself gifted me with it."

Her voice sounded pained, higher and quicker. "Put it away. Please."

Unsure of himself, he slid the knife into its sheath, the steel seeming to sigh as it went into the darkness. He blustered, "It's worth more to me than the cost of it, and certainly more than the cost of an unneeded guide."

He walked away, knowing by the slant of the evening breeze and his inborn knowledge of the land the direction he wanted to go. His carriage upright, his steps sure, he hoped the two ladies realized how useless he found their pity. He went on feeling that way, right until he tripped over a stone that should not have been there.

As Conn lay sprawled at full length on the ground, it

seemed to him that the earth throbbed beneath him, as though it were an anvil being struck with hammer blows. Suddenly, the air seemed full of voices, whispering a chant, too low for him to grasp the words. As the song grew, he wondered if he wanted to know the meaning. There was menace in the song, formless now, but if the singers knew he was there . . .

As he sat up, brushing himself off with a scraped and stinging hand, he felt as he had as a boy, on his first sojourn to London. Everything was so unutterably strange that he felt like a foreigner in his own nation. He could not tell friend from foe or noble from base.

"My lady, the moon!" the older woman said urgently.

"Yes, I know."

Then she was beside him again. "Listen, you must leave here now, before the moon rises. Will you put your trust in me?"

"I'm only turned about," he said. "I'll soon find my own way."

"You haven't time. Leave the dagger, and I will help you."

"Why should I?"

"Oh, he's a fool! Leave him, my lady. Such men don't deserve your kindness."

A soldier can never mistake the note of command. He heard it now, not a whit incongruent coming through a woman's voice. "Do you want to die?"

"Sometimes," he answered honestly.

"Now?"

"No." His answer surprised him. This morning, he'd longed for death. "Not now."

"Then throw it away and come with me."

Conn found himself freeing the sharp blade again from its sheath. He could all but feel her reaction, as though the shudder that went through her passed through his own body. His fingers opened, and he heard the clang as the dagger fell to the ground.

He felt a cool smoothness come around his shoulders and breathed in her fragrance as heavy cloth enfolded him.

"That's just my mantle around your shoulders," the younger woman said. "It will keep you safe. Hold on to it, and do not try again to touch me."

The other woman said something, another protest no doubt, but Conn could not hear her. A strange humming had come into his ears and a dizziness clouded his mind. He could not feel the ground with his feet anymore, though he went on walking as before.

Her voice, however, he could hear. Not with his ears, but in his mind. "Show me your home."

The front gate appeared in his inner vision. Hanging with chains, forged of iron bars with overlapping plates of steel, it might have belonged to some earl's castle. Instead, it served as the defense of a fortified manor, the first addition Conn's Norman grandfather had made to the place after conquering it for William the Bastard.

She said quickly, "Not that. Show me something else."

So he pictured the garden, his mother's garden. The fountain, its spring long dry, made of the same black stones as those that clung to the hilltops. The green mist that had returned with the spring to cover the brick walls, the only hint that the roses and vines still lived. And his hands, digging in the rich soil, turning over the beds where once herbs and vegetables had grown and would, one day, grow again.

"Ah," the girl sighed. "That I can do. Pity the fountain is dead."

"I'd ask you to fix it, but if you charge a silver-bound dagger to see a blind man home, I doubt I can afford a miracle."

"Oh, miracles are very inexpensive." Her laughter rang out full and merry.

He could still hear it when he awoke, and the smile it had brought to his lips lingered a moment longer. He sat at the foot of the fountain, his body heavy and stiffened by long sitting in one position. The edge of the basin had left a line across his back where he had leaned against it as he slept.

"A most curious dream," he said to himself, rubbing his hand over his rough cheeks and across his dry mouth.

"Master!" someone shouted, and Conn heard running footsteps.

"Gandy?"

"Yes! Oh, master, we feared ... Lord Robert is like to turn the world over to find you, and here you sit. But how ... not that it matters. Where is Arundel, my lord? Not hurt?"

"I don't know. I ..." He must sound like the very fool the older woman had called him. But no, that was a dream. Only in dreams could a man travel from Beldry Tor to his own bailiwick by flying through the air. Conn tried to shake off the memory of it. "I am well," he declared. "But I am in no mood to listen again to my father's rantings. Tell him I will wait upon him in the morning."

He did not need eyes to realize he'd lost his servant's attention. Very little indeed could prevent Gandy, son of a Welshman, from putting in his oar. Yet he didn't remonstrate with his master, urging an instant meeting with Lord Robert. "What is it?" Conn asked.

"Naught, master, only ... I never should have believed you'd make that fountain work again. Didn't they say the spring was dried up as an old cow?"

"That's right. It ..." Unmistakably, his ear caught the trickle of water coming from behind him. He put his heavy hand on his servant's shoulder and, giving him a slight shake, demanded a description of what he heard.

" 'Tis but a bubble, my lord, rising from the center and rinsing away the dry slime."

"Clean?"

A pause while the servant groped for the wooden scoop that still hung on a rusted hook driven into the stone. It had a long handle to reach into the freshest water at the center of the old fountain. Conn remembered his mother dipping up sweet water for her son, tired by his games.

Gandy rinsed his mouth and spat. " 'Tis noble," he said in surprise.

It served to wash the worst of the dirt from his hands

and face. When Conn lifted his cupped hands to his lips, the water was sweet, cool, and fresh. Conn did not spit it out. It seemed to cool the fire in his heart, his anger toward his father, his anger toward fate.

He said, "I didn't do it. This fountain was dry today when I left here."

His servant laughed. "It must be a miracle. Be careful, my lord, else you'll have hordes of pilgrims coming to wash in it."

"I'll be first in the line," Conn said wonderingly. Had it been a dream? Or . . . witchcraft? He lifted his hand to cross himself but let it fall, the gesture uncompleted.

Two

"Please, Anat?" Sira gave her nurse her most appealing glance, opening her eyes to their fullest extent and cocking her head cunningly to the side. As always, the stern shell of the older woman cracked.

"Oh, well, I suppose it won't do any harm. Mind, if your father asks me straight out, I'll not lie for you."

"Oh, thank you, Anat," Sira said humbly. "You are truly the best of my friends. After all, it's not as though I'm ever going to see him again."

"Perish the thought! A hulking brute like that! If he had realized who you were, he'd have held you for ransom. Wishes, most likely, that's what they usually want."

"He didn't seem brutal," Sira said, picking up her wooden brush. The back was totally carved and incised with runes promising to protect her beauty.

The brush was plucked from her hand before she could do more than pass it once through the length of her hair. Anat began to wield the brush, lecturing and scolding all the while.

"Don't be fooled. Just because he wore that bandage over his eyes doesn't make him any less a brute. He laid hands on you, did he not?"

"He tried," Sira said, chuckling as she recalled the look on the mortal's face when he found himself grasping a handful of nothing.

"There, you see! He tried. If he'd had his eyesight, he would have succeeded, and where should you be now, may I ask? Captive to that smelly, violent . . ." Anat clicked her tongue against her teeth. "And who would your father have blamed? Me, and rightly so. You think you know everything. Well, let me tell you. . . ."

With the ease of long practice, Sira let the diatribe go by her unheeded, practically unheard. She thought about the son of man she'd seen last night. Everything about him had been so different from the males of her own people.

"Great lumbering feet tramping all over . . ."

"He was tall," Sira said quietly. Taller even than her father and with those broad shoulders. . . . She wondered if such muscles came from lifting the heavy steel that constituted their formidable weapons. Among her people, only the harpists seemed to have strong arms, and she couldn't think of anyone with such firm-looking thighs. Glancing at herself in the smooth reflecting surface of the waterfall that poured down one side of her airy white room, she saw that her cheeks had heated.

Anat continued, "But what's worst is all that hair! They grow it on their faces, their arms—hideous sight!"

Sira had noticed a certain roughness to the mortal's cheeks and had wondered at it. Would it feel rough and coarse against her fingertips? She curled her hands together in her lap, as though to keep them out of mischief. The long, black hair that grew from his head in sleek waves had not looked coarse but smooth and thick. She tightened her hands' grasp on each other.

"Yes, well, there's no need to be going on—"

"And I'm sure you noticed the *smell*, my lady. They don't bathe, you know. They really don't—not enough, anyway. You'd think they were afraid of water."

"He didn't seem to be afraid of anything," Sira said. "Not many mortals would be so bold under the circumstances. A blind man, alone on a hill, suddenly meeting two women whom I'm sure must have seemed very strange to him . . . Even I might have cowered if our positions had

been reversed, and still he tried to take mastery of the
situation.''

"He couldn't see us, remember. He'd have crouched in
fear if he'd seen us."

"Why? Am I so terrifying?"

"You don't know these creatures as I do. Their ignorance makes them fearful until their greed makes them
bold."

"Yes, you're probably right. He was bold, wasn't he?"

Working from the crown of Sira's head, Anat began to
braid the back of her hair, working it into a fantastical
coronet. Sira tried to relax under her nurse's care but
glanced again into the waterfall mirror.

What would have been his reaction if he had seen her?
Her People called her lovely; certainly enough odes had
been addressed to her face. What would a human male
make of her? In form, she was not unlike their own
women: fairer and more delicately molded perhaps, but
similar in all features. She even carried small, high breasts
under her gown, though they would never nurse a child as
she'd seen the human women do, all those long centuries
ago. She wondered if they still did that.

Sira lifted the wings of her hair to peer at her ears, the
small lobes a-jingle with tiny silver bells. Raising her tilted
brows, she turned her face this way and that to look at
herself from different angles. What would a mortal think
of her eyes, changeable from blue to green like the sea that
had called her into being at her father's command?

"Sit still, Sira."

"Yes, Anat." She held a regal pose, her lips twitching,
suddenly prey to a vision of herself at a hundred thousand
years of age, Anat still fussing and scolding. The thought
made her sigh but with a smile for all the services her
nurse performed with unending and unyielding love.

"Anat," she asked, "don't you ever get tired?"

"Tired, my lady? What do you mean?" The pull and
tug of Anat's nimble fingers paused.

"Restless?"

"No. Never," she declared, her tone filled with finality.

But then she asked, "What could I possibly long for? There is nothing that the Lands of the Living cannot instantly supply."

"Yes, I know. But—didn't you tell me once that long ago you went to the regions of endless ice and snow?"

"Yes, I did. But I have no wish to go back."

"Why not? It must have been so interesting. The ice palaces, the great blue caverns, the snow diamonds . . ."

"Whatever desire I had for travel was satisfied long ago. It is profitless to leave the Living Lands. The outside world brings only sorrow to meet those who visit it. Wasn't that poor man example enough? He, no doubt, set off with a light heart on whatever adventure he thought worthy. I wonder what he thinks of it now, now that he's blind. Without their sight, humans are helpless."

Resolving to find out more about Anat's trip all those centuries ago, Sira rose from her chair without answering her. Yet she longed to whisper, "He wasn't helpless."

The ceiling of the long council chamber was interspersed with carved medallions and beams that told the long story of her People. As a child, she'd spent hours lying on her back, deciphering the crossed lines. She always felt as though old friends watched her with kind eyes when she came in.

Her father, Boadach, sat on his low stool, a three-foot-long clear crystal held across his lap. He smiled when he saw her and waved her closer, though Sira felt certain he'd been looking very dark a moment earlier. Certainly the half-dozen council members who stood in a loose semicircle before him looked crestfallen as though they'd been admonished.

"See to it, my friends," Boadach said, staring at each of them in turn from beneath the overhang of his majestic brow. "Leave no stone unturned. I want to know how this happened."

Male and female, the counselors bowed low and departed. Before they'd taken three steps over the tessellated floor, Boadach had turned to his daughter with the special smile he kept only for her. "Did you enjoy the ceremony, Sira?"

"Very much, Father."

"You were late." He held up his hand to forestall her hurried words. "Never mind. I'm just glad to see you safe."

"Safe?" Sira sank down to sit on the raised dais beside his knee.

"I'm tempted to send all those on guard duty last night to the bottom of the sea. Maybe a hundred years spent swimming back will teach them to be more cautious."

"You're very severe," Sira said, thinking busily.

"None too severe, if the truth be known. Look at this!"

Boadach turned the perfect form of the crystal so that Sira could look down into its very heart. There, like a jewel in a casket, lay a dagger, the hilt wrapped in silver wire. Swallowing hard, she tried to sound suitably impressed. "What is it?"

"Steel. Still warm from the human's clasp. Where do you think it was found?" He didn't wait for her answer. "On the very hill we chose to hold our revels! Well may you be speechless! The thought of a human being spying on us fills me with disgust. I have spoken with great severity to my council and to Forgall the Wily. He'll not rest until he discovers who it was that helped the human escape."

"Escape? Father, I . . ." She hesitated. The one thing in the universe that daunted her was the expression in her father's eyes when she gave him cause to be disappointed in her. It made her feel very cold inside. Nevertheless, she gathered up her courage, only to lose it. "Perhaps it was left there a long time ago. Years even."

Not listening, Boadach stroked his short beard, still dark brown despite the endless ages he'd lived. During all the years of her memory, only his eyes had changed, growing ever deeper and warmer with the passage of time. Only on one point was he less than just. Her father's hatred for humans had not lessened over the years, despite the edicts

he'd issued and the bard's songs he commissioned dwelling on the iniquities of the human race.

"Eh? No, the guards went over every inch of ground
the day before. It was not there then. Nor when the guards
searched again tonight. It came with a human—rot him!
A sneaking, prying, peeking . . . You didn't see anything
out of the ordinary this evening, did you?"

"I, Father?" Sira struggled with the truth. She did not
like to lie to her father—it was disrespectful and damaged,
however slightly, the love between them. Yet sometimes
when he was being unreasonable, she felt she had no
choice.

Her hesitation turned her into a liar by omission. Boadach turned the crystal in his hands to glare at the knife.
"The bottom of the sea is too good for them," he muttered. "A fine Beltane *this* is turning out to be. Humans
spoil everything."

Sira could not allow the blameless sentinels to be banished in some desperate fashion. She said softly, "Father,
I can explain everything."

The king turned his fathomless eyes on his daughter.
"I'd like to hear that explanation."

His voice had something of the quality of a tame lion,
deep and purring, growing all the more so when a mouse
runs between his paws. Sira gave him a sidelong look.
"You already know, don't you?"

"I? I know nothing. Least of all how my daughter—
great princess, lofty arbiter, lamp of her people and light
of my life—could possibly allow a mangy, vicious . . ."

Sira hated it when he started reciting her titles. "Father,
I had to help him."

"You know the penalty for a human caught at our revels. It may sound cruel—" He held up his hand to silence
her. "It may sound cruel, but consider what would happen
if we let them alone. Our refuge would be overrun by
greedy hunters. They wouldn't be content learning the secrets we shelter. They'd want our lives. It's happened before, Sira, and it is my first duty as king of our People to
see that it never happens again."

Boadach hadn't needed to remind Sira of the terrible massacres of years past. His queen, her foster mother, had been involved in such violence centuries ago while visiting her sisters in Gaul. Her spirit had been so undone by the dreadful sights witnessed and the assaults committed on her that she'd never recovered. However, not even the memory of the queen's sorrow, which had struck Sira like a knife of frost in the spring of her youth, made her hate humans with the same passion as Boadach. The strong human hand she'd grasped last night had not committed such a crime.

Boadach said, "You know where this human lives?"

"Yes, I took him back there. But we have nothing to fear from him."

"If you were as wise as you are beautiful, my daughter, you would not say such things. All humans are a threat. He will talk of what he has seen—"

"He saw nothing. Didn't your spies mention that this man is blind already? There's no need to strike him down. He saw nothing. Not even my face."

Boadach mused in silence. Sira had time to repent accusing her father of setting spies to watch her. She'd long ago realized that while she could have anything her heart desired merely by asking for it, from unicorn hair to make a gown to the apples of knowledge, a princess could never have privacy. Her lightest action was a source of interest to her people. Glimpsed from a distance, however, even the most fascinated watcher would not have been able to tell that the Son of Man could not see. Sira herself would never have guessed it from his posture or the confidence he seemed to exude.

The king said, "You swear to me that is the truth?"

"By whatever power you invoke, I swear it."

Boadach kept his narrowed gaze upon her for a few more moments before accepting her word. "Very well. I trust you were discreet enough to leave him with the impression that he merely had a strange dream."

"Oh, absolutely." Sira decided not to speak of the spring she'd persuaded to fount again. Remembering what

Anat had said, she hastened to add, "Besides, the poor man is very nearly helpless, Father. You would not wish to blight him further when fate has already been so unkind."

"No, I don't suppose I should."

Sira smiled up at him trustingly. "Shall I call in Forgall and tell him to stop searching?"

"Yes, but . . . there is still the matter of this thing." He tapped the crystal containing the dagger. "We cannot keep it here. Even shut away in this, it has disrupted our harmony. It must be returned. I shall tell Forgall to do it."

"Wait, Father. It is my fault the dagger was on the hill. I couldn't take it with me when I returned the human. Let me take it back now."

Once again, she bore her father's penetrating gaze. She would put the dagger in an inconspicuous spot, someplace where it might plausibly have been lost. Before she returned to Mag Mell, she'd make the fountain as dry as it had been before, with only a few dead leaves in the basin. Then there would be nothing to make the mortal believe his dream had any basis in reality. It might even be possible to catch a glimpse of him, just to reassure herself that he'd suffered no ill effects from his brief acquaintance with the Wilder World.

"Very well. But be cautious. This human may not be as feeble as you claim."

"Oh, he isn't!" She caught herself. "Isn't dangerous, I mean." She gave the king her most winning smile and was relieved to see that his sharp suspicions had not awakened again.

"I'm so bloody *helpless*!" Conn muttered as he sat alone in his room. A bowl of savory-smelling stew sat on a board across his knees. A wooden spoon clasped in his right hand, Conn used his left to hold the bowl steady. "Come on," he said. "A man doesn't need his eyes to feed himself. Just open your cursed mouth and put the cursed spoon in it!"

When he'd first come home three months ago, his father

had held a welcome for him, inviting all the tenantry and
the neighbors to fete the returning son. Conn had only sent
word that he was returning, giving no hint of his condition.
He could still hear the cheers, suddenly choked off, the
gasps from the men and the sound of sobbing from the
women when he'd been lead through the gate by Gandy.

That had been bad enough, but the feast that followed
had been a nightmare. Ideally, one shared a trencher with
a neighbor, making for good fellowship and camaraderie
while enjoying a succession of dishes, each designed to
delight the eye, and only incidentally the palate.

Conn had been unable to share in that, and his attempts
to eat neatly had ended with his father, as well as himself,
splashed and mired. Helen, his betrothed, already distraught by the sight of her bridegroom, had been sickened
by his failure. Like so many others, she'd become confused, thinking his blindness had made him deaf. She had
not lowered her voice when she spoke of her disgust.

Now Conn ate alone, each mouthful a difficult conquest.
The board he used as a table and the front of his tunic
caught the rest. He put down the spoon and groped for his
goblet. The turned oak felt solid in his hand. Wine he
could manage without spilling.

"Gandy!" he called, knowing his servant had taken to
lurking outside his door after bringing him his food.

"My lord?" The answer came after a brief hesitation.

"Where's the God-rotted spoon?"

"Here, my lord." The voice seemed to come from the
floor, and Conn knew he'd dropped the thing on the rushes
again.

"More wine."

The liquid sloshed and gurgled from the jug. "You
know, I could just live on wine," Conn said. "That would
solve my problem."

"My lord, if I may—"

"Not offering to feed me again, are you?"

"No, my lord." He could tell by the rustle that Gandy
was rubbing his head. Blindness had not entirely ruined

Conn's aim. "I was going to say that if you were to pick up the bowl . . ."

"I won't be turned into an animal, Gandy. Not even for my own needs."

"No, my lord." In a brightening voice, the young man, son to one of Conn's fallen comrades, said, "I thought you'd like to know that Arundel came back. Morse found him in his stable this morning, sound as a nut. His furniture had all been taken away and he'd been rubbed down, though Morse swears he didn't do it himself. Though I understand he was so drunk last night that a horde of horses could have ridden in and he'd not have noticed."

"Dipped deep, did he?"

"All the way to the bottom of the well. Margery says—"

"Margery?"

It wasn't hard to picture Gandy's eyes rolling ecstatically. Conn had seen that look often enough. For a man of no particular good looks, his servant had caused many a young maid to lose at least her heart to him. He would have been despicable were it not for a heart soft with romantic longings.

"A heavenly creature, my lord. She's a cousin of your father's steward. With the kindest heart. She's been helping me find my way around."

"Pretty?"

"Yes, my lord. Eyes like sapphires and the sweetest mouth . . ." Gandy sighed as he poured more wine.

Conn sipped and then asked, "Any sign of my dagger?"

"I've asked the servants, but no one has admitted to having seen it."

"Damn. It's one I'd rather not lose. I wonder . . ." Conn shook his head. He might have lost it on his ride or dropped it into the mire. In his dream, he'd left it high on the tor, but now he could not be certain that he had even set foot there. Conn squared his shoulders. If he let on how confused he'd been yesterday, there'd be no reprieve from the monastery. As a blind man, he might yet find a way to keep his manor. A madman didn't have a place anywhere.

Conn could feel his soul gape open to expose the black abyss of his loneliness. He knew no one who was blind; certainly he'd never met a blind knight. Only mendicants, who used their infirmity to beg on some corner, squatting in the filth of the passing crowd. He knew no one who could tell him how to live as a blind man in a world that valued only strength—and then only strength of a very particular kind.

He flexed his fingers, hungry for the numbing weight of a broadsword. Once he'd been able to fight in the sun for hours, never wearying of whirling the four-foot length of steel. Sometimes in the night, he could still hear the clash of sword on shield echoing in his dreams. His own sword had been taken from him on the field at Lincoln, when he'd been forced to yield. "I should have died," he muttered. "It was a good day to die."

Conn stood up abruptly. The board that had held his frustrating meal tumbled down with a crash that made him startle. He'd forgotten about it. "I'm sorry, Gandy."

"No, it's nothing. The food was all but gone, anyway. Oh, I almost forgot. My lord, your father wants to see you."

Conn laughed shortly. "Do you give me nettles to divert my mind from my bleeding wounds?"

"Doesn't it work?"

"Not very well."

Gandy dropped his voice conspiratorially. "Then if I might suggest . . . Cassandra FitzSimmons."

"Cass? She's in London. Panting in attendance on the empress, if I know Cassandra."

"Well, my lord . . ."

His blindness was hard on Gandy, too. Not just because of spilled food and dirtied clothing but because he'd been used to communicating with nods and winks, shrugs and smiles. After a moment in which Conn could imagine his body servant going through convolutions like a man suffering from Saint Vitus' dance, Gandy said, "Mistress

FitzSimmons is said to have a wonderfully loyal nature, my lord. I feel she'd hurry to succor a knight such as yourself. I mean, a noble, brave, *well-endowed* knight . . .''

Conn could well imagine the broad wink that went along with this advice. He couldn't help chuckling with rather more humor than he'd shown before. "Cassandra is a rare armful. You think then that the tender embrace of a lioness would distract me from the nettles?"

"My mother—may the Lord God have mercy upon her—told me once that if a man doesn't lie with the maids often, he'll never have health."

"I'm glad to know you've taken your mother's advice with such filial constancy, Gandy." He grinned. "You at least need never fear illness."

Conn took a moment to consider Cassandra Fitz-Simmons, a dark beauty who was fond of wearing a low net headress in all weathers and during all activities, even in the friendly warmth of her bed. She'd smelled of musk, morning, noon, and night, anointing herself with the precious oil as if with holy water. Even her bed had reeked of it. He'd found it pleasant enough at the time, but now, thinking of the heavy air that surrounded her, he felt he could hardly breathe. He longed for some other scent— like the wind blowing over the high tor bringing with it the fragrance of a thousand flowers.

"I am a good son," Gandy said complacently, "and my mother never lied to me. May God rest her. But, my lord, it has been some time since you . . . Some of your father's maids are not uncomely. None so fine as Margery, may-haps. I think on little Lucy with the hot eyes, but there are others. Let me make a choice for you."

With a rueful smile, Conn refused. "But you may chose another tunic for me. This one—" He shrugged. "Then go to tell my father that I will attend him in the hour before the evening meal. If that does not meet his pleasure, you will be unable to find me to tell me of it."

"As you will, my lord."

So far as manor houses went, Hamdry had many com-

forts. The original hall, huge and echoing, had been the
sole building when Conn's Norman grandfather had come
home here. He'd brought ideas from France and added, in
addition to extra hearths, a new wing that housed offices,
family chambers, and servants' rooms. The stone for the
narrow, winding stairs that connected the two sections had
come from a tor fort. In contrast to the gray walls of rough
stone, the stairs were black, with a subtle shine. A curb of
rounded stone set in the wall as a rail might have been
designed specifically for a blind man. Conn wondered if
he would have forty years here to smooth a groove in it
with his questing fingertips. Or would it be better to die
now?

Conn pushed the thought away with the effort he would
have used against a huge boulder set to crush him. He'd
made his choice yesterday. The easy way of suicide was
not for him.

He paused at the bottom of the steps, his head cocked
for noises. Faintly, almost more as a vibration than a
sound, Conn recognized his father's voice, blustering
away. Who was he hectoring now? Not Ross, his only
hope for an heir. Mayhap Lord Robert merely voiced his
frustration with his older son. Conn could almost pity his
father. He'd learned much about frustration in the last few
weeks.

Conn reached the side door without being hailed by anyone. Outside, the air was heavy and slightly dank. He felt
the cold touch, gentle but inexorable, of mist on his cheek.
With a shiver, he followed the path of flush-set stones,
their tops slippery with moss. At the end of this walk,
walled off and secret, was his mother's garden, an oasis
of peace and remembered sorrow.

His grandfather had built with stone, replacing much of
the wattle and daub construction of earlier times. But he'd
had war and defense on his mind. Only when his beloved
daughter-in-law asked for a little square of her own to
make a garden had he realized there might be more to life
than war. It was a lesson Conn wished had been taught to
his father.

"Is anyone here?" Conn asked, pausing in the act of closing the squeaking wooden door. The laughter of the fountain was the only answer.

Then he heard a gasp. "I—"

"Who's there?"

Silence. Conn said, "If you are a maid attached to the house, you needn't be afraid. I won't tell anyone you were here, though it isn't your place to be here at all."

Was that sound the whisper of a long skirt over the grass or the sighing of the breeze? Conn began to doubt his remaining senses. Perhaps he hadn't heard that startled intake of breath and a half-begun word.

Then the voice came again. Giving the impression that the words were forced from her by a sudden impulse, she asked, "Have you been blind long?"

"You must not be listening to the gossips. I'm sure that's all anyone in the kitchen's talked about since I returned."

"I never listen to such stuff. Is it interesting?"

"More interesting than the truth, in any case. Come, don't be shy. You can admit that you listen." Where had he heard her voice before? It had a musical lilt to it, a different stress that made her seem slightly foreign but not obviously so. It wasn't the Devonshire accent that the rest of the servants had.

"I do have a friend who loves to tattle."

"Ah!"

"But I try not to pay too much attention. I don't want to know what's bad about our People. I prefer to think all is light."

"You must thrive on discouragement," Conn said sourly. "There is little light in the world. None for—" He broke off. Soliciting pity ranked as Conn's most reviled sin, placing above even such crimes as murder, desertion, and borrowing money from his father.

"To answer your question," he began again, "no, I haven't been blind long. Just a few months, really. Hard to believe it's been such a little time."

"You seem to manage quite well."

"Because I'm not led by the hand? I don't need to be, not here."

"How did it happen?"

"In battle. In February." She must be near the fountain. The cool sound of the water seemed to mingle with her voice. Together, they made a wild kind of music. Conn started toward her, slowly. He could hear the skittishness in her tone. He thought of a horse unable to decide between flight and curiosity.

"Battle must be a terrible thing," she said.

"It's not so bad. Especially if you can't see the enemy."

Did she laugh at his callous joke? "You don't seem very—if I lost my sight, I'd be terribly bitter and angry."

"When the leeches first told me that I'd lost the sight of my left eye and was likely to lose my right, they tell me I all but broke apart a dungeon door three inches thick. I was lucky not to have shattered my bones."

"Why were you in a dungeon?"

Her questions and her reactions to his answers were as innocent as a child's. Perhaps she was a child, wandered in here to play. He tried to answer as simply as possible.

"That's where they put you when you fight on the losing side."

"Oh. You *are* bitter."

No child then. "Not bitter," he answered and laughed. "Why would I be bitter? I have nothing left but this place, and even this I may yet lose. My father . . ." He broke off, aghast at how much of himself he was giving away. Were the walls he was building around himself so weak that a single blow from a girl could shatter them?

She asked, "Is that why . . . ?"

Conn knew he was quite close to her now, within an arm's length. Making a sudden grab, he demanded, "Who are you?"

Once again, his fingers closed on empty air.

Three

"Damn it!"

Sira cocked her head, half-smiling with curiosity. "What did you say?"

He spun on his heel, turning his head like an animal to catch her voice the better. Swift as striking lightning, he made another grab, the roughened tips of his fingers all but brushing the trailing sleeve of her gown.

"Stop that!" Sira demanded, only to jump aside when he tried again. "I mean it! Stop that, or I will leave and never come back."

"I hope you won't do that," he said, turning unerringly in the direction of her voice. He seemed to lift his nose as though to catch her scent the way she'd seen foxes sniff on cool mornings, the scent of prey carried on the mist. "But let me touch you."

"No! Why?" Sira held herself ready.

"To prove to myself that you are real."

"Of course I'm real!"

"Not to me. I can hear your voice, smell your perfume, but I could be a madman, dreaming all this. I had a strange dream last night. It seems to me—"

"You're not mad," Sira said quickly to prevent him dwelling on his adventures and perhaps remembering her; her voice, or the way she'd vanished. Humans were gul-

lible, her father had said, ripe for any trick one of The
People might choose to play.

She said, "I assure you that I am real as you are."

"That's no comparison," the human said bitterly. "I'm
hardly real at all these days."

"What do you mean by that? No!" she said, jumping
back without losing her solid form as he swept one large
arm through the air. If she'd been a thought slower, his
knuckles would have grazed her cheek.

It was fatal to allow a human to touch one of The People. The freest heart, so the story went, would be in thrall
until the human chose to release "the fairy" he'd caught.
No worse fate could befall one, for the humans never released anything that could be of benefit to them. One had
only to look at horses and dogs to know what fate one of
The People could expect.

He said, "Since I've been blinded, my father wants me
to surrender my rights to my younger brother."

"That's foolish. A man is more than his eyes."

"Not to Lord Robert of Hamdry."

Why didn't he look to be out of breath? Her heart was
beating rapidly and her mouth was dry from exertion. He
looked as though he'd been for a leisurely stroll, instead
of chasing her around the garden.

"Being blind doesn't seem to have harmed you otherwise," she said, stepping quietly back out of reach.

"Yes it has. If I had my sight, I would have caught you
by now."

"If you had your sight, I should not be here to be
caught."

On the last word, Sira realized that all this time, the
human had been herding her like a lost lamb into the angle
where the walls met. Now he was in front of her, his
brawny arms outstretched, brushing the walls on either
side. She could possibly duck under his arms, but having
seen with what speed he could move, she didn't dare.

"Pray stop, sir," she said, sounding very much to her
own ears like a bleating lamb. "We have gamboled
enough for one afternoon."

Still he came on, inexorable as a glacier, only far warmer. She could feel the heat beating out of his big body, bringing with it a whiff of some totally male scent. Sira found herself breathing more deeply, and not because she was tired.

"I just want to be satisfied that you are real. If I am mad, then my father is right to order me away for the good of the land. If I am sane, then I will stay and fight for what is mine."

"Please . . ." she said, feeling the rough wall at her back.

To her stunned surprise, the human stopped, only inches away. "What is it? You sound . . ."

"Please . . ." she said again, the magic of the word seeming to hold him back. "Please, I beg you not to—"

He dropped his arms, a puzzled frown showing above the white strip of bandage around his eyes. "I'm not going to hurt you. I'm certainly not going to . . . to do anything you don't like. It was just a game. You're the fastest woman I've ever met."

"Fastest?"

"The trick you have of jumping away silently. Or is it that you throw your voice like a jester? A strange talent for a woman, my lady."

"Why do you call me that?"

"Come, you'll not pretend again to be a simple maid from the kitchens!" He chuckled warmly.

Laughter changed him, turned him into something more civilized, less the hunting beast. Sira, on her toes to flee at need, relaxed a tiny bit.

"Come now," he coaxed. "Tell me your name. Did you come with Helen? Are you her friend from the north country? She said someone might come to visit her."

Who was Helen? Sira wondered. His voice had not given away his feelings for this unknown woman. If only she could see his thoughts! Perhaps she should ask her father why she could not. No, that wouldn't be wise at all.

Not quite answering his questions, Sira said, "I came out of curiosity."

"To see her blind betrothed?" Again, she heard the
sharp tang of bitterness in his voice.

"To see his garden," she answered calmly, though in
her heart she knew that if she'd come only to return the
dagger at her father's order, her visit should have been
over long since. She had wanted to see this man again,
and she still did not know why. She didn't even know his
name.

"My garden?" he echoed.

"Yes. But this isn't all your work, is it? Who was it
that loved flowers so?"

"My mother. This was hers, long ago." He turned away
as if he would look around the walled plot. When she had
successfully looked into his memories yesterday, he had
been thinking of it as a green and pleasant sanctuary, neat
and orderly, with a tinge of green sweeping in over the
gray remnants of winter.

Sira saw a well-planned arrangement of neat, square
beds, but only as one glimpsed the underlying form of a
tree beneath the withered leaves of autumn. Dead stalks
still protruded among the freshening green of the rising
plants, whereas in other beds, the only green was the en-
croaching grass. Several apple trees had a neglected air,
with never near as many blossoms as they should have
had. And the roses should have been cut back long ago,
instead of keeping their brittle branches like broken-
toothed saws.

Yet there were signs that someone had been at work
here. Earth had been spaded and turned to show its lush
potential. The earth around the lilies, only just sprigs now,
had been cleared of all weeds and grass.

"Have you been working here?"

"There's nothing else I can do, or rather am allowed to
do." She heard the bitter hatred of his condition rise in
his voice, only to be choked down again. "So I work here,
when I can. I'm afraid it only confirms my father's belief
in my uselessness. Wars are for men; gardens are women's
work. Or peasants'."

Swiftly he turned around to stare fixedly at the closed

door in the wall. Only by standing on her toes could Sira see over his broad shoulders. "What is it?"

"Someone called my name."

Sira blinked in surprise. She had quick ears, but she'd heard nothing. In a moment, however, the door opened. The human male put his hands on his hips, squaring his shoulders even more. At first taken aback by the change in his attitude, she realized that he was trying, rather gallantly, to screen the sight of her from this new person. She was touched, surprisingly touched, by his consideration. Nevertheless, she thought it wise to fade, to become a shadow painted in colored mist.

"Good morrow, Conn."

"Ross."

The newcomer seemed a younger man, similar in coloring and appearance to the first human, but then, they all looked so similar to her eyes. This new one, this Ross, bore a fleeting resemblance also to the males of her own people. He was slender and pale-skinned. His dark eyes were restless under straight brows. Even though he had his full senses, he moved with less confidence than the blind man.

"I'm surprised to find you alone. I thought I heard you speaking to someone."

"Did you want me for something?"

"I thought you'd like to see Helen. . . . I mean . . . Helen's come over with her father . . . I think . . . I think *our* father arranged for them to come."

"Yes. I understand you are to be congratulated."

Sira saw Ross take a step forward, his mouth opening as though to protest. But he only lifted his hands in a helpless gesture and let them fall.

"Helen's a fine girl," he said without enthusiasm.

"Beautiful."

"Yes, and thrifty."

"So her father says."

Watching, Sira saw the exact moment the younger man decided to take the risk of plain speaking. "Helen is the most loyal and honorable girl in the world, Conn. She'd

never renounce your betrothal over something like . . .
like . . .''

"Like the fact that her bridegroom repels her. Don't
bother to deny it. I've heard the way she looks at me.''

"Heard the way . . . ?''

"If by some mischance she glances in my direction, I
hear how she sucks in her breath through her teeth as
though she saw a fearsome apparition.''

"No, I'm sure—besides, how do you know if she's even
looking at you? That noise might be caused by the sight
of me. She's never liked me, Conn. Even when she does
talk to me, she only wants to talk about you. I'm only
interesting to her because I'm your brother.''

"Father won't care about that.''

"I do. Do you think I want to be just a substitute for
you all my life?''

It no longer surprised Sira that Ross was thinner than
his brother. Wrestling every day with the serpent of jealousy that gnawed him must leave him little time or appetite
for food. Easily, she looked into him and saw that the
serpent had not yet won. She felt possessed of a tremendous curiosity to see what this Helen was like to set two
brothers quarreling over her.

Conn didn't respond to Ross's sharp tone. He said,
"You go back to the hall. I'll join you there soon.''

"Father said I shouldn't come back without you. He
doesn't like the answer your servant brought to him earlier.''

"Nevertheless, go on and wait for me.''

Ross, his suspicions aroused, glanced with seeming casualness around the garden. When his eye lit on the fountain in the center, his face brightened. "*Helas!* It's true. I
had heard you started this working again. How did you do
it?''

He hurried over to peer into the depths of the stone
basin. His expression of joyful expectation turned rapidly
to one of disappointment.

"It stopped again,'' Conn said, and Sira glanced at him
in surprise. When had he noticed that? Almost as though

in answer, he said to Ross, "I didn't hear any water when I came in here. I think the spring must have had a brief resurgence and is gone down again."

"Maybe it only flows at certain times of day." Ross groped for a loose pebble and dropped it down into the basin. "At least there's some water in the bottom, and it's not green with slime anymore, though it's here on the walls."

Conn said, "If Gandy hadn't seen it himself, I'd be thinking I'd only dreamed it was working again." When the younger man sought another pebble, Conn sighed with impatience. He murmured, "Don't move. Don't speak. I'll tell him to leave."

He had shifted his body to continue to screen her from his brother. So gallant, though quite unnecessary. Sira smiled at the big man, pleased by his concern for her honor. She'd heard that the Sons of Men were very protective of their women, even fighting terrible wars to preserve their honor. She thought it rather silly—as though women couldn't be honorable without a man keeping watch—and yet touching.

Conn said more loudly, "Ross, do you—" but his brother broke in with an exclamation.

"There's something in the water! Something shining . . ." He got one knee up on the basin's edge, peering forward into the water. The sun had shown itself through the clouds and a stray beam struck right into the depths of the fountain.

Remembering where she'd put the big man's dagger, Sira caught her breath. Instantly, Conn turned his head as though catching the sound. But that was impossible. When she was incorporeal, only thoughts could pass. She'd already tried and failed to see into his mind for reasons she could not fathom. She admitted that this made him even more interesting.

Some instinct told her that it would be wise to leave here, to leave him. She'd done what her father had asked, and a little more than that. Time to go. Safe in the Living Lands, she would soon find it hard to remember the human called Conn, and in a few decades, so brief was his life, he'd be gone to wherever it was Sons of Man went to when they met their deaths.

Taking a last look at his garden, she wondered if he would ever have a son to care for this plot of land. Ross didn't impress her as a man who troubled his head about apple trees. Perhaps his wife—this Helen—would.

Sira decided that it would not hurt anything if she appeased her curiosity about this Helen creature. Did she really love Conn enough to defy her father? Or would she be meek and obedient, giving up her blinded lover for his younger brother?

Looking at the fountain, Sira saw that Ross still knelt on the rim, trying to retrieve the dagger. The tight sleeves of his red undertunic were wet to the elbows, stripes of green algae marking the fabric. "Faugh," he said, grimacing. "This muck stinks worse than a guarderobe. I only pray it doesn't stain my clothes forever."

Yet he persevered, leaning forward again to make another grab.

Quickly, Sira made herself solid. "Conn," she whispered urgently, his name already familiar on her lips. "Conn, he's going to fall . . ."

A splash, quick and flat, punctuated her words.

Conn did not hasten to rescue his brother from the fountain. The water was not deep, though more than four feet down. A soaking would do him no harm.

"Ross," he said, reaching the basin. "Give me your hand. I'll pull you out. Ross?"

He leaned over, patting the roughened stone as far down as he could reach. The lady spoke at his shoulder. "He's not moving. I think . . . mayhap he struck his head?"

"Do you see any blood?"

"No, but his head's in the water. . . ."

"In the water? Is he drowned, for God's sake?" Conn still found himself straining to *see* through the linen of his bandage, though he knew it was hopeless.

"No, he's just lying there. But his eyes are closed."

Conn stepped back and stripped off his outer tunic, leaving him in his shirt. As his hands went to the laces, he barked a sharp order to the lady. "Go at once to the house and summon servants. Tell them to bring a hurdle. And send someone for the leech in the village."

"But I—"

Impatiently, Conn threw his hand at her, meaning only to push her in the direction he wanted her to go. His fingers tangled in some soft cloth and, without his willing it, sought for the warm flesh beneath. His hand met only nothingness. Bringing his other hand up, he groped wildly at the empty air. He turned in a circle, seeking her, determined this time to prove to those senses that remained that this woman was real.

"Christ and His angels!" he swore, swinging his arms wider and wider.

Her voice came at him, shaken with a tremor of fear . . . or was it laughter? No doubt he looked a fool, stumbling over his own feet, his arms swiping through the air as though he were imitating a bird, drunk on fermented fruit.

"Where are you?" he demanded.

"See to your brother, my lord Conn. I'll gather your servants. Keep my veil in memory of me."

After swearing after her a moment more, Conn swung himself over the rim of the well, steadying himself with one hand on the fountain. He managed not to trod his brother under when he landed, up to his boots in water. He thrust his hand inside Ross's shirt to place his palm over the breast. The slow pulse made him thank God for his mercy. Conn lifted Ross out of the wet, no sooner glad for his brother's life than fearful of losing it to the water.

Now, feeling the water wick up his legs, he cursed the slowness of servants. He had no doubt that the lady would summon them as she had said. Yet would she herself return? She'd left her veil, she'd said, for a memento. Did that mean he'd never hear her voice again?

Suddenly, Conn was shaken with an intense yearning to hear it. He could not have said what it was that made her voice fall so much more gratifyingly on his ear than the voices of other women, no more than he could describe the sound of a lute most sweetly played. But he had gone back again and again to hear a maid play cunnningly on the lute in an inn in Spitalfields, drawn there by a desire beyond that of the gross body.

He frowned, striving to recapture something of what she'd said. The words were there in his memory. The strange rhythm of them, though, the lilt of her voice . . . these were things he could not recapture. Yet he recalled that she'd spoken his name, and the thought warmed him beyond its measure. He did not know her name, not yet. It seemed right to call her The Lady.

Then the servants were there, and his father. "Reach down your hands," Conn called, and not a moment too soon. An instant later, and he could have walked out on the heads of all those who were wishful to climb down with him.

Conn slung his brother over his shoulder and reached up to grab a strong hand. Half-pulled, half-walking, his legs at an angle to the wall of the well, he came out. He was not surprised to find that the hand that had aided him belonged to his father.

"Is he dead?" Lord Robert demanded.

"Nay, Father, nor me neither." Tenderly as a mother, Conn lay his brother on the grass.

"Stand back, you fools," Lord Robert roared to the servants. "Take these wet clothes from him, Gandy. Where's the woman with the hot bricks? Damn his soul, is that leech to be found yet?"

"He's not drowned, Father," Conn said. "He may have struck his head when he fell in."

"And how did he come to fall in? By God, if this was your doing . . ."

"Mine?" Conn said in wonder. "How should it be my doing?"

Then he understood and rose to his feet from where he'd been kneeling at his brother's side. "Do you accuse me of encompassing his fall?"

He heard how the servants, gabbling and blessing themselves in wonderment, suddenly turned silent. Conn could not tell if the sun had vanished behind a cloud though it seemed as though it ought, rather than to witness a father accusing his son of murdering his brother.

"You have the most to gain from his death." Lord Robert's voice was cold as a wind from the north.

"I have naught to gain. All I have, I shall keep and require no more. Ross is no threat to my place."

"He will be, if he lives!"

Then Conn caught the sound of the slow shuffle and panting gasps that never failed to accompany the exertions of Walter de Burke, friend and neighbor to Hamdry and to the family. Enormously fat, he affected the long gown and close-fitting cap of a scholar, though he'd been a notable warrior in his day. As a mere boy, he'd been in the train of a follower of the Conqueror. He'd been heard to boast that he'd been thin as willow windle and just as whiplike. But that had been long years and many a meal ago.

Now he paused, breathing hard, only to say, "What's this? Arguing? And the boy not yet cold?"

Conn heard another voice then, shaken by tears, and felt a blush of shame for his unseemly anger go over him like a flame. Helen de Burke, as slim and fair as her father was gross and bald, rushed forward over the grass, calling Ross's name. "Oh, God, not dead? Not dead?"

Of all the men that stood there, it was left to Gandy, quicker-tongued, to say, "Nay, my dear. Stunned only. Only stunned, you know."

"Yes," Conn said. "He struck his head as he fell into the well."

"The well?" She must have turned toward him instinctively when he spoke, for once again he heard plainly that little intake of breath that told him well what she thought of marriage to a scarred and sightless block.

So that she would not have to look at his face, Conn turned and walked to the sloping wall that surrounded the fountain. "He said he saw something sparkling in the water. He tried to reach it."

"That makes no sense," Lord Robert said, coming over. "The water's too far down for him to reach it. He would not have even troubled to try. And if he had, a simple push . . ."

Walter de Burke said, " 'Tis folly to speak so. A heedless boy, who could say what he might do?"

Conn said, "The water was deeper when he reached; he complained of the slime on his arms."

"Come," his father said, chuckling without mirth. "Does water rise and fall in an instant?" In a lower tone, as though he turned toward his friend and muffled his mouth, Sir Robert said, "Is this not proof enough?"

"Not yet," de Burke murmured. "See to the boy, Robert. There's yet time enough for the truth to show."

Conn kept his face a blank, not wishing for his father to know that he had heard. He asked, "Is Ross yet lying on the grass?"

Instantly, his father began to bellow again. "Carry the boy to his chamber! What are you all about to stand there in that stupid way? Hurry now, or I'll have your noses off!"

A timid voice said softly, "By your leave, mistress, here is your veil."

" 'Tis none of mine, girl," Helen said haughtily. "What do you see, Father?"

Judging by his voice, de Burke now stood beside the fountain. He snorted with surprise. "By God, there *is* something sparkling there. Ah, me. I'm too fat by far to climb down and fetch it. You . . . you boy?"

A stable lad, milling around with the other servants, came when called. A moment later, he was conscripted into climbing down again. " 'Tis a rock,' he called, then whistled low with amazement.

"Come up, then," Lord Robert said impatiently. "Damn his eyes, is the leech arrived yet? Send him up to the boy when he comes, the instant he comes."

Taking no interest in whatever it was they'd found in the well, Conn called to the maid. She sounded young, and shy. "What have you there?" he asked.

"A . . . a veil, sir. I found it lyin' in the grass."

He put out his hand. "Give it to me and tell me of its like."

It lay smooth and heavy in his hand. He ran his fingers over the sleek surface and felt the fibers catch on his callused fingertips. "What like is it?" he demanded again.

"I . . . I cannot say. I have never seen aught like it."

"The color then. Tell me that."

" 'Tis blue, like the sky, but never such a blue sky was a-dance with stars—"

"Stars?"

"Aye. Worked into the stuff, yet how can it be so light as I can see through it?"

"Can you see through it?"

"As though 'twere the air . . . oh, the queen herself must not own aught so fine and fair."

Confused, Conn let the cloth dangle over his arm and ran his hand over it again and again, listening with his head cocked to catch the soft rustle. He brought it to his face to breathe in a hint of the fragrance that clung to the folds. Flowers and a breath of sweetness like air untouched by any living thing . . . and the memory of all that had happened the night before came back to him. He remembered the night, and the moor, and the girl who had helped him. Here lay a mystery, indeed.

"Witchcraft!" The word slashed through the air like a whipcrack.

Conn turned, realizing he'd been hearing sounds of a quarrel all along but too involved in his discovery to pay heed.

Sir Robert said, "I tell you plain; no one man unabetted by devils could have made such a thing!"

" 'Tis most rare and strange, but not outside the reach of some master craftsman."

"Craftsman? Wizard, rather. How did he make such a thing without join or seam? Eh? Answer me that."

"I've never seen anything so beautiful," Helen said, her voice full of a yearning awe. "But how did the knife come to be within it?"

"Knife?" Conn asked. "What knife?"

He rolled up the veil—it made a surprisingly small bundle—and hid it in his sleeve. Someone, probably Gandy, pushed his tunic into his hand. As he walked toward his father and his neighbors, he pulled it on over his head so Helen would not be affronted by the sight of his body through the fine linen shirt.

Walter de Burke was kind enough to describe what they'd found. "Place your hand here. . . ."

Conn let his fingers explore. The surface was cold from the water, and hard. Sharp edges met his touch, coming to a point at both ends. "Rock?" Conn asked.

"Indeed. Rock crystal. Fine as glass and without a single mark of having been cut. And within it, lies a silver-bound dagger of most handsome style."

"Witches . . ." Lord Robert hissed.

Four

Conn had been present at enough banquets of his father's giving that he did not need his eyes to picture the torch-lit scene. The great U-shaped table would be crowded with men while a haze of smoke and steam drifted above their heads like a misty cloud ringing a mountain. Sweating servants would bring in great slabs of meat, crisped and savory from roasting, to place at intervals around the table. The meat would be hacked at with knives, while a chicken per man would be ripped apart with greasy hands. No man would take time to point a mocking finger at Conn's clumsy eating, for who among them had not dripped fat down their fronts while ale frothed out the sides of their mouths?

The singing and the drinking would go on until dawn. Lord Robert's hospitality was a byword, yet Conn recognized that there was more than the usual revelry tonight. The thirty or so guests and men-at-arms that sat at his father's long table were so noisy that Conn could only hear the sharpest notes that the minstrels picked out on their lutes and flutes.

Ross had recovered from his accident with no more to show for it than a bump on his head and some wet clothes. He also had to suffer a certain amount of rude chaffing from his friends and his father.

"You'd think one baptism would be enough for anyone!'' That was the family priest, Father Maynard, a rollicking fellow who'd come to the Church because he had been the third son of a minor nobleman. He and Lord Robert had been foster brothers together.

"Oh, the ladies love a man who bathes . . ." Lord Robert began to bellow the song and the other men joined in, leaving the minstrels still playing "The Crown and the Adder." Their mild tune was drowned out in a great roar as the singers reached the chorus.

"Not one of them is pure at all! All before money fall! Come, offer coin, and love like any king!"

He heard earthen mugs crashing together. Conn flinched as a slosh of ale hit his shoulder, cold where it sank through the thick fabric. He sat at the high table at his father's left hand with Maynard beside him. Between the two, they could drink the Thames dry, provided it be flowing with good ale.

At the end of the song, there was much cheering and an attempt to start another by a few isolated voices. But most of the guests realized they'd gotten behind in their guzzling and had better uses for their mouths than music.

Father Maynard, his voice muffled with meat, said, "So, my boy, have you heard the news from London? My cousin Allsop writes to me—you know Allsop, do you not?"

"Yes, Father. You were kind enough to recommend his house to me in London. What is the news he sends?"

"Oh, bad, I fear. A church council has declared King Stephen deposed—"

"Deposed? By what right do they dare?" His fist struck the table, making the knives jump. Beside him, his father cursed.

"Look what you've done! My tunic is awash in ale!"

Conn turned his bandaged eyes toward his father's voice. "My pardon, father. This news from London—"

" 'Tis no business of yours any longer. This household will accept the right of the Empress Matilda when it is profitable to do so."

"I will serve the king and no other—" Conn began.

His brother's milder voice interrupted. "My lord, what matter is your tunic? Have you not already spilled enough ale to fill a hogshead, and half down your throat? And how came my brother by the stain on his shoulder if not from you?"

A low growl from Lord Robert was his response. Conn, glad not to belabor an issue for which there was no answer, grinned a bit tiredly. "Well said, Ross. But we are more fortunate than you. Better to be baptized with ale than water."

Father Maynard shouted with laughter. Conn felt a splatter of half-chewed food strike his left arm. Sweeping it off with the edge of his hand, he added, "And a morsel of meat to follow."

"Better meat than bread, Conn!" The priest laughed.

"Go on and laugh, Maynard," Lord Robert grumbled. "It's plain the favor of heaven no longer shines on us. Misfortunes pile on misfortunes like fever victims flung in a pit."

Ross said lightly, "All this agony over a damp tunic, Father? Give me leave to send your servant for another one."

"Nay, 'twill serve. But think you on this . . ." Conn heard the slurping sound of his father's drinking go on until one would think he'd drown. From long experience, he knew Lord Robert would grow more morose with every cupful that passed his lips. He'd passed the point where he could match jest for jest. Soon he'd order the minstrels to play only solemn songs and pass from frowning to weeping. Few would be sober enough to see him unman himself and fewer still would care. It was no disgrace to drink oneself insensible.

Once, Conn would have carried his lord father to bed. He supposed that task now, with so much else, belonged to Ross.

"Think on this," Robert went on. "What has caused so much to go wrong of late? Half a storehouse of winter grain disappears so that I must buy more for the spring planting, putting the house in debt. Then my fine mare comes up unmated after covering. . . ." He sighed heavily. "What causes these things to happen?"

"Bad luck?" Conn ventured.

"Was it bad luck that caused you to lose your sight and me my son?"

"I am still your son," Conn said between gritted teeth.

"Aye . . . aye." Lord Robert patted Conn's muscular forearm as though he were reassuring a child. "But no longer the good right arm I relied on. My only blessing now is that I have another son to do me honor."

By the sound of Lord Robert's voice, Conn could tell he had turned his face toward Ross, sitting at his right hand. In a tone flushed with embarrassment, Ross said quickly, "I could never take my brother's place. . . ."

Conn wanted to say that Ross already had, that to sit at their father's right hand had always been his privilege. That was a minor matter—other things counted for more. He must chose his battles with care now.

Lord Robert drank again. "Now," he went on as though there had been no pause. "Now my other son is nearly lost to me by drowning in a fountain that has been long dry. Why?"

Like Conn, he slammed his fist on the table, ignoring the mugs that fell and broke for his own was emptied. Conn heard a muffled curse from Walter de Burke, sitting on Ross's far side. He wondered whether de Burke's cup had been full or empty.

"What say you is the reason?" Ross asked.

His father's voice dropped, speaking Norman so that the lesser men could not understand him and be afraid. "Witches. I guessed it the instant I saw that accursed rock in the water. The witches put it there to mock us."

Father Maynard said, "Hold hard, Robert. As the voice of the Church, I must say—"

Lord Robert was too deep in his cups to listen. "No. 'Tis witches. They've been seen. Haven't they, Maynard?"

"That ass Nicodemus? He's just a lying boy. No one

has asked him what he was doing at the pasture so late. No good, I'll be bound.''

''He's old enough to know what he saw,'' Lord Robert said stubbornly. ''Eight witches, riding each other like horses under the full moon.''

''But he's a monstrous boy, full of deceits! The times I have absolved him for telling tales outnumber the stars. I shouldn't take his word if he told me it was snowing in January.''

Lord Robert said solemnly, ''To lie about such things is to in-im-imperil the boy's soul. If it were his word alone, I should scoff, but taken with all these other signs, 'tis plain there's witchcraft about. Foul deeds have foul causes.''

Conn said nothing. What had he interrupted up on the tor? Had it been some obscene ceremonial dedicated to the Black Arts? Remembering The Lady's soft fragrance and gentle voice, he could not believe it. What reason would a witch have for saving him from the wrath of her king? If she were abandoned to evil, she would have handed him over and laughed to see him die in torment.

Surely she would not have come again today if her soul was possessed by the Evil One. Her laughter had been sweet, even as she evaded his touch. Only when he had her trapped had her laughter faded to be replaced by a note of pleading that even now made him ashamed to think of. He had no right to treat her so, whoever she may be.

Her veil, softer than down, nestled in his shirt. No place in his chamber had seemed fair enough to shelter the cloth, so he'd tucked it next to his skin. It had shifted and fallen against the band that gathered his shirt close to his body. Conn could feel it there, like her touch against his side. Was this to be all he would ever have of her? If she never came again, it would be his own fault for his brutishness. The thought pierced him with an exquisite pain, as sharp in its way as that he had felt the moment when he'd re- alized his blindness.

''Are you well, Conn?'' Father Maynard asked in a tone pitched for his hearing alone.

"Well? Well enough." He realized he sat stiff as a stone saint and threw a brief smile to the priest as he lifted a morsel to his lips. She had to come again; that much was plain. Conn prayed silently, though he could not be sure who he prayed to: *Let her be wicked, let her be ugly as a black dog, let her be whatever Heaven or the devil allows, but let her come again.*

At the far end of the table, a couple of men-at-arms began to play a rhyming game. It became noisier as others joined in and soon drew attention from the high table. Ross and Walter de Burke called encouragement while Lord Robert drank on, sullenly.

Conn, turning to the priest, said, "Go on with the news from London, Father."

"Outside, my son," the priest answered. "Let us not disturb your good father more."

Willingly, Conn stood up to follow. He felt Maynard's fingers touch his elbow. "It's all right, Father. I don't need to be led."

"We all need a guiding hand now and again. There's no shame in it."

Cheerfully, Conn answered, "True. Yet in this instance, I need no such guidance." As he pulled the oaken door open, he said, "There. I have brought you, Father, instead of you me."

Outside, despite the stink of horse manure and wood-smoke, the air seemed sweet after the rancid reek of the hall. He heard the breeze whirling some straw around in a corner of the walls and the bleating of goats penned near the gate. Conn took a deep breath and said, smiling, "Wash day tomorrow."

"How do you know that?"

"Smell the soap fat cooking? The maids will be up all night stirring the pans. The first great washing of the year begins tomorrow, and not an hour too soon."

"Are you grown so nice then, my son?"

"I grew spoiled in the army, Father. There were always washerwomen following in the king's train. For a half penny and the heel of a loaf, they'd wash my shirts and my overtunic, too.''

The worldly priest laughed. "That's not what washer-women would do for a half penny in my youth! Saucy wenches they were, always smelling of hot water and tallow." He sniffed the air in quick breaths like a fox scenting for the hounds. "Aye, I smell it now. How it takes me back!''

Conn walked on a step or two. Without the wall to guide him, he knew he'd soon find himself lost in the center of the courtyard, unable to get his bearings again until a wall stopped him or he tripped over a rut or a forgotten stick. Yet he longed to feel the air more fully on his face and to breathe freely. The news from London was not good; better to listen to it here in the fresh air than in the clatter and confusion of the hall. Outdoors, he could believe himself again on the battlefield in the clear light of day. Dark and stuffy rooms were the rookeries where plots and treason hatched.

Instead of asking the priest to go on with the news from his cousin Allsop, Conn found himself saying abruptly, "It is my father's wish that I leave Hamdry and enter the monastery at Closebeck.''

"Ah, good old Windom! He'll make the son of his old friend comfortable! He has a nose for good wine! But then these Cluniac orders are famous for good living. If it were a Cistercian order, it would be a different matter!''

"I have nothing against Abbot Windom. I remember him well.''

"A good, godly man, an honest abbot with a true care for the monks under his orders.''

"I'm not going, Father.''

"Not . . . ? But if it's your lord's wish . . .''

"Nevertheless. I had hopes once of a glorious death in battle, but as that has been denied me, I will not now choose to dwindle my life away in the Church. I will stay in the world and make something of my life.''

The priest gave a wry chuckle. "How like me you are, my son." He put his hand on Conn's sleeve. "Come, don't

stand there in that bullheaded fashion. Come and sit you
down.''

Conn allowed Maynard to lead him to a bench set
against the courtyard wall. The two men sat down together,
the priest sighing. ''My head's as hazy as a foggy night.
I doubt not I'll have a hard time opening my eyes come
the morning. But 'tis well we have left the hall. I fear at
times I drink overmuch.''

''Not you!'' Conn answered, grinning.

'' 'Twas a habit your father and I fell into in our youth.
He who was our master then used to punish us by taking
away our ale. Given nothing but water to drink, we drank
all the more ale when allowed it. Now that we may drink
all we like, we do drink all we like.''

When Conn laughed, Father Maynard squeezed his arm.
''Good it is to hear that again. When you came home, I
thought the laughter had died in you.''

''It lives,'' Conn said, thinking that he would not have
answered so yesterday. Had The Lady brought that to him
as well? He slid his hand with seeming casualness over
his tunic, feeling the coolness of her veil against his skin.

''I am glad. Preserve your laughter, my son. If you stay
here, you will lose it to your father's grief and your own
jealousy. Go to Closebeck and take the gift of the noviti-
ate.''

''Never.''

''Listen to me. I have known you from the hour of your
birth. It was I who stood at your mother's side when she
felt her pangs come upon her and I who baptized you.
Don't I know that you are as masterful as your father, as
resourceful as your grandfather, and moreover burdened
with the compassionate soul that you received from your
mother?''

''Father, I—''

The grip on his arm tightened as the priest shook his
wrist for emphasis. ''Take these gifts to God. In the embrace of the Church, you may yet rise to greatness. The
lack of your eyes will not matter. In the abbey, there are
learned men and boys to read to you and to write letters

for you. On their shoulders, you may rise as far as any man might. I should not despair of seeing you one day with an archbishopric or higher office yet.''

''Do you council me to embrace the Church only to advance myself?''

''What better way now that the brotherhood of arms is closed to you? And it is not so very different. The Church has need of her soldiers, too.''

The priest sighed and Conn heard a flat sound like someone slapping a slack drumhead. ''I, alas, am too old, too fat, and was ever too indolent to serve her as well as I should like. While my memories are not all bitter, they are none of them as they should be. I have drunk and whored away my best years. If it were not for your father's kinship and kindness, I do not know what should have become of me.''

Made sharply uncomfortable by these emotional revelations, Conn said, ''Father Maynard, I have—''

''I never wanted to take the cloth, you know. I wanted to be at court. Whenever my brother Gaspard came home, all he could speak of was the wonders of the court and the splendor of the young prince, William Aethling. I followed Gaspard's every word as though he described a mystery play. The prince seemed like a veritable Saint George.'' Maynard sighed again. ''I might have gone to court, you know, but for him and all the young men drowning like that in the White Ship. There was no more merriment to tempt me hither after that.''

''I, too, regret the young prince's death. If not for that, we should be at peace now. King Stephen has it in him to be a worthy king, or so I believe. Yet I could wish William Aethling had had enough sense to stay on dry land and inherit his father's throne, instead of leaving the succession in doubt.''

''Well,'' Father Maynard said with a return to his hearty manner, ''there's no profit in thinking about the past. What's done is done. Time to consider what best to do for your future.''

''I shall stay here at Hamdry and—''

"Stubborn as your father! Can't you see that . . . I didn't mean . . . of course you can't . . ."

Conn spread his hands wide, absolving the priest for his slip of the tongue. He said, "As for the Church . . . save your breath for your next cup of ale, Father. I was born at Hamdry; I shall die at Hamdry. Not at Closebeck, Canterbury, or even Rome."

"You'll not be swayed?"

Conn only shook his head, smiling but sure.

"Very well then. I shall say no more on it." The priest stood up, his hand resting a moment on Conn's shoulder.

In a much softer tone and in Norman French, Maynard said, "Look to thyself, then, my boy. Thy father surely means to unseat thee as his heir if he must barter his soul into Hell to do it. Thou shouldst comprehend that well, for what wouldst thou not do to keep this land thine own?"

"I am no danger to this land or its people," Conn replied in the same tongue.

"Couldst thou hold off an army as thou art now?"

"Could my brother? I at least have some knowledge of arms, while he has stayed at home to mind his books."

Maynard clicked his tongue wryly. "What a debater the Church has lost! Go with God, my son."

"And thou, Father."

For a long time after the great door had creaked closed behind him, Conn sat on the bench outside his father's hall. He guessed that Father Maynard was even now reporting his failure to Lord Robert. This would not be the last skirmish over his retirement from the succession. He had no doubt, however, that he would be the eventual victor.

Only when the muffled shouts of revelry from the hall had ceased entirely did Conn stand up and return to the main hall. He hoped that Gandy had found a sup of ale and a bite of pasty for an evening meal. Conn also hoped that the neat little man was not waiting up to help his master to bed. He yearned to shrug off his clothes, slip under the coverlet, and find his sight again in cool dreams. The last thing he wanted was to listen to whatever gabbling gossip Gandy had sniffed out in the course of the feast.

His luck ran against him. He had put his foot on the first step of the winding stair when he heard Gandy's light, shuffling step behind him. Gandy's voice was subdued, for him.

"They've all drunk themselves into sleep, my lord. A near thing, it was, too. Seemed as though once or twice it would be knives out and no quarter. It came to naught, though. None but silly fellows breaking wind in each other's faces."

"I'm for bed," Conn said. He would have said more had not a sudden yawn cracked his jaws. Conn didn't trouble to cover it; he could be sure Gandy was busily making the sign to ward off the evil spirits that were said to leap down a man's throat while his mouth hung open.

"I shall light your way . . . I mean . . ."

Conn put out his hand to clasp the servant's shoulder. He missed at first. Gandy stood still as a stork in high water until Conn touched the padding that gave Gandy's shoulder a modish peak. "A kindly thought, but no, I thank you. Go to bed. I need nothing more tonight."

"I will come with you, my lord, to see to your—"

Conn scowled. Though Gandy was a troublesome servant at times, froward and garrulous, he rarely disobeyed a direct order. Nor did he impose when Conn's uneven temper lead him into unspeaking solitude for an hour or a day. Now he was doing both. Conn wanted to demand what the man meant by it when his heightened senses caught a voice at the top of the stairs.

Gandy started to say, "If you—"

Conn held up an imperious hand, commanding silence. The voice had been female, and urgency had filled the single syllable it had spoken. "Ross . . ."

His voice hardly a breath, Conn said, "Do you carry a light?"

"A tallow dip," Gandy replied just as softly.

"Extinguish it. Stay here."

Using his hard-won ability to walk without making a single betraying sound, Conn mounted the stairs. Had his ears fooled him? He certainly heard no voice now.

As he neared the top of the stairs, however, other sounds

told their own story. A murmuring sigh, a sudden gasp, and then a sucking sound like two dampened palms separating. A whisper in his brother's voice, his breathing ragged, reached Conn.

"By all the saints, Helen, have you lost your mind?"

"Mayhap I have. If my father knew . . ."

"Never mind your father. If Conn knew . . ."

"Ross, I can't bear to marry Conn. He never appreciated me, even when he could see. What good is my beauty to him now? Touch me, Ross. Touch my hair and my skin and my body. I'll give all of myself to you."

"Helen . . ."

Her voice was sharp with desperation. "Could you give this up to Conn? And this. Please, Ross . . ."

Conn heard his younger brother groan and knew that Ross was completely in thrall to Helen de Burke's beauty. Conn could hardly blame him. She was the loveliest creature he'd ever seen, with her proud, sulky mouth, hair like a black silk banner snapping in the breeze, and the long body and high breasts so valued by artists and troubadours.

He wondered at himself. By rights, he should feel a blaze of jealousy so hot that it could lead him to take up arms against his own brother. Helen de Burke was *his* betrothed, a bond sanctified by the Church, as binding in its way as wedlock. Yet listening to the young couple as they kissed and embraced, Conn felt no rage, only a bone-deep weariness.

A step behind him told him that Gandy, curious or tired of waiting, had come up the stairs. Conn held one finger to his lips, enjoining silence.

"That's enough, Helen," Ross said. "Will you or nil you, you belong to Conn. I can do nothing to change that, nor would I if I could."

"Then I am lost. You were my last hope. My father won't see that Conn's blindness is grounds enough to dissolve our betrothal."

"Your father is right. Conn's still alive. If he had died in battle, I should have rejoiced to take you for my own. It's all I've wanted since that day by the church."

"Oh, yes! If only we could be children again."

"But Conn lives. While he lives, you are his. You will never be mine. Please, Helen, don't tempt me anymore. No more secret meetings. No more messages."

"While he lives . . ." the girl muttered. Conn clearly heard his shocked hiss as Ross breathed in. Helen must have seen the dismay in Ross's eyes, for she hurriedly said, "I wish him no harm. If only he will choose Closebeck, the last obstacle to our happiness will go with him."

"Conn will never go to Closebeck," Ross said bluntly. "Nor would I, were I in his case. Conn will never leave Hamdry."

It was good to know that at least one member of his family understood the seriousness of his intent.

"Then it's hopeless. I will have to marry him, to share his bed, and to bear his children. . . . I can't. I can't." Helen's voice quavered along the ragged edge of hysteria.

Conn reached out and tapped Gandy on the arm. With a single gesture of his forefinger, he told the lackey to climb the stairs and interrupt them. It was not fitting that Gandy should eavesdrop on his betters. Besides, at this rate, Helen would soon be screaming, which would only bring more witnesses to their meeting.

As he hoped, the appearance of a lowly servant stiffened Helen's sense of restraint. The close-knit communities of manor life made displaying strong emotion most unseemly. The only way to create even a semblance of privacy was to keep one's thoughts concealed as much as possible.

Helen said coolly, "My thanks to you, Ross, for guiding me back to my apartments. You need trouble yourself no further. This lackey can direct me thither."

"Gladly, my lady," Gandy said. Conn could imagine the flourish the neat man gave to the words. He could trust Gandy not to give away any hint that he'd heard Helen offer to betray, if not to murder, her betrothed husband.

No doubt Ross contented himself with merely bowing as Helen walked away. A moment later, however, Conn heard a deep sigh come floating down the stairs like a lost spirit. Then slow, thoughtful footsteps moved away.

Five

The worst thing, as well as the best, about working in the garden was that Conn had no sense of the passage of time. He could not check the sundial nor did he particularly notice the change as the sun crossed from one side to the other. If he were paying attention, the distant sound of the church bell tolling away in the village could give him a hint, but frequently, absorbed in some task, he'd miss it. More often than not, the growling of his empty belly alone told him that six or eight hours had passed since he had broken his nightfast.

Then he'd straighten up, feeling the good pain in his back that meant his day had not been wasting in fruitless repining. Steady labor made the day hurry on. No longer did Conn wonder if he'd taken on an impossible task. Though it meant crawling on the ground like an infant, his bare hands digging into the soil, he'd begun to learn by touch the difference between a harmful weed and a valuable plant.

Fortunately, the herbs he'd uprooted the first week, chervil, saxifrage, and rosemary, had all survived the necessary replanting, though the saxifrage had needed extra watering. Now when in that part of his mother's garden, he was careful to crush a leaf between his fingers before determining what stayed and what could be pulled out.

Over the last four days, the hours had gone by even

more quickly. He had the sound of his Lady's fountain to
charm his ears while he worked. He could imagine it, sparkling and merry in the light of the sun. The strange crystal-
encased dagger had been taken to the church, where it was
soaking in a tub of holy water. No change had yet been
reported in stone or in dagger. Father Maynard was mull-
ing over a letter to the archbishop, asking for advice.

Hearing the squeak of the garden door, Conn sat back
on his heels and turned his head in that direction. "Who's
there?"

For a moment, Conn tensed, wondering if this could be
The Lady. One word later, he was disappointed again.
" 'Tis Lucy. Master Gandy sent me with a basket."

"A basket?"

"Aye, half a chicken, a loaf of Mistress Allen's bread,
and a bottle of wine."

"A blessing on Gandy, then, for I'm sharp-set. And on
you, too, for bringing it."

A maidenly giggle answered him. It should have
charmed him; he even smiled without thinking. Yet as subtly as a shift in the wind, Conn became aware that the
maid had moved a little closer than was usual. He froze
into immobility, his brows twitching down. The maid
moved off.

"I'll just be layin' it out on the grass, then," she said,
and just as if he could see, Conn knew what kind of a
glance she was giving him. It would be a slow upsweep
of her eyes, her head held at a slight, enticing angle. "You
can come and take it when you've a mind to it."

"You're very kind," Conn said. "May I know your
name?"

Again the giggle teased his ears. "My father farms at
Calderford. My name's Lucy. Me and Master Gandy are
friends."

"Thank you kindly for the basket, Lucy. Tell Gandy I
thank him for his thoughtfulness, but I won't need anything else today."

"I don't mind staying t' take the basket back. Such a
sun I don't often see, tewing away in the kitchens for all

I'm worth.'' Her scent, grease and onions, reached him. She said boldly, ''Master Gandy tells me I could be a stillroom maid if I work to please you.''

As Conn sought for the words to refuse what she offered without offending her, she settled down on the gravel path near to him. Suddenly, her work-hardened fingers circled his wrist. ''By 'strewth, you're a big one, my lord. Strong in the saddle, too, I'll be bound!''

Most men would have taken all she offered. Conn, still striving to be decent, said, ''In truth, Lucy, I have no wish—''

''It's no mind to me that you can't never see. Most men close their eyes when they mate, don't they? Leastways, all the ones I been with does.'' She placed his hand over her breast with a simple matter-of-factness.

Conn pulled back at once, breaking the hold of her strong, roughened hand. ''I don't wish for what you offer, girl. Though I thank you.''

He heard puzzlement in her tone as she rose to her feet. ''Master Gandy said you'd tumble me quick 'cause it's been so long since your last bout.''

''It's not you—'' he started to say.

''Oh, I know that! I could have 'em on me like flies on a honeyjar if I snap my fingers.'' He heard the dry click of her fingers snapping. ''Master Gandy's goin' t'be that let down over this. He was certain sure you'd tumble me.''

Conn resolved to have a stern word with Gandy. He'd given plenty of homilies on the health benefits of frequent bouts, but this was the first time Gandy had gone beyond advice.

Lucy of the hot eyes had been in the nature of a physic prescribed by his loyal servant. Conn didn't know whether to laugh or to be angry, but it had to be stopped. As inventive as Gandy had proven in the past, he would whistle up a caliph's harem next. From what he'd heard from former Crusaders, the Eastern women might prove even more tenacious than Lucy.

The food, however, was most welcome. The flesh melted in his mouth, the bread was still warm from the oven, and the wine slipped gratefully down a parched throat. Afterward, Conn felt no immediate desire to return to the work he'd begun.

He lay back, the grass tickling his skin through his shirt and breeches, his arms spread wide at his sides. The weight of the sun's heat fell on him, pressing him down. Long ago, he would have seen the veined red of his eyelids as the sun shone through them. Now, though he lay in the full heat of noon, all was as dark as a midnight without a moon. The darkness dwelt in his soul, a yawning pit of cold night so deep that not even the scorching of the sun on his skin could warm him.

Had he fallen asleep? All he knew was that it had been silent and now he became aware again of birds singing and the sighing of the breeze. He sat up, his head thick and aching. His back itched from the crushed grass beneath him, and he thrashed his arms around, trying to scratch an unreachable part of his spine.

Giving that up and remembering that he had work still to do, he lurched in the direction of the roses. Setting off so carelessly, his sense of direction muddled, he soon found himself tripping over the bricks that lined the walkway. The laughter of the fountain sounded suddenly much nearer.

Conn forced himself to pause, to rub his face briskly until he could be sure he was awake. Then he proceeded with greater caution. He'd already learned the pain of stumbling into a rosebush.

They'd been his mother's, planted by her own careful hand after being brought by messenger from France. The withered sticks had bloomed as if by magic in the rich earth of the walled garden, the warmth of the sun reflected down into the beds by the stone walls.

After her death, they'd grown wild, sprawling in untamed splendor over the walls that had nurtured them. Conn had occupied himself since his return with trimming out the dead wood, narrowly avoiding being pricked to death by the thorns. Yet he'd not truly minded the cuts. They'd brought him the reassurance that he still dwelt among the living.

For all his work, he'd not yet been rewarded with flowers. What buds there were had been withered by cold, blasted by disease, or bored out from within by insects. Father Maynard had recommended chopping the intractable canes back to their roots so that fresh growth could create new roses. Conn had resisted that advice, good though it might be. He hoped that with patient tending, he'd bring the blighted plants to life once more without destroying what had grown already.

Yet now as he approached, a wave of fragrance swept over him. The sharp, sweet scent of a thousand flowering roses pierced his heart. It had been his mother's scent, attar of roses, crushed from the heart of the flower. He put out a questing hand and encountered a velvet petal.

"Ware thorns!"

He couldn't help turning his head to search for his Lady. "Thorns don't trouble me. It's only a scratch when all's said and done."

He wanted to hear her speak again. Mayhap he'd only imagined her voice. It could be that he still lay asleep on the grass. Yet he did not believe himself to be dreaming. He could feel her presence like a touch at his shoulder.

"I find roses to be the best balm for a troubled heart," she said, her strange, soft accent making music of the words.

"Is your heart troubled, my lady?"

"Not mine," she answered, yet there was a sigh behind her laugh. "Not now."

"It seems monstrous that such a woman as you should know even a moment's sorrow."

"One would not think, to look at you, that you have such honey on your tongue, good sir."

"Because of this?" he asked, touching his bandage. Strange that he wasn't furious or wounded by the suggestion. Had Helen made it . . . but then Helen made no attempt to hide her disgust from him. His last meeting with

Helen had gone badly. He'd been unable to dismiss from his mind the memory of all he'd overheard.

The Lady laughed, a low ripple of merriment that made Conn's lips curve despite himself. She said, " 'Twas not the bandage that I had in my thoughts. Yours are not the shoulders of a courtier. Somehow I misdoubt that you have ever bent the knee to a lady nor strummed a hymn to her beauty."

"I bend my knee to no one but my king," Conn said sternly. Then he grinned. "As for music, were you ever to hear me play, you'd soon call for silence."

"Vile, is it?"

"Monstrous vile. Yet I like to listen to a lute well played or a verse on some worthy subject."

"A worthy subject being war?" she asked, a teasing note in her lilting voice.

"More worthy than a tale of mawkish romance."

"Now, I prefer a courtly tale of love to one of battle. No woman really minds having her profile praised or her lips compared to the rose. Courtiers are at least good for one's pride, if bad for one's vanity."

"Do you know court life so well then? Which one do you favor: the shrew Matilda or our king, Stephen of Blois?"

He could tell by the sound that she'd turned away from him. "What matters not is king or queen but that the kingdom lasts. Whom among your claimants to this throne has an heir?"

"They both do," Conn said, displeased. Even a witch, if witch she be, should understand that Stephen alone had the right.

"Well then." He didn't need eyes to tell him that a pair of female shoulders had just dismissed the entire war with a careless twitch. "Let he that survives worry over the matter. Much wiser to have one king for all time and let the rest acknowledge his sway."

"But you must see that—" He swallowed the words. After hoping day and night that she'd return, Conn felt that he'd be a fool to drive her away by babbling about

the succession, a subject of notorious disinterest to women.
Their intellects, the scholars said, were not equipped to
deal with serious subjects. As for their souls, many great
minds joined in the opinion that women did not possess
any such thing.

With a hint of apology, she said, "This is not what I
came back to tell you, my good sir."

"My name is Conn," he said, interrupting. "I make you
a gift of it to use as you will."

"What does it mean? Conn. Such a hard sound and at
the same time . . ." She said it again, holding the *n* against
the roof of her mouth so that it hummed. It made a sudden
shiver run over him, as though she'd tapped him like a
silver bowl to hear the vibration spilling from the metal.

"I never heard that it had a meaning. It's a Saxon name.
This land belonged to them before we Normans came."
He wondered at his telling her this. Surely she must know
it already, whether she be witch or Christian.

"Belonged to them? Yes, and to the ones who lived here
before them, and those before them as well."

"What about you?" he asked, glimpsing an opening
into the world of questions he wanted to ask her.

"Me? Oh, I am neither Saxon nor Norman."

"Neither? That's impossible—" Then Conn recalled
that she might very well not even be flesh and shut his
lips.

She laughed softly at his embarrassment, as though she
had guessed at his thoughts. Something soft and sweet
pelted him on the cheek, then tumbled and clung to his
loose linen shirt. Conn instinctively raised his hand and
felt the open, flat petals of the small rose. He laughed out
loud and sent it skimming back toward the sound of her
voice.

Her laughter drifted off into silence, and Conn knew she
had gone. An instant later, he heard men's voices on the
other side of the wall.

Instinctively, he stepped forward, seeking her. He
touched only the wall and a flower. Conn stood there in
amazement, the rose clasped in his hand, as Ross entered

the garden. He said, "The last time I came in here I went home soaking wet."

"Be more careful this time," Conn said.

"I didn't thank you for getting me out of the fountain. Everyone told me that you did it."

"I did little enough."

He heard his brother's boots stomping over the grass and the awe in his words. "I've never seen so many flowers on this wall. The whole surface is alive with them."

"Is it?"

"It's wonderful. I don't remember there being so many colors. But I was so young when our mother died."

"What colors?" Conn tried to keep his frustration from taking over. "Describe it to me."

"Oh, I'm not good with words."

"You do well enough," Conn said, remembering.

"It looks like . . . as if . . . not to be fanciful, but as though a wizard came in and brought every bud to life with a wave of his hand and a word. I can see every color of rose except mayhap blue. There may be one yet. You know, Conn, I thought roses were mostly red or white, but I can see yellow, mauve, pink, even some that I cannot put a name to the shade. It's almost . . . it is like magic."

The excitement died out of his voice, leaving only confusion. Ross added, "My lord father is troubled. He is adamant in his belief that there are witches at work in our manor. What do you think, Conn?"

Conn clutched the rose in his hand more tightly. "Are you asking if these roses are the work of the Devil?"

"No! No. Of course not. Besides, the rose is sacred to Our Lady."

"My Lady, at any rate," Conn murmured. There'd been nothing holy or awe-inspiring about her today. She'd been playful, though she'd hinted that she had something serious to say to him. He imagined her as younger than himself but with a serenity that came from inner certainty. If only he could catch even a single glimpse of her face . . .

Ross had not heeded what his brother had said. "There's no doubt that something strange is happening. That stone

with the dagger . . . it's like a legend come to life. Father
has forbidden me to go near it as he's afraid it's witched,
but I should like to take another look at it. I only saw it
for a moment before Father Maynard took it away. It
looked . . . familiar.''

"You must obey Father," Conn said. "It's your duty."

"Of course."

"Speaking of Maynard, I wonder if you could ride as
far as the church with me. I have some things to talk over
with him. While you wait for me, mayhap you could offer
up a prayer or two *inside* the church itself."

"Eh?" Ross coughed affectedly. "Ah, yes. I do feel the
need for some extra prayers. Tomorrow, Conn?"

"In the morning. I will work here after the noon meal."

"I should be happy to assist you here at any time,"
Ross said. "I know Father does not think it suitable for a
man . . . that is . . ." He floundered, trying to recover from
his tactlessness.

Conn only smiled bitterly. "Well I know it. But it matters not. He will learn differently."

"I hope he will. Conn . . ." All in a rush, the younger
man said, "You know that I do not covet your position,
either as heir to Hamdry or my father's favorite. It's all
his doing."

"No, it is not those things you covet."

"Conn . . ."

As though nothing had been said, Conn said gently, "I
thank you for your offer, Ross, but I prefer to work alone
in this garden. There is much I can learn here, and it is
my own hands I must use, not another's."

"I'll not trouble you any more, then, brother." Ross's
steps moved away, then he paused. Conn waited, wondering if Ross would admit he loved Helen. The younger man
said, "Tomorrow after we breakfast?"

"Tomorrow."

The next day, Gandy finally found the courage to speak.
His master sat before the opened window in his chamber,
one ankle resting on the other knee, his foot waggling too

and fro to the tune he whistled, a bawdy air that had been making the round of the king's army just before the Battle of Lincoln. The sunlight awoke the red in Conn's dark hair and made the white bandage around his temples gleam. A breeze freshened his chamber, bringing with it a scent of spring that stirred the heavy tapestries. Golden motes of dust danced as joy must dance in the very air.

Conn stretched and said, "A fine day, indeed. Too fine to ride into the village. I should like to bed out those new herbs, trusting that there will come no more cold nights." He shrugged his broad shoulders and said, "It shall have to wait until Ross and I return. If anyone comes in search of me, you must tell them I shall be in my mother's garden later."

"I need say nothing of the matter, then, my lord. All the world knows where you spend your days now."

His master's head turned as though the blind eyes sought him out. Strange how one still felt scrutinized, even though no one knew better how sightless his master was. Though Gandy swore his conscience was clear, he still felt a need to babble out his sins when Conn fixed his attention on him.

Conn said, "You sound disapproving."

"Not I, my lord. Though others have wondered at your sudden interest in the garden."

"There's nothing sudden about it. I have little enough else to do. My father sees to that."

"Aye. 'Tis a cursed shame to this house."

"Ross is helpless in this." After a moment, Conn added, "You have not spoken to anyone of what you heard Ross and Helen say?"

"May the Lord strike me down if I utter a word of it," Gandy protested and drew an elaborate cross over himself to prove that he spoke the truth. His master could not see that and yet he smiled just as he used to at his servant's posturings. It was this kind of thing that unnerved Gandy more than anything. How *could* his master understand so much while seeing nothing?

Conn said, "See that you do not. They have much to

bear, the two of them. They shouldn't be gossiped about
by servants.''

"Oh, I never said they were not gossiped about. Only
that I had said nothing.''

"You mean there is talk about them?''

"Not a great deal. Some. It has been noticed that Master
Ross's eyes follow her whenever she and her father visit.
Moreover, he has been melancholic and but toys with his
food. His servant, a knock-kneed codswallop named Hub-
ert—not a one I'd care to have near *me* in the night!—he
tells us that his master does not sleep well but tosses and
moans aloud. This disloyal dog has boasted that he has
listened to his master's night words but has heard no
names that can be understood.''

"This you call *some* gossip? It appears to me that poor
Ross is the chief topic among you.''

"Nay. There is another of greater interest.'' Gandy
waited for Conn to pick up the hint he'd let fall, but his
master returned to—one almost might say—watching out
the window.

Gandy sketched another cross over himself as he moved
about the room, flicking away any dust with a cloth. Clicking his tongue for shame, he bent to pick up a shirt from
the floor. "Look at this stain, green as grass,'' he said.

"Did you speak?''

"Nay, my lord.''

"I thought you did.''

Gandy struggled with silence but could not keep it.
"Only it makes my heart glad that you took my counsel
at last.''

"Which council? You offer so much.''

"Why, to ease yourself upon the body of the maid I
sent to you yesterday.''

"What makes you say so?''

"Signs upon this shirt declare themselves. 'Tis plain you
have rolled about the grass in it.'' Gandy held it up toward
his master as if even a blind man could see the proof. "All
is well and much explained.''

His master chuckled. "Thus from nothingness does all

the world come into being. I've heard tell of such a Genesis but did not expect it from you.''

Gandy stared at Conn. ''Was she not to your liking, master? True, a most ardent nature beats within her—all too ardent, the old women would say. Yet what more arousing to a man than an maid eager to know all manner of pleasure?''

''You thought of everything, Gandy,'' Conn said with that gentleness that always meant trouble. ''Except one thing. Your master will not sleep in soiled straw. Nor do I tumble with maids of my own house, for it leads only to jealousy, pride, and ill feeling. Besides, my taste no doubt is flawed. I sent her away at once and will thank you to send no more.''

''Then why so do you look this way?'' The question burst from Gandy. He'd longed to ask since he brought Conn meat last night.

At once, Conn put up a hand to adjust his bandage. ''What way? I look no different than yesterday.''

''But you do! I cannot say how nor speak to any one point. Everyone who saw you yesterday remarked on it and wondered. You do not look so troubled today, my lord. You ought. We both know what cause you have.''

Conn stood up, and Gandy feared he'd overstepped even the liberal bounds his master granted him. Other men of a soldierly stamp might beat an insolent servant. Experience had taught Gandy that Conn would disdain to use his fists. He inflicted damage enough with a cold word or a cutting look. All the same, there might come a first time. With infinite relief, he heard Conn speak sternly.

''Teach them then to mind me not. You have a good right arm, Gandy. Use it. When they respect you, they will not speak of me. I will not have them peeking and prying nor gossiping. If you cannot silence them—''

''I shall, my lord. I vow it. Only . . .''

''Only?''

''Take heed, master. This jaunting about with only your brother for company I cannot like. If you are dashed from your horse, injured or killed, there is only his word to say how it came about.''

"You and my lord father should speak to each other, Gandy. He fears I may murder my brother, and you fear that Ross will murder me. Yet we are both milder than you. Neither of us has any such thought in our hearts."

"For your heart, my lord, I will stand surety. But Master Ross? The love of a fair woman has driven other men to murder, since you will speak the word so plain."

"I am not afraid." Conn walked to the bed, paused, and felt his way along the surface to the flat pillow at the head. He thrust his hand beneath it and sought with his fingers. When he spoke, his voice had dropped to a freezing register. "Gandy. What have you done with the veil that was here?"

"Veil? I saw no—"

His master's blindness had not affected his speed. In an instant, Gandy found a massive fist grasping the front of his tunic. "M-M-Master . . ."

"It was here. Blue, spangled with stars, sheer as still water. . . ."

"No. I've seen naught like that. It—it must be wondrous fine."

Gandy watched fearfully as his master's tight jaw unclenched and his fist opened. "Who else has been in here?" Conn demanded, though in a milder tone.

"No one. Just you and I. Oh, and Lucy. I thought . . . you couldn't have sent for her as I had thought."

"Get it back from her."

"As you will, my lord."

Conn turned away and started for the door. Even in his confusion and hurt, Gandy noticed that his master grew more confident by the day. If it were not for the bandage he still wore, a stranger would have been hard pressed to realize that this was a blind man.

At the doorway, Conn paused. "If it is any comfort to you, I shall ride warily."

"I pray you will." Gandy, prompted by relief and the devil, added with a sniff, "It would not please me to take time to train another master."

"Nor I another servant. Be content."

Six

"This is outrageous! What your father would say if he knew!"

"He doesn't know. I hope he won't find out. *I* won't tell him." Sira drew a deep breath, almost intoxicated with the scent of the roses. "Didn't I tell you it was beautiful, Anat?"

" 'Tis well enough. Though there are too many colors. That brilliant yellow rose clashes with the purple. But I expect no better from a meedless human."

Laughing quietly, Sira said, "You must blame the roses on me. Mortals haven't learned to make those colors of their roses yet. It's a good thing, perhaps, that Conn is blind. He'd know the truth."

"You said his brother saw them. Didn't he say something about the colors of the blooms?"

"Not he. He's not the kind who notices such things." She reached up and brought an especially succulent rose down for a long, euphoric sniff. Sighing with pure pleasure, she added, "Such a lovely day."

Anat squinted suspiciously at the sky, drawing her warm woolen stole more closely about her thin shoulders. "I suppose . . . if you like that sort of thing."

"He'll be here soon," Sira said to her companion. "Then you'll see there's nothing at all objectionable in my meeting him here. It's as harmless as though he were a pet lamb.''

"Have you told him who you are?"

"Certainly not. I don't want him to think me a mad-woman.'' Sira remembered how warmly he'd spoken to her. "He thinks I am a lady from another manor. We spoke of courts yesterday. Yes, I'm sure that's what he thinks. Just a lonely mortal like himself.''

"Ugh, how insulting! Well, it's to be hoped we won't need to stay here all day. Such an uncivilized spot!"

"It's not so bad."

"Not bad . . . ?'' Anat began, then said, "Do you hear voices? Is your human bringing a female along?'' She sniffed. "So much for innate nobility.''

Sira knew instantly that it was not Conn approaching. Conn's mind had been closed to her after the first glimpse she'd had of this garden. It still troubled her that she couldn't look into his thoughts. The male who came now, for instance, had a shallow mind, as easy to look into as a bowl of water, and the things she saw concerned nothing but images of carnal excess.

Clearing her head with a shake and hoping that Anat wouldn't wonder why she'd changed color, Sira faded into conscious nothingness. Anat looked disgusted but copied her.

A moment later, the door in the wall opened. A young man, none too tall but with a certain undefinable *air,* entered, hand in hand with a girl.

"Don't be so slow, Margery,'' the young man said with a tinge of impatience.

"Don't be in such a hurry,'' she shot back. "No point in a-hurrying me, m'dear. Margery goes at her own speed.'' The girl, brown-haired with merry blue eyes crinkling in her round face, glanced around the garden. She caught her breath. "Ain't it lovely, then?''

The young man grinned. "It's all yours, my lady,'' he said with a flourish. "At least, yours until my master comes back.''

Sira made herself a trifle more solid so that she could

listen without the roaring in her ears that came when she stood between mortal reality and her own. The shade Anat had become gave off a frowning emanation that Sira felt rather than saw. She paid no mind. Had the mortal, Conn, left Hamdry for the monastery? A strange hollow feeling settled behind her breastbone.

Margery asked, "Oh, shall I say it's mine when he comes back sudden like?"

"My master's a good heart. He'll not begrudge a faithful servant a dalliance with the loveliest maid in all the shire."

"Go on with you, Master Gandy, do! I'm not one to lend my ears to such lies." She tossed her head, setting her glossy curls to bouncing under her stained kerchief. Sira saw how Margery rolled her eyes at the young man and the sudden spark that leaped into his eyes.

Gandy started toward the girl, slowly, one foot solidly on the ground ere the next one lifted. She, on the other hand, began to back away, faster and faster. Sira was reminded of one of The People's festival dances, only the glow between these mortals made it very different. This was no formal, sacred salute to eternal powers. Something even more elemental was going on.

The girl's smile turned to laughter as she retreated more and more quickly across the grass. It seemed certain that the young man would never catch her, when she stopped, thrusting her arms out in front of her, hands held up, as though to keep him off her. Gandy took her wrists, one in either hand, spread her arms wide and stepped between them. She gave him a warning glance, which he ignored.

An instant later, they were tightly embracing, their lips crushed together. It looked most painful. Judging by the moans that escaped them, it must have been. Yet if they were hurt, why should they continue? If they stopped, they only gazed into each others' eyes and started up again.

Sira drifted a bit closer, curious to better see this strange ritual. She noticed that their hands seemed to have a part in whatever it was they were doing. Gandy ran his hands up and down over the girl's back, bringing forth even more of the strange moans. Then his hands stopped, low, and seemed to press the girl's lower body forward. The sounds they were making increased in intensity. Sira threw a confused glance at Anat.

Striding forward, nearly visible, Anat hissed, "Come away from that savage spectacle! In a thousand years, I've never seen anything so vile—not since we had the Rhine Maidens' visit with that nasty little Nibelung creature who panted all over them."

"And you . . ." Sira added absently. The two mortals lay on the grass now, the male over the female. His fingers were surprisingly nimble as he unlaced the ties of her simple gown.

Opening her eyes, Margery lifted her head a moment and said, "You're sure Master Conn won't be back from the church for a good while? I feel like there's somebody standing over us."

"Once Father Maynard gets to talking, my master won't be able to get away 'til sundown." They laughed together so warmly that for a moment, Sira felt a sharp pang of what she greatly feared might be jealousy. Instantly, she dismissed the notion.

Never be it said that she, daughter of Boadach the Eternal, cared to be tousled and tumbled like a kitchen wench. Yet something in the sound of their shared laughter had pained her as though she saw a half-tame bird fly out of sight forever. They seemed so happy lying there together.

Sira spread out her arms over the entwined couple. "Oh, Mother," she said, calling on the source of all things. "Let this union be pleasing to you with its fruitfulness."

Then Sira gave in to Anat's increasingly desperate signals to depart. As they floated over the wall to the dreary outer garden, Anat flatly refused to stir another step beyond the borders of their own kingdom.

"I'm not inflexible, I hope. I can accept innovation as well as the next. Am I not the first to praise every change you have ever made in the court's attire? Don't I hasten to obey every edict the king hands down?"

"Yes, Anat. Of course. You are a very faithful friend."

"Very well. Then you can't accuse me of prejudice when I say I would rather join the Sleepers than ever witness such a ghastly display again! Far rather." She closed her thin lips tightly, but Sira did not cherish a strong hope that this would be Anat's final word.

Sure enough, a moment later, she'd thought of something to add and unsealed those joined lips. "No good can come of your association with a mortal, Sira. You may think this Conn is a gentle, refined sort. Yet you tell me he was a warrior once, a wielder of cold iron and even that thrice cursed steel. How does that tally with *your* perception of him?"

"He's different now. Do you think I can't tell?"

"I think you're toying with things better left alone. I only hope it's but a phase you are passing through, as when you had an absolute passion for those little dragons. You outgrew them; you'll outgrow meddling with humans as well."

Before Sira could open her mouth to protest, the older fay took herself away. Sira told herself that Anat was wrong; Conn wasn't like that. She'd prove it today.

Half an hour later, as humans reckon time, Sira sat on the edge of a low stone wall half-grown with lichen. She kept her eyes closed and her face lifted to absorb the sun's healing light.

The green mounds of the graves lay unevenly scattered in unmown grass behind her. The church stood on a slight rise, casting its shadow over the dead men. She still wondered at the human tendency to keep the dead handy but gave them no particular thought. She swung her feet from side to side and waited with what patience she could.

Today, she fancied, she looked truly mortal, as ordinary as coarse bread. She wore a simple satin gown tied up the sides over a loose silk blouse. A kerchief with the tiniest border of doves embroidered in silver caught back her hair, though long braids spilled out from beneath it, tied with more silver cord. A dark blue mantle went over all, fastened at the neck with a paltry chain carved from sapphires and fastened with a small cabochon ruby.

Sira had modeled her clothes on those of that Helen person. True, she'd substituted finer materials but so subtly that no one would look twice at her. A fat priest had done no more than nod absently as he hurried past her on some errand, his sandals flapping in the dirt.

Sira didn't know how humans stood the slow passing of the minutes. So much easier to be one of The People to whom time was like a river in which they occasionally bathed. Humans were steeped in time for always, dragged down by its weight, battered by its relentless sweep onward and onward. No matter how they fought it, sooner or later, every human was lost in the mists. How difficult it must be to live never knowing which moments were wasted and which were of value.

At last, Sira heard the sound she'd been waiting for. Flipping one braid forward, she licked her fingers to comb the flowing ends until they lay smooth. She shook out her skirt to discourage a beetle that had landed there. Then she remembered that Conn was blind and all her effort would be to no avail.

Instead, she started to sing. Perchance it was Anat's mention of the Rhine Maidens that had put the tune in her head. The People had taught it to them and the river goddesses had made it their own. A song without words, it followed the road, and Sira's mind went along with it.

Ross was first to draw rein. "What is that? I've never heard aught like it. . . ."

"The miller's daughters sing as they grind the grist," Conn said glibly.

Sira wondered if he recognized her voice. She softened the notes but strengthened the power of her song. Concentrating, she watched as they came closer to where she sat, half a mile away, on a stone wall. Alert both there and here, she could feel the sun still warm on her face and see and listen to Conn and Ross, all at the same time.

Conn said, "Let's ride on."

"I've heard the miller's daughters a thousand times. They sing like old crows from the dust in their craws. This is . . . like an angel's voice."

"She's no angel," Conn muttered. Half a mile away, Sira laughed.

Ross crossed himself. "A devil then? A witch?"

"No, not that, either. Just the miller's daughters. Or strolling players. Yes, that's it! Strolling players on the way to Hamdry who have stopped to practice before appearing. Father's always looking for new entertainment, and the gypsies all know it. No doubt we'll see the singer tonight as we sup."

"If that's an itinerant minstrel, I'll eat her lute, ribbons and all!"

"I wish you good appetite, brother!"

Sira didn't want Conn and his brother to argue about her song. The Rhine Maiden song was supposed to steal a man's will, make him hasten to her side though untold dangers bar the way. Willing slavery for life was usually the outcome. Though she didn't in the least wish to enslave Conn, for she thought he'd be much too difficult to handle, she did want them to hurry up. Mayhap she wasn't doing it right. It had been a long time, even by fay terms, since the maidens' disastrous visit.

So she stopped and glimpsed on Conn's face an expression of agony, as though he'd been stabbed to the heart. She reached out to him with healing but was taken aback by his continuing to banter with his brother in a light although somewhat hollow tone. Had she mistaken a pain of the body for one of the soul?

"Too bad, Ross. I believe you've lost your heart entire to the unknown singer. What a shame for your true love should you prove false!"

Ross gave a sudden start that set his horse to dancing. Leaning forward to pat his mount's glossy neck, Ross's laughter sounded forced. "A shame, indeed. But as I have no true love as yet, she is spared much pain, whoever she may be."

Conn mused, "Do you imagine the singer to be dark or fair? A queen among lesser mortals or a slovenly beggar? If we see her, you must describe her for me. But, somehow, I doubt we'll catch a glimpse of her."

They rode on, to Sira's relief. Deciding to stay visible, she sat up straight on the wall, as they came within un-assisted sight. The young man dismounted to open the gate, handing the reins of his horse to Conn.

"Good morrow to you, good sir," she said in a voice as soft and purring as a baby dragon's. She couldn't resist turning her gaze toward Conn, sitting at his ease in the saddle on the back of an immense horse.

Ross barely glanced at her. "Good day, Mother." He threw a question to his brother. "Are you coming in?"

"No, I can't see the miracle, so am likely to be unim-pressed. You go. Do tell me if you see your singing lady."

"I will. Meanwhile, mayhaps this good woman will keep you company and perchance fetch you a cup of water to cool your throat? Eh, Mother?"

"What woman?"

Sira didn't think that Mother was a respectful way to speak to a woman Ross didn't even know. She was seri-ously considering turning him into something slimy when Conn asked again.

Ross, with a half-embarrassed glance at her, walked quickly back to his brother's side. Conn leaned down in answer to a tug on his boot. Though Ross whispered al-most too low for Conn himself to hear, Sira caught every word.

"There's an old crone sitting on the church wall, Conn. A hideous creature with a wen on her cheek the size of an apple. She's wrapped about with stinking rags, and I swear I saw spiders in her hair."

"A frightful sight," Conn whispered back, though with a chuckle buried in the words. "Makes me glad I'm spared it."

The younger brother gave the boot another tug. "Father may be right about witches being nearby, for she's surely one if ever there was. So gruesome . . . I swear she smells of graves!"

Nervously, Sira passed her hand over her cheek and found it as smooth as ever. Just to be doubly safe, she ran her fingers over the length of her shining braid. No creatures of any kind. Tightening her lips, Sira whispered fiercely, "Anat!" and could swear she heard her companion's emphatic "Humph!"

Conn told his brother to go on into the church for safety. For himself, he'd sift the old woman and find out if she was a witch in truth. "No, I'm not afraid. I've met many a witch in London, though there they pronounce it differently."

Sira bestowed on Ross her most charming smile as he edged past her. He winced and averted his eyes. Sira wondered how many teeth Anat had deleted from her mouth to complete the illusion of her repulsiveness.

Then Conn asked, "Has he gone?"

"He is running up the path . . . there. He's entered the church."

"We should move on, my lady. He might come back with a vial of holy water."

"How . . . how do you know it is I?"

The powerful shoulders lifted and fell under the buckram tunic. "My brother is not the most discriminating of fellows. If there is a smell of graves here, it comes from the churchyard. You always smell of flowers."

She slid down from the wall. "Will you walk with me, Conn?"

Though she knew little of such things, his grace in dismounting pleased her eyes. He lifted the reins over the horse's head and asked, "Will you tie them to the gate? You won't be afraid?"

She looked into the eyes of each of the mounts, their half-aware brown eyes acknowledging an age-old debt. "They'll not stray. They are noble and true and quite dedicated to you and your brother. It is their pride and joy to obey you."

Sira turned to find Conn laughing at her. She demanded the reason. He said, "My brother is gone. Why do you persist with this disguised voice? It was not thus when you sang. Unless . . . have you caught a chill sitting on that wall so that you croak like a frog?"

"I—I croak?" She let out a fuming breath. "Excuse me

a moment. . . ." Quick as thinking, she stood again outside her chamber in the Living Lands. Conn's village church was built practically on top of an old doorway. Long abandoned, it yet remained a viable passage to the Lands. Only the end of time itself would close the gates. Or the end of The People themselves, which was unthinkable.

"Anat!" she demanded, walking into her chamber. "Undo this glamour at once!"

"Why should I?" her companion asked. "Your mortal cannot see you, and it is protection against the others. Do you know how unwise it is for one of The People to walk openly among mortals?"

"I do know," Sira insisted. "I've heard the tales over and over. And it's not as though there were mortals to see me."

"Three have done!"

"Two. The old priest and Ross. Conn is, as you have said, unlikely to guess by seeing. Now, kindly take away the illusion you've slung about me and make me as I am. I can do it myself, you know, but you wouldn't like it."

Anat nodded slowly. "Very well. At the least I can tell your father that I tried to save you from the consequences of your headstrong folly." She unfocused her gaze a moment and the thing was done.

Sira narrowed her eyes suspiciously. "You haven't made me worse still, have you? Shall I look in the waterfall?"

Sighing, Anat let her gaze go out of focus again. "There. You are in all respects exactly as you know yourself to be."

"Thank you. I have to go back now. I left him waiting."

Anat said, "Don't let him touch you."

"I won't. He hasn't yet." She felt a trifle of guilt over not telling Anat about how he had tried.

Conn had turned about and was now resting, his elbows on the warm stone. For her, minutes had passed. For him, something less than a single minute. For all he knew, she'd simply stepped out of earshot, nor would he have believed the truth. Humans were tremendously tenancious of their ideas about reality. Everyone said how hard it was to convince any mortal that he'd actually captured one of The People. They always wanted proof.

"Where shall we walk, my lady?" he asked.

"Do you have a favorite place here?"

He made no move to lead her. "You must know the way yourself."

"No, I don't." Something about the quality of his silence struck her as disbelieving. "In truth."

"That night, by the standing stones, you saw into my mind, didn't you? Easily."

"Yes, I did."

He nodded, as though he merely heard confirmation of what he'd been thinking. "So, you can do it now, too, can't you?"

Instinctively, Sira began to shake her head. Remembering, she spoke her denial aloud. "I could at first. Not since then. I can't figure out why the scrying doesn't work with you. I should ask Anat; she'd know."

"Oh, yes. The friend who wanted to throw me to your king. King of what, my lady?"

She noticed then that his hands were fists and his muscles stood out, bunched under his shirt. "Don't be afraid," she said quickly and saw him smile bitterly.

"I'm not afraid of any dark power," he declared. "What can you do to me that has not already been done? Only take my life, and it will do neither of us any good."

"What about your soul? I could take that."

"My soul is my own. I might barter it away, but there's nothing I want."

"Not even . . ." She couldn't complete what she'd thought to say. It would be too cruel even to mention restoring his eyesight. She could do it—at least, she thought she could, but she would have to touch him. That she dared not do.

Though she'd found herself wondering again and again what the rough hair on his body would feel like under her palm, and sometimes her hands would itch suddenly with a curiosity over whether his skin was smooth or coarse, it took more than inquisitiveness to overcome twenty-two hundred years of custom and upbringing.

Looking at him, with the sun glinting off his hair and gliding lovingly over his skin, she realized that even twenty-two hundred years might not be enough.

She said suddenly, "This is the last time I'll come to see you, Conn."

"What?"

"It's too dangerous. I don't dare come anymore."

"I would not have thought you a coward."

"Oh, but I am." More loudly, she said, "I must do one thing before I go."

"I shall help you if you tell me what it is."

"I must take away the crystal that surrounds your knife. I shouldn't have left it behind; I should have taken it back after I returned your knife. If my . . . king finds out that I left it, he'd be angry. All the more so since I have returned twice now without correcting my earlier folly."

"Why didn't you?" He seemed to have accepted her bare word that she was responsible for the crystal that encased his dagger. She felt too grateful for it to marvel at his acceptance.

"I don't know why I didn't. I can't say that I forgot . . . exactly. I was confused . . . your brother falling into the water like that and you . . ." She smiled shyly, though he could not see it. "You were chasing me to see if I were real."

"I know now," he said with something like a laugh. "You are real. It is myself I now have doubts about." Before she could ask his meaning, he nodded decisively, saying, "Very well, then. Let's go to the church and deal with this difficulty."

He held out his hand with such a careless yet commanding gesture that Sira had almost reached out to take it before she recollected herself. Conn had a habit of taking obedience for granted that must have come from his soldiering days. But that was no excuse for her.

"You go on," she said.

He held the gate wide for her at her request, and Sira

slipped through without touching the iron fastenings. She dared not tell him why she took such precautions; even the meanest serf knew of The People's aversion to iron or steel.

"Is this your church?" she asked as they walked up the winding path among the grave markers.

"Well, my parents were married here in the porch, and I was carried to the font here. But it has been many a day since I or my father came down the hill for Mass. Father Maynard comes to the manor to our lady chapel."

"Father Maynard? A fat priest?"

"You've seen him?"

She couldn't help laughing, though she did not answer when he asked her what was amusing her. Now she knew why the hurrying priest had not thrown her a second glance. He was most likely on his knees right now, praying that the hideous creature no longer perched beside his gate. Though her People had as little love for the Christian priests as for the iron their soldiers brought, Sira had thought the priest in Hamdry had a kind face, though not kind enough perhaps to stop and speak to a possible witch.

Sira had put her silver-shod foot on the doorstep of the church when she drew back with a hiss of breath. Every nerve in her body sizzled like hot stones thrust into cold water.

"What's wrong?" Conn asked from within the dimly light doorway. He came back out to her.

"Nothing," she said, while she swept the threshold with her gaze. There, half-buried in the dark gray rock, still rough with the marks of the hammer and chisel, was a date wrought in iron.

"Did you hurt yourself?" Conn asked. "I've stubbed my toes a score of times on this old stone. It's cut too thick for the purpose."

Her quick wits supplied her with an answer. "I just recalled that your brother is within. I don't wish for him to see me."

"Though he will not now see an old crone? Will he, my lady?"

"No," Sira admitted. "He would see me as I am."

Conn nodded as though she'd revealed more to him than she had intended. "I have a thousand questions to put to you. I dare not ask even one."

"Dare not?"

"You have said you will not see me again. Is it not better then that I do not ask?"

She looked up at him, seeing not the bandaged eyes nor the lines of pain about his mouth. She saw rather that rarest of mortals, one who could understand that it was not for evil that The People acted as they do, nor even for mischief. It was for double protection: mortal from fay, fay from mortal.

Sira did not for a moment expect Conn to accept her protection willingly. In his world, a woman did not protect a man. Yet she would keep him safe so far as lay within her powers. She vowed that now, silently.

She did not answer his question. Instead, she asked, "Will you bring the crystal out to me?"

"With a right good will, my lady."

Following him with her mind, she saw him enter the empty nave and caught the edge of his wonder that Ross did not answer his call. Conn walked more slowly, sliding his feet over the stones that lined the aisle. The solid stone walls kept out the warmth of the sun except where it slanted in, in long falling beams of gold, from slits so high up that their tops brushed the roof. "Ross?" he called again.

"I'm here!"

Conn turned toward his brother's voice. Sira saw that the younger man's hair no longer lay neatly waving over the closed neck of his overtunic. His cheeks were flushed and his breathing quick and shallow.

"Where were you?" Conn asked. "I thought you'd be rapt in wonder at the miracle."

"Oh, that. Most wonderously made, I vow."

"Let's take it outside so you might look at it in the sunlight. Where does it lie?"

"Within six paces, on the altar step." Ross went to his

brother and took his arm. "But you can't mean to remove it from the holy water."

"For a moment only."

The crystal lay within a stone vat filled to the brim with water. Disregarding Ross's repeated protest, Conn plunged his hands into the trough. "There," he said, lifting his dripping hands. "Guide me again to the door."

"But Conn . . ." Even while continuing to bleat, Ross did as he was told.

Sira, about to recall her consciousness, became aware of a movement in a side chamber off the chancel. Instantly, she reached out with her thoughts and recognized the woman, Helen, crouching there like a mouse eyeing a cat. Like Ross, she breathed as though she'd been running, trembling as she inhaled and exhaled.

Realizing Conn was carrying the crystal over the doorstep, Sira returned instantly to her self. Ross's eyes widened as he saw her. He said in a choked voice, "My God! Is it an angel?"

Conn said, "Describe her now, if you please."

"Now?"

Sira reached out with one hand, fingers spread open as if she tried to clutch a ball bigger than her hand. "Hold," she said calmly.

Ross froze on the doorstep of the church as though he had turned to stone. His eyes were blank, his mouth opened on a word that would not be spoken.

"Ross? Ross?"

To Conn, Sira said, "He should not see this. It might make trouble for you."

"What have you done to him?"

"Nothing of lasting harm. Do you trust me?"

"I—"

She came up to where Conn stood, cradling the long crystal in one arm. "I should have been wiser," she said.

With a stroke of her fingers, she left him holding only his own steel blade, the hilt wrapped round with silver wire. "It is yours," she said, immediately stepping away.

The knife, baptized more than once in blood, burned her even more fiercely than the iron or steel alone.

"I will go now, Conn. And—"

"No, my lady, stay. Or promise to return."

"I cannot. But I will always remember you. Always."

He reached out for her. If a scream had not arisen from the church steps, his fingers might have grazed her face. But the scream made him start in surprise, turning toward the sound. Sira let herself become unseen; bad enough that Ross had seen her in her true form. If only she had listened to Anat!

Remembering Ross, but never taking her gaze from Conn, Sira waved her arm to free the younger man from the hold she'd placed on him. The woman, Helen, stood beside Ross, screaming. One word only was clear.

"Witch! Witch!" Her shaking finger pointed at Conn.

Ross, blinking as though he'd awakened from a long sleep, said, "Conn? What is it?"

The girl turned and ran back into the church. Ross, bemused still, stared at his brother. "What happened to the crystal? Did you drop it?" He looked at the ground stupidly as though expecting to see shards there.

Then Sira heard the sound of hoofbeats racing away. She cast forth her thought again and saw the girl, her long black hair slipped free of its bonds and whipping behind her, riding hard across the fields. She asked, "Does she flee to her parents?"

"My father, more like," Conn said.

Ross asked, "Did she call you witch? Why did she?"

Sira said, "I shall stop her."

"No! No one will believe her. I will say we found the knife like this, with the crystal melted away by the holy water."

"What of Ross? He saw it whole."

"He will say that he saw no crystal here."

"Will he?" Sira glanced at Ross, who, still recovering from the effects of the spell, was gazing blankly at the ground.

Conn slid his dagger into his belt. "I can be very eloquent when the need arises. I shall convince him to tell the same tale as I do."

"I wish . . . I wish that I had not meddled with you."

"Don't wish that," he said, the lines about his mouth faded for a moment. "You have brought me things that I never dreamed of before. I cannot regret them now." He sighed. "You must go. But promise that you will return."

"I—will try."

"Then I am content."

Ross, rubbing the back of his head, asked, "Conn, who are you talking to?"

"No one. No one at all."

Seven

Sira sat alone in the great hall, wrapped in a shadow of deep thought. The firelight from the open pit in the center of the hall traced a shifting embroidery of flame along the hem of her white gown; or was it golden thread cunningly worked? Before the evening's songs had faded into silence, Sira knew Anat would be besieged by the maids of the court, demanding to know which it was. Sira could trust Anat to return a sharp answer.

Moving her foot to set the embroidery to shimmering all the more, Sira thought, *What a frivolous creature I am,* and shook her head slightly. As long as she lived and no matter what trouble came, she would always cherish pleasure in the trivial delights of life. A new gown, a fresh fashion of the hair, or a trinket brought from the ends of the earth made her clap her hands in glee like any child.

Then a slight frown creased her perfect brow. She felt it there and pressed her fingers against it. What business had she with thoughts of trouble or age? These things fell not to her portion. Her heart had always been given, *should* always be given over to pure joy, and if that meant at times an overinterest in the trivial and foolish, so be it.

Sira sighed, knowing what was troubling her most. She would never see Conn again. If by some chance she should, he'd be an old man, withered away, broken by the heavy press of years.

If he survived at all. The charge of witchcraft, even laid to him by a hysterical girl, was not one mortals took lightly. On the contrary, the tales of their viciousness to those weakened by age or infirmity were terrifying.

She saw again in her mind's eye the ripple of Conn's smooth skin, the flex of his muscles as he moved with that infinitely masculine grace, and above all, the merry fortitude of his smile. How warm his skin must be, how resilient and strong his arms.

"Shall I sing a song to the lady who kindles fire in all our hearts?" said a voice from beside her.

Sira started, her frightened gaze flying up. Then her tense shoulders relaxed. "Oh, it's you, Blaic."

"Pray contain your rapture lest my self-conceit become overwhelming."

"Too late," she said with a mischievous smile.

"For your smile, my lady, I'll sing forever."

"Must you sing at all?"

"Crushed again," he said, bowing.

"I meant that I should rather talk with you."

"I am at my lady's service in this, as in all things."

Blaic had the fair hair of The People as well as their agelessly smooth skin, but having come from the Westering Lands, his skin was darker than most in the court, and his eyes gleamed forest green instead of blue. His father was an underlord to Boadach and had sent his son hither to learn the ways of the high court. He was among the most notable of Sira's admirers, yet she could never quite tell how seriously he felt toward her. He had taken her father's rejection of his aspiration to her hand surprisingly well for one who professed undying love.

He stood beside her. "Sad, my fair?"

"I?" Sira resolved yet again to push Conn from her thoughts. "Not out of reason. It's always dull after a high festival."

"I shouldn't have guessed that you ever found life less than delightful."

Sira looked up into Blaic's dark eyes, puzzled by the

tone of his voice. He sounded wistful, as if her capacity for pleasure daunted him.

He added, "I looked for you earlier. Were we not this day to go into the sea together?"

Stricken with guilt, Sira said, "Yes, we were. I'm sorry. My lord sent me about some business, and I could not return in time." Better to place the blame on her father than to admit that she'd utterly forgotten. "I should have sent you word."

Blaic dismissed the subject with an easy shrug. "I do not see your lady dragon guarding you tonight. Shall I take advantage of her absence to kiss your hand?"

"Please . . ." Sira held out her hand toward him, the least recompense she could make for being so rude.

He took it with much tenderness, holding it lightly on the back of his own. Slowly, he sank down onto one knee, gazing down at her slim white fingers with a reverence far deeper than any she'd seen on his face before. She caught her breath, more with dread than anticipation. For a moment, even the sound of the snapping fire seemed to die.

Sira felt an entirely instinctive longing to snatch her hand away. As though it had been foretold, she knew that a moment of decision had arrived. She wanted to face it with courage, yet her heart failed at the thought of hurting him.

He raised his head to look into her eyes. What she saw in the depths of his gaze made her realize that she had not known him before now. He had been light in words, merry in deeds. Though he'd approached her father to propose, Sira had thought only that he was acting as *his* father would wish. Marriage was rare among The People. Her marriage would be cause for celebration and festival unrivaled in the Lands of the Living since Boadach took a wife in the Long Ago Before.

Now she knew Blaic felt for her a passion so deep and strong that she felt frightened, for she knew she could never answer it. Yet what folly. He was as near to the perfect mate for her as could be imagined. There might never be another. Perhaps she should agree. . . .

She thought of Conn. Not as beautiful as one of The People, more rugged, more violent. She could not imagine him going on his knees to any woman. Even defeated in a human war, blinded, he still bore himself as a conqueror. It seemed as though his entry into her life had been a blessing. Though a human could never be a fit mate for her, or indeed for any of The People, Conn had shown the truth within her own heart. Never could she marry one who did not fulfill her dreams.

Blaic lowered his gaze. Without touching his lips to her hand, he let it go. The moment had passed. Sira blessed him silently, grateful for the reprieve. He said, with a return of his light tone, "I hope they'll not make new music for us tonight. You know how fond I am of the old songs."

"Go to Cuar, then, and tell him that I wish to hear some of my mother's songs. I don't believe you have ever heard them."

"I obey at once."

Again alone, Sira now took no pleasure in the play of light on her gown. She cherished no hope that the moment between Blaic and her had gone unobserved. It must have been obvious to all eyes that Blaic had been on the point of offering her his whole heart and that somehow she'd forestalled him. Her only wonder was that it had not already been reported to her father.

Anat came bustling up, the keys at her waist jingling. "I've told you again and again that if you are going to flirt with the young lords, you must expect this kind of thing. A most embarrassing moment! I had thought better of the Westering prince's manners."

"It's not his fault. He loves me."

"Humph! You see how any contact with mortals corrupts you! Among them, that kind of talk might be proper, but you should be ashamed to use such language in your father's own court. Blaic has no business feeling anything of the sort for you."

"He didn't ask me tonight."

"I should hope not! Your father would be right to banish him forever if he offered you such boorishness. As it

is, I shouldn't be surprised if this is the last we see of him
for some time. He'll be going home to his father, if he has
any decency."

Sira leaned her cheek on her hand, knowing Anat would
continue to fuss and fume until she'd said all she had
stored up, and some of it more than once. She sighed, "I
wish . . ."

The first ravishing notes of an ancient air shimmered
through Boadach's great hall. At that, every voice stilled,
as the haunting music stole into every mind. Even those
in midstep paused, turning toward the wizened figure of
Cuar, greatest harpist in all the Living Lands. He seemed
less to strum the strings of the harp nestled into the curve
of his arm than to conjure the song from the shimmering
air. Oldest and greatest of their song makers, he followed
his lady's wish and sang an air of her mother's.

> Oh, spirits of spring descend on me,
> Give me all your greenery. . . .
> The blooming flowers, petal and leaf,
> For winter brings me only grief. . . .

The rule that held Sira still had not chafed her so much
since her impetuous girlhood. Yet it would be the worst
kind of bad manners to leave the hall in the middle of even
the poorest harper's song. To walk out on Cuar would be
an inconceivable insult, especially during a song she had
requested herself.

For how many evenings had she sat here, half-dreaming
while the countless songs carried her away? Tales sung of
the Long Ago Before, when the First People peeped in
wonder at the first dawn. Tales sung of their warriors, male
and female, of terrible beasts and fabulous wonders, of
loves and lives, of battles lost and won. All around her,
The People sat and stood, rapt, the images of the songs
filling their minds, until it was as though they walked
through those days once more.

But the magic did not work for Sira this night. She
feared the unsettled feeling that kept the music at bay but

was too restless to force herself to listen. Her gaze fell on the arm of her tulip-shaped chair. All furniture and utensils in the Living Lands, right down to the ladles used in the great kitchens, were carved with symbols, pictures, and runes. Some were spells for protection or increased skill. Others, like the carving on her chair, were mere decoration.

Here, incised deeply into the reddish wood, smoothed but not worn away by the touch of her hands over the last five hundred years, was the story of Alamac the Fair and the mortal woman he'd won away from her own people. It had occurred long before Sira's own making, though not as far back as the Long Ago Before, in the days when her father still allowed some congress between the mortal world and the Wilder World.

Sira traced her finger over the tiny forms. It showed the moment before Alamac had saved the mortal woman from the fearsome bear beast that had menaced her. The woman fled, her outstretched arms a mute testament of terror. Her tiny face was turned to stare back in stark horror at the creature tearing up bushes behind her. The woman didn't know yet that her fated lover waited in those trees just beyond.

Looking more closely at the beast behind the woman, Sira frowned slightly. It stood on its hind legs, massive forepaws beating back the brush as it hunted for its prey. And yet, surely, it had not meant the woman harm. Something in its look was lost and the hunger on its face was not that of the body. Sira recalled the way Conn had looked when, against all sense, he had tried to see with eyes forever darkened.

Sira pursed her lips and blew ever so gently on the figure of the bear beast. The fur rustled and feathered over the massive body, blowing away. A man, alone and naked, stood in the woods, watching his beloved run to the arms of another.

Suddenly ashamed of herself, Sira stood upright. Instantly, the music ceased and all eyes turned toward her.

Feeling heat rise into her face, Sira stalked proudly out of
the great hall without a word or meeting a single glance.

The household at Hamdry retired with the sun. Most of
the servants slept communally, the strongest and most senior closest to the fire, the spit boys and slavies the farthest
away. Gandy slept outside his master's door and sometimes enlivened the night with murmurings and sighs, living his conquests again in sleep.

For Conn, however, all hours were the same. He, at
least, had no fear of anything walking by night that did
not walk by day. Even if the most horrible demon appeared, he'd have to see it to be afraid.

He lay on his bed, the covers drawn to his waist. In his
hands, he held the veil his mysterious lady had left behind.
Again and again, he let the supple scarf slide through his
fingers. He'd never touched anything so fine. Gandy, when
he'd returned it, had told him that it was as beautiful as a
summer's night.

He let the veil puddle on his bare chest, cool and
strangely heavy for its sheerness. How had she worn it?
About her shoulders? Trailing from a headpiece or lying
like snow on her hair? And that fragrance . . .

He raised it again to his face and breathed deeply. It
might be that she'd worn it as the ladies of the court sometimes wore such finery, draped about the low neckline of
a gown to shade their breasts with all apparent modesty,
the ends of the veil thrust down between them. Was this
scent hers, never created in an alchemist's lair of ambergris
and attar of roses, but rather brought to life by the warmth
of her own body?

Conn moved uncomfortably beneath the rough blanket
that covered him. Though the stone walls of his father's
house kept the rooms pleasantly cool, he felt warm arousal
prickling his flesh. He had not given way to desire for
months, first too busy at the wars and always too fastidious
to slake himself on the willing but filthy bodies of the
camp followers; now he was growing aroused by no more
than the smooth slide of a woman's veil through his hands.

Conn smiled at his folly even as he smothered a groan of frustration.

Suddenly, the slight fragrance emitted by the cloth seemed to grow stronger. As if he heard an alarm, Conn raised up on one elbow, listening to the darkness. "Who's there? Gandy? Did you pick the lock, man?"

"No," came a soft voice from the night.

Never minding his nakedness, Conn reached out a fumbling hand for the bandage he'd removed from around his forehead. "Wait! Don't strike a light."

"There's no need. I can see you well."

Conn clapped a hand to his forehead, covering his left eye with the palm. He could feel the scar, rough and pulsing hot with emotion. She must have seen the horrid white stare of his filmed eyes.

"Give me my bandage," he muttered, turning his face away.

The strip of linen fell into his lap as softly as the shed feather of an angel. Swiftly, his fingers more clumsy than he was used to finding them, Conn smoothed the linen over his face from brow to cheeks, then tied a knot behind his head.

He said, "I apologize for the sight, my lady."

"And why?" Her voice was cool.

"Such hideousness is not for your eyes."

She laughed, as merry as a bird's song in spring. "But you are so ugly already that a scar more or less hardly matters."

For a moment, Conn bridled. He had heard a thousand polite dismissals of his fears, yet always with the sickening sound of pity behind the voices. The appalled gasps of his betrothed were no more revealing than those lies. Hearing his Lady's laughter increase at his anger, he had to smile at himself.

"One might even argue that a few scars improve my face, serving as a distraction from the rest."

"Now, if you could but contrive a limp . . ." she said.

"To disguise this ungainly body? I shall send for a crutch at once!"

Her laughter was like brandywine; it went to his head. He threw aside the covers, feeling despair leave his body. It wasn't until he felt a whisper of a chilly breeze that he recalled his nakedness. *She* had not said a word, nor had she screamed. He did not hear the sound of her footsteps fleeing over the rushes, either.

Conn snatched the blanket from the bed and draped it about his hips. "I—" he began.

"Not so ungainly," she said and it seemed to Conn that her voice had gone a tone higher.

He'd become an adept at judging emotion by the sound of a voice, yet he didn't need his newfound skill to tell him that she looked at him differently now than when she'd come in. No pity or laughter there now. Curiosity, yes, and mayhaps . . . could it be that his mysterious Lady, who appeared and disappeared like mist . . . could she desire him?

He asked the question almost the nearest to his heart: "I have asked you before to tell me your name. Will you now?"

"I have many names."

Conn had been walking toward her, slowly. At this answer, he stopped. Again he demanded, "Tell me at once and for always! Are you a demon? Is this some game of the devil's to drive me to madness?"

"No, of course not!" She wasn't angry; she was incredulous. Her answer had flashed back quickly, carrying a light sting of contempt that he could even consider such a thing. Somehow that alone reassured him.

"Then for the last time . . . and for the love of God . . . who are you?" he asked again and could not despise himself at the plea that broke his voice.

"You may call me Sira."

"Sira . . ." Her name soothed him like a healing balm. Conn could feel the heat in his chest fade, the hot anger that had been there all day, that had in truth burned in his heart from the hour of his capture.

He said, more steadily, "When you came before, you

had a purpose. What is your purpose now?'' Then he said her name again: ''Sira.''

''I don't know what I want. I am hoping that you'll be able to tell *me*.''

''I haven't an answer. I have only a hope of my own.''

Her head to one side, Sira studied the mortal, from the black hair tumbling around his face, over the blanket he held to his waist like a shield, to the broad feet below. Without his clothing, he looked more formidable than ever. The contours of his brown body flowed sleek and strong, despite the sprinkling of black hair over his chest and stomach. The men of her People were smooth, so she should have been disgusted by this indication of the brute nature of mortals, but disgust was the last thing she felt. Curiosity was more like it.

She spoke slowly at first, then the words came more easily, flowing forth. ''From the moment I first saw you, I have asked myself why I care what becomes of you. You were nearer to death than you knew. If my lord father had seen you there at the site of our revels, you would have died where you stood, blasted into the nothingness of eternity. I should have told him of you; my honor demanded that I tell. And yet . . .''

She took a step nearer, almost within reach of his hands. Had he put out a finger, would she have stopped him touching her? She couldn't answer that. ''And yet I saved you,'' she said. ''Can you tell me why I did that?''

''Who are you?'' His deep voice was ragged; the words were whispered. ''What are you?''

She stepped away. ''What happened today? After I left you?''

''Nothing of any importance. Tell me, Sira. . . .''

''No. I want to know. Did they believe that silly girl? Have they hurt you?''

He turned away from her. ''If you try the door, you'll find it locked. This evening they sifted the evidence. My brother lied in their faces, saying he'd neither seen nor heard anything out of the ordinary, and he has no notion why Helen is saying these things.''

"This does not please you."

"No. My father is torn between doubt and relief. Doubt because he knows his son."

"And relief?"

"If I am in a league with the devil, then my father is free of the responsibility of removing me as his heir. He can hand me over to the Church and the law and have his wish that Ross follows him, without ever suffering a shred of guilt."

He couldn't hear her. Wondering if she'd gone, he turned toward where he believed her to be standing. But when she spoke again, her voice came from nearer to, almost in his ear. He could have touched her; he did not try.

"The door is locked?" she asked.

"It's locked. They have sent for Father Maynard, but they have not found him yet. My father won't attempt to condemn his own son without an approval from the priest. When Father Maynard comes, he will defend me against this charge they dare not speak aloud in my presence."

"You are sure he will save you?"

"If any mortal man can."

Conn felt heavy folds of cloth around his shoulders and the swing of a mantle touched the backs of his calves. He shuddered away, fearful of her touch. Had he boasted to himself that he would not be afraid of what he could not see? Folly. He felt nearly unmanned with terror and yet he found wit enough to say, "I pray to Jesus Christ and His angels to protect me. . . ."

"Please do," Sira said politely. "And if such a thing is possible, bid them protect me, too. When my father finds out what I am doing, I shall need all forms of protection."

"What are you doing?"

"Taking you with me, I think. It can be done, though it has been long years since anyone was foolhardy enough to try."

"Take me where?"

"Do close up the mantle at your throat. I shouldn't wish it to fall off. I really don't know what would happen then—nothing pleasant, I'm sure."

Conn lifted his hands and passed his fingertips over the slick, cool surface of a clasp. It did not feel like any metal he'd ever known. Concentrating, he realized the clasp was in the form of some kind of animal, sharp-toothed and with a curling tail. He found that his fear was passing off, leaving behind a devouring curiosity. "Where are we going? Is it far?"

"I don't know," she answered. "It cannot be measured in miles or in time. We will be there before long. Tell me . . . What tales did your nurse tell you when you were a boy?"

"Tales?"

"You said she told you of these lands, this . . . England as you call it."

"You *are* a foreigner! I knew . . ."

"Oh, no." She was laughing at him again, and yet the sound made him wish to weep. If laughter could be sad, hers spoke of tears. "We were here long before your people came. Before the fires of men ever burned here. Before your first footprint fell on the sand, we dwelled by sea and by shore. By the tide and by the sand. By stone and by wood. By root, branch, and swelling root. By the flower, by the fruit, by the falling leaf."

Conn felt dizzy and sick. His mouth went dry, so that when he tried to lick his lips, his tongue dragged over his teeth. Though there was no pain, he felt prickling all over, like a thousand small fires set in his flesh.

Over a sound like a rising windstorm he heard her voice, chanting now the words of some spell. A horrible feeling of falling overtook him, and he wanted to cry out. He felt he did, but now he couldn't hear his own voice. Another instant would be more than his mind could bear! He felt madness beating at the door to his sanity.

All at once, everything was still. The tide of blood that drummed in his ears faded. He felt a fresh breeze on his skin and smelled the salt of the sea. Conn found he could lick his lips and they, too, tasted of salt. Yet all could be an illusion of her making or of his own. Had he gone mad? Which would be worse, madness or enchantment?

Then Sira's voice came again, ripe with the satisfaction of work well done. "I am the daughter of Boadach the Eternal, King of Mag Mell, Master of the Wilder World, Lord of the Living Lands. And this is my home."

Eight

For months, Conn had seen nothing but a blackness so deep, so intense, it was as though night had swallowed his whole life. Once in a great while, his darkness would be lit by red or gold flashes, brief as falling stars. The surgeons of the king had shaken their heads over this delusion when he described it.

Only one, an Arab, had said, "You do not see these flashes with your eyes, my friend, but with your mind. Your mind is hungry for sight and so creates it. The mind of man is a remarkable creation. Let us praise God for it."

Had his desire for sight given him what he now saw, a blur of white instead of a cage of black? Were his eyes open or still sealed? Ignoring everything else, Conn stared with all his might at the captivating play of white across his vision, here brighter, there darker. He turned his head back and forth to catch the merest flutter of a change in intensity. Then he saw a hint of pink and caught his breath as the faint color seemed to glow, growing stronger, mingling with the faintest wash of blue. Whether real or not, the sight delighted him.

"What's happening to me?" he demanded.

He felt her touch on the back of his head, so lightly it was merely the sense of her fingers in his unbound hair. She tugged gently at the knot in the scrap of fabric. "In just a moment . . ." she said, her voice full of joy.

"Wait . . . don't! What are you . . ." He turned his head abruptly as the bandage over his eyes fell away.

The world rushed at him as though he were falling toward it from a great height. In a confused deluge of images, he saw the sea below him, blue and gold in the sunlight that tortured him with an agonizing dazzle. The sky held great mountains of cloud that seemed to burn though his brain in glowing cascades of white. The grass beneath his feet was like a green flame. He stumbled in a circle, gazing with tearing eyes at the ghastly beauty of the world. Then he halted, his mouth falling open, as the forces of madness again pounded in his temples.

In the sky above his head, an immense vortex whirled, howling with a song of birth and death. A glowing pale purple, it beat its way through the sky in a wild dance of power. At its base, it absorbed stars with constant tiny explosions that must have been enormous and only appeared small in comparison with the immensity of the thing that destroyed them. At the highest point, where the vortex opened out like a horn of plenty, new stars were born with a radiant violence.

"My God," he whispered. "This cannot be. What have you done to me?"

Sira watched in hurt amazement as Conn dropped to his knees, covering his eyes with the bend of his arm. As though that were not protection enough, he collapsed into a huddled ball, his face pressed to his knees. She heard a deep sob, instantly muffled, break from him.

She gazed about her in confusion. She'd always loved the high cliffs above the sea here at the end of the Living Lands. She could watch Il-na-ilith, the star vortex, for countless hours, losing herself in its endless melody and finding serenity in its absolute reality. No trouble of her own could seem devastating when compared with the vastness of space. The making and unmaking of worlds was far more important than a struggle of wills with Anat, disappointing her father, or even her mother's decision to abandon her duties, her husband, and their child.

Sira looked at the man huddled at her feet. "It is that I

am a fool,'' she said with a sigh. ''What one has known from birth may well be overwhelming to a stranger.''

Sitting down beside him, she drew a fold of her mantle over his curved back. Then, hesitatingly, she put her arm around him. With a gasp, he clutched at her with one broad hand, as though she were the only thing keeping him anchored to the world. As she suspected, while they stayed in the Living Lands, his touch had no power over her. And yet she was not unaware of it.

Rough and heavy, his hand burned through her close-fitting sleeve. Her first instinct was to pull free, and she even tried to. But she couldn't repel him in this moment of need.

Sira moved closer still to the huddled man and gently urged him to put his head on her knees. Under her breath, she sang to him and to herself, a song for children, in the simple, gentle language that all were taught first. There were no words in this speech for harsh or wicked things. Every living thing could respond for all had been young once. As Sira sang, she felt his breathing grow calmer, his heartbeat slowing.

After a time in which they were silent, she asked him softly, ''How did you come to lose your sight?''

Without raising his head, he spoke, his voice no louder than hers. ''I fought for the king in his war against those who would take his throne and give it to the German empress, Matilda. He is a good man, openhearted and generous, and what is she but a meddlesome, haughty, and brawling woman, not fit to be Lady of England. He is her captive now, and she treats him with all severity. Yet when he had her well besieged, he released her into her brother's care at once.''

''That was not wise.''

''No,'' he replied with a ghost of a chuckle. ''The king is not always wise. But he is always my king. I lost my sight in his service, and it is little enough.''

''You said you were blinded in a battle?''

''Earl Randulf of Chester and his brother, William of Roumare, took Lincoln Castle to hold in revolt. We went to lay siege to it, but the earl slipped out and returned with the whole of the enemy forces. That black-hearted Earl of Gloucester, Matilda's half-brother, rode at its head. It was Candlemas Day. I remember . . .''

He shook his head against her knee. She felt the weight of it, the prickle of his hair through the soft, clinging folds of her gown. Between the grip of his fingers and the touch of his cheek against her thigh, she felt less trapped than she would have thought. On the contrary, she felt . . . claimed.

When he spoke again, she seemed to see rather than hear the things he told her.

''The army betrayed the king and fled, pell-mell, tripping themselves with their own pikes, fouling themselves with their fear. The king stood alone, only a handful of men about him. We had no horses, no mail, nothing save shields and helmets. The Angevins threw all they had at us, charge after charge. The press of horses was so thick, they could hardly reach us and their frustrated rage was like a wave threatening to carry us away. And the king! He stood like a lion, his legs wide. If a man came within his reach, he lay dead in an instant. I, myself, did some good service with my broadsword. When the king's sword broke, he took up the ax and with it laid Randulf of Chester in the bloody mud. There were but five of us still standing then.''

''And you?''

''A blow across the face with a sword drove the nose guard of my helmet into my right eye. The inflammation spread from there to the other. I know now that I must have been blind within a few days. I did not realize it until they brought me up from the castle dungeon into the dim sunshine of February. The king was by then in Gloucester and went from there to Bristol, where still he lies in a dungeon.''

He shook his head in disbelieving wonder. ''And now I am mad,'' he said, ''and there's nothing for me but the death I have thus far eluded.''

''Mad?''

"When I see such visions with my sealed eyes as whirl-winds in the sky? Better mad than enchanted."

Somewhat insulted, Sira said, "I only thought it would please you to have your sight again. I didn't stop to think what it would mean for you. Forgive me."

He drew himself upright, and she saw that his lids were still closed. Tears had left his lashes spiked, and she wondered if it hurt very much to cry. Her People did not do such things. His voice was choked as he said, "You ask for forgiveness? I give it freely. Shouldn't I forgive the thing I have invented myself?"

She was insulted for certain. "You haven't invented me! I was here long before you. I told you that I am the daughter—"

"It is all part of the same malady," he said, and she saw him smile at himself, mockingly. "A maiden who appears and vanishes, who makes me fly with her through the air, and who speaks with the voice of a tender angel . . . you cannot be real."

"I am very real. Are you not touching me?"

"Now I am. But what about yesterday? I reached for you and you were not there. A creature born of my fancy only."

"That was because . . . forget that now. If you look at me, you'll see that I am real."

"I could look at you, believe you real, and yet know you are nothing more than my mind seeking for something it will never find again."

"Look at me! I demand it!"

Conn shook his head. "Not yet. I don't quite dare. You might be as terrible as that thing in the sky."

"A few have called me cruel, but never terrible. I have not had cause."

Sira reached out and caught between her own palms one of his hands. She could barely contain it and knew that if he wished, he could break her grip in trying to escape. Urgently she said, "Believe that I mean you only the best, Conn of Hamdry."

His hand twisted to capture what had captured him. "If you are not my invention, then tell me. Are you an angel?"

She laughed. "No. No. Nor ever shall be, I fancy."

"Then you cannot be a devil, for we are taught that devils are angels that have fallen." He gathered himself and rose to his feet, still holding her hand.

Perforce, Sira stood with him. She realized that though his legs trembled, his back was straight, and she understood what true bravery was: this power to face on his feet what he feared most. She lifted his hand, slipping his arm around her shoulders to offer support. At once, she felt too warm. How could he bear having a body so overheated all the time?

The wind pulled at them, for they were more exposed now than when they'd huddled on the ground. Conn turned to face her, his body close to hers. She wished he'd open his eyes so she could read their expression. He began to draw her nearer yet.

Sira yielded to the pressure of his arm on the back of her neck only because she had too much advantage over him with her eyes open. If he lost his balance over the cliff edge, she did not know if she could save him. Would a human die, even in the Deathless Realm where such evil never came?

She said, "Let us go from here, since you dislike this place. In a moment, we can travel wherever you please, back to your home or to the ends of my world."

"Not yet."

Holding her, he began with his other hand to trace his fingers delicately over her face. Sira froze, every muscle tense, for no one had ever touched her like this. She might have been a harp, played by a master hand, judging by the vibration that went through her.

After a moment, he no longer needed even to hold her fast. With both hands, he combed back the heavy wings of her hair, stroked the softness of her temples, and smoothed the tiny hairs of her brows. It was as though he brought her to life with his fingertips, inventing her even as he had said. She closed her eyes as he slowly drew the

back of his hand over her cheek and over her lower lip.
He paused there, tracing with a fingertip the tender flesh.

She concentrated on the rough drag of his finger over
the smooth sensitivity of her mouth. Sira felt a quiver deep
inside that startled her as she realized his touch had indeed
power over her. She who never accepted the authority of
any but her father now waited to know a mortal's pleasure.

She opened her heavy eyelids and found Conn staring
down at her, his brilliant amber eyes reflecting his shocked
surprise.

Sira wanted to vanish from his sight in an instant, but
having brought him here, she could not abandon him. Bad
enough if her father found him in his realm by his daughter's side. Sira did not care to think what would happen to
Conn if the king found him without anyone to defend his
presence here. Because she owed him protection, Sira
faced Conn's frown.

"You're beautiful," he said, as though the sight brought
him only disquiet. "Like a dream. Is this a dream?"

"You are neither mad nor dreaming."

"Tell me the truth! And you may begin with your true
name. Enough of this nonsense of kings and evil spells. If
you are a witch, then tell me so."

"I am no witch as you mean the word."

He did not seem to hear. "If you are a witch, then my
soul is damned already. You are beautiful enough to en-
snare men's souls eternally. If I am damned, then nothing
I do matters. Tell me the truth of this place, or I'll show
you my strength." Yet his hands as they cradled her face
remained gentle.

Sira noticed that he kept his eyes averted from the vortex endlessly spinning in the sky above. She realized his
sudden descent into blustering threats was his way—perhaps his people's way—of dealing with his fear. She decided to be patient and wondered at that as well.

In a soothing voice, she said, "My name is Sira, and it
is as I have told you. You stand on the farthermost shore
of the Lands of Fragrance. Among you who dwell in the
mortal lands, we are sometimes called the Folk of Mag

Mell. My father is Boadach the Eternal, king of my people for always and forever.''

"These are the names in the tales my nurse told me. . . ." He shook his head as though throwing off a noxious insect crawling on his cheek. "No. Such things don't exist now, if ever they did.''

"Because you have banished the night with your torches, does it no longer live? The world is wider than you know, Conn of Hamdry, and it contains much of which you are ignorant. Shall I show you?''

What did men mean when they talked of beauty? Conn had sat through a thousand firelit conversations where men argued the merits of one woman over another, much as they discussed the fine points of their horses. The women most admired were those who could raise their families, raise their husbands in the sight of the world, and raise a siege, if necessary during these dark days when Christ and His angels slept. Physical beauty was a mere afterthought in the woman one sought to wife.

Helen de Burke, his betrothed, was brought up by her parents from birth to be all these things to the man she married. In addition, her beauty had made her well-known and much sought. Conn had felt proud of her for that, as he'd been proud of his name and of his manor, which made the thought of losing her to his brother all the worse.

Looking into Sira's face made him forget why he'd ever thought of Helen as beautiful.

In the weird purple glow of the sky, her hair had a satin sheen like cloth-of-gold. Remembering the slide of his fingers over it, he knew the satin was not of appearance only. Beside her small ears, short strands curled into tendrils that echoed the artistry of the twining vine necklace she wore, the flowers entirely real. He touched a flower, his hand appearing brutishly coarse next to the lilylike fragility of her throat, and saw the ornament tremble with the next breath she took.

Under swallow-wing brows, her eyes were a soft blue, like shaded moss. Almond-shaped and fringed with golden

lashes, they gave away her uncertainty, though the uptilt
of her determined chin told him she was too proud to show
fear. Knowing what he looked like, heavily muscled beside
her slimness, weather-beaten beside her glowing fairness,
Conn was only amazed that she'd returned after their first
meeting. He remembered how she'd spoken of her confusion over why she had done so. Now his desire to know
why was as strong as her own.

"My lady," he said, pushing his hair off his forehead.
He went silent as his fingers explored the ridge of his scar.

"Merciful God," he murmured. Though still there, the
scar had lessened. No longer did his faltering fingers dis-
close a twisted rope of traumatized flesh slicing through
brow and nose.

"It's not that I am vain," he said, frowning lest she
think him no more than a popinjay, proud of his feathers.

"Of course not."

"A man has no use for vanity. It's only . . . in all my
years of warring, I have seen many men with scars beside
which mine was nothing. A warrior without scars has no
honor. But this—" His fingers sought again the ridged
flesh they recalled so well and found only a shallow line.
"Had I not won it in defeat or at the price of my sight, I
could have boasted of it."

"You sound as though you miss it. Do you want it
back?"

"No, I thank you, my lady." He grinned at her, accepting for the first time that miracles could still happen.

He said, "I wonder how I look."

Sira handed him a mirror, an understanding smile dawn-
ing on her warm, pink lips. Conn took it in his hands, a
heavy circle in the shape of a sun in splendor. The glass
was as true as a still lake. With it, he confirmed that his
scar had faded to a smooth, even white, still cleaving
through his dark brow, but without making him hideous.

Conn started to give the mirror back but almost dropped
it when he inadvertently touched the silver surface with
his fingertip. A ripple began at that point and spread across
the surface as though he'd dropped a stone into a millpond.

Wonderingly, he touched the mirror again, his fingers sinking slightly into the cool water. "In the name of God . . ." he began.

" 'Tis just a mirror," she said, a laugh in her voice like the ripple on the water.

Then Conn realized Sira had conjured it out of thin air. She could not have concealed it; her white robe, though flowing, had no room to hide so large a mirror, especially one that was not silver-backed glass but water.

"God-a-mercy," he whispered, and his right hand fluttered up to sketch a cross over his body.

Her smile widened, showing her small white teeth. Though she was still beautiful, Conn thought he saw a darkness in her eyes, a witch's shadow, and feared his soul was in peril. Dashing the mirror to the ground, he grabbed her by the wrist and dragged her close to glare into her brilliant eyes.

"Let me go," she demanded, her first touch of real fear sending her voice high. She twisted her arm, striving to be free.

It surprised him how much strength he had to exert to hold her without hurting her. "You claim to be of the faerie kind?"

"I claim nothing. I am who I said I am."

"Then if I hold you, I can bend you to my will. True?"

She didn't answer, only tried to kick him while flailing her free hand at his face. He only laughed when she made contact, though the mark on his cheek stung. Her bones felt light under his fingers, as though he held a bird that beat its wings against his hands, demanding to be free. "Is it true?" he asked again.

"My lord was right about you mortals. Greedy, rude, ungrateful . . ."

Conn pulled her against his side, trapping her within his arms. She struggled a moment more, trying to get her hands up, but his wide biceps held her arms down. She tossed back her head to challenge his gaze. She met the heat of his body with the scorching strength of her pride-fueled anger. It was a wonder it didn't blind him all over

again. Her beauty, heightened by rage, was nearly enough
to dazzle him sightless without magic.

"Is it true?" he asked again, more softly yet.

"It's true. In your world, if you can catch one of us, we
must obey you in all you order us to do." She wriggled a
moment more, her teeth clenched. Then she added, "But
this is *my* world, Conn of Hamdry."

Conn did not feel the force of her will being cast over
him. What he felt was the binding strands of a new desire,
woven from the fire in her eyes and the sweetness of her
scent. When she moved against him, he could not resist
finding out what it was like to kiss such a woman.

He took her lips under his. Feeling a shock run through
her, he tightened his arms to prevent her from struggling.
But she didn't try again to break free.

She stood frozen within the circle of his arms, only her
soft, quick breaths on his face giving away her apprehension. Her breasts were small, yet he could feel them against
his chest, warm and firm. Conn longed to deepen this kiss,
but first he wanted for her to melt against him, to show
him that this desire was equally felt. Nothing less would
satisfy him.

For the first time in this world he said her name. His
whisper was ragged. "Sira, don't you like this?"

"I have seen it done," she said, her voice soft as well.
"Your people seem to take pleasure in it."

"Don't your people do it?"

"No, never." Her alabaster forehead crinkled with
thought. "Why do yours?"

He'd never thought about it. "We just . . . do. How do
your people show . . . affection?"

"That is private—not for an outsider to know."

Conn released her when she made another effort to be
free. If he had not let her go then, he felt as though he
never would have. However, before she could step away,
he again took hold of her hand. He rubbed his thumb over
her knuckles as he looked down at the delicate structure
of her long fingers.

"I'm very confused, Sira. Everything I know tells me

that you are trying to enslave me. All the stories I have heard . . . the things the priests tell us in the church . . . I should condemn you and say prayers for the salvation of my soul.''

"And yet?"

He looked into her eyes. She was still hesitant about him and simmering with anger from his aggression. Conn said, "Never think for a moment that I am ungrateful, Sira. I'd do anything you ask of me in gratitude for restoring my sight, even if it does not last beyond today. Forgive me my confusion."

He waved his hand at the twirling vortex in the sky, hoping she'd understand that this was the symbol for all that held him in amazement.

Sira softened. "Oh, I forgive you. I hope that I have done well."

"You have made my life anew. I can never repay that."

"Don't thank me yet," Sira added, drawing her hand out of his grasp. "You have yet to meet my father."

"Is he so terrible?"

"He can be. And he does not love mortals. He has cause to hate and fear them."

"But you do not?"

"I hate no one. Nor do I fear any creature." Again he saw the flash of pride in her eyes. But at the same time, he noticed that as she turned away, her fingers brushed over her mouth. Not as though she wiped away the memory of his kiss, but more in wonder, as though she asked herself again what he meant by it.

Conn wondered at himself. He'd never taken more than what a woman had freely offered. His control was a by-word among the king's men. They often boasted of the women they'd taken in some captured town or of a wench they'd tumbled without troubling about her name. But Conn preferred a willing and familiar partner, for he'd never understood how a man could take pleasure without giving some in return.

Never until now had he been possessed by a desire to taste one particular pair of lips, willing or no. In the past, if one charming woman had refused him, well, there were others. Remembering Sira's cool lips beneath his own, he could not recall kissing any other pair. For a moment, he froze as he felt the winding tendrils of enchantment clutch him more tightly.

Then Sira smiled at him over her shoulder, with laughter trembling on her lips. She said, ''Come with me. You've only seen the beginning of my world.''

Conn bent to collect her mirror from where he'd thrown it down, but his fingers closed on nothing, for it had disappeared as though it had been absorbed by the earth. Resolving to go more carefully, for there was so much here that he did not understand, Conn followed.

Nine

"A human? Have you lost your senses?"

Sira shot a quick glance toward Conn, hoping he hadn't heard Anat's voice, which carried like a hawk's cry above a field of wheat. He hadn't seemed to hear, though he wore a frown as he walked around, picking up her small things in his big hands. She noticed he kept a wary eye toward her waterfall mirror as though he suspected it of forming distorted pictures of him behind his back. She threw it a warning glance herself, just in case it got any ideas. Then she turned again to Anat.

"Speak softer," Sira urged her companion. "He'll hear you."

"I don't care! If your father finds out . . ."

"Then lower your voice so my lord father *doesn't* find out." Sira held out pleading hands. "Anat, what else could I do?"

"You didn't have to bring him here. You should have left him in his own place and time. He's a human; he doesn't belong in Mag Mell."

"Mortals have come into the Land of Promise before this. Alamac the Fair brought his bride . . . and there have been others."

"Yes, and a great deal of trouble they caused, too! They're nothing *but* trouble. They don't know how to behave themselves like civilized people. Even their women were unable to adapt to our ways. Clumsy creatures with tangled hair. No music, no arts, nor even any manners. But this is one of their males! Brutal, smelly, rude! And such a big brute!''

"Yes, he is." Sira did not mention the kiss. Anat would have run at once to Boadach, screaming that Sira had been assaulted by a mortal. Knowing her father, Sira didn't imagine Boadach would stop to ask any questions. Conn would be blasted into nothingness or, if her father stopped short of the crime of murder, be turned into some sightless, speechless, broken thing.

She found herself touching her lips, recalling the scrape of Conn's whiskers against her cheek and the surprising tenderness of his lips on her own. She glanced at him again, intrigued by the difference between the delicately feminine surroundings and the utter masculinity of the mortal. She saw that he held a small pot of earthen make in his hand and was peering cautiously at the contents. Laughing, she turned from Anat.

"That's my perfume," she said, taking the pot gently from where it nestled in his palm.

"I like it. That's why I first thought you were real. I might imagine a woman, but I couldn't have invented the flowers.''

"But it isn't flowers," she said, confused. "This is my winter scent: clove and rosemary.''

He grasped her wrist, and Sira felt a tingle as if lightning had run up her arm. Conn raised her arm to his face and inhaled the fragrance of her skin. "Definitely flowers," he said, his voice low, rumbling in his deep chest.

Anat let out a frustrated scream and came rushing in from Sira's bedchamber. "Let go at once!" she shouted, chopping her hand down across his thick wrist.

Uninjured and amused, he released Sira. Turning to Anat, he looked her over. "I recall you from the other night on the tor," he said. "You are younger than I thought.''

Sira stepped in before Anat could choose among her

arsenal of blistering retorts. "Anat is the nearest to a mother I have. Without her, I would be lost."

Anat scolded them as though they were naughty children. "The pair of you should be ashamed of yourselves for telling so many untruths. I'm not one to be swayed by honeyed words."

"One can see that at first glance," Conn said.

"Believe me, mortal, 'tis not by *my* will that you see, nor will the king take pleasure in your sight or in the sight of you! My duty is clear. I must go to him at once and tell him that his daughter's lost her mind and brought a mortal through the Veil."

Yet Anat hesitated. Sira knew it had never been Anat's wish to drive a wedge between Boadach and his headstrong child. Sira, from infancy, had often taken advantage of her nurse's warm heart. As a mature adult, she'd felt guilty for all the times she continued to use Anat's devotion to get her own way. Yet she had to choose those methods that worked best.

Deliberately, Sira said, "You know what will happen if you tell him?"

"Don't start—"

"He'll be angry with me. Angrier than he has ever been. Do you want to be the cause?"

Anat bit her pale lip in confusion. "But, my lady," she protested weakly.

Then Conn dared to interfere. "That's enough," he said, his deep voice decisive. "Don't talk to her that way. She's older than you, and deserving of your respect."

Sira shot a dagger glance at him. "Do you dare to correct me?" She'd meant to overawe him, yet she knew she sounded too surprised to succeed.

"You are mistress, no doubt," he said, bending his stiff mortal neck in acknowledgment of her rank. "Yet you are wrong."

"You don't understand," she said dismissively.

"I know it cannot be right to speak so to this lady. She is in a difficult position—torn between her loyalties." Conn smiled at Anat. Sira saw how his brown eyes could

look as warm and bright with sympathy as they had looked
hot and dark in the moment when he'd raised his head
from their kiss.

Anat simply appeared stunned. She murmured, "Yes,
very difficult. Sira is so headstrong—always running ahead
of her good sense. But the king's anger is a frightful
thing."

"If I were you," he said kindly, "I should tell the king.
Your first duty is always to him."

"Oh, but . . ." Anat spread out her hands helplessly.
"You don't know him. He despises all the mortal breed.
If he knew you were here . . ."

"You can't hide my presence forever, nor do I wish it."

Sira said abruptly, "You speak foolishly, Conn. My father will destroy you."

"I'm not afraid."

"You should be," the two immortal women said in the
same breath. Then they glanced at each other.

Anat said more tolerantly, "You can't hide him. Even
if he were smaller, he could never look like one of our
People."

"Never," Sira said, throwing a cutting glance at Conn.
She might agree that she'd been too sharp with Anat, but
she didn't feel the slightest need to apologize to *him*. On
the contrary, he should learn not to meddle with her.

He only grinned at her, impudently. Yet his smile gave
her the same strange tingle she'd felt when he'd taken her
hand. Sira promised herself she'd assess that feeling at her
first opportunity. In all her hundreds of years, she'd never
known anything quite like it. She wasn't certain it was safe
to feel something so new.

Anat studied this man, two fingers pressed consideringly
against her cheek, her head tipped to the side. Sira guessed
what her companion must be thinking. Anat had no hope
that she could conceal Conn's presence for long, yet there
could be a difference in the king's reaction if presented
with a clean, polite mortal rather than an uncivilized creature who stank of sweat, both human and equine.

Sira muttered to Anat, "What do you think?"

"Oh, don't ask me! I wash my hands of the whole matter." But Sira knew too well that this would not be Anat's final word. She waited to hear more. "I know this much. He can't stay here with you. That shame would destroy you, my lady."

"I never intended—"

"I wouldn't even if I—"

Conn and Sira smiled at each other, then she encouraged him to go first. He said, "I know full well, Lady Anat, that I can't remain with your mistress. But I am not yet ready to return to my home. There are so many wonders . . ."

He gazed around her chamber, and Sira saw it as though through his eyes. The golden tracery of runes over the walls shimmered in the warm light of the suspended center lamp while the endless music of the waterfall charmed the ears. The velvety soft covers of the bed promised that the luxuriousness of sleep would be guaranteed even without the magic spells carved into the white head and foot boards of alder and ash. It had been her home for all her life, and she'd never grown tired of it.

Anat clicked her tongue impatiently. "Wonders? It'll be a wonder if you live through the night. But since the pair of you are so determined that he should stay . . ." She paused as though to hear them deny it. When they did not speak, she sighed, raising her hands as though to declare the coming disaster to be none of her fault.

Sira said, "What we need is a friend. I wonder . . . Anat, go and ask Blaic to come here. Tell him I have need of him."

"Blaic? No, Sira, I don't think that would be right."

"He's trustworthy."

"I don't mean that the prince of the West isn't loyal. Only that he will surely feel that going against your father's wishes would be an evil."

"He won't be going against the king. I have every intention of presenting Conn to my father tonight when we are gathered in the great hall."

"Tonight?" Anat pressed her hand to her chest, her eyes wide. "He'll never be permitted!"

Conn studied Anat. Though her skin was unlined, her hair not grayed by years, something told him that she was by no means as young and fresh as Sira. Mayhap it was the more somber hue of her robe or the way that it concealed her body. When a man looked on Sira, he saw a ripe creature, eager for life. Anat, however, seemed more wary, less openhearted, as though she were judging from a darker experience of the world. If she went in awe and fear of their king, then Conn could do worse than to carry himself with caution and to persuade Anat to help him.

Instead, however, he found himself asking, "Who is Blaic?"

"A prince," Sira said, as if that were explanation enough.

"A prince? Are all here royal then?"

"No, of course not. Why do you say so?"

"You are a princess, are you not? And surely Lady Anat is of royal blood."

The older fay simpered a bit. "On my father's side . . ."

Sira looked as though she might laugh. Conn decided he must be more subtle with his admiration. His Lady seemed to understand him all too well. Yet he shared her smile without hesitation. Then he asked, "Blaic is your brother?"

"No. I have no brother, nor sister neither. When my father called me from the sea, I came alone."

"Called you . . ." Conn rubbed his eyes with one palm, feeling that swirling sense of confusion again. He clung to the one fact he desired most to know. "Then who is Blaic?"

"As we told you, he is a prince from the Westering Realm. He has come to court to pay his father's tribute."

"Prince Blaic has also done my lady the honor of—"

But Sira cut Anat off rapidly. "I hope he'll serve me by aiding you, Conn. We cannot show you where to bathe, and I have never had good fortune at creating men's clothing. Try as I might, it always comes out in my size."

"That won't do." She wasn't small, exactly, though the delicacy of her build made her appear ethereal. Actually, she was not much smaller than Ross. Their voices had seemed to come on the same level that day in the garden. Strange how long ago that felt. For all he knew, of course, she could have been floating one or two feet off the ground. Could she fly?

She said, laughing, "If you could but see the results of my labor when I tried to make something for my lord father's last holy day . . ."

"I could try."

"No, Anat. Your tunics always come out with four arms. It's a good thing, too, because the guardians always need clothing, but they won't do for him."

"Guardians?" Conn echoed, trying to force his mind to imagine something humanlike with four arms.

Sira paid no attention. "Bring Blaic here, Anat. He can help Conn prepare for tonight."

The fay prince, his muscular chest and arms partly revealed in a leather vest, turned to Sira after studying the human. He shook his golden head slowly, regretfully. "Aye, I'll help you. I'll help you by sending this . . . man back where he belongs."

"And if I choose to stay?" Conn said, not liking the possessive glint in Blaic's eyes when they looked upon Sira.

"You have nothing to say to it, mortal."

"No, Blaic," Sira said. "He's going to stay. I don't want him to leave yet."

Blaic's green eyes were cold as he bowed ironically. "If you choose to keep a pet, my lady, I will show you where the lion cubs may be found, or if that does not please your sense of danger, there are griffins in the hills of my country. Even a basilisk or a sphinx—no, they talk too much, yet less than he will."

"He's not a pet," Sira protested.

Conn said, "I would gladly show you my teeth, good prince. Or my sting."

"You weren't mad enough to let him bring his sword, were you?" Irritatingly, Blaic paid no attention to Conn's veiled threat beyond an impatient glance.

Conn decided to make his presence felt. He stepped between Blaic and Sira, telling himself that he wanted only to stop them treating him as if he were in truth no more than a cat or dog. Yet he was also aware that if Blaic were looking at him, he could not look at Sira as though she were his.

"I have no sword," Conn declared. "Yet I am not unarmed."

Blaic's lip curled in a sneer. "I could swat you like a fly, mortal."

"You could try."

Blaic lifted his hand. Conn caught the prince's arm as it raised and held tight. Seeing the rage well up in Blaic's cold eyes, Conn set his muscles and was prepared when the prince struggled to be free. Conn laughed, fanning Blaic's rage.

Then Conn felt the tingle of magic in his body. Setting his lips, he tried to force Blaic's hand down. He noticed that the prince's gaze had gone past him and that alarm had replaced anger. Conn's senses were suddenly sharper. Blaic's scent of wood and smoke filled his nose while his eyesight, newly restored, became astoundingly acute.

The two males' eyes met. Conn had only an instant to recognize that the prince's pupils had elongated. Each realized that they were equally helpless in the moment before they dwindled and shrank.

"Anat! Change them back!"

Conn only dimly understood Sira's words. The reek of another male lynx roused primitive instincts. He arched his back, turning sideways, and growled, his mouth open. He felt his ears flatten against his skull while a strange prickling along his back told him that his hackles were raised, his tail twice its size as every hair stood on end.

The sleekly handsome mountain cat before him also took a position of menace. His tail lashed his hindquarters while a stuttering yowl roused Conn's fighting instincts to a painful pitch. He still felt, though in a more elemental way, that he could take on the other and win.

Blaic lashed out with a paw, the black scythes of his claws exposed. Conn ducked and began to circle the other, who turned with him, not daring to let him get behind. The yowling increased as Conn joined in the battle song. His human thoughts faded as instinct, dark and intoxicating as fine wine, flowed in his veins.

This time, when Blaic sprang at him, Conn did not try to evade. He closed with the other lynx, rolling on the floor, biting and clawing with unholy glee. He felt the other's bites and scratches only as an incitement to his own violence.

They careened across the floor, first one on top and then other, screaming and roaring, a whirlwind of claws, teeth, and striped fur. Knocking into Sira's dressing table, tiny bottles fell, bouncing and rolling, spilling fragrant lotions and liquids. Conn, as cat, sneezed, but hatred of his rival more than outweighed his outraged nose. He made a feint with one paw and swiped the other across the eyes. Catching an ear in his teeth, he rejoiced in the other's scream of agony.

"Anat! Stop this, or I go to my father myself!"

"Very well."

Sprawled at full length on the floor, his fingers dug into the fay prince's upper arms, Conn saw his own human face reflected in the tiny mirrors of Blaic's eyes. He threw himself off, rising at once to his feet. Shaking his loosened hair from his eyes, he extended his hand to Blaic, still lying on the floor.

For a heartbeat, the fay prince hesitated. Then, with a grin as frank as any mischievous boy's, Blaic accepted Conn's hand. "I would have beaten you in another instant," he said, as he came up.

"Without a doubt," Conn conceded. "I know I had the upper hand for only so long as you'd allow it."

Blaic swiped at the front of his leather vest, clearing away the dust. He wrinkled his nose as a hunk of fur drifted down. "I do not like cats," he said. "Not even when I am one."

Knowing Sira listened to every word, Conn said, "Any man who fights over a woman is a fool."

"Were we fighting over a woman? I thought it was because I do not like you."

"Nor I you," Conn answered. "Yet I do not say I cannot change my mind."

Blaic bowed to him a bit ironically. Rising, he flipped his fingers toward Conn's torn sleeve. "I have drawn your blood, mortal. Come with me. I will show you to my chamber. There you may bathe—if you are not afraid of hot water—and have your wound tended."

Glancing down at his upper arm where a stinging scratch showed tiny beads of blood, Conn said, "This is less than nothing; I do not regard it. Yet I should be glad of a bath. You yourself must have that ear seen to."

Blaic dabbed his fingers at the lobe of his left ear and gazed in disgusted surprise at the smear of blood that resulted. He looked coldly at the two women. "My lady Anat, I would suggest you do not carry your sense of humor so far next time."

"Would you indeed? And have you any other advice for one who is much your senior?"

"Only that you think long on the fate of Eitche."

Sira caught her breath. "Blaic, you go too far."

"Oh, don't trouble to defend me," Anat said coldly. "I do not believe the king your father would punish me for such a minor thing as outraging the dignity of this little prince."

The older fay turned on her heel and went toward the bedroom. She said over her shoulder, "If you are quite done playing with your pets, you should prepare yourself for tonight."

Sira said, "I shall be there in a moment." To the two men she said, "For my sake, be friends. I have perhaps acted hastily with you, Conn, but—"

"I have no complaint to make. I can see. I know to whom I owe that."

"I have cause for complaint," Blaic said dryly.

Conn did not like the way Sira's eyes pleaded with the prince. "I know it," she said. "I can only offer my regrets."

"With that I am content." Once more, Blaic bowed. Conn could do no better than to imitate him, though he realized with what clumsiness he did so.

As they left Sira's quarters, Conn asked one of the many questions that burned in him. "Who was Eitche?"

"A female of our People who chose, unwisely as it turned out, to set her power against our king's. The battle raged for many days, each throwing the might of their power against the other. Eitche lost, eventually, tricked into a surrender. She is the only one of us who has ever died as you humans die."

"How is that?"

For long moments, Blaic was silent as their footsteps echoed over the smooth stone of the passageway. Conn was on the point of repeating his question when Blaic answered with every appearance of distaste, "She died of old age."

"How do you ordinarily die?"

"We do not die. We live on. I am myself nearly twenty-six hundred years old. As you reckon time."

Conn stopped as he tried to comprehend what he'd just been told. "And the Lady Sira?" he asked, through a throat suddenly thickened with dread.

"It isn't well done of me to discuss the age of a lady, yet I will say she is not so old as myself."

Blaic's face showed no warmth of compassion as he looked on Conn. He said abruptly, "She is not for you, mortal."

"I had not thought of it," Conn said, knowing he lied.

"Do not let desire for her grow in your heart. She will still live when the last-born descendant of your body has faded beyond the reach of even the longest memory. She will bring fragrance and delight to our People forever."

Stunned by the ideas that any woman so fair could be so old, Conn noticed nonetheless that Blaic had mentioned

Sira's special scent. Curiosity warred with a jealousy he had no right to feel.

He asked, "You desire her?"

Blaic said, "For a hundred years now. You cannot even promise her that much of life, let alone such devotion."

"No, I cannot offer her that."

"Come with me," Blaic said and started again down the corridor of black rock. The walls of the same stone met overhead in a pointed arch that seemed to extend endlessly in both directions. Sometimes they came to a crossing where more corridors could be seen, bending out of sight around a corner.

"It's like a rabbit warren," Conn said. "My nurse told tales of a people gone underground, into the fairy mounds that can be seen on some hillsides, even more in France than here."

"Some of our doorways are in such hills, but not all. We do not live in the mounds; that is a foolishness perpetrated by silly old women. We live in the Realm—infinite and eternal."

"And dark. And cold."

"Do you find it so?" Blaic stopped at a conjunction of two corridors. "Go down there and tell me what you think on your return. I shall wait for you." The prince leaned against the wall, his well-defined arms crossed over his middle. The blood that had dripped from his ear onto his vest left a shiny gleam of red on the dark leather.

Distrustful, Conn hesitated. Would he find some nightmare creature waiting to rend him apart? Would a death trap tilt beneath him, sending him sliding into a pit for a lingering doom? Catching a glance from the prince's scornful, challenging eyes, Conn straightened his shoulders and followed the twisting path.

He could only hope Blaic would keep his promise to be waiting. Ordinarily, he possessed a strong sense of direction, but so much had been happening to him that he did not know if he could find his way back to Sira's chambers. He might find himself wandering aimlessly in this maze until he dropped.

Even so, he felt strongly that, come what may, he would always be able to find Sira. He knew that a river would, sooner or later, find the sea, meeting its destiny with a great roar and crash. The river would drive through any obstacle, from a mountain to the habitation of man, to reach the sea. He had seen such overwhelming floods and the patient power of the cataract in his travels. He had no more explanation for Sira's effect on him than he had for tides. He closed his eyes for a moment and saw her, bright as an afterimage of the sun, branded on his inner vision forever. It gave him strength to go on, undaunted.

At the end of the passageway were several doors set into the walls. Over each crawled a pattern of runes, meaningless to his eyes yet rhythmic in their procession. Only here and there did a knothole insufficiently smoothed betray that these were doors carved of wood. They did not possess a latch or string to open them by, nor could Conn see any hinge.

Reaching out, he touched the nearest door. It opened inward at the first brush of his fingertips, swinging silently. Conn looked out into a dark night, the sky a-swirl with stars. Dimly, in the distance, he saw bivouac fires and heard the far-off throb of war drums. The beat was strange to his ears, as was the chant floating across an infinite plain. Yet it called to him, bidding him come and fight in the battle that morning would bring. Conn took a step forward, unable to resist the lure of war.

At the last instant, he remembered Sira and threw himself back. The door closed, shutting off the drums, the sight of the fires, and the strange, wavering call of a night bird.

Turning, he inadvertently touched another door. When it swung wide, he saw only blue for a moment, a moving, living light that made him half-close his eyes until he realized the smell of salt water filled the passageway. His feet were wet as water splashed over the threshold. When his sight adjusted, he saw that the blue light was full of moving things: fish, seaweed, the never-still water, and something huge that rose up before his view to wink the massive and alert eye that looked on him.

Startled by the sight of the whale, Conn stepped back. The door closed. He couldn't wait to open another.

Ten

When Sira received the summons from her father, she felt trapped. She knew that Boadach could be harsh, even cruel, but she'd never been the target of his anger. She felt shame and guilt at having disobeyed him, for she knew from long experience that the hardest punishment to bear was her father's disappointment.

Peering through the gauzy silk curtains that screened the parapet from the king's lavish chambers, Sira saw Boadach storm back and forth across the long stone gallery. From here, he could observe all of the Living Lands with the help of his crystal eye.

"You summoned me, Father?"

"Sira." His deep voice rumbled like approaching thunder. A hale and powerful figure, Boadach carried his unimaginably long life on broad, squared shoulders. Alone among The People his shoulder-length hair had begun to shine with threads of silver. He wore no crown, nor were his robes of velvet-silk. Many a foolish mortal had mistaken the great king for no more than a simple woodsman, traveling through the forest.

Glancing out toward Il-na-Ilith, always aglow in the distant sky whether by day or by night, Sira wondered how much her father had already witnessed with his magical sight. She felt sure he'd not seen Conn kiss her, or she'd not be standing here now. Her father would not hesitate to send her off to some unimaginable distance to keep her safe from a mortal's hands.

Thinking of Conn, Sira couldn't repress a shiver of wonder. He had touched her lips with his own, awakening her to new possibilities that both excited and frightened her. She asked herself if she were willing to choose a mortal man's kiss over everything she had to lose.

Her father said, "I have asked you to come hither, Sira, for a most important reason."

Under his gaze, Sira felt a compulsion to blurt out all she had done since she'd seen her father last. Boadach spoke again just before the need to betray herself overwhelmed her.

"As Lady of this realm, you know you have only to speak, and whatever protection you need is yours." His deep-set eyes, dark with ancient wisdom, studied her. "Why then do you not come to your father—I who would pour out my heart's blood for you—when troubled by this Western prince?"

"What Western prince, Father? Do you mean Blaic?"

"I neither know nor care what his name is."

Sira knew that wasn't true. Her father had often gamed with Blaic.

Boadach continued, "If he is not aware that such an approach is unwelcome, I shall teach him in such a way that he will not soon forget!"

"But, Father—"

"Bad enough to force his affection on some lesser female, but to approach *my* daughter with his demands—"

"My lord, Blaic did nothing. He did not speak a single word of his feelings for me."

"That is not what your companion has told me."

"Anat spoke to you?"

The wrinkles in her father's forehead deepened. "I asked her why you left the hall so suddenly in the middle of Cuar's song. She told me that this princeling disturbed your harmony with his emotional insults."

"She had no right to say anything of the kind," Sira

said, though less vehemently than she might have yesterday. There were so many other things Anat could have
told. "She did not stand near when Blaic and I spoke. He
said nothing to me of his wish for our marriage. Nor would
he. He has spoken only to you, as is right and proper."

The king held up his hand to deter her. "You should
know nothing of that."

"I am not a fool, my lord. Half the court expects an
announcement at any hour. Am I alone to pretend ignorance? I have no love for such mealymouthed ways."

"Well I know it," Boadach muttered. Meeting her eyes,
he smiled with an outflowing of warmth that never failed
to thaw the resentment she often felt at being hedged about
with so much precaution. "Nevertheless, it is unseemly for
a maid of The People to speculate on her future. Your part
is to be joyful."

"It is not all joy," she said, thinking of Conn. She wondered if he and Blaic were still tearing at each other like
wild beasts. Blaic's actions she understood; he loved her
and did not like to see her stand on intimate terms with
another.

Sira walked to the edge of the parapet and looked down.
The wind tugged at her silken hair, making it fly like cirrus
clouds. She saw the pleasure houses, their multicolored
thatched roofs sparkling in the clear light, and the beautiful
People going in and out. What would Conn, a mortal with
a violent past, think of days spent in courtly games and
nights wrapped in blissful song?

"Father? Have you ever met someone whose mind you
could not see into?"

"What?" Boadach had been rolling his crystal eye from
hand to hand. He stopped now and put it up to his face.
Studying something in the distance, he said, "Guard?"

His form only to be guessed at from behind the curtain,
a guardian stepped forward and raised two hands in salute.
The other two remained at the ready, a bow in one and
stone-tipped arrows in the other.

"Go to the Shadow Forest and inform Forgall the Wily

that the brothers Cett and Craife are cheating at proles. But speak only to Forgall so that the brothers do not hear you.''

The guardian nodded and vanished. Boadach laughed. ''I've just increased Forgall's reputation for cleverness.''

''Is that how it is done, Father?''

The king lifted his shoulders in a shrug. ''It cannot do harm to make him seem greater yet than he is. He himself taught me that lesson when he supported my claim to the kingship.''

There had been but the three then: Boadach, Cuar, and Forgall the Wily, the first to see the miracle of the risen sun and the awe of the night-dancing stars. They had come first, and all the rest after.

Sira asked again, ''Have you ever met someone whose mind is closed to you?''

''Yes, long ago.'' He stood motionless for a moment, his scrying stone still held up to his eye. ''Now and again, one is born among the mortals who can command himself enough to conceal his thoughts from one of us. They are rare; you never find one without some of our own blood mixed in him.''

Then the crystal eye turned toward her. ''Why?'' King Boadach asked. ''Why do you ask me that?''

A quiver of alarm shook her. Was this the time to tell her lord father everything? With a forced smile, she said lightly, ''No reason at all. A legend I remember . . .''

''You are certain this prince's unmannerliness did not distress you?''

''No, Father. I am well.''

''Yet you seem troubled.''

She hesitated and chose the lesser of her difficulties. ''I am concerned about Anat. I love her dearly, but she meddles.''

''Then she is doing that which I have asked her to do. Have you never asked yourself, Sira, why you alone among all the young maids of my court must be so often accompanied by another?''

''I know why that is, Father. There is no need to ask.'' The smile she gave him was not forced but open and loving. She put her hand on his sleeve, crushing softly the black velvet that trimmed his robe. "Your love and care for me is the one constant mark in a changing world. I rely on that. . . ." Her father's eyes dampened as he patted her hand, yet the focus of his loving observation did not fade.

"I understand, which is why I tolerate Anat's meddle-some ways. Yet if you could suggest that she not turn my friends into wild cats nor cast a glamour over me to make me hideous—"

"What? Wherefore should she do such a thing?"

Remembering an instant too late that Anat's reasons for these actions would only turn her father's fury against her-self, Sira stammered, "I—I meant only that she should not. . . . She can, but she ought not to."

"I have given her these powers to keep you safe. That you find the world so often troubling concerns me. You, above all, Sira, should be without any shadow."

"Surely, a life without shadow becomes meaningless. But you are right. I should not wish for such things." Her gaze turned again toward the brilliant vortex on the hori-zon.

Boadach's eyes narrowed. His hand tightened over hers. "If you do not care to wed this prince, tell me which of my subjects do you choose to marry?"

"Must I marry, my lord? In truth, I cannot recall the last marriage among our People. Was it Dua-nach and Dor-nolla? No, I'm sure it must have been Scibur and Blatnat. Remember? They'd been promised for ever so long, but he had to labor in the vineyard until her father would give his consent. Oh, 'twas a happy day. I remember wearing my rose-colored silk with the diamonds dancing on the trim. A modest gown, but I'd no wish to outshine the bride. How happy she has been since, sweet Blatnat."

Her inconsequential chatter had its intended effect. Her father lost his suspicious look and even smiled. "Go on to your friends, Sira. I have affairs to tend to. The Lady of the Eastern Marches sends that there is some unrest among the dragons—talk of a mutiny. I may have to travel there myself to remind the worms of our treaty."

"Take the Great Worm a cask or two of our own ale, Father. That was what kept the peace the last time. No doubt he has run out and the fire in his belly grows hot once more."

The king chuckled. "Indeed, you may have struck it! I shall do as you suggest."

Sira escaped her father's presence, feeling both ugly and tired. What a loathsome creature she was to turn on he who had always shown her the warmest love; to lie, to plot, to care more for some chance-met mortal than for her king and her father. Yet what good could come of telling Boadach that she'd brought a human into the Living Lands? Let him go to the Eastern Marches. She'd keep her human for a few days only. The king need never hear of it, or at least not until Conn had gone. Sira did not ask herself why the thought of losing Conn so soon filled her heart with unaccustomed depression.

When Conn bowed to her at the Silver Pavilion at the edge of the wood, Sira feared she'd stood agape like any child. Her court, the young and merry among The People, had gone silent at his approach, moving out of his way as he walked up to where she sat enthroned. She heard the sharp intake of breath, almost a screech, from one young maid, but she had not looked around to see who had made the sound. Sira barely noticed Blaic, smirking with self-satisfaction, in the background. Conn stole all her attention.

His hair, still darkened with damp, was drawn into a neat tie behind his head and looked as sleek as a seal's. In fresh clothing of forest green laced with amber, his leather breeches showed every muscle in his hard legs.

His was not the charm of an enchanted prince. He was a jagged bolt of dark lightning in her sun-dappled kingdom. It wasn't just his skin, tanned by the sun of the Upper World, nor his hooded eyes that made her wonder what storm of violence he might bring with him. The darkness

lived within him in a way that none of The People could
match. He had fought, drawn blood, and shed his own.

He took her hand, not waiting for her to offer it, and
bowed over her fingers. She felt the lightning strike her
and grasped his hand hard to keep from falling. Sira fought
to remember that of the two, she possessed all the power;
that if it were not for her, he'd still be blind and lost.

Then he looked straight at her with his strange, amber
eyes. She read there, just as though she read his thoughts,
the hunger he felt for her. It was a blaze in his eyes that
heated her flesh wherever his gaze chanced to fall.

Her voice sounded strange to her own ears as she said,
"In the name of the court, I bid you welcome. You are
our guest, and your only concern is to find what pleasure
you may."

"I dedicate myself to that—and to your service, my
lady."

As though a spell-spun bubble burst, the members of
her court began to chatter and to move once more. Sira
realized how very lovely many of her female attendants
were. Would Conn look at any of the others as he'd looked
upon her? She told herself that it mattered not and knew
she lied.

She'd ordered him food, rare delicacies from the ends
of the earth. He ate well, making no complaint that there
was no meat offered to him, neither flesh nor fowl, nor
even any fish. She heard him give polite thanks to those
who served him and saw the sidelong glances of the
younger females. To prove to herself that his interests were
nothing to her, Sira put more animation into her own mild
flirtations. Yet every time Sira would glance at him down
the long table set in the open air, she would meet Conn's
eyes and fall silent.

Blaic had stood up and pledged her with a raised goblet.
The others, wanting perhaps to show the human what loyalty they bore her, echoed the action and shouted her name.
Conn said nothing, only looked at her, more promises in
his eyes than on the lips of all the courtiers, and she felt
the heat of her blood in her face.

She walked away from the table to cool it and found him behind her. Anat had been on the point of following. When Sira looked back, it was to see her companion talking to Blaic. Was the prince delaying Anat on purpose?

Knowing it was wicked, Sira had gone a little farther into the wood with Conn, teasing Anat. Yet when she found herself utterly alone with him, she made no excuse to return to her own kind. Instead, she told him of the interview with her father.

"You haven't told him?" Conn asked.

"No. As I have said—"

"If you are trying to protect me, my lady, let me say again that I fear no one."

They stood alone in the deep shade beneath a canopy of golden leaves. She turned toward him abruptly, challenging his gaze. "You say that, but what do you know of fear? Merely that which a man might feel in the moment before the clash of armies."

"If you had ever seen such a thing, you would not speak of it so dismissingly."

"No," she admitted, "I have not seen men at war, but I have seen what my lord is capable of and it terrifies *me* whom he would no more harm than himself. You have no protection here but mine, Conn of Hamdry. So do not say you are not afraid."

To her surprise, Conn smiled at her, not just with his lips but with his heart. He said nothing so that she had to demand, "Why are you smiling like that? Don't you understand?"

"Yes, I understand. But whenever you say my name like that, it makes me want to laugh."

"How so?"

"Conn of Hamdry. As though you must make it plain to which Conn you are speaking. Are there so many here who carry my name within your borders?"

"There are none." She continued to walk away over the brilliant emerald grass, thinking, *There are none like you anywhere.*

•   •   •

She was not alone in thinking it. Once the court accepted
Conn's presence among them, many of the maidens began
to pay him extraordinary attention, flirting and teasing like
flower buds dancing with the wind. Though the young
lords looked black at this, Conn himself seemed only
amused. Though he would bow and talk to the maidens,
he was as quick to join in the pastimes of Blaic and the
others.

Conn led them all at tilting, even teaching Blaic a pass
or two, though he had long been the only one to carry off
the palm. Though he could not sing, and his dancing contained none of the grace of The People, he had an ear for
music. As Cuar said, "There are times when appreciation
is of more value than even the wisest critiscm."

As a rule, the elders took little notice of the mortal in
their midst. Anat could never be cheerful when Conn was
near. For the most part, however, the elders seemed to
assume that Boadach had approved Conn's presence, pur-
suaded to overlook his prejudice by his daughter's plea.
Sira was careful not to disabuse anyone of that notion.
Sometimes, when she met the eye of Forgall, she wondered
how much the cleverest of The People had guessed, and
she made it a study to keep out of his way.

As the quicksilver days slipped past, Sira learned what
it meant to have a friend. She'd never known the pleasure
of catching someone's eye and thus silently sharing a
thought or a smile. They could laugh together without need
for explanation. Quiet moments could also be found, when
he lay beside her on the grass or by the sea, neither feeling
the need to speak.

She showed him the wonders of her world, pleased and
gratified by his reactions. His near panic had turned to
delight when she gave him a temporary power to breathe
underwater while visiting the creatures of the deep. They'd
flown like eagles to the highest peaks of the wild North,
where the men wrapped themselves in rough blankets and
took better care of their weapons than of their wives. She'd
taken him again to her favorite place, and the vortex in the
sky had not been nearly so appalling on a second viewing.

Today, as on the first day, she held her court in the shadow of her father's palace. The sun shone down, dazzling the eyes where it landed on her cloth-of-silver pavilion. The young of the court were off playing some game that required much searching high and low for strange objects—no conjuring permitted. Conn stood beside her, dressed simply in brown. After the first day, he'd rarely dressed in bright colors. His somber attire made him stand out all the more from the others, who preferred the brilliancy of rainbow shades.

She asked for the second time in a very few minutes, "Are you certain you would not rather join the game?"

"I hold myself in readiness to do your bidding, my lady. If it is your wish . . ."

"No. But I do wish you would not merely stand there! Tell me . . ." She had been on the point of asking for one of his tales of mortal life, but something in his expression made her change her request. "Tell me of what you are thinking."

"I am thinking how beautiful your realm is and of how loath I am to leave it."

"You like it here?"

He stood beside her, his hands on his hips. He often stood that way, and sometimes his hand would seem to seek after the pommel of a sword. He said, "I saw some books once, long ago. Irish priests had drawn them to while away the hours in some distant monastery. I think those monks must have visited your lands once upon a time. I swear I see things here as though in those books."

"What things?"

He tilted his head back to look at the trees at the edge of the meadow. "The interlacing of those branches, it may be, or the two-tailed birds I saw singing among the leaves. The colors . . . the winding of the lines . . . the perfection. Everything . . . and nothing."

"The Living Lands have been long in the making. It should not be amazing that something of what we have done here has reached the world beyond."

"The Living Lands? That's a new one. I've heard this place called many things in the days I've resided here."

"This realm has many names indeed, even among us. Some call it the Lands of Promise. Or Tir Tairngine. Or even the Lands of Fragrance. Only my father knows what its true name is, and he may well have forgotten."

"Mag Mell . . ." Conn said wonderingly, as though mouthing words heard in a dream.

"Yes. That is another of them."

He shook his head, and again she saw him smile, this time in wonder at himself. "Mag Mell" he said again. "I find myself wrapped in a dream from which there seems no waking."

"Is it so dreadful to dream a while? I think . . . I think there has been little that is pleasant in your dreams of late."

"Not since . . . not since . . ." Conn paused and pressed his hands to his eyes. "I can't remember," he said from behind his fingers in a voice full of amazed hurt. "What was the name of the battle? I can see the castle and the smoke. I can all but hear the roar of my enemies' voices as we took the charge."

Sira rose from her throne and came near to him. Reaching up, she brushed her fingertips over the back of his hands. "It doesn't matter now. Come with me. We will play."

He'd taken his hands from his face and somehow, with some turn of his wrists or speed of hand, he'd captured her fingers, interlacing them with his. Lifting, he pressed them together against his chest.

"No," he said in a voice changed and deepened. "The time for games is past. I am a man, Sira, and must, for my sins, act the part."

Sira felt his heart beating in his chest and in his hands, proud and strong. It commanded and drove the beat of her own, but she couldn't seem to summon a wish to break free. She struggled a moment and then went still as she met his clear-eyed gaze. A sudden quiver shook her body and she knew he felt it, too.

He said, "You've ruined my sight forever, Sira."

"Ruined? I—"

When he shook his head, a lock sprang free from the thong that held it, tumbling over his brow. "You've ruined it. Before you, I saw flashes of light. Now when I close my eyes, all I can see is you."

Somehow then, his hands were around her waist, flicking aside the long fall of her braided hair to encircle her. By the same magic, he made her clutch at the stuff of his shirt, as a feeling of falling swept over her. Half-frightened, she saw his eyes close as he tilted his head. Then she couldn't think any more, only feel as his lips moved on hers.

The last time, she'd felt desperation in his kiss, as though he kissed her more to prove something to himself than for desire. This time, she had no ability to stand apart and analyze what was happening. Wave after wave of sensation assailed her, sweeping her away in a fierce undertow of bodily desire.

Conn had understood his motives for kissing her the first time after but a moment's reflection. He'd been confused, torn from everything familiar, given almost carelessly the thing he most wanted. He had kissed Sira in a foolhardy attempt to prove that he still had some mastery over the situation in which he found himself. He had been determined to prove that a knight of England could hold his own under any circumstances. He'd almost hated Sira when he'd kissed her then. But it was not hatred he felt now.

He hardly recognized his own voice. "Kiss me, Sira."

"I am . . ." He heard a hint of a question and smiled.

"There's more."

"There is?" The pupils of her eyes were hugely dilated. Even the tight-tied braids of her glorious hair were springing free in what seemed a spontaneous invitation. He felt a quickening in his loins that told him how ready he was to accept.

Hardly able to speak for desire, he said, "Much more."

She blinked at him owlishly, as though she'd drunk too

much wine. Conn felt a surge of anticipation hardly dis-
tinguishable from fear. He wanted desperately to be Sira's
lover, yet wondered even if he had twice his strength,
would he be prepared for the challenge of making love to
a woman at least two thousand years old? She must have
had lovers by the score.

Looking down into her superbly innocent eyes, Conn
knew she was untouched. Not one of the handsome, brilliant young men of her father's court had ever succeeded
in winning her, not even Blaic. Conn wouldn't have been
human if he had not felt a thrill of victory. His resolve
solidified. "It may have been a long time," he said, "but
that's because you've been waiting for me."

Conn cradled Sira's face in his hands as though he
cupped a golden goblet of fine wine. Then he sipped from
her mouth, tasting and relishing all her flavors. She was
eager, not realizing perhaps the solemnity of this occasion.

Then desire took him like a jab to the heart. He couldn't
wait to teach her more.

Coaxing her lips apart with gentle thumbs, Conn flickered his tongue into her sweet moistness. He felt her instinctive recoil and then, triumph burning in his blood, felt
her slow return for more of the strange, exquisite sensation.

Conn tightened his arms around her. She was slender
and pliable in his grasp. Then as she clutched at his shoulders, Conn lost his fear that he might break her. Her
strength was not the same as his, yet he was humbled by
it just as though she'd wrestled him to the ground.

"Sira," he said, a catch in his voice. "Sira!"

He gathered her more closely still. Her breath came fast
and short. Her eyes were nearly closed, only a glitter showing behind her sweeping lashes. She kissed him, lifting her
face, her arms slipping around his neck.

Conn wanted desperately to pick her up and take her to
some secluded spot. He had not meant to kiss her here,
where any of the returning game players might see them.
His body, sharply aware of her warmth and the insistent
press of her small breasts against his chest, urged haste,
though a voice of wisdom inside his head still required

caution. Yet the voice grew muffled as Sira opened her mouth to him of her own accord.

"By the Horns of the Moon!"

Conn looked up, dazed by the unexpected delight of Sira's unbridled response, and saw a plainly dressed, heavy-set man staring at them. Though his stocky figure and strong arms made him seem no more than a simple farmer, something about the domineering way he stood told Conn that this was the true ruler of all the Other Realm.

Sira turned her head. "Father!"

The brilliance of the sky dimmed to the mysterious paleness of moonlight. The scented breeze died, leaving the air heavy and dank. Then a lurid glare began to flicker out of the ground, casting strange, sick glows over everything.

For a moment, the woman he held in his arms possessed a skull for a face while the king seemed a very demon. All Conn's superstitions rose up—even those he'd believed he'd forgotten—and besieged his faith.

Yet Sira's hands were still gentle on his shoulders, and he could still smell the lily and rose fragrance of her beautiful hair. She gave him a smile of reassurance, though Conn could read fear in her eyes. When she faced the king, Conn knew that he'd never before seen bravery, not even in the depth of battle, and worried that he'd never be worthy of her.

"Father," she said again. "And what of the Worms on the Eastern Marches?"

"A ruse, which you see has worked." There was undisguised triumph in the king's voice. "I have been watching you all this time. You see how my suspicions are justified!"

Conn noticed that Sira stood between him and her father's wrath. Though she did not spread out her arms in any grand gesture, it was obvious that she considered herself a shield against anything Boadach might do. Looking at him, Conn recognized that power lived and throbbed inside the king's stocky frame in the same way that fire lived in the heart of wood. Conn realized that anything he might say could prove to be the ember that set the king blazing.

He wondered what the penalty was in the Living Lands for the high crime of kissing the king's daughter. Less, he assumed, than the penalty for making love to her. He regretted with all his heart not being qualified to suffer the greater punishment.

Yet, no matter what vengeance the king took, Conn was surprised to find that he was content. He had taken what no other man had, and if he did not have Sira's love, he could yet be happy knowing she had desired him. However, he could foresee that shame would be his portion as well as death if he continued to hide behind her skirts.

Conn stepped out. "Here I am, Your Majesty," he said, bowing low. "Do as you will with me."

A deep voice, which seemed to come out of the air and the ground and the sky all at once, replied, "I shall."

Before Conn lifted his head from the bow, he found himself staggering blinded in a howling world of snow.

Eleven

The cold lashed at Conn with tiny knives, ice forming instantly in his nostrils and mouth. The fine silks he wore offered him no protection, and even the leather on his legs was not proof against the slicing wind.

Wrapping his arms about his body instinctively, Conn peered into the heart of the storm. He saw only dazzling flakes of white streaming past him in endlessly altering patterns. He could not distinguish sky from earth nor up from down. No clue told him which way to go. He might as well die where he stood.

He stumbled forward, bent over like an old man. Every movement took tremendous effort as he lifted each leg high to break through the crust. After only a few steps, his leg muscles began to cramp. The hollows his boots left in the snow were instantly filled.

The wind was pain. The cold was pain. His face burned with cold, his eyes watering from the lash of the wind, the tears freezing on his cheeks. Only the determination to die while *doing* kept him moving forward.

All too soon, he stumbled over something hidden beneath the mass of snow and fell, sprawling. Half-expecting to shatter as he hit, Conn couldn't even put down a hand to brace his fall. He lay there and knew he did not have the strength to rise. Strange, too, that lying in snow could feel so warm. It muffled and comforted like the sheep's fleece that he slept beneath on winter nights.

Conn struggled faintly against this mysterious sensation, feeling somehow that he had literally fallen into a snare. Was the king watching him now, taking some perverse pleasure in seeing him freeze to death? Conn wished for hot anger to flood him, to give him the strength and warmth he needed. He called up the glimpse he'd had of King Boadach and tried to fan his anger. Somehow, though, he couldn't make his rage blaze hot enough. His lids began to close as he hungered for sleep.

The snow falling since he'd tripped had all but covered him. Now the wind could not touch him so sharply. He had a small space by his nose to breathe. It would be so easy to fall asleep here in the midst of this wilderness. Were there people here? Would they discover his dried-out corpse when the spring came? Did spring ever come here, or did the snow fall ceaselessly all year round?

He hoped that whoever discovered him would give him a decent burial. Furthermore, Conn found himself hoping that it would not be a child or a woman who made the gruesome find. A middle-aged man, mayhap, on his way to a fair? Or a priest, if they had such things. Someone at least to whom his discovery would not haunt in nightmares ever after. Conn thought of his fine, useless clothes and hoped they'd be of more use to his discoverer than they'd been to himself.

Somehow, these morbid thoughts turned to dreams of Sira, and Conn smiled, cracking the ice crystals on his cheeks. Sira—so different from any woman he'd ever known, yet sweet in spite of her strange ways. How few women, even of his own sort, would have treated a hated stranger with the tenderness she had shown to him?

He'd been wrong to kiss her, wrong to shatter her innocence with his base desire . . . yet he could not regret it. If he had one wish in the world, he would want to see her face again. Not because he hoped for rescue, just so that he could die with her face before him.

Conn seemed to hear her voice, not carried on the wind,

but warm and close. He knew, of course, that she had not followed him into this bitter land. What seemed to be her voice was no more than his dying mind playing a last joke. Nevertheless, his longing to look on her once more grew so intense that he struggled to cling to life for one more instant. Whispering ''Sira'' so softly that even he could not hear it, Conn tried to force open his eyes.

His lashes were frozen to his cheeks. Slowly and with intense mental effort, Conn lifted his blue-nailed right hand and rubbed beneath his eyes with his icy knuckle. He couldn't feel the friction, yet he broke the ice free. Knowing Sira could not be there, calling himself a fool, he yet raised his head just enough to look above the crust of snow that covered him.

Either the wind had died or he was so cold now that he could no longer feel its stinging lash. At any rate, Conn could look steadily across the top of the snowy hillocks and see clearly. What he saw so surprised him that he forgot his body's agony.

Snow continued to fall from the sky but not in fat white flakes. Whole blocks tumbled down, shaped and squared like the stones of Hamdry Manor. Each fell seemingly haphazard but landed with accuracy one atop the next. A small house took shape, the blocks creating clear window space and forming an arched doorway. Flat plates of snow layered like fish scales onto a sloping roof, peaking along the front to shelter the entrance. Sheets of ice whirled out of nowhere to form sparkling windows.

As though some great creature tunneled beneath the snow, a pathway appeared, the loose powder flung aside to leave only a hard-packed surface. The end of the path sought this way and that, like a dog seeking a scent. It paused, and Conn knew it searched for him. No sooner had the thought crossed his mind than the end of the path seemed to leap forward and rushed over to him.

Conn had only to rise and walk along the path. The house glowed from within, a golden light that wavered and danced. He recognized firelight and knew that he had only to rise and walk to find shelter and warmth. But he could no longer feel that any of his extremities belonged to him. Even the hand before his gaze, blue and glittering with hoarfrost, had no connection to him. Exhausted, Conn watched his hand fall nervelessly away.

It fell with an audible clunk on the very edge of the path, his smallest finger touching the flattened snow. Conn closed his eyes and waited for death.

The first sensation was that of a drop of water running over the sensitive skin on the back of his hand. Though he'd never paid a great deal of attention when the priests had discussed the ways and means of eternity, Conn did not think any priest or philosopher would say that death's first harbinger was supposed to tickle.

He tried to fix his thoughts on the eternal. All he could see in his mind, however, was Sira's beautiful face smiling at him. A second drop traced its way down, stirring up response. Without thinking, Conn turned his hand over to rub the irksome spot on the snow path.

Startled, he flexed his fingers experimentally. They did not hurt. Conn stole a peek. The skin on his hand had regained its usual brown tint, the veins showing in bold relief across the back where the blood flowed strongly. Yet ice still clung to his sleeve and his lips were still frozen to his teeth.

Almost crying with the strain, Conn dug his fingers into the snow path. Agonizingly slowly, he dragged himself forward a scant few inches. He felt life, warm and invigorating, flow back into his wrist and then surge up his arm. Again he struggled to drag his body forward.

Inch by painful inch, Conn brought more and more of himself onto the path. It became easier when he could use both hands. Long ago, he had gone hunting in the northern hills. Trapped by a sudden snow squall, he'd stumbled into a tinker's hut. He well recalled the sharp torture of the blood heat returning to his limbs, the prickling and burning.

He felt none of that here. Though when he pressed his cheek to the smooth path it felt as cold as the wild snow at the edge, his body had recovered its warmth. When he sat up, he inadvertently put his hand in the piled snow and jerked it back as the cold bit to the bone. So long as he stayed on the path, the wind was not as piercing, though it still blew the snow about in a mad shower of sparkling white.

"Magic," he said and accepted it.

When he reached the snow house, he reached out toward the sheet of opaque ice that served as a door. Then he paused with his hand in midair. Though his heart longed for the woman he guessed awaited him, he could not in honor go breaking in on her like a ravening wolf.

Conn rubbed his face vigorously to remove the last of the ice crystals and smoothed back his tumbled hair. He straightened his damp silk tunic and brushed the snow from his leathers. Banging his boots against the doorstep knocked off the crust that clung to them. Then he lifted his hand again and knocked.

While he waited for an answer, Conn realized why he'd taken such pains. To be so finicky was not his way but Blaic's. That fay male's smile when he'd first beheld Sira's "pet" had lashed more deeply than Conn had known at the time. To borrow some of Blaic's manner in wooing a fay princess would merely be good tactics.

But when Conn saw her, all thought of strategy flew from his mind to be replaced by a warmth and tenderness more painful than the cold.

"Thanks be. . . ." she said as she opened the door. "I was so afraid," she whispered as he came in.

"Afraid? No, lady. Never fear for me."

"I couldn't help you. My father forbade me to help you."

"But all this?"

"You had to come to me," she said. "I could not save you without your help."

Conn looked at what she had created. Though only one room, the snow house had all the elegance and more of a great noble's house. A fire roared in a fireplace that, had he not known the truth, he would have taken for white marble. A long table covered with a white damask cloth overflowed with the finest foods, though he noticed there was still no meat. Rich hangings, worked in white and silver, covered the walls and floors. A bed of birch wood dominated the corner, heaped high with furs and fleece, all of the purest white.

And Sira, her long, pale hair flowing unbound with but one strand braided, wore a loose robe of pale blue, the color of a shadow on snow. Diamond clips glittered on her shoulders as though they alone held her gown against her body. Warmer than the fire, more beautiful than magic, she looked at him with a worried frown. He felt she was no longer the proud, merry princess but a woman: one that he could touch, hold, and possess.

She reached out to brush her fingers over his shirt. "You are cold. Come nearer the fire."

Conn captured her hand, holding it to his heart. "Not cold now," he said. "Not while you are with me."

She held very still, like a deer hoping to blend in with the forest so that the hunt would go by. "Oh . . ." she said with a voice like heartbreak.

"What is it?" He reached out to gather her against him, his mind in turmoil at the sight of her haunted eyes.

She went into his arms as though she were helpless. She trembled, shaking him with her fear. "I thought . . . no, I didn't stop to think whether this was your world or mine. It's yours."

"Mine? But the snow . . . it's spring in my world."

"Have you never had a late snow before? One long after winter had passed? Chances are it was faerie made."

Conn couldn't tell if she were laughing or crying. His arms tightened. "Why should it matter which world we are in? As long as we are together."

"You don't understand. If a mortal touches one of The People, he or she owns us until we perform what task is asked of us. That is why we are always so careful."

"Yes, I remember chasing you around the garden. A blind man chasing a butterfly." Conn put a finger under her chin to tilt her head back. He wanted to look into her eyes, but she would not meet his gaze. "You have nothing to fear from me. I shall not ask anything of you."

"Nothing?"

Conn hesitated before giving her reassurance. He knew of one thing he wanted of her—wanted desperately. But to ask that would be to change her life forever. He forced himself to speak lightly. "Nothing at all."

He saw a smile tremble on her lips. "You lie, Conn of Hamdry."

Sira broke from his arms, gently and slowly, but he felt it as a wrench, nonetheless. She walked toward the fire, and Conn's mouth went dry as he saw her slenderness outlined through her robe. The flare of her hips and the rise of her breasts were imprinted on his memory. If he lived to be a hundred, he need only close his eyes to see her again as she was now.

She knelt down on the carpet, her head bowed submissively. Her hair swept down in a silken curtain from the crown of her head to her knees. "Ask what you will, mortal. I am bound to obey."

Fighting with his feelings was far more difficult than facing any battle-ready Goliath. It would have been easier if all he had to combat was lust. He had to do battle with his love for Sira and the first engagement was to realize that love was what he felt. He wanted to care for her, to protect her, to keep her with him. He wanted to make love to her and to create a shared future.

Yet to do these things would be to destroy her.

He strode to the table and sought among the treasures there for a decanter of straw-colored wine and a goblet decorated with snowflakes incised into the crystal. Conn poured and drank while she waited for his pleasure. Then he splashed more wine into the goblet and carried it to her.

Kneeling, he said, "Drink."

Sira took the goblet and sipped, still without meeting his gaze. Then she said, "I can make you king, if you wish it."

"That's not a gift I crave, though I thank you."

"Wealth, then? That is power enough in your world.
With wealth, you could make and unmake kings."

"What makes you believe I lust for power, Sira? What
have I said or done to give you that notion of me?"

Now she looked at him, but aslant, out of the corner of
her eye. "Renown in battle then? Shall you wish to be the
greatest warrior of your age? At a word, armies shall flock
to your banner. Will you secure the throne for your king?
Conquer all Europe to the capital of the Rus? Or . . . or
will you drive the 'infidels' into the sea and take the Holy
Land in Rome's name?"

"Now you tempt me, lady. Any man who did such a
thing would win renown indeed and no doubt sainthood
thereafter. And yet . . . and yet I have not heard from those
who went on Urban's Crusade that the people of the Holy
Land long for our interference."

"But sainthood . . . you would be raised among your
most high. Think of that, Conn of Hamdry."

He chuckled. "Being a saint means no rest in the
hereafter. All those people soliciting your favors for their
needs. It makes me understand your reluctance to deal with
mortals, lady."

Again, he saw the flicker of her glance. "It is some
woman or other that you wish for, then? I could bring any
beauty in the world to your side in an instant: An empress?
A queen? Name her, and you shall own her heart forever."

"Shall I name her, Sira? Or do you know her name
already?"

He received the full impact of her gaze and read there
a yearning that matched his own. Conn slipped his hands
down over her arms, feeling with what sweet passion she
responded to his touch. Taking her hands, he pressed each
one to his lips. She sighed, a whisper of surrender.

"Sira, I dare not wish for what I want. But I can bring
myself to ask. Sira, will you be my wife?"

She had believed herself prepared for anything. At Conn's
touch, the weight of the ancient Law had fettered her spirit.
She had turned unthinkingly to hide herself in the

arms of the very mortal who had so enspelled her. Yet even as Sira took comfort from him, she was raising her defenses. Her People's songs and stories were full of the incessant, unreasonable, wicked demands of mortals.

Now he asked for nothing that she had expected him to. Her walls crumbled, leaving her helpless. She could only stare at him in amazement. When he swept her into his arms, she responded fully as the leap of hope in her heart expressed itself.

Conn laid her down on her back next to the fire, cupping her face in his hands. "Will you? Please say that you will and free me from this doubt."

Afterward, Sira knew she should have stopped to consider all she was giving up. Just then, however, she could only think of all she was gaining. She reached up to run her hands along the broad strength of his shoulders, clutching him closer. The desire and love in his clear eyes was more than she could resist.

"I will . . . I will."

Then she gasped, more in surprise than in pain, as the transformation began.

"Sira! What is it?"

She hadn't breath or words to tell him. She could only hold him with all her strength as the changes took place. Conn hissed as her nails sank into his shoulders, but he didn't thrust her away. He held her close, his thoughts racing in his head as he stared down, his anxiety unbearable. Had he slain her with a word? He felt thick and slow, stupid and incompetent.

Then her sweat-slick body shuddered against his. She rolled onto her back slowly. Conn let her go, holding only her hand. With her eyes tight shut, she seemed to be surveying herself from the inside. He knew that look; he'd worn it often himself on awakening from some clout on the head after a skirmish.

Sira opened her eyes and saw Conn above her. She wondered if she had grown haggard and hideous. Did all her years show on her face? Would he recoil in horror, finding himself in the arms of a incredibly ancient creature?

Conn asked simply, "What happened?"

Sira sighed in relief that he had not fled. "I am one of you now."

"One of . . . Human? Mortal?"

She nodded slowly, trying to resign herself while her fingers itched for a mirror. Gazing at him, she saw herself reflected in the tiny mirrors of his eyes. Though she could see no details, the expression in his gaze had not changed. Sira was reassured. Moreover, she felt ashamed. What would Conn think if he realized her first thoughts on becoming mortal were not of him and the bliss they might share but of herself?

Conn said, "You look just the same. As beautiful as a dream."

"Do I?" More than her cheeks warmed under the expression of his eyes. Had she caught a fever so soon?

"I wish that I had a mirror so you could see."

"Oh, I can . . ." Automatically, Sira put out her hand to call one forth. Then she remembered. "No, I can't."

"It will take some getting used to," Conn said. "I will help you all that I can."

Then he kissed her, and her doubts fled before his gentle claiming.

Sira wound her arms around his neck, enjoying as before the difference between the hardness of his chest and the softness of her breasts. She reveled in the way his breath sounded in her ears and the dazed glitter of his brown eyes when he looked down at her. Yet after a few nearly silent moments, she withdrew from him, saying, "I don't understand. Something is different."

He shook his head, not understanding, and returned to tenderly plundering her mouth. A strange, new tension built in her body, something she couldn't recall feeling before. It made her want to twist against his body, not in protest over the way he crushed her into the tapestry but to be more a part of him. She kissed him in return, hard, then dragged her mouth away.

"It wasn't like this before," she muttered. "This is the third time you've kissed me. Why is it so different?"

His hands moved on her shoulders. At the touch of his human fingers, the diamonds let go their hold on her gown. With a tug, the dampened silk slid over her skin and he pushed up on rigid forearms to gaze down on her. Sira felt the heat flame in her cheeks again. She put her hands up to cover, not her bare breasts, but her face.

"Shhh," Conn whispered. "Don't . . . We'll stop here but . . . my God, you must marry me as soon as we return to Hamdry. I'll go mad else."

As though he couldn't help himself, he bent down to kiss the soft satin swell showing between her raised arms. A moment of sweet sensation and then he withdrew, clenching his jaw as though it were only by force that he could control himself. "When we are married . . ."

She said quietly, "I saw, not long ago, two humans lying in each others' arms, kissing as we do now, holding each other. He lay atop her as you have lain with me, but they did not stop."

Conn lowered himself so that she had only to turn her head to whisper in his ear. "Who were they?"

"Members of your household, I assume. They were in your garden, at any rate."

"Gandy, I'll be bound," he said as though to himself. "The base . . ." Meeting her eyes, he explained, "A pair of servants may do as they like, within reason. But you and I are not a varlet and a slut. We do not make love on grass. At least, not until properly blessed by a priest."

"What of this feeling? So restless . . . so hot. I have never known anything like it and yet . . . Is this what a woman feels when she lies with a man?"

Conn turned his head away. Sira saw the struggle for control continue within him. Suddenly sure she'd made the right choice, indeed the only choice, she reached out to him.

At the first brush of her fingers over his cheek, Conn shuddered. With his eyes closed, he might as well be blind again, but even in the depths of his real blindness his senses had never been so alive. Her scent surrounded him, the same floral that had first told him whenever she was near, yet now underlaid by a warmer scent that was of her aroused body.

Without opening his eyes, Conn caught her hand. "You can't know what you do to me."

"I want to know."

Her voice created havoc within him, it was so warm and eager. He glanced at her, almost afraid. She dazzled him with her anticipation. "Sira," he began, searching for the right words. "You say you are a human now. How do you know?"

She pressed his hand to her breast and Conn licked his dry lips. "I can feel it in my heart. Things have changed within me and . . ."

"And?"

"Elsewhere," she whispered and the pink in her cheeks became bright again.

Conn realized he'd never seen her blush in all the weeks—How long *had* it been?—that he'd stayed in the Living Lands. Now she'd done it twice in a matter of moments. He repeated her last word. "Elsewhere?"

"We of the fay are not formed like you humans. Oh, outwardly, I suppose, our faces and our limbs are similar, but we do not . . . we do not *love* as you do. Even as we do not die as you do."

"You said something once—about being called from the sea when you were born."

"I am sea-born, that is true. My father went to the sea and asked for a child. I was given forth to my parents. We were very happy until my lady mother chose to retire from the realm and join the Sleepers."

"Leave her husband and her child? Why?"

Now it was she who could not meet his gaze. "She was ravished by a human."

"Oh, God!"

"It was long ago, by your reckoning. There were soldiers from some distant land pillaging Gaul. They wore strange armor decorated with birds and beasts and walked behind eagles."

Conn recalled his boyhood lessons. "Romans? The Roman Empire? A thousand years ago!"

"Yes. My father could never forgive you."

"Me? I would never—"

"He holds all you humans responsible. You cannot say that man has changed so much that such things do not now happen."

Thinking of all the horrors he had seen, Conn could not argue with her. "Your father was furious with me for merely kissing you. What he would say now, I dare not think."

"I am more worried by what he will do."

"Are you afraid of him?"

Sira smiled, but tears glittered in her beautiful eyes. "No, never. But this defection of mine will break what is left of his heart."

Conn held out his arms. She nestled against his chest and he felt a hot tear slide down, dampening the silk of his shirt. He brushed a clinging strand of her hair aside and turned to kiss her brow and then her lips. It was she who pulled him strongly against her as she let herself lie back on the carpet.

His weight atop her was maddening, both confining and liberating. Though she couldn't move freely, she'd never felt more unrestrained. Nothing seemed impossible now. Remembering the lovemaking she'd briefly witnessed, Sira ran her hands under his shirt. His skin scorched hers. Conn made a sound of pleasure in the back of his throat, though he didn't lift his mouth from their kiss. She found herself making the same sort of noises as she trembled, the beats of her human heart shaking her whole body.

When he stopped, she protested wordlessly. He gazed at her with strange, hard eyes that frightened her for a moment into thinking he was a stranger. Then he bent his head to explore her face and throat with his lips. He found a tender spot and laved it with his tongue. She gasped, twisting now beneath him as unbearable excitement flooded her. Conn stilled, his groan not that of pleasure but of pain. His arms tightened around her, his soldier's strength crushing her, yet her thoughts were all for him.

"What is it?" she whispered. "Have I hurt you?"

"Not yet."

Conn couldn't find the words to tell her what the slide of her cool skin did to him. He thanked heaven that her silk gown was twisted around her hips, offering her some protection against the rigid evidence of his well-nigh killing desire for her. "One more kiss," he muttered. "Just one more."

He could trust himself that far but not a step farther. To lie atop her, to feel every inch of her against him, and to know with body, heart, and soul that she was his for the taking was the sweetest torture he'd ever known. He made love to her mouth, his hands gripping the carpet either side of her head.

She called his name, offering her throat again to his lips. Images flooded his mind, of drawing the tight nipples he could feel against his chest into his mouth, of his roughened hands sliding upward over her smooth thighs.

Then Sira raised her knees, cradling his leather leggings against the very source of her heat. Her gown was no protection now, and he knew the innocence of her spirit would not protect her for very much longer. Even as these thoughts passed through his mind, his body demanded more. He flexed instinctively against her, seeking completion.

She moaned into his mouth. Her eyes half-closed, she whispered hoarsely, "Help me, Conn. Show me what to do."

"No." The sound tore from his throat as Conn rolled away from her. He flung his arm over his face. For a moment, there was no sound but the snapping of the fire and his ragged breaths, the broad planes of his dark-furred chest rising and falling. Lifting his arm, he stared at the medallions on the ceiling. He said firmly, "This stops here. It must."

Sira shook her head almost lazily as she sat up. "I have

never heard that humans were so noble-minded. Or is it just you?''

Sliding her fingers into the hair at his temples, she bent down to kiss him, her perfumed tresses falling around him. Then, her lips busy with what he'd taught her so far, she gently tugged at his hands, once more sunk into the carpet. He could not resist her without hurting her.

"You like it when I touch you. . . ." she said quietly. "Will I like it when you touch me?"

Realizing that he watched her every move through slit-ted eyes, she once more brought his unresisting hand to her breast. They seemed fuller now that she was human and much, much warmer. Without a word, Conn caressed her, reaching out with his other hand as well.

Sira had expected a mild pleasure, not half what she'd known from his mouth. That was before his thumbs, still slightly rough despite his days living like a prince, dragged across the most sensitive part. Sira's eyes flew open in surprise as the languor of passion fled, supplanted by flame.

Then he drew one unbearably tightened tip into his mouth. Had she saved him from freezing? Sira would not have known it by the heat he caused to bloom everywhere in her skin. She was shaking as he swirled his tongue over her nipple, drawing it deeper into the suction as she leaned over him.

"Please, Conn. Oh . . ." Forgotten, all forgotten, her dignity as a princess, her power as a faerie, her duty to herself and her father. For the first time in her life, she longed for something that only a mortal, only *this* mortal could give to her.

She found herself again on her back, Conn beside her, Conn's hands everywhere on her. His previous restraint had been maddening; his need drove her past all control. With her fumbling help, he was within moments as naked as she. The first sight of his proud manhood stole her breath. Was the shudder that racked her from fear or de-sire? Even Sira didn't know.

Conn saw her eyes widen. Though he possessed the

power to please even a demanding woman, he knew he
was large for a virgin to take. Sira was more than a virgin
in body; her spirit had known nothing of passion until now.
He tried to smile and made a feeble joke. "I'm only human, Sira, but if it is your wish to stop. . . ."

"The one I glimpsed before . . . didn't look like that! It
was much smaller and pink. Harmless, or so I thought."

"I cannot promise that I will be harmless. The first time
can hurt."

"I would never hurt you," she said, looking up at him.

His smile was rueful. "Not for me. But for a
woman . . ."

"And I am a woman now."

"Yes. So much a woman . . ." He smoothed his hand
over the sensitive skin of her stomach and watched the
muscles dance. Then lower, to brush the soft curls that hid
her secrets.

"That's new, too," she offered brightly, then held her
breath as she watched his hands' progress. She gasped as
he pressed downward, seeking to know her completely.
Without thinking, she rolled her hips forward, welcoming
his touch. Something she recognized dimly as ecstasy began to spiral through her body, twisting tighter and tighter,
driving her higher and higher in response to his hand.
Sweat broke out, making her slide against him slickly as
she threw her arms around him. What pleasure in the Living Lands could compare with this?

"Oh, my beloved," he gasped as she clung to him, limp
in the aftermath of her first climax. "All will be well, I
swear it."

He laid her gently back, as he moved over her, poised
at the entrance to her body. She opened her eyes as though
she waked from a long sleep. Then she reached out, drawing her fingers down his spine. She vacillated a moment
before stroking the hard rise of his muscular buttocks.
"You are so magnificent," she said. "I'm not afraid."

Conn tried to move slowly, to give her time to adjust,
but he could not stand against the living fulfillment of all
his wishes. She lifted against him at the same instant that

he flexed forward, surging irresistibly into her tightness. Conn heard her soft cry of pain.

He would have far rather taken a pike through his stomach than hurt her. He wondered if he could recall the discipline that had fled at the first foray. Looking down at her face, at the tear that seeped from under her closed eyelid, he realized that for Sira, he would do anything, though it killed him.

Through gritted teeth, he offered, "Shall I stop?"

"There's no point in stopping now, is there? What is done is done." He saw nothing of the martyr in her true gaze. On the contrary, it was with a light of wicked courage that she said, "I am hoping that something good will yet come of this."

Determined to fulfill that hope, Conn took up the ancient cadence. In a moment, Sira began hesitantly to match it. She lifted her feet to cross them on his lower back. The change in depth, the increase of tightness, was nearly enough to send him over the edge. Only the realization that Sira, too, had begun to climb toward her own peak kept him going.

The sight of her beautiful face as she found her pleasure, combined with her calling his name, rushed through Conn with the force of a conquering army. He surrendered completely to the power that swirled through him.

A long time later, he returned to his senses, the sound of her voice in his ear. "I have a heart now," she whispered. "It is yours if you want it."

Twelve

At some time during the night, Conn carried Sira to the bed. Expecting to feel once again the storm of his love-making, Sira said, "Is this wise . . ."

"Regrets already?" He let her slide down his body, skin awakening skin, as he stood her on her feet again. He threw back the covers of fur and marvelously soft blankets. Indicating that she should get in first, he watched her with a lazy gleam in his eyes that made her all too aware of her nakedness.

She said, "No regrets. But a little . . . tender?"

"I am sorry." He settled himself beside her, the bed sagging beneath his weight. She rolled toward him, well content. He added, "Though not so sorry that I regret what we have done. That I never shall."

Sira ran her hand up his arm, her fingers appreciating the definition of his muscles. "If you only knew how often I had wanted to touch you before . . . when you were blind and so lost."

"Lost? Did I seem so to you?"

"You did." Sira raised her hand yet higher and let her fingers brush the mark which was all that remained of his scar. "What a pity your honorable wound no longer shows."

"I have scars enough."

"I saw." Indeed, he bore many marks of his service.

One, slicing down across his chest from left to right, made a permanent trail through the thick hair on his upper body. She followed the path with her finger and heard him suck in his breath sharply. "Hurts?"

He cleared his throat. "Tickles."

"Tickles? What is that?"

In an instant, she was on her back, convulsing with laughter as she'd been shaken before with passion. She fought off his tormenting hands with little success until she carried the battle into his camp. When she twiddled her fingernails against the sole of his naked foot, he sued for peace. Looking up the length of his hard body, she saw the evidence of his renewed desire and offered easy terms.

Conn awoke the next morning, smiling. The little house of snow glowed as though he resided in the heart of a great pearl. His breath steamed above the edge of the fleece drawn over his chest, and he realized that his exposed feet were nearly numb from cold. "Sira?"

"I'm here." She hurried to his side, bearing two apples in her hands. "Breakfast," she said, tossing him one.

"What became of last night's feast?"

"All gone. I don't know how long the rest will last." She cast an assessing gaze over the walls. "You notice the fire is out?"

"I noticed." He took a bite of the crisp, chilled flesh. It had a tang far surpassing any apple he'd ever eaten before. Not even in the Living Lands had fruit tasted so vibrant. He said something of his thought, and Sira laughed. "It's a real apple. Not one of ours. I have always preferred them."

She wore her loose gown, but no brilliant diamonds held it closed at her shoulders. Instead, she'd tied rough knots that stood up like knobs. Her hair hung in hanks, unbrushed and less than fresh. Under her laughing eyes were the faintest rings, signs of the sleep she'd lost to their mutual pleasure. She yawned and stretched, her breasts thrusting out against the fabric.

"Lucky for you it is so cold," Conn said. "I have not given you good morning, my lady."

Her kiss welcomed him. Conn suddenly found the chill
to be less of a deterrent than he thought. Until a cold drop
of water on his back convinced him otherwise.

"Conn," Sira said, freeing her mouth. "The house is
melting. We should leave."

"Later. . . ."

He took her mouth again, lingering even though he
knew she was right. Conn did not care to find himself up
to his knees in melting snow, not before he put his clothing
on.

In a little while, he stood beside Sira, snugging a fleece
around her shoulders. The silken gown she wore gave her
no protection from the wind that now slithered through
fast-widening chinks in the bricks. Even as he watched,
their bed dwindled into half-melted ice. He snatched up a
few sheepskins before they became soaked. They were
real, too, though far whiter and softer than any he'd seen
from Hamdry.

"Let's take the tablecloth as well," Sira said. She
started toward the remains of the table, and Conn noticed
that her small feet were pale with cold.

"Don't you have shoes?"

"They were under the bed," she answered with a quick,
humorous grimace. She plucked the fine cloth and napkins
from the slush. They still looked as though they were made
from snow. "We'll keep these in memory to cover our
own table."

Conn frowned over her feet. "You can't walk home in
bare feet. Your toes will freeze black. I could carry
you. . . ."

"All the way to Hamdry? We don't know how far that
may be."

"Do you think I can't do it? You weigh nothing at all."

"There's an easier way," she said, after he'd swept her
off the ground. She pressed her mouth to his, all too
briefly, then added, "Though I don't mind this."

"What easier way?" Conn asked.

"A horse."

"You have one made of snow?"

She chuckled deep in her throat. "No, foolish mortal. You have one in your stables. What was his name?"

"Arundel? How could he be of any use to us now?"

Conn saw a shadow cross her bright countenance, quickly thrust away. "My lord father told me that, since I could not reach your mind—"

"My mind? How do you mean?"

"It is an easy matter to read a mortal's mind. As easy as seeing what lies at a distance beyond one's own eyes. Easy, that is, unless he has some fay blood in his veins. My lord father told me so. Therefore, since I could only read your thoughts with your assistance . . ." She must have seen disbelief in his face. She gave the little sigh of impatience that was hers alone and said, "Why is it you can believe all this magic I have done, yet you cannot believe that I could look into your thoughts? Don't you remember the first time we met? You thought of your garden, and I took you there."

"I had forgotten, as one forgets a dream on waking."

She sniffed. "I would have hoped you'd remember our first meeting with a *little* more clarity. I remember it so very well. You wanted to kill Anat and me with your inflexible pride." Sira kept her face turned away from him, hurt vanity warring with an irresistible urge to giggle. When Conn, properly chastised for his lack of romance, pressed a hard kiss into the white side of her throat, the giggle bubbled up.

Conn tossed her up to settle more comfortably in his arms. She clutched the fleeces and the cloths as he strode out of the house through a dripping gap that had not been there an hour earlier. He stepped gingerly, expecting to feel again the soul-killing cold of Boadach's storm. Instead, he saw the snow melting away in tiny rivulets, while all around was the snap of ice breaking and the whisper of snow falling from bent branches.

Taking heart and suddenly filled with a causeless optimism, Conn prompted, "Go on with what you were saying."

"My lord father said that if I could not see your

thoughts, it meant you possessed fay blood. Even if your ancestor had lain with one of my blood five thousand years ago or more, you would still carry enough in your veins to make your mind impervious to our minds. Not that we could not work our will on you!''

''That you need not tell me.''

''What it means is that you might be able to call your horse and have him hear you, no matter how far off. Those of the fay bond well with animals, and I noticed that your good horse seemed to bear you in affection. Call him.''

Conn took a great breath only to find her slender fingers flat against his mouth. ''You need not deafen me with a shout,'' she said softly. ''Call gently. You need not make him hear your voice except the voice of your heart.''

He was more than a little glad that there was no one nearby to witness his folly. ''Arundel?'' he said, letting the name resonate within his chest. ''Arundel. Come to me, boy. Come on!''

Conn waited, half-expectant despite himself. He laughed a little at his own unreasoning disappointment when no thunder of hooves answered his call. ''I think the mingling of blood happened far too long ago to lend me any magic.''

Sira said, ''It seems I must teach you patience.''

''Teach me as I walk then, my lady.'' Clearing his throat, he said, ''Pick a direction, my lady, and I'll carry you thither.''

''How shall I choose? Without knowing where we are, I could send us miles away in the wrong direction.''

''At this moment, it matters but little. Choose.''

''Very well. West. 'Twas ever a lucky point for my people.''

As he carried her, Sira told him tales of The People to keep his mind off the weariness of his arms and legs. One apple was not very much for such a man to support himself on. The sun mounted into a sky as blue as cool waters.

As they progressed, Conn saw that wildflowers, oppressed under the sudden weight of the snowfall, were straightening up while the fox that stopped to sniff the air as they passed seemed entirely undismayed by the late storm.

Conn nearly dropped Sira when she called a greeting to the fox over his shoulder. Then she pushed what she carried into his hands and said, "Wait a moment. Let me down."

She left footprints in the thin crust of snow that remained on the ground. When she knelt in it, Conn was moved to call a protest. He had no wish to lose her to an inflammation of the lungs now that she was mortal.

The fox did not take fright as she approached, merely stood by and panted like a dog. Conn glanced in wonder at this marvel before giving all his attention to Sira. "Up," he said, taking her elbow. "It's too wet."

"Oh, yes." She brushed absently at her gown, her knee having made a round wet spot on the now-bedraggled gown.

When Conn turned, Blaic stood beside him. About his compact body swirled a cloak composed entirely of fox fur, every color from black to silver. The prince stared at Conn, his upper lip curled in a sneer, wonderment and contempt equally blended. "Do you have the remotest concept, oh mortal, what you have done? Can you conceive of what enmity you have earned? Or do you flatter yourself that this is some little matter of your love epic and all the rest of the Two Worlds can make a May game of themselves?"

Conn, knowing he had won, could restrain himself in the face of Blaic's derision. "Not that, certainly. And yet . . . I cannot weep for being happy."

"It is not his fault that I love him," Sira said.

"What of those who love you?" Blaic said. "Your lord father and Anat? Notice, won't you, how I say nothing of my love for you."

Sira's eyes sought Conn's, offering him herself as a safeguard. "My father is no doubt very angry."

"No," Blaic said. "Not angry now. Wounded. Wounded to the heart. He sits on his throne and though he weeps no more than you, mortal, I believe that his heart weeps blood.''

Conn felt the shudder of pain and grief that shot through Sira. Yet she asked only, ''What of Anat?''

''She went on her knees to Boadach, begging his forgiveness. He withheld it. She has offered to go to the Sleepers in redress for her carelessness in allowing you to flirt with the mortal world. He refused.''

''Allow me? How was she to stop me?''

''I believe she feels she should have appealed to your sense of duty. I told her you had none.''

Sira's cheeks were flaming. Her pride would not stand this sort of address. ''You are not wrong!'' she said, flinging back her head. Her loose hair flicked Conn on the cheek. ''What do I care for my duty when I am in love?''

Defending her, Conn said, ''She owes her duty to me now, prince. I am sorry for the grief of her family, but I will not surrender her.''

''Then you know you have condemned her to death? Look at her. Already the mortal's doom has made a claim on her.''

''I know it,'' Conn said. ''That sight grieves me more than any words you can throw at me.''

Sira only laughed. ''You cannot reach me with guilt so you try my vanity, Blaic? It won't work. Nothing will change my heart. It is fixed on Conn of Hamdry.''

''Then there is no more to be said.'' Blaic bowed, still with irony. He swept off the flowing cloak of fox fur and slung it over Conn and Sira both. ''Accept this as my wedding gift. It is not perhaps all I could wish, but faerie gold is of no value in the mortal world.''

The prince turned and disappeared as though he were a candle flame blown out. Conn gaped. Sira, snuggling under the fox cloak with a sigh that was part sorrow, part enjoyment of luxury, said, ''He took a secret way. You saw some of the other entrances, I believe, your first day in our . . . in my father's land.''

''Sira, do you regret?''

She shook her head fiercely and drew the cloak more closely around his neck. "No. But I must ask you . . ."

"What?"

"Do I look so very bad? You say you can see mortality in my face already? Have I become less pleasing to you?"

Conn chuckled at her anxiety, letting her feel the rumble of laughter in his chest. "If all your poets sang for ten thousand years, they would never create anything half so lovely as you. When you slept beside me last night, I gazed on you for hours. You are so . . ." He shook his head at the paucity of mere words, adding, "To think I touched you. . . ."

Sira kissed him, not once but a hundred times until Conn said, "Enough! Or your next bed will be that pile of leaves."

He carried her onward, tiring a little, yet so pleased to have her close that he disregarded the low ache in his arms. Her head lay on his shoulder. He thought she slept.

When he saw Anat, sitting on an ancient way stone in the midst of a frost-sharpened field, he knew that he'd been expecting to see more of his bride-to-be's "family." He only wondered why Anat had not taken on some other form. Then he saw her exhausted, confused eyes and realized she had not the strength either to change or create an illusion. Her rich, sober raiment and the costly veil that floated from her graying hair made her a target for any passing villain, the chance for wishes aside. Only the wooden necklace around her throat, each link polished to satin by age, seemed homely, though the interlaced star-shaped pendant was cunningly carved.

"Sira?" Conn roused his lady love. "Sira, get her to conceal herself, for it is too dangerous for her to be here alone, dressed like that."

"Dangerous? For her or for any who find her?" Then Sira looked more closely at her former companion and added, "Oh, yes. You're right."

Sira wiggled down from Conn's warm arms and ran over to Anat. Going down on one knee, her head bent, she said only, "Anat, I am sorry."

Anat reached out her hands to Sira, she who had been all but her own child. Then she gave a cry of despair. "I cannot even touch you!"

"Please . . . please . . . don't . . ." Sira, too, reached out, also stopped by an invisible barrier that could not be breached without breaking more hearts. The two women, young and old, knelt together, arms outstretched, as though separated by a panel of ice.

Words broke from Anat's lips, loud and sharp enough to break the ice, had it really existed. "Come back, Sira. Come back to us!"

Slowly, Sira's arms dropped to her sides. "I cannot. He has wished and I—I have chosen."

Conn saw then that not being able to weep when sorrows overwhelmed one was perhaps the heaviest burden The People carried. He could well believe that Blaic had not exaggerated when he'd said the king's heart wept blood. Anat's cheeks had sunk in over the course of a single night, her eyes deep in their hollows edged with deeply purple circles. Suddenly she looked like an old woman instead of the satisfied, middle-aged one Conn had come to know and respect.

When she saw the tears slipping from Sira's eyes, Anat said, "You are lost for certain." She pressed her hands to her chest, clasping the pendant tightly, and her lips moved in what seemed to be silent prayer. "There is nothing to be done."

"Please believe that I am happy," Sira pleaded. "Tell my father . . . I am happy."

"He will not speak to me now." Anat rose, with the simple elegance of her kind that not even great age could steal. "You will not wish to go empty-handed to your husband's home. I leave you a fit gift for a princess."

Anat held out her hand. Blood glittered on each finger where she had clasped the sharp edges of the star. Large scarlet drops rolled off her fingertips to land smoking on the ice-glazed carpet of moss by her feet. Conn stepped forward with a band of cloth he'd torn from his shirt, intending to offer it as a bandage. He stopped in wonder as each drop of blood hardened into a ruby.

Sira took the cloth from his suddenly nerveless fingers. "Bind your hand, Anat."

Anat ignored the offered bandage. "I will not forget you. I bid you to think of me. If only now and again."

Like Blaic, Anat turned away and vanished. Yet her disappearance seemed slower to Conn, and he could have sworn the lady looked back as she faded out like a shadow under sunrise.

Wiping her cheeks with the bandage, Sira knelt down to collect the stones her dear friend had left behind. At first, Conn hesitated to touch the smoothly gleaming gems that lay on the white-tipped green patch of moss. The drops varied in size from big enough to cover the pad of his thumb to smaller than the tip of his littlest finger. Each cabochon looked as though it had been cut by a master's hand, uniformly shaped into ovals, and flawless even when held up to the weakly shining sun.

As Sira tied the last stone into the cloth, Conn stood up and offered his hand. About to sweep her up again into his arms to keep her little feet from the icy mud, he heard a strange, rhythmic sound coming nearer. Turning, he half-expected to see an army of four-armed guardians bearing down on him. Impossible to think that Boadach wouldn't make an appearance as his daughter wended her poignant way home.

Instead, he saw a magnificent stallion racing away over the thin crust of snow. His white-blond mane streamed out behind him, his fawn-colored coat agleam with sweat despite the temperature. He looked like a creature out of legend as the steaming breath blew from his nostrils and the feathers around his hooves flew like wings.

"Arundel!" Conn cried and clapped his hands.

At once, the huge horse wheeled and came toward him. Aware of Sira, smiling with satisfaction behind him, Conn moved at a near run toward his horse. Something must have scared him to make the charger run like that. If he decided to bolt away . . .

But Arundel came directly up, slowing every step until man and beast met in the middle of a barren field. The barrel-like sides heaved, showing the ripple of muscle under the slick coat. Yet he had spirit enough to push his huge head into his master's chest.

"Rogue!" Conn, used to the trick, fell back a step. Though priests had told him often that animals possessed no souls, surely Arundel appreciated his own jokes. There was a light as of laughter in the heavily lashed brown eyes.

Catching hold of one cheek strap, Conn saw the rope trailing from the headstall. He reached for it and noticed the broken, frayed end. Letting go of that with a snort of disbelief, he rubbed the pale velvet nose. "What were the fools about, to tie you? I could have told them it does no good. What rope could you not break?"

"Any but that which ties him to you." Sira came up behind him, the cloth swinging lightly in her hand.

"Don't come too near," Conn warned her, even as he continued to caress the horse. "Arundel is not fond of women."

"No? Why is that?"

"I don't know. A smell, or their higher voices, perhaps. But whenever a woman came near him in the camp or even in a stable, he'd shy." Thinking of Helen for the first time in what seemed forever, Conn added, "Of course, when he showed he didn't like it, sometimes a woman might scream and then . . ."

"Any sensible male would flee from that, of course." Sira stepped around him and stood gazing up at the horse. Arundel towered over her, her head not even reaching the huge shoulder. She said, quite as though she were speaking to a person, "Do you remember how, long, long ago, we raced the wind together and rode it down? Lightning could not catch us, nor were there any who stood between us and the end of the world. We showed the herds the sweetest grass and the water; you taught us the meaning of freedom. Do you remember?"

Not even the creation of the house of snow or the visitations of Blaic and Anat had stunned Conn so much as this moment when his mount, whom no one had ever had the training of save himself, chose to bend his great knees to his master's bride. He had seen horses trained to give such courtesy to queens, but he had disdained such frivolity always. Yet here was his horse offering homage without prompting.

He was so surprised by this that it was some time before he recalled that because the horse had come to him, what Sira said must be true. Somewhere in his ancestry, he must carry fay blood. His mother's people had lived for so long in England that he supposed it must be one of them who had taken a faerie lover. Looking on Sira as she laughingly stroked Arundel's face, he could only be glad.

Sira said, "There was not time to show you my father's stables. Twelve snow-white horses, none of whom have ever known bit or bridle but whose manes are braided with precious gems and whose hooves are burnished like glass." For the first time in many hours, Conn heard Sira laugh. "He may in time forgive your stealing of his daughter, but had you taken a horse, he would have hunted you down with the remaining eleven." Idly, as she rubbed Arundel's nose, she added, "They possess speech and often sing while pulling his carriage."

Conn found words. "You were right when you said he would come to me."

"At least now you need not carry me." Looking up at the horse's eyes, she said, "But first, I think, we could all do with some water. Is there a stream near at hand?"

Arundel tossed his head in what a human would be a nod. He began to walk toward the line of trees on the horizon. Sira reached out for Conn's hand. "Come along. Horses can smell water, you know. It's very useful."

"Yes, I know." To be following his horse to water seemed more dreamlike than his days in the Living Lands.

They came back to Hamdry while the sun stood at noon, though it seemed they'd been traveling for days. Conn wondered but did not ask how much of their trip had been taken through the Realm. Even Sira seemed to find it hard at times to know which world she stood in. Though Conn

kept a sharp eye out for the king, they had seen no more
changeling foxes or appearing and disappearing women.
Yet Conn knew that any tree might hide a spy or that at
any moment he could find himself wandering again in a
world of myths and legends.

Approaching his father's manor, Conn gazed at it as it
appeared against the blue sky. "Look," he said. "It's not
as grand as your father's palace, but it is as snug and well-
built as any in England!" He knew he did not have to tell
Sira what his home meant to him. She knew full well. He
added only, "I will be glad to be at home again."

She smiled down at him from horseback. He walked
beside her, for there was no need to guide Arundel. "I
hope your father will like me."

"He will," Conn said, though with such determination
it sounded like a vow. To himself, he added, *Or else.*

There was no breeze to make the pennons stand out in
welcome, nor did any voice cry greeting as they stepped
onto the entryway into the manor. Conn said, "There
should be at least one guard on duty. And where are the
servants?"

He felt a cold touch against his soul at the emptiness
and silence of the courtyard. Suddenly, he recalled one of
his nurse's tales: a man was taken into the Living Lands
where it seemed only a day had passed, but on return to
his family, decades had gone by. His wife had changed
seemingly overnight from a fresh-cheeked housewife to a
crone; his children were grown with children of their own.
Conn looked up, frowning at Sira, silently demanding an
explanation.

"Do you hear music?" Sira asked, her head cocked to
the side.

As the blood tide faded from his ears, Conn did catch
the sound of pipe and drum. Then a door burst open and
the music spilled into the courtyard as dancing, laughing
people burst out of doors. The men-at-arms wore armor
decorated with knots of ribbon, with flowers twisted about
their pike staves. The women of the household, dressed in

their ragtag finery, followed out, skipping and laughing
while the children raced underfoot.

Out came Lord Robert, splendid in a velvet surcoat, his
best hat on his head. Behind him, fat Sir Walter de Burke
followed, a yard wide in a scarlet-sleeved robe, his face
agleam with sweat and smiles.

The men-at-arms formed a rough avenue, lining up either side of the threshold, though it was plain from their
weaving and their lopsided grins that much ale had flowed
down their gullets this day. Next to emerge from the great
hall came a young couple, bridal in attire and in the shy
smiles they gave to one another. The bride's dark hair
flowed like a silken river over her gold-embroidered dress.
The groom, as he escorted her down between the guard of
honor, seemed to have no eyes for anything save her love-
liness. Then some other sense made him look up.

"Conn!"

Leaving his bride, Ross hurried at a near run toward his
brother. Conn, too, started forward, feeling his joy leap up
at the thought that Ross was not an old man, that no one
he had left behind had changed. That thought was all that
was in his head; he would have taken his oath upon it.

Some, it seemed, thought otherwise. For even as Conn
reached out to embrace Ross, he found Father Maynard
standing between them, saying urgently, " 'Fore God, let
there be no blood shed this day!"

Thirteen

~

Conn stared in stunned amazement at the priest. "Blood-shed?"

"You were believed dead, my son. Your betrothal was broken. You cannot blame your brother, that he wished to—er—console the Lady Helen."

"Was marriage the only consolation she would accept?"

Father Maynard opened his mouth as though to contest hotly, only to have the words dry on his tongue. Ross, too, halted the confused words with which he tried to form explanations and stared in wonder at his brother. Looking from one to the other, Conn let the smile within him break forth.

"It's true," he said. "I can see. As well as ever I could."

The priest found words first. "Give praise, for God is mighty! I shall write at once to the Holy Father to proclaim a miracle. Ah, to which saint did you pray, my son?"

"Save your ink, Father. If it was a miracle . . . perhaps it was, but not *directly* of heavenly making."

"Ross! Stand away!" Lord Robert recovered from the paralysis that seemed to have gripped all but Ross and Father Maynard and started forward. He pushed through the assembly as though desperate to save Ross from a devil in disguise.

Slowly, as those present recognized who it was that had arrived, the marriage merriment had drained away, leaving them standing in tense and unnatural postures. The men-at-arms were plainly unsure of how to act. Some stared, some were evidently embarrassed by the unwarlike additions to their weapons and began stripping off the ribbons and flowers. Others, with lovers or wives among the women, sought to stand before them, to protect them in case a fight broke out. These men knew Conn best and knew to the full his dangerous abilities.

Lord Robert knew also and stopped some few steps off. "Ross! Come here at once."

Ross turned his head and said joyfully, "Look, Father. It's Conn come home again. And he can see!"

"Do as you are told, boy. That's not Conn!"

Ross's happiness faded into confusion. "Not . . . ? What's wrong, Father? Has Conn regained his sight only to have you lose yours?" He gave a chuckle, but it died in the face of his father's anger and unmistakable fear.

Conn looked at Father Maynard, silently demanding an answer to his questioning thoughts. The priest said, "It seems your father believes you a witch taking on Conn's likeness."

He held up his hand to hold Conn in silence. "You did vanish most mysteriously, my son. Even your faithful servant did not hear you go. He vows that he is such a heavy sleeper that you could have walked on his back and he not feel it."

Conn asked, "Where is Gandy? I don't see him."

Ross answered that. "He was sent off this morning with your horse. Father determined to sell it, for it ate more than any four others." He nodded toward the entryway. "I see you have fallen in with the animal again."

"This is not all you see," Conn said proudly. "Unless your eyesight had begun to fail as well."

Ross's eyes flickered in unmistakable recognition. "The crone?" he whispered with a grin.

"None other."

"Ross!" Lord Robert called again. "Do not speak with him. I forbid it!!"

Then Helen added her mite to the increasing murmur from those assembled. "Ross! Ross, I'm afraid. Please come here."

"Your bride," Conn said. "I congratulate you with a full heart."

"We thought you were dead."

"So, as Father Maynard has said, you console the bride?"

A flush of color rose into Ross's cheeks. "She is very lovely, and our fathers were of one voice in urging an immediate marriage."

"None too soon, I fancy." Conn winked at his brother. "For I have found that a lady of determined nature will use fair means or foul to gain the man she sets her heart upon. Now you will not have to meet in doorways and churches."

"You knew?"

"Even a blind man might have seen that much," Conn said, matching Ross's grin.

Then the brothers embraced. The servants, high and low, gasped, expecting perhaps to see the younger lord carried off into the dark regions by the fiend masquerading as Conn. They were all well aware of Lord Robert's thinking, as were Helen and her father. Helen's moan was sharp enough to cut through the sound of the others' surprise. Not a few crossed themselves, chief among these, Lord Robert.

Conn turned toward his father. "It is truly me, my lord. Returned as you see me."

"If that is true," Lord Robert said, his eyes narrow as arrow slits, "then tell me where have you been these last twelve days?"

"Twelve days?" Conn glanced toward Sira. He had spent part of the day casting in his memory, and he could recall at least a month's worth of days, though they blended now in his memory like a tapestry, each glittering thread a part of the whole.

Conn said, "It seemed more than that."

"Answer me," his father said. "I demand that you tell me."

Raising his hand, Conn silently asked Arundel to come forward. The huge hooves could move almost soundlessly. Father Maynard and Ross stepped back as Conn lifted up his arms. Sira swung down from the horse. Conn supported her as her cramped knees bent.

"I have been with my lady," Conn said, steadying her with his hand at her slender waist. Sira nodded regally, acknowledging the stares and whispers that greeted her. Conn felt a stirring of pride almost as great as his love. Though dressed like a wandering player in a now-ragged robe of silk and the magnificent cloak of fox, though bringing nothing to her new family but a rough bag (for they were not to know it contained no less than a king's ransom), she had lost no trace of her charm or dignity.

Conn laid her fingers on top of his extended hand and led her forward. "This is the Lady Sira. My lady, welcome to the manor of Hamdry, my home and now yours."

He gestured to Lord Robert who stood silently glowering twenty feet or more away. It was his part, as lord of the manor, to welcome her, yet he said nothing. Conn knew another surge of pride in his bride-to-be when she dipped his lordship a curtsy and said, "I am honored, my lord," just as though Robert had spoken a proper welcome.

Lord Robert's brows knitted in consternation. The unexpected appearance of a woman at the side of his lost son threw him into complete confusion. Conn could not recall ever seeing his father at quite such a loss before. He'd always seemed to know what to do, even when he was utterly wrong. He never backed away from his position once taken. He'd been absolutely certain that it was right to disinherit his son because of his blindness. Would he, rather than admit that he had to change his mind, persist in this folly about witches?

One thing Conn determined at once: His father's lunacy would not touch Sira. If it came to his choosing between

Sira and Lord Robert, his lordship would suffer his first defeat.

Conn took Sira's hand and laid it in Father Maynard's. "Father, I ask you to marry me to this lady with all the speed you can muster."

"No!" Lord Robert shouted. In his tone was a warning. "Conn . . ."

Father Maynard looked deep into Sira's eyes. She returned his look steadily, having heard much this day of the priest's love and care for Conn. She used no arts beyond her smile.

As the priest took her hand, Sira realized that his were the first human eyes she'd ever looked into, save for Conn's. Though somewhat lost in deep pouches, the brown orbs were steady and clear-seeing. When she'd seen him for the first time, he'd been hurrying on his way, and she had been disguised, thanks to Anat, as a hideously bent and gnarled creature. He had hardly glanced at her then. Now he studied her, as if to determine her worth.

Her smile was brighter for remembering his previous haste. He could not help but respond to her warmth. "Are you of a mind to marry with this good-for-nothing fellow? So fair as you are might bestow her hand with honor upon a prince of the blood Royal."

"I will marry Conn of Hamdry and no other," Sira declared, her voice ringing out over the assemblage. She turned her gaze toward Lord Robert and saw his face darken as the hot blood rushed to his cheeks. She gave him an absent, gentle smile, just as though she had not this moment defied him.

Father Maynard, absently retaining the refined fingers in his grasp, whispered, "Don't be frightened by his lordship's black looks—"

"Frightened? I?" She lifted her shoulders carelessly, and the fox cloak slipped. Quick as winking, Conn caught it before it could so much as brush the ground. His fingers caressed her shoulders even as he wrapped her up. Sira's courage, which despite her brave words, had dimmed in the face of Lord Robert's obvious wrath, grew stronger.

She said gaily, "How soon can we be wed?"

"At once! Today!" Conn grinned over his bride's head at the priest. "Please?"

In a lower tone, Father Maynard said, "For all of me, my son and daughter, you could be wed this moment, here under the eyes of heaven. But you must consider your father unless you mean to *live* under the eyes of heaven."

"He won't disown me. He's already tried that trick. As for me not being who I am . . ." Sira saw Conn shake his head, to all appearances entirely unconcerned. "He'll soon give that up and all shall be as it was before I went away to war."

Sira tightened her grasp on his hand. "We must try, or there'll be no peace here."

She let her eyes plead with him. She knew he was proud; he'd held on to that even in the Living Lands. Furthermore, she had guessed how deeply Lord Robert had hurt Conn when he'd tried to make him give up his rights to this land. Nothing would shake Conn loose from what he saw as his duty. When duty mingled with love, it made a bond impossible to break. But she could not tell if the bond held him more strongly to this land or to his father.

Then she saw his eyes light up as he called out, "Gandy?"

Sira saw a small man, young in his face, but carrying himself with a bent back as if heavily burdened, walking along the courtyard wall. He paid no attention to the festive trappings around him. He scuffled his feet as he walked, his eyes on the ground. Even when Conn called his name, he didn't look up.

Then Conn drew a deeper breath and shouted loud enough to wake the echoes and startle even Arundel, "Gandy, thou lazy brute! Where's my sword? My armor? By this day, if you've let them get rusty . . ."

Long before this diatribe was over, the servant was on his knees before his master, tears carving tracks in the dust of his cheeks. "Master . . ." he cried, not troubling to wipe the drops away, for he would then have to stop gazing at Conn. "You *are* alive."

Here was the welcome that Sira had looked for, more for Conn's sake than her own. Who could be glad to see her, a stranger brought from who knew where to be Conn's lady? But someone, she thought, should have been eager to welcome him back to his own home.

Yet his brother had been prevented from embracing him until the impulsive moment had gone by. The priest, whom Conn loved, had greeted him only with a panicked desire to avoid a killing. Lord Robert still stood a few paces off, stony-faced, his arms crossed and an ironical jut to his lower jaw as he took in the servant's rapture.

Gandy clung to Conn's hand, though his master had raised him to his feet. "Alive and well? All well?"

"Better than that. Now I can see what you have been up to since I was gone away."

Something of a guilty look appeared in the dusty fellow's reddened eyes, to be banished in a moment by wonderment. "Is it a miracle that you can see?"

The priest said, "He tells me that it was not. Yet I wonder how—"

"Some special ointments I had of my mother," Sira answered. She met Conn's laughing look with a serious mien. He did not take her warning but laughed aloud.

"One look at her face completed the cure," he announced. "Have you ever taken fairer medicine, Father Maynard?"

"Nay. Most is as nasty to the eye as to the taste."

"Not to mention the nose," Ross returned to the conversation, turning a sullen shoulder to Helen, who had advanced as far as Lord Robert, but no farther. He bowed now to Sira. "A hearty welcome to my new sister. If my brother ever mistreats you, turn, I beg, to me."

"And you'll do exactly what?" Conn asked, draping his heavy arm about the slighter man's neck.

Ross staggered playfully under the weight. "Why, challenge you, blow for blow. Or, failing that—"

"Fail you would!"

"Failing that, I say, I could pour into her ear a tale of

all your misdeeds from boyhood so that she'd never grant you an hour's peace thereafter.''

''Oh, now you do threaten me! I shall treat my wife with more tenderness and respect in consequence.''

Sira knew as though she had been told that this playfulness was compounded in part of relief at Conn's safe return and part in defiance of their father, standing by so cold and silent.

Helen stood beside Lord Robert, her face stamped with so similar an expression that they looked more like father and daughter than he and Conn looked like father and son. Sira prickled with embarrassment and pride at the scorn of their glances. She remembered that she had more right to pride than they. Not only was she of royal blood, though not mortal blood, but she had won for her own a man of noble worth.

Sira said, ''I wonder if I might rest myself before the ceremony. It has been a long day indeed, though the sun stands at but noon.''

Gandy, with an eager look, said, ''May I offer my lady a maid servant? You recall my little friend, master? She'll make an excellent tire woman to my lady.''

''Would it please you?'' Conn asked her.

Sira smiled up at him. '' 'Tis little enough she'll have to wash for me. I have nothing but what I stand in.''

Helen's voice was as lovely as her face, though at this moment every bit as cold. Only Sira's quick eyes had seen the purposeful shove Walter de Burke had given her from behind. ''I have gowns enough and to spare.'' Once again, a heavy hand prompted her to speak more graciously. ''If my lady would deign to use them?''

Sira bowed her head. ''You are too kind.''

''Sweet Helen!'' Ross said, smiling at her with pride and love.

Sweet Helen tossed up her chin petulantly, yet in her gaze Sira saw something of the hurt she felt at her husband of hardly an hour's neglect. ''Follow me,'' she said to Sira and began to walk toward the manor's main door.

Sira started to follow when her hand was captured by

Conn. "Go if you must," he said in a voice for her ears alone. "But not like that. Not without one word or a kiss."

"Kiss you? Before so many?"

"You'll kiss me before them all in an hour, more or less, so what does it matter?" He drew one fingertip under the line of her jaw and every atom of her body thrilled to it. Conn bent and kissed her, tenderly enough but showing just a hint of the strength he possessed. Knowing she could tame him whenever she wished, she enjoyed showing him how submissive she could be. Yet, before he raised his head, before he could feel too much in control, she nipped secretly at his lower lip. He was still rubbing it, a smile peeking through, as she walked away.

Inside the stone walls, it was dark after the dazzling sunshine of the courtyard. Smells assailed Sira's nose—woodsmoke, greasy odors of a thousand meals, onions, hot tallow from a few smoky candles—that the crushed rushes underfoot did little to quell. Nor had the flowers that had lately been carried here prevailed over so many different aromas. Sira felt almost faint but told herself that was a consequence of a long journey with little refreshment. Let her eat and she would be well.

Through an archway, she saw a long table littered with the remains of a lavish meal. A few dogs chewed bones beneath the table. One with tall, pointed ears looked up as she passed and thumped his tail in friendly fashion before returning to his chomping.

She sought for something she could eat. The bones told her that the barbaric tales she'd heard of meat-eating men were in all probability quite true. Surprisingly, she felt little or no revulsion, though she did not think she could bring herself to pick over what they had left. But if she could find a piece of fruit or a heel of bread . . .

"Here now . . ." A softly burring voice made Sira turn. She saw a plump young woman, dressed in a simple brown gown with a clean but much-stained apron over it, standing in the doorway. Her brown hair curled and frizzled beneath her simple kerchief. "Where's the rest of your company then?"

"My company?"

"Aren't you one o' them acrobats Lord Robert hired? Pleased as ol' jackdaw he be at them kind of goings on. Not me. Church be play enough for Margery Fletcher. Have you a stomach?"

Sira couldn't restrain a smile. "I believe I have, now that you mention it."

"Come with me, then, and I'll be pleased to find you better than they broken meats. Not fit for the piggies after them soldiers been at it, and with this marrying today, they be worst than ever. Fair sick with drink, the lot of 'em."

Commenting and grumbling, the young woman lead Sira away toward the kitchen. Though she knew Helen must be waiting in some upper chamber, Sira felt in no hurry to enjoy a private conversation with Conn's formerly betrothed wife. Whatever bitter words Helen wished to hurl at her could keep. Besides, there was something familiar about this Margery that tugged at Sira's memory. She wondered what it could be, for she'd seen few mortal women.

The vast kitchen was empty. Margery gave vent to an angry sigh. "Those dogs," she said. "Cooks, maids, scullions, spit-boys all. The instant they can, they flit away, leaving all to be done."

She pointed to a low stool and stood with arms akimbo until Sira seated herself. Then the maid began to bustle about, cutting a slice of bread, scooping out a savory-smelling broth from a great cauldron steaming over the banked fire. She poured the broth into a wooden bowl after setting the bread in the bottom.

Putting it down in front of Sira with a spoon beside her, she stood back. "There. And no thanks to that great booby that it's not scorched black as the devil's eyebrows."

"You do not care for your fellow servants?" Sira blew on the broth to cool it. She saw a bit of stewed green leaves and a chunk or two of what might have been turnip floating in the depths.

"They be well enow, if you hearken to rogues and simp-
kins. They rob his lordship blind and steal all the best
meats for themselves."

"Have you told his lordship this?"

"Me? And me taken up for a thief myself? Nay. I be
not that kind of fool. Though . . ." She tightened her rose-
colored lips as though damming up the words that wanted
to burst forth.

Though the soup had none of the rich, rare flavor that
Sira was used to, it was hot enough to chase the last of
the spring rawness from her body. The bread tasted faintly
nutty and was remarkably filling. She thanked Margery for
her generosity.

The servant girl had been studying Sira even as she fluttered about the kitchen, cleaning a table here and wiping
a dish there. While apparently in the depths of her work,
she asked, "Do you like your roaming life? Seeing new
faces and places?"

"I have traveled farther today than ever before in my
life," Sira said.

"Ah, you're newly taken on?" She pushed back the
curls that had snuck from under her kerchief to brush her
eyes. In a softer voice, she asked, "Didst thou run away
from home, then?"

"In a manner of speaking," Sira said. She had still
failed to remember where she'd seen this girl before.

Margery sighed wistfully. "Thy master wouldn't have
a place for a girl like me? I can cook and sew as fine a
seam as any lady born. Though I know not what manner
a player I should prove—"

"Why do you wish to leave Hamdry?" Sira asked.
Conn thought that this manor was paradise on earth, as she
had heard in his words and seen in his mind the one time
she had been allowed to look in. This being so, she wondered at Margery's unhappiness. "Is it because the others
are unkind to you?"

"No. I don't mind them fools. 'Tis my own foolishness
that I can't bear with."

She looked up, a light in her eyes, when a ringing voice

called Margery's name insistently. Sira saw the girl yearn
to answer, yet almost at once she hardened her eyes and
mouth. By the time the slight young man appeared in the
kitchen, she had banished every hint of soft emotion.

"There you are," Gandy said. "I've been searching
high and . . . never mind that cookery, my lass!"

"Now, then, Master Gandy, away with you! Margery
hast no time to give thee now."

"Margery, don't be that way." Conn's manservant
hadn't noticed Sira yet, being entirely taken up with getting Margery to look at him. Though he caught at her
hands and waist, she kept herself stiff in body and turned
half-away, her face averted from the kiss he tried to place
on her cheek.

Was he the foolishness that Margery had mentioned?
Even as Sira peeped at them, she recalled where she'd seen
them before. This was the man and the maid she'd seen at
dalliance in Conn's garden the day she'd met him at the
church. She stared down into her soup, a trifle embarrassed
to think now of how much of their lovemaking she'd
seen—more than a kiss or two!

Gandy stopped trying to kiss Margery. Still holding her
hands, he said, "Such great news! My master has returned!"

"Eh?" Margery held still, though not relaxing her
stance.

"Yes, he's home. And no more blind than you or I!"

"What's this? Have you been sucking down the mead
so early in the day?"

"Oh, I'm not drunk. Not yet." He tried to swing her
around in a dance, but she was having none of him.
"That's not all," he said. "He's brought back a bride from
wherever he has been. And such a bride! Skin like a snow-
drop, hair like . . . like fairy gold . . . oh, she made our dark
Helen look no-how. A black witch, she is, but cast into
shade by Lord Conn's bride!"

"A beauty?"

Sira ducked her head down farther toward the soup.

"Aye, a rare beauty but in need of a neat-handed maid

for, poor lady, she has no goods with her, nor any atten-
dant, neither. So, methought, who shall serve her but my
own sweet Margery.''

"What color did you say her hair?"

"What does that matter?" Gandy frowned now, for obviously this news had not delighted his own sweet Margery
as much as he had imagined. "Did you not hear? You are
to be my lady's tire woman. No more smoky kitchen, no
more greasy platters to wash, no more black-faced scullions underfoot. You shall serve in the noblest chambers,
and we shall see each other every day."

He turned his hard-thinking lover about and began to
pick at the knot of her apron strings. "What times we shall
have! Never in all my days have I seen my master so in
love. He stood and watched her walk away when she came
into the house with such a look in his eyes as I have never
seen. He hardly seemed to hear what Father Maynard said
to him and even when Lord Robert began to rail at him,
my lord scarce blinked."

"Lord Robert is wroth with your master?" Margery
asked. She suddenly seemed to realize what Gandy was
doing and, wheeling about, slapped at his hands. "You'll
tangle it in a worse knot yet! Why are you here, if your
master is new come? Get to him, where thou art wanted."

"But Margery, I thought you would be pleased."

Sira saw the girl soften toward him the instant his crest
fell. "So I am," she said, kissing him on the cheek.
"There, and there, my dear lad."

But when his hands crept toward her waist, she stepped
abruptly out of range. "That's all you'll have of me, Master Gandy, as I told you. Now, away with you. I'll present
myself to my lady just as I am. If I suit her, then I'll serve
her."

"It's all arranged," Gandy said, still trying to please his
prickly darling. "My master has already bidden my lady
take you. He did it to please her, and she agreed to please
him. Oh, his love is not unrequited, that I will vow before
Heaven."

" 'Tis well. I should not wish for any man or maid to love without being loved. 'Tis too lonely.''

"That you never need fear," Gandy said, drawing her head to his shoulder. Margery's arm slipped about his waist. She closed her eyes and rested against him but only for the space of a half-dozen heartbeats. Then she pushed away.

"Have done, now, do! Be away to your master and leave me to my lady."

With wounded eyes, Gandy went away. Sira, sitting up, said, "You are hard on your young man, Margery."

The maid servant hunched her shoulders and sniffed scornfully. "I don't doubt but that he'll live. There's a-many and a-many maids even here would do him ease if Margery don't. Gandy takes his pleasure where he likes."

Then the sky-bright eyes fixed on Sira, and Margery added, giving each word weight, "Your man is none so light, my lady."

"I had not taken time to wonder if Conn will be faithful or not. I think he will."

"If he takes a vow, he keeps it," Margery said, adding, "My father served this house before I ever was born. He says the same. Master Conn keeps his word and does his duty, stand or fall, whether to king or to the last boy in the stables. There's few indeed in this wicked world as could have so much said."

Having taken off her apron, Margery wiped her sturdy, work-reddened hands on it. "If you've supped, my lady, I'll be guiding you to your chamber."

"The Lady Helen is waiting for me. She offered me the use of some of her gowns until . . ." Sira paused, suddenly wondering where a woman acquired gowns in Conn's world. At home, she would simply imagine . . . but no. She had to stop thinking of the Living Lands as her home. Hamdry alone could carry that name now.

"Lady Helen offered you something of her own?" Margery sniffed. "If she has, it's the first time. A little hand but tightfisted, that one!"

Sira found herself liking Margery very much. "I didn't say it was entirely her own idea."

"I'm glad you told me. Now I can sleep at night without wondering if the sun'll rise on the other side."

Sira rose and followed the maidservant from the room. After a very few steps, she realized that without a guide, she would have soon been irretrievably lost. The manor was not so large, yet between the near-darkness of the interior and the twists and turns, staircases that seemed to go only upward without so much as a landing to turn on, and the innumerable chambers opening out of each other, her head spun and she could not tell her direction.

"Ross has moved into a larger chamber, now he's taken a wife. Second only to Lord Robert's it is, with a warm southern breeze to stir the humors. Now that Lord Conn is come, the younglings will have to find a new nest."

"I don't want to throw them out. . . ."

"Take a word of warning. B'ain't right for the younger to have it better than the old. And a soft answer won't do you good with *her*. Spoilt she is from being her father's darling."

Margery led the way out of the kitchen. "And if it's rags and tatters you're offered, don't say 'twasn't me as warned you."

Fourteen

～

"This woman . . . this woman from nowhere. You disappear from your chamber only to appear with this woman and announce that you mean to wed her." Lord Robert frowned, more as though he were trying to understand than in anger.

"And I shall."

Though Conn could wish that his father had been willing to accept Sira merely because he loved her, he knew in his heart that this was too much to hope for. Lord Robert was consumed by the desire to benefit his dynasty, as personified by Ross and himself, even if it meant the sacrifice of the very sons whose blood he was trying to save. Ross had fulfilled that expectation handsomely. It was only his good fortune that his marriage had also fulfilled his own pleasure.

Conn had been standing by the door to his father's solar in an attitude of profound filial respect. Now he crossed the room to lean his shoulders against the smooth nap of a dark red tapestry. He was tired, and no one in his home had thought to offer him so much as a cup of wine. He hoped Sira had found refreshment. How he had hated having to watch her enter Hamdry Manor without him at her side.

"Do you pay heed, Conn?"

His father's voice broke into his musings like a brick

hurled into a mill pond. "I beg your pardon, Father. I'm tired. We had a long journey and a . . . restless night."

"The woman's bewitched him! There's no argument to that, Maynard!"

"Now, my lord, be at ease." Father Maynard pushed up the sleeves of his cassock, a gesture left over from his days when wrestling had been his chief sport. Years of the priesthood had not broken him of it. Conn smiled to see it still, for it had always meant Maynard was about to wrestle in spirit.

"Conn," the priest said. "I beg you to be reasonable. Your father's request is sensible. Pray deliver a sensible answer."

"I'll do my best, but you ask a great deal of a man in love. I don't feel sensible at all."

"There!" Lord Robert said. "You see! He admits it."

Maynard threw the friend of his boyhood a quelling glance. "Sit down, my lord. Or summon your butler for wine. Yes. Wine will cool our hot heads and make us all see reason."

Frowning, Lord Robert stomped over to the door, jerked it open, and bellowed down the stairs, "Wine! Wine, you dogs." A faint echo of a question came back to him and he shouted even more loudly, "I don't care! Bring the whole tun!"

Then he hurled himself into the only chair in the room, which creaked and groaned as he thrashed into a comfortable position. "Go on then," he said with irritated impatience. "Go on, and tell the priest how this woman enchanted you."

Conn straightened up and bowed, mimicking something of Blaic's irony as he did so. "You took the very word from my mouth, Father. I am enchanted. You have eyes; you must have seen the wherefore of it. Who could look upon *her* and not be enchanted?"

"True, she seemed most lovely," Father Maynard said. "But there is more to a woman than her face."

Conn's father said, "I saw her. Don't tell me she's some cottager's daughter or even the daughter of a knight, like poor wronged Helen. She's not from Devon, of that I am certain."

Conn suddenly surmised that if his blood had faerie mixed in with it, then his father's must as well. Did something in Lord Robert answer to the mystery that Sira trailed behind her like the elusive scent of her perfume?

"She's not from Devon exactly, and yet I believe her family to have deep roots in this country."

Father Maynard said, "Where's that wine? My head's going around like a top. Speak plain, Conn. Before I undertake to make her your bride, I must know more. What of her father? Have you his permission to marry her?"

"I don't require that, surely."

"Then I am to assume you have it not?"

"Her father . . . her father has entrusted his daughter to me, with certain scruples. I do not deny that I have in some measure eloped with her."

"A stolen bride?" Lord Robert sat up straight. "She is not without property?"

"Only what we could carry," Conn said.

"No lands?" Lord Robert sat back, his fingers entwined across his stomach. "No gold?"

"I cannot hope that my answers have pleased you, my lord. Believe me, there is much that perplexes me as well. But this I know above all: I love her, and I shall marry her this day, if the good father will act. If he refuses, I shall carry her to London and marry her there, or wherever true men of King Stephen's cause forgather."

"I will act," Father Maynard said. "I confess that I have long wished to see you shackled, rogue that you are!"

"I give you thanks," Conn said with a grin that banished the formality from his words. He looked toward his father. "My lord, I know it grieves you to have your plans for me overset. If you are concerned for de Burke's wounded pride, I will sue for his pardon. Yet I cannot but think that he is well satisfied with Ross as husband to Helen."

"You don't understand. . . ." Lord Robert muttered.

"I do, indeed. I am your son, and I do understand. You wished for the enlargement of our lands. De Burke has no other child, and with his lands falling under our name, Hamdry would grow ever more prosperous."

"Now it is all undone. De Burke will leave his lands to Ross as Helen's husband and what then of Hamdry?"

"It will be safe, my lord, under your charge. One day it will be safe under mine."

At that moment, as Lord Robert's sullen gaze rose to meet Conn's, the butler entered, carrying pitchers in either hand. A boy followed him, carrying the goblets and savories on a salver. Amid their bustlings, Lord Robert tightened his lips on his answer.

Father Maynard rid them of the servants by waving blessings at them in such a way as to shoo them from the room. Then he himself poured out three overflowing measures of good red wine. "Come. Drink. Drink, I say. I myself shall propose . . . to the health of Conn's lady!"

Conn caught up the goblet on the word and drained it off. Father Maynard cried aloud in his disbelief and pride, "Well done! Hah, he learned that in the field, eh, Robert? Drink heartily for the day comest when we shall go dry."

The priest joggled the lord's elbow and said, "Drink, you fool, for in tournament between bride and father, the bride will win. 'For a man shall leave his mother,' er . . . and so on."

"To the health of Conn's lady," Lord Robert said slowly and touched his lips to the wine. Maynard rolled his eyes to heaven while downing a hearty bumper. Smacking his lips, he said, "Ah, a proper vintage, that! Come, Conn. Fill your cup again."

As Conn leaned down to offer his goblet, the priest muttered, "We'll drink him into a warmer mood, if we empty the cellars for it!"

"Not so much as that. I need a clear head," Conn said lightly. Though talking to Father Maynard with every sign of interest, he remained aware of his father, who cradled his goblet to his chest and stared into its depths as though hoping to scry the future. Whatever he saw there did not

seem to cheer him. Yet, after taking a drink, he broke into
Father Maynard's description of the last Communion when
a goat had wandered into the church by accident.

Lord Robert said gruffly, "Some call it accident; I say
it's all of a piece with the evil work that has been plaguing
these lands. What other explanation can there be?"

" 'Twas my own goat," Father Maynard protested.
"You don't fancy that *I'm* in league with the Dark One?"

"Nay, nor any other whom I know well. But these are
unsettled times, and there is much talk of strange portents.
That snow we had yesternight, for one."

"Come now ... there have been such storms before
now. Mind when we were boys and how a freak storm
kept us from being punished for stealing your father's
hunting mare? Why, if it had not been for that late snow,
we should have been cleaning the stables unto this day!"

"How did that keep you from punishment?" Conn
asked.

"The heavy snow caused the roof of the stables to fall
in. No one was injured, thanks be to God, but there was
no point in mucking it out after that!"

A half-smile had crept onto Lord Robert's stern face
during these nostalgic moments. "Aye," he agreed. "A
fortunate snowfall for us. But we were not cured of trying
to ride the mare. How my father beamed when I succeeded, though he beat me for it! 'Twas after that he gave
me my own first blood horse."

Winking at Conn, the priest said, " 'Tis ever so with
those of your blood; courage brings its rewards. I seem to
recall Conn and Ross cleaning a stable themselves."

"I remember that!" Conn said with a heartfelt grimace.
"Only Ross wasn't there. He'd broken his arm a month
earlier by falling out of one of de Burke's apple trees,
where he had no lawful business. Neither did I, as it happened, but I at least did not break bones when I fell."

Lord Robert stared with narrowed eyes at his eldest son
but not in censure. "You brought him home on your back
and that black-haired girl sore berating you every time

Ross moaned. Was it then, do you think, that she chose him over you?''

"It may well be, my lord. Helen was ever one to know her own mind.''

"Yet it seemed to me that she was not happy to see a bride beside you, even if today she married Ross.''

"Was it my bride she did not wish to see or myself? The lady Helen, meaning no disrespect, would have preferred to marry the heir of Hamdry, whether it be myself or my brother. When I was blind, she turned to Ross, whether out of disgust at my condition or long affection for him, I cannot say. It may well be that she herself could not tell you.''

Father Maynard snorted. "Women have little gift for self-discovery. That is only one reason why we men must do their thinking for them.''

"Do not say so to Sira, I beg you. She knows her own mind to its depths.''

"You imagine yourself to be 'in love' with this woman?'' Lord Robert asked, putting a world of disdain into the words.

"Yes.'' The single word, he saw, carried more conviction to their minds than any passionate protestation.

The priest and the lord exchanged a glance. Clearly, Father Maynard prompted Lord Robert to be benevolent.

"You truly wish to be married to her, though she is unknown to your family and your people, a stranger who seems to have neither rank nor family?''

"Yes. In time, they will come to know her and love her as I do.''

"Even though she is without property—even without *shoes*?''

Now Conn laughed as he forced out another *yes*. Trust his father to notice!

Lord Robert caught the end of his mustache in his mouth and nibbled at it. "Very well,'' he said at length. "Marry the woman with my blessing, and may you have strong sons to follow me.''

Conn dropped to his knee and pressed his lips to his

father's outstretched hand. "That I can promise you, my lord. The getting of sons will be my first task as a married man."

Helen had bundled up the luxuriant length of her dark hair and put aside the radiance of her bridal gown. Though still very lovely in her simpler cotehardie of plain blue cloth, her eyes were hard as she looked on Sira. "If you would deign to look over my poor wardrobe, my lady, I hope you may discover something you can suffer until your own gowns arrive."

"I have no gowns to arrive," Sira said quietly. She heard Margery click her tongue disapprovingly, whether at the fact she stated or over excessive honesty in the face of her enemy, Sira couldn't say. "I have nothing but what I stand in. I should be most grateful if I could borrow a gown or two from you, Lady Helen, until some can be made for me."

Helen stared disbelievingly. "Yet he married *you*."

"Does Conn take much notice of what a lady wears?"

Margery jumped in quickly, before Helen could choose among the cutting remarks on her tongue. "T'others and I'll start on some clothing for you at once. There's some old 'uns of her late ladyship's that we'll make over in a twinkling."

"You are very good, Margery," Sira said. "I'll leave the choice to you. I am, I'm afraid, very ignorant about hu—what is being worn."

"Half the fine ladies at court turn old into new, going by what Gandy has told me."

"Cease nattering, wench," Helen said abruptly. "If you would make your mistress a gown, then be about it!"

Startled, Margery dipped an instinctive curtsy. As she headed for the door, she threw Sira a look compounded of warning and encouragement. Sira only said, "Thank you, Margery. I know I can trust your taste."

As soon as the maidservant had gone out, without even waiting to be sure she was out of earshot, Helen said, "You allow her too much liberty! That kind of treatment spoils a servant faster than cruelty, or so my mother used to say.''

"Conn, on the other hand, tells me that as I am to be lady of this manor one day, I would be wise to find what friends I can here. After all, I have much to learn.''

"Men don't know very much about that sort of thing,'' Helen said, putting her charming nose in the air. "They think servants like them, when all they do is kiss their feet. You can't have friendship without equality, and there can never be equality between peasants and gentry.''

Helen crossed the room to throw open a chest of clothing that had been placed beneath the only window in the room. The only other furniture was a large bed curtained with plain linen decorated with a stiff Tree of Life. Helen glanced over her shoulder at Sira. "Where *did* you say you were from?''

"Oh, I am no peasant, my lady. We can be friends without crossing any barriers.'' She, too, came to look into the chest. "What lovely things,'' she said politely, reaching for a high-waisted overdress of pale green wool.

"I'm sure it will become you far more than it ever did me.'' Helen ran her finger over the leaf design embroidered around the low neck. "I don't know what possessed me to have it made up. I look ill in anything green or brown.''

"Those are among my favorite shades,'' Sira said. "How lucky that neither of us need ever be jealous of what the other wears.''

Helen nodded her head regally. Sira wondered if her not-so-subtle meaning had been understood.

The young bride reached again into the highly carved wooden chest, pulling out a darker green undergarment with tight-fitting sleeves. "You wear this under that gown. We are quite similar in size, I think.''

"Oh, do you think so? I should say you are far slimmer.''

For the first time, Sira saw Helen's frozen face thaw into a smile. Helen said, "I try to keep slender, but it's very difficult. My father loves to set a good table, and he frets if I do not eat and eat. He is himself somewhat portly. He thinks it wise to be fat in lean times."

"I believe I noticed him, but there was such a crowd. I have not yet congratulated you on your marriage, Lady Helen. I hope that it will be long, happy, and fruitful."

"The same to you, Sira." Though Sira noticed that Helen left off the honorific, she pretended not to. If they were to become friends, such minor annoyances must go unmentioned.

After putting on the green gown, Sira incautiously asked, "Where is a mirror?"

"A mirror?"

"Yes, a looking glass? I should like to see how this gown becomes me."

Margery, who had returned to help her mistress dress, exchanged a glance with Lady Helen. She turned her raised eyebrows on Sira. "My lady, there's not a mirror in the world large enough to show all of you."

"The Empress Matilda herself hasn't such a glass," Helen added. "My father brought me back a small mirror from London, but it's no bigger than your hand."

" 'Tis packed safe away, I trust?" Margery asked.

"Yes, with my jewels."

"Jewels are fine things."

"You have some, I suppose," Helen said, her upper lip curling in a sneer.

Sira stared. "That quite spoils your beauty," she said. "How do you do it?"

Margery turned a laugh into a cough. "Shall I fetch some wine for your ladyships? Sorting clothing is thirsty work."

Helen nodded abruptly while Sira said, "Thank you. I should like it above all things."

When Margery opened the door, she caught her breath in surprise. Conn stood there, his fist raised to knock. "Is my bride fit to be seen?"

"Judge for yourself, my lord," she said and stood out of the way.

Sira jumped up to meet him, feeling as though they'd

been apart for days rather than minutes. "Well, sir, am I fit?"

Conn didn't answer. He held her out at arm's length and said, "There's something different about you."

"I brushed my hair. . . ."

"That gown is becoming to you, my lady. I believed you beautiful before, but after every parting, you dazzle me afresh."

Helen sniffed. "She said you wouldn't notice."

Conn chuckled. "I notice everything . . . about her. Thank you for the loan of the gown, Helen."

"She may keep it if she wishes. It became me not."

"Lady Helen has been kindness itself," Sira said, eager to soothe this first private meeting between the formerly betrothed man and girl.

"I don't doubt that Ross thinks so. He's been roaring this past hour for his lady wife to come to him. 'Tis a shabby way to treat a bridegroom. You should be kneeling in adoration at his feet. Or so Ross would have us believe."

"Is that your model for how *I* should behave, sir?" Sira asked with deceptively innocent eyes.

"No. As well you know. I long only to worship you." He drew her forward, a clear intention to kiss her gleaming in his dark eyes.

Fighting her own inclination, Sira held him off. She angled a laughing glance at Helen. "Oh, he's willing to worship me now, I grant you. But in an hour's time when we are wed? Do you think he'll turn tyrant?"

"I doubt not that you'll be well able to bring him to heel." Helen, however, heeding her own husband's summons, moved busily about the room, packing up her scattered clothing.

As she pulled a wimple from the bed, a glittering thing of glass and silver fell to the floor, landing unbroken by good fortune on a woolen cape that had floated there. Helen bent to collect it. "Why, what . . . ?"

She paused, half-crouched, as she stared at the flat crystal frame in her hands. Let into one side was a looking glass of surpassing clarity, surrounded by pure crystal cunningly shaped and deeply incised to make it sparkle. Helen said in a whisper, "Even the one my father bought for me makes my face wiggle, and it was very expensive."

Sira looked up into Conn's face. "I swear I do not know how it came here," she said quietly.

"Did you ask for one?"

"Aye, but only of Margery."

"Are any of your People listening, do you think?"

"It's possible. Perhaps my father . . ."

Conn crossed the room to take the mirror from Helen's hands. " 'Tis a fair gift," he said. "It's for our wedding day."

"Where did it come from? For I swear it was not there a moment since."

"Of course it was. My bride did not come so empty-handed as you might think."

"I swear she had it not when she came in!"

"I didn't," Sira said. "I—"

"I brought it," Conn interrupted swiftly. "I laid it here myself."

"When?"

"Before you ever came into this room. I had brought it back with me months ago for the lady I would make my bride."

"Then it is mine," Helen said, "for I was to have been your bride."

"Ask a new glass of your husband, for this one is none but Sira's." He laid the looking glass in Sira's hands and added, "It is yours, my lady. As is my heart."

Helen swept out of the room, flicking a icicle-sharp glance at Conn. Sira sighed. "We were agreeing somewhat better before you came in, my dear one. But it is not your fault but the fault of whichever generous person left this mirror. It is a magnificent gift."

"I thought your People did not use metal."

"They do not. Yet . . . do you remember how your sword was encased in crystal not unlike this? No doubt some great lady of fabulous wealth is presently unable to find her mirror.''

Sira raised the glass to inspect her face. To her relief, she saw no lines carved on the flawless skin of eye or forehead. Her lips were as soft and as pink as ever, her eyes as bright. She smiled at her reflection, tenderly, as she said, ''Only one among us can work such a deed. Our king.''

''Then this is your father's gift for our wedding? He is generous.''

Shaking her head, she said, ''I don't know. I can only hope that this is a sign that he had accepted my choice. Until I hear further, I can do nothing but hope.''

As she looked more closely, she saw beneath her lower lashes a hint of darkness, a shadow perhaps of future decay. Worried, she pointed out this defect to Conn.

He laughed. ''That is nothing but a reminder of a sleepless night. You'll see that circle again tomorrow, God willing.''

Glancing again into the mirror, she saw a deeper rose tint come into her cheeks. ''And what, pray tell, is that?''

''A blush, my love. I can make that brighter yet.'' Bending near, he whispered in heated words a reminder of all that had happened in the night. Sira watched the blush grow brighter indeed, just as he said.

''Enough! Or lock the door.''

''You should learn now not to tempt me, Sira. I feel strongly that I shall always answer yes. Shall I lock the door?'' he murmured, bending to kiss the side of her throat.

''Yes . . . no! Margery's coming back.''

''Oh, she won't be insulted if she can't get in. . . .''

But Sira trotted over to open the door when Margery came back. Her face was shuttered as though against the wind. Sira saw why when Conn's jackanapes servant followed close on Margery's heels. As the two laid out the small table that Gandy carried with an assortment of viands and good wine, Margery snapped and snarled at poor Gandy. Every time he tried to make a joke or arrange the smallest item, she would scowl, or slap, or scold. Then she marched out, Gandy following hangdog behind.

Glad of Conn's arm about her waist, Sira whispered a question as soon as they were out of sight. "Why is she so cruel to Gandy? For she surely loves him."

"Some women play cruel to make their kindness the more kind. I am glad you are not like that."

"No, I am not clever enough. I should lose my place and be kind all the time."

"Be kind to me now, Sira."

She laughed as she kissed him on his bristly jaw. "There. And there. Now, be content. . . ."

"Not until you are all mine. Body and soul."

"Soul?" She put her hand to her cheek and stared at him with dilated eyes. "Do I have a soul?"

"I never thought of it. You'd know better than I."

"I suppose I must, now that I am a human being. Dear me. I never thought of it."

"Come here, Sira." Conn shut the clothing chest and sat down upon its cushioned top. He drew her onto his knees. She clasped her hands lightly behind his neck to keep from falling off.

Studying him closely, she realized that he had laughed more since last evening than in all the time she'd known him. Even in the Living Lands, where every dawn brought some new delight, he had stood apart as much for his seriousness as for his humanity. Now his laughter had gone deep inside him again, and his dark eyes were shadowed with solemn reflection.

She said, "I cannot tell if I have a soul or not. Your greatest scholars cannot tell whether a human born of a human mother possesses a soul, so how can I tell, who have been human only this day?"

"I cannot tell, either. I only know that I loved you long before you changed."

"Did you?" Sira couldn't help feeling pleased.

"I did. From the first time I heard your voice I was enchanted."

"Oh. Were you?"

He shook her lightly between his hands to dispel her disappointment. "Not that kind of enchanted. I only knew that I had to meet you again. You were kind enough to come back. Why did you?"

"I wanted to see you again. I cannot say why." She leaned her forehead against his. "Is it very uncomfortable to have a soul?"

"Sometimes. When you want to do something that you know is wicked."

"As long as I am with you, I do not want to do what is wicked. Or rather . . ." She smiled, a slow, tempting smile.

"That doesn't count." Conn answered her smile with a long stroke of his strong hands down her back. He wanted her again, desire mixing with the yearning to have her wholly his. "I wonder what that priest is up to."

"The one who is to marry us?" she asked softly, pressing her lips again to his beloved face. Then a new thought struck her and she sat up straight on his knee. "That is another matter. I know nothing about the proper way to marry among your people."

"Hmmm, that is a problem. What do they do among yours?"

"It's been many years since we had a wedding. The king joins the two who want to be together. It only takes a moment, usually at a high festival with everyone looking on. Then we all drink a cup of the special mead. You must drink in one swallow to confer good luck."

"Well, the drinking will be the same. For the rest, just watch what I do. Be careful not to cross yourself backward or with the wrong hand. Much can be forgiven you as a nervous bride, but my father sees witches everywhere he looks these days."

"Why?"

"Need you ask? When magic follows you wherever you go?" He slipped one hand behind her neck and brought her face down for a kiss. "I will protect you from him, but you must be careful."

"I will."

"That is also something to remember for our wedding. 'I will.' "

"So much to remember! So much to learn!" She looked about her. "Not least of which is this. . . ." She folded her hands in her lap and looked very prim, to the delight of her bridegroom. Then she leaned forward 'til her lips were a scant inch from his ear and whispered a delicate question.

Conn, with a grave face for which she was most grateful, whispered the answer in turn. Sira said, "Ah! Yes, that's best. I shall go now, if you please. But this house! I vow 'tis enough to confuse a rabbit."

"Shall I accompany you wherever you go?" Conn asked. Even as she moved from his lap, he could not let go of her entirely, clasping her hand, holding her waist.

"No, am I a child? I have been a rabbit and never gotten lost in the most twisted of warrens. I have been an ant and found my way through the countless chambers of a queen's palace. One human dwelling will not turn my head."

"Very well, my lady love. Rest assured that if this dwelling or any other should prove too much, I will always search for you. I will always find you."

As she left the room, she glanced back, her eyes appraising and enjoying the sight of her soon-to-be husband. With his dark hair tumbling onto his brow and the set of his broad shoulders, he resembled in every detail the man she would have conjured up if she'd ever thought to create a mate for herself. Something of her thought must have shown in her eyes, for he started toward her, an answering light of desire shining in his. He reached out to gather her up in his arms.

Sira turned and fled away, laughing. Her shoes, borrowed from Helen and slightly too large, betrayed her. She slipped on the unevenly cut stones at the threshold, falling to her knees.

"Sira!" Conn stooped over her. "God help us, are you all right?"

"Yes." She winced as she stood up, pushing up with

her hand on the top step. She wondered how she'd fallen so close to it.

"You could have struck your head on these steps. You must be more careful."

"Yes, I . . ." Pushing the loosened hair off her face, she looked up at him. "Don't worry so, Conn. I am entirely well. I just slipped, that's all."

"You could have been . . ."

The dimness at the top of the stairs prevented Sira from seeing his face. But his frozen posture and sudden silence told her what he had been about to say.

"I could have been killed?"

Just then, Lord Robert called up the stairs. "What's amiss?"

"Nothing, my lord. All is well," Conn called back, setting the echoes to work. "Come," he said to Sira, sliding his arm under hers. "I'll help you up."

"I'm not an old woman," she said, trying to laugh. "I can do it myself."

"If you're sure . . . ? Very well. But for God's sake . . . no, for *my* sake, go carefully, Sira." He went back into the room, leaving the door ajar.

Her heart twisted at the sound of his apprehension. She suddenly realized that to love was not all merriment and sweet passion. It meant that forever she must fear for him, strain her heart if they were separated, and petition Heaven daily for his safety. Though every parting might be their last, she must let him go and show a cheerful face. Even now, he might be lost to her forever due to a falling bit of stone or a chance bolt of lightning.

Sira wanted desperately to run after Conn, to spread the mantle of her protection around him. Bitterest of all her losses, even greater than that of father or friends, was the loss of her ability to shelter Conn from danger. Had she been even the least of The People, all she need do was hold out her hand over him and he would be safe. As a mortal, she must let him take his chances. How did these humans bear this dreadful sense of helplessness?

If only there were someone to talk to, to share these

feelings. Anat would have understood her. Even Blaic would be a comfort, cruelly straightforward and unsympathetic as he could at times prove. The only one Sira did not wish for was Boadach. To see him now would be too heartrending, for he would surely beg her to return.

It struck her forcibly, standing in the cold, dark hall that was to become her home, that when Conn was away from her, she was truly alone.

Fifteen

Helen, though not the most cheerful of attendants, was of more help than Sira might have imagined. She herself brushed out Sira's long hair, weaving a few strands that sprang from her temples into an encircling web that constrained the rest. A few blue flowers tucked among the silver gilt gave the impression of a crown. Sira smiled with delight as she looked at herself in her father's gift.

"It's marvelous," she said.

" 'Tis a pretty conceit," Margery agreed, bundling up the clothes the two ladies had left strewn about the chamber earlier. "I'll borrow that, if ever I weds."

"Is there any doubt that you will?" Helen asked, forgetting perhaps her mother's dictum of treating servants like friends. "I heard a tale about a certain young man-servant. . . ."

Margery sniffed. "Don't you be listening to such idle prittle-prattle. Margery has no time for young jack-at-warts who love today and then away!"

Sira exchanged a glance with Helen, standing above her still. The two young ladies smiled at each other, recognizing false bravado when they heard it. Sira turned her face again toward the mirror. "A few more, do you think?"

"One or two."

"Who helped you get ready?" Sira asked Helen.

"Oh, my old nurse came with us last eve'n. She's attended me since I was a swaddled babe, as I have no mother.''

"Neither have I," Sira said. "I had a companion once, though. I wish she could be here now."

"It is hard to be married among strangers. I am glad I have known Ross and Conn for so long. Some girls have never met their husbands until the day they marry, so all taken in all, I am a very fortunate maid."

"As am I. Though I have not known Conn long at all."

"No," Helen said, taking a small pot of dark glass from her trailing sleeve. "If you smear a fingertip of this on your lips, they'll be red for the ceremony."

"Is it usual to do so?"

The other girl's dark eyes flickered as she worked the stopper free. "Not usual, perhaps. My nurse gave it to me to use. She said that on such a day a maid should look her best."

Margery said, "She needs none of that, then. Neither of you do, and you should be ashamed to try to improve God's handiwork. Put that away, Lady Helen. Master Ross would chastise you sore if he caught you with that witches' work."

"Chastise?" Sira caught the one word and felt a chill come over her heart.

Helen hid the small pot away again. "Ross will never beat *me,*" she said confidently, "though he has the right."

"The right to beat you?"

Neither Helen nor Margery looked the slightest bit shocked, except by her ignorance. Sira said lamely, "I hadn't realized. . . ."

Margery said, "Mind, now, they don't *all* do it and there are some who do so only once."

"That is little comfort," Sira said.

Going on in a musing tone, Margery said, "They do say Lord Robert struck his wife once. The late steward told how Lady Edith had spilled wine on his lordship and he struck her with his hand across her face. I never knew her, but from what they say, she was not the kind to bear such use. She picked up a twig broom and chased him thrice

around the great hall. He said the lady gave his lordship
such a basting that he moaned for three days and never
struck her more.''

Helen sighed and said, ''I know I shall never need a
twig broom to defend me against Ross. He is in all things
a gentle-hearted man.''

Sira pursed her lips, then said, ''Margery, when you go
again into the kitchen, search out such a broom for me. I
should rather be safe than sorry.''

''Oh, thou hast nowt to fear from Sir Conn. For all his
warrior ways, he has never lifted his hand to any here at
Hamdry. Even the children know they can go their length
with him and find no harvest but a stern look.''

A knock interrupted this plaudit, though Sira would
have gladly heard more. Margery opened the door and listened for a moment. Nodding, she closed it and returned.

''They are ready for you now, my lady.''

Sira tried to rise, but it was as if she'd been frozen to
the stool. A tremor passed through her. She tried to speak.
She saw her lips move in the mirror yet she made no
sound.

''There, now,'' Margery said, putting her rough, red
hand on Sira's shoulder. ''It won't be so bad as all that,
will it, Lady Helen?''

In answer to Margery's fierce glower, Helen said
quickly, ''No, not at all. A few minutes' ride to the church,
a moment in the porch while Father Maynard speaks over
you, and all is done. Then back here for a feast.'' She
glanced at Margery, a second thought in her eyes.

''Oh, the feast they are preparing downstairs! Wonderful
cakes and a whole roast pig. Mayhaps a few less dainties
than they made for you, Lady Helen, but a good, hearty
meal to send us all to sleep with full bellies. Come, Lady
Sira. Your lover is awaiting thee.''

The thought of Conn brought Sira to her feet, cold
though they were. They seemed to ache within the too-
large shoes as she walked carefully down the twisting
stairs. She dimly heard Margery whispering to Helen as
they followed her.

He stood in the doorway, the sunlight casting red into his hair while his shadow stretched across the floor toward her. He looked very tall and quite like a stranger in his freshly sponged overtunic of quilted red wool. Then he smiled at her, his eyes staring straight into hers, and the cold fled from her bones.

Conn himself set her on Arundel's back and took the flower-bedecked bridle in his hand to lead her to the church. The rest of the party followed, walking in the unusually bright sunshine, even Lord Robert himself. Ross and Helen walked hand in hand, he singing snatches of the songs that the lower members of the household sang, she looking at him with dream-filled eyes.

The serfs setting out plantings in the new-turned fields waved and cheered as the procession passed by. Some little girls, dirty, their dresses tattered at the hems, were yet laughing as they played in the churchyard. They stood up as Arundel stopped outside the church gate. Sira well remembered waiting here for Conn to come. She told him of it as he lifted her down.

"Don't worry," he whispered back. "Father Maynard won't recognize you today. I hardly recognized you, myself. Is it possible you've grown more beautiful in a day?"

Conn clapped his hands together, breaking echoes from the church stones. His guests turned to him, a passing breeze rustling the extravagant sleeves the gentry boasted. Happy with their attention, Conn said, "Before I wed this most wonderful of women, it is customary for the bride to bring a gift to the house into which she marries. My bride's beauty, grace, and wisdom are perhaps gift enough, but lest she be thought ungenerous, she offers these as well."

Conn handed the rough bag of torn cloth to his father. Some laughed at the miserly look of the gift, but Lord Robert heard the crunch as the stones knocked together. He poured them, tumbling with cold weight, into his open hand. The red stones took light from the sun and broke it into a thousand glimmering coruscations. It looked as though he held a handful of live coals.

"What are these?" His voice was drowned by the gasp

of astonishment that rose from their guests. There was a scuffle at the back of the group as some fought to see. A low whistle arose from Gandy.

"My bride's gift to your house, father. A rare gift, one that a prince might envy."

"You said she had nothing!"

"Nothing but the clothes she stood in and those stones."

"Is she a thief then? No woman born ever had such a fortune! Or are they false?"

Throwing her voice against the whispering crowd, Sira said, "They are not false stones. Nor did I steal them. Yet if you do not believe me, then I shall take them back again." She held out her hand and advanced upon Lord Robert.

He fell back, clutching the stones against his chest as though he feared she'd snatch them from him. As though to himself, he said, "With these, I could buy my way to any position I liked. I could be marshal of England. I could bribe my way to acquire a license for crenelation and build the castle my father dreamed of."

Sira glanced up at Conn. The happiness in his eyes had gone away as he looked on his father. She said for his ears alone, "Fairy treasures bring but little good. Give them to children for playthings for that is the best use for them."

Conn carried her hand to his lips, but absently. "There are too many who have seen them. I had hoped they would ease your way into my father's heart."

"You cannot buy a heart with rubies, Conn. We were wrong to think we could."

A shout from behind them made them turn. Father Maynard, aglow in a white surplice embroidered with gold, came down the slight hill from the church. "What's amiss? The climb too much for you?"

"Not a word!" Lord Robert said sharply before Father Maynard came close enough to hear him. "I'll give the church its share in due time."

He jerked open the drawstring on the leather bag he carried on his belt and dropped the stones in. Coming to meet the priest, he said quickly, "My new daughter felt faint a moment, Father. Come along, sweet child. I'll not have my son perish from a further thwarting of his desire."

Sira saw no tenderness in Lord Robert's expression as he looked on her. She saw amazement, however, in Father Maynard's round countenance. Conn simply cast his eyes heavenward as though offering his responsibility to the God that dwelt above the clouds. When he met her gaze, he said, "I never thought I should see the sky again. But even the sun doesn't dazzle me the way you do."

"I see you have taught my son to be a courtier. The wenches around here used to complain that he would never make a pretty speech, though he was never behindhand in other ways."

"Indeed?" Sira shot another glance at Conn, walking on the other side of his father as they followed the priest.

"Aye. There was a weeping and wailing when he went off to war. You'd think he was the only stallion in the shire."

" 'Fore God, my lord, that's a pretty speech to make a bride on her wedding day." Conn looked as though he'd been dipped in boiling water. He wiped sweat from his brow and tugged at the snug collar of his tunic.

"Oh? I wouldn't expect her to buy a horse untried without some word on what training he'd had. She's no fool."

"I hope I am not, my lord. But fool or no, I intend to marry your son the moment we stop."

She did not understand why they did not proceed into the church itself but stayed within the portico. The font was a few steps farther in, but it was here, the door left open to accommodate their witnesses, that Father Maynard stopped, raised his hands in benediction, and began to marry them.

Her clearest memories were of the priest's beaming grin and Conn's voice, low and unsteady, as he made his vows to her. She found the words strange, yet they rang with her love as she spoke them in her turn.

"I take thee to my wedded husband, to have and to hold, for fairer, for fouler, for better, for worst, for richer, for poorer, in sickness and in health. . . ."

She paused, unable for the moment to believe her ears, and gave Conn a questioning look. He nodded, biting his cheek to keep from laughing. With rueful agreement, she went on repeating the vows. "To be blithe and obedient in bed and at burden, 'til death us depart."

Conn brought out a golden ring, as fair as any devised by man. Sira couldn't help a small gasp of pleasure as she looked at it. Tiny crosses held in circles linked all the way around the gold, deeply incised. The design would last a lifetime and more.

"It was my mother's," he whispered. Then more loudly, he said, repeating after the priest, "With this ring, I thee wed, and this gold and silver I thee give, and with my body I thee worship, and with all my worldly chattel I thee honor."

Sira hesitated before she extended her hand. This was a more profound hesitation than before she'd spoken her promise to be obedient in all things. She knew that beyond this last portion of the ceremonial rite, there could be no going back. Whatever doubts she had must be forgotten from the instant the ring touched her finger.

Conn sensed her apprehension. He did not seize her hand and force the ring on, nor did he give any sign of impatience. He waited for her to give him her hand. The moment stretched on, while the priest's smile dimmed and a whisper arose from those who stood by.

Yet it was not their whisper that Sira heard. A beloved voice called out to her, a voice used to command, now breaking with an unaccustomed pleading. She glanced back, out the open church door.

There, in the bright sun, stood the figure of a man, taller than a mortal and surrounded by a cloud of white that both obscured and illuminated him. He raised his hand, beckoning to her while waves of sorrow rolled from his heart to hers. A tear stung Sira's eye and ran tremulously over her cheek.

Conn said nothing though she felt that he, too, could see her father standing there, begging for her return. She turned toward him, unable to put into words the indecision

that tormented her. He said softly, "Go if you must. That
you loved me for even an hour will be the only thing I
shall remember of my life. I want more, but if this is all I
am fated to have of you, it will serve."

Sira laid her hand in her husband's.

The People were never too hot or too cold. They never
had to think about their bodies, for they grew tall and
healthy, strong and sweet-smelling without ever bothering
to think of it. They clothed themselves how they pleased,
with simplicity or with opulence, for sport or for high occasion, in whatever struck their imaginations. They need
never trouble themselves with worry or alarm. All in the
Lands of Fragrance was delight to the senses.

On the other hand, Sira thought, pushing aside a rough
and rumpled blanket, there were some pleasures that those
of the Wilder World knew nothing about.

She rolled onto her side, her head cushioned on her bent
arm, enjoying the enticing view of her husband tending the
embers of the fire that burned in his chamber. The hairs
that dusted his flexing thigh were backlit into red gold as
he coaxed the embers into flames once more. Then there
was the firm mound of his buttock as he leaned forward,
the ridged lines of his back, and the winglike flare of his
scarred shoulder blade.

Sira sighed luxuriously. She'd seen myriad beautiful
things—from butterfly wings to the great star vortex—but
what had ever drawn her more deeply into the heart of
beauty than her husband?

She toyed with the ring on her finger without looking
at it. She'd not gotten used to it yet. It still felt too tight,
though it was not a bad fit. Then she smiled, as a sensual
memory overcame her. Some things were a perfect fit, she
thought, as her stomach tightened with mingled memory
and anticipation.

"Conn?"

"Hmmm?" He leaned forward a bit more to blow some
air under the small log he'd placed atop the embers.

"I love you."

He turned his head, still half his thought on the fire. Sira shut her eyes quickly, so he wouldn't realize she'd been openly ogling his body. But she knew already how hard it was to fool him.

His bare feet made no sound on the floor. Though she kept her eyes closed tightly, she felt him loom over her and it was no surprise when the bed shifted as he put one knee on the mattress to lean down. Where he put his lips, however, made her squeal and tense.

"Conn!" She clapped her hand to the spot, sure she felt teeth marks.

"I didn't taste a morsel at our wedding feast—or at least, nothing so sweet."

She lay between his arms like a bird between the paws of a cat. His eyes looked hungry, though one would think he'd had enough at his first course to last. Sira smiled with something of a feline air herself. She'd taken her fill not an hour since, and *she* was certainly ready for more of him.

They had been white-hot, filled with a desire so obvious to anyone with eyes that they'd been spared the usual jokes and japery that accompanied a first consummation. Margery had explained about that, saying that it was usual and an eagerly anticipated part of a wedding. Sira had listened wide-eyed and more than a little appalled by some of the cruder pranks played in the past.

There had been a little of that, mostly directed to Helen and Ross. The jests had been mostly of how patiently Ross was bearing the extending of the time between his wedding and his bedding. Ross had responded good-naturedly enough, saying he was so glad to have his brother home that he would have delayed longer yet—but not much longer. For proof, he'd kissed his crimson-faced bride before all the company, until Helen, stiff and shy at first, had seized him in her strong young arms and taken over the kiss herself. It was Ross's turn, then, to turn as scarlet as a pimpernel.

Conn stroked her shoulders with the rough pads of his thumbs. "What are you thinking of?"

"Whether Helen enjoyed her first night as a married woman."

His caress paused. " 'Tis a strange thing to wonder."

"Why?"

"I should never wonder so about Ross. What happens between a husband and wife should be unspoken."

"I didn't say I was going to ask her."

His fingers began to move again, his eyes slightly troubled now as they gazed upon her gleaming skin. "I would ask though whether *you* enjoyed your night?"

"Need you ask?" Her own hands smoothed his lower back, pressing upon the triangular muscles that inset his waist. "It may be that half the manor knows by now that Master Conn's wife enjoyed herself. That door is only wood, and I doubt kept back the sounds of pleasure I made."

"Does the thought disturb you?" The trouble fled from his expression as he, too, remembered the cries that had broken from her lips, the sighs, the gasps and eventually, the demands. He slipped his fingers down from her shoulders to caress the rapidly hardening tips of her fair breasts.

"Nothing—" she began then broke off to catch her breath. "Nothing that increases my lord's honor could ever abash me."

He chuckled, his body vibrating against hers. "And hearing you express your pleasure rebounds in some strange way to the increase of my honor?"

"Oh, yes." She raised one knee, sliding the arch of her foot over his calf. The hairs tickled, but his expression was not one of glee but of desire reanimating, just as the fire had awakened from embers. "They'll be whispering of your prowess for days."

"Many days," he agreed. "Every night will bring its own tale, until they'll begin to hope my virility will flag. Little do they know it is not my strength but your beauty that they should blame."

"Nights only? Didn't you say something about the days?"

"I wonder how long it is now until dawn?"

Sira moved restlessly beneath him, feeling the sweat begin to trickle between her breasts. There was little need after all for the fire he'd rebuilt; Conn gave off heat like an oven. Yet it was not his heat alone that roused her this way. She could feel him against her thigh now, heavy with passion. Yet he made no move to drive their lovemaking along. He seemed content to rest on his elbows above her, talking like this.

She shifted her hips, rubbing against him. Then, trying to gauge his mood, she asked, "What will we do tomorrow? I . . ." She tried to stifle her sigh of frustration as he continued to lie quite still. She said, "I don't know what you do with your time. Do you work in the fields?"

"No, certainly not. I am no serf. Before I was blinded, I would put Arundel through his paces, train in arms, and the like. When the larder grows bare, I hunt with the other men. We hold hunting rights from the king. You know all the deer in the royal forests are his?"

"Are they? How unusual." She knew she was having *some* effect on him. Peeking between their closely aligned bodies, she could see the effect very plainly. She trailed her fingertips over his back and felt him tremble.

Yet he answered quite complacently. "For anyone who has no right to, killing a deer is a hanging offense."

"Hanging?" She stilled.

"There are many such offenses. Here at Hamdry, we don't inflict half the punishment we should by law. But we are a small manor, and it would not pay us to execute many of our people."

"You think of them as 'your' people?"

"Yes, of course. We are responsible for them, and they look to us for leadership. I've been trained for war, but my heart is here. All the more so, now."

He looked down at her with eyes that held a strange, heady combination of humor and hunger. "If you want me," he said in a husky whisper that caused every inch of her body to tighten, "you may use me for your pleasure."

"I—I may?"

"You know what to do, Sira. Take what you want."

Her curiosity about the serfs faded as another interest took over. Running her hands over his rippling sides, she reached between their bodies with one hand to brush ever so slightly his arousal. She laughed softly as he groaned, closing his eyes.

"My agony amuses you?" he asked through gritted teeth.

She touched him again, feeling him lift off her so she could reach him more completely. Sira had become well-acquainted with the hardness he could achieve, but she had not realized what a delicate and sensitive touch could do to him. His breath came short and fast, while his arms trembled with the effort of keeping his upper body suspended.

She wanted to explore this new world of sensation and power, to take and to give with greater and greater urgency until she could no longer tell who submitted and who conquered. She rolled her hips again, raising herself against him to brush him lightly.

To Conn, the sight of Sira's face, intent with concentration as she worked out what would please him and her the most, was more stimulating than the admittedly maddening things she was doing to him. His strength was nothing compared with the desire he felt. Though he'd assuaged his longing for her before, it had not diminished. If anything, the memory of all their doings added fuel to the fire. The fantasies he'd indulged in while falling in love with her were cold and colorless compared to the reality.

As sweat broke out on his brow and his locked arms trembled, he stammered, "You'd better . . . that is, if you want me . . . I love what you're doing, but for God's sake . . ."

Sira looked up at him, her blue-green eyes glowing with an amber light. The dark golden lashes fluttered, yet she held his gaze as she opened to him. He thought of the end of battles, when swords slipped safe into scabbards and decided that peace had definite merits. Then his thoughts were whirled away as she moved beneath him.

A long, long time later, as Sira and Conn lay curled

together like two leaves swept away by the wind, he realized he had his hand on her stomach, which rose and fell
to her sleepy breaths. He stroked her skin, feeling the tiny
hairs like the nap of a fine cloth beneath his fingertips.
Conn whispered his idle thought. "I hope we made our
child tonight, don't you?"

"Did you ask the fire for it?"

He didn't move, his hand stilling. Was she talking in
her sleep, mumbling a nonsensical answer to a question
half-understood? "What?"

"Did you ask the fire for our child? I don't mind if you
did, though it is more usual to discuss such things with
your wife. A fire child is very nice, though."

"A fire child? Sira . . ."

She rolled onto her back, her body golden on the dull
ivory ticking of the mattress. Her eyes were still closed
and her voice heavy with sleep. "I'm a sea child, myself.
Blaic is of the earth, which is why he has so many moods.
What are you? Funny, I never thought to ask you that
before, and it's very important."

"Sira, you remember how I told you once that mortals
don't get their children from the sea . . . or wherever?"

"Hmmm? No, did you? Where do you get them from
then?"

"Our wives."

"Wives? Is it a mystery then? A secret a woman doesn't
tell her husband? I'll have to talk to the others. Do you
suppose Margery knows? Oh, do you think she and Gandy
will wed? I believe she likes him better than she admits."

Sira smiled dreamily, and Conn felt a heavy coldness in
the pit of his stomach, as though he'd swallowed a stone.
"Sira, wake up. This is important."

"I am awake," she said, "but it's hard to open my eyes.
I feel like I'm drifting away. . . ."

"Sira," Conn said again, trying to get her full attention.
"Sira, we mortals mate."

"Yes, I know." She turned over toward him, her long,
slim leg draping over his hip. Conn couldn't help wanting
to touch her. He dragged the back of his hand over her,

from her pink cheek to her softly rounded kneecap. Every inch of her was satiny, with a gleaming light that seemed to emanate from her skin.

Then he took his hand back. "Sira, we mate like this, and then we have our children. They come from the woman's body. They grow inside her. There could be one inside you now."

It was as if she hadn't heard. Conn tried to think of how to state the facts even more simply.

Then he saw the tear seep from under her eyelid. He put his arms around her and held her against his chest, feeling each tear burn him to the soul. In the end, he could only say, "I thought you understood."

Sixteen

A tentative knock the next morning awoke Sira from a heavy slumber. At some point in the night, Conn had covered her with a blanket, though her head still pointed more toward one bottom corner of the bed rather than the head. She opened her eyes, temporarily unsure of where she was. The knock came again.

Sira sat up, gasping at the stiffness of rarely used muscles. "Come in," she said, glancing around for Conn.

A neatly covered head poked around the edge of the door. " 'Tis Margery, my lady. I brung thee a morsel to break thy fast."

"Oh . . ." Sira blinked. Holding the blanket to her chest, she came up onto her knees, making sure she was covered back and front. "Where is he?"

"He rode out this morning on that fine big horse of his'n. Proud as a dunghill cock, to look at him. And Lord Ross not a hair different. Men!"

Margery put the tray she carried down on a flat-topped chest. She pushed open the shutters, letting in light and a cold breeze. Sira drew the coverlet more closely about her, more for warmth now than modesty. Margery didn't seem to notice the drop in temperature.

Bending, Margery scooped up several cushions that had tumbled off the bed or been hurled aside in the course of the night's exertion. Piling them against the headboard carved with a tree of life, she gave them a housewifely pat. "Now, sit here, my dear, and refresh yourself."

There were sliced apples, half a loaf of fair white bread served with a small dish of soft cheese, and a shapely pewter mug of sweet brown ale. Though it had never been Sira's custom to drink anything but water first thing in the morning, she didn't wish to send Margery all the way back to the kitchen to serve her whim. Besides, the drink was heartening.

"Do you know where Conn has gone to?"

"Nay. Hunting for deer, it could be. They took no hawks with them, though it is a good season for hawking. I should say it was high spirits alone that sent them out today."

"High spirits? I should think Conn would be too—"

"Oh, 'tis not so tiring for a man as 'tis for a woman. They sleep hard afterward and that refreshes them."

"It seems a woman bears all the burdens," Sira murmured.

"Never mind," the maidservant said soothingly. "Margery'll send up bathwater for you, bathwater scented with lavender. That'll wash the sting away."

"What about you?"

"I? I don't take your meaning, my lady?"

"You and Gandy . . ."

Margery suddenly became even busier about the room, clicking her tongue over Sira's gown, lying on the floor, and the broken lace that Conn had cast off. "A fine way for him to treat good cloth! No need to defend him, my lady. Well, I know you never left such stuff to fall willy-nilly where it may! That's man's work, right enow! Thou shouldst see the condition of Lady Helen's things. A shocking want of heed paid to the trouble they cause us women!"

"Where is Gandy this morning?"

"Margery knows not, nor cares she a whit! Tending on his master, if he's wise, or more'n likely luring some poor wench on with his cunning ways."

"Is that what he did to you?"

"To me?" Margery echoed, and the scarlet tide of shame rose over her face. "I'm not one to be taken in. No. Indeed, no."

Sira understood this human signal now. She busied herself with food and drink, giving Margery a chance to recover her poise. Sira felt that Margery could make a valuable guide to the strange ways of mortals, especially mortal men. Some deep instinct told her there were questions she'd never be able to discuss with Conn, dearly as she loved him. Men seemed to be as far removed from the female kind as mortals were from The People.

"Margery . . ."

Margery held a half-folded cloak in her hands. She smoothed it repeatedly as she spoke, keeping her gaze on the tightly twisted wool fabric. "My lady, I couldn't resist him. From the day he came here, riding with his master, I—oh, 'tis hard to put into words. He was so gay and merry withal, though many another would have been cast down through having so much to do for his master. Gandy seemed so good!"

"He does not seem so now?"

"Tach! 'Twas a green girl I was then, a fool! Many a man had tried to catch Margery and never the glance I'd give 'em. A clout on the ear, maybe, or the sharp side of my tongue. Then I go and gi' myself to a man with a thousand hearts, half of 'em give away before he ever saw my face."

"Yet he seems most attentive toward you. He is made merry when you are kind and seems broken-hearted when you are cold."

"Seems? I dare not trust his seeming, no more than were he some mountebank player wandering through. That's a sure path to Weeping Cross."

"You don't trust him at all, then?" Sira raised her eyes to the other girl's face.

"Not now."

"Why not?"

Margery shifted on her feet and looked everywhere but into Sira's eyes. "I lay with him, my lady." Then, with defiance, she stared back at Sira. "I lay with him, and I was glad."

Remembering what she had witnessed of Gandy and Margery together, Sira felt a touch ashamed at having forced Margery's confidence. She said, "Well, that's not so bad . . ."

"My lady? Did'st thou not know? I am the daughter of a villein. A—a serf."

"Are you?" Sira ate the last bite of bread, but what she heard Margery answer made it stick in her throat.

"My body is not mine to give. It belongs to Lord Robert. If he knew. . . ." She shook her head as though for something dead.

"Your body is not—"

Margery went on. "My father could never pay the layerwite. Two shillings it was when Agnes lay with the boy with the black goat. Her family nearly starved that winter."

"You mean if you make love with someone they charge your father money?"

Margery nodded. "Aye, to pay the lord out for my virginity. Don't they do this in your village?"

"No, never. No one there belongs to anyone else."

"Then how does your lord pay for what he owns?" Margery didn't wait for an answer, busy with her own thoughts. "No, 'tis best I stay cold toward poor Gandy. Now, no one knows what we did, but were I to show as being with child . . . ! My father could never pay for my doings and the bride ales as well—two in one day. 'Tis a wonder such as never been seen in England. Near enow to a miracle what with Sir Conn gettin' his eyes back 'n' all."

"Hand me my gown, please, Margery," Sira asked.

"Oh, are you done then?" Margery took the tray off Sira's knees. As an afterthought, she dipped her knee briefly and asked, "My lady . . . you won't be telling aught of what I said? My tongue wags like a dog's tail at meat. 'Tis a fault of mine. I've no wish to be whipped for makin' too free."

"You have nothing to fear from me. *Nothing*," she emphasized. "No, I thank you, but I can dress myself. Please see to having someone bring up that bathwater you mentioned."

"Aye, at once." But the maidservant stared. "Won't you be wanting your overdress, my lady?"

"No, I'm not going out. I thought I'd spend a few moments with Lady Helen before my bath. Do hurry, Margery."

Sira rapped on the door on the other side of the dark hall. She glanced up and down the corridor. As yet, besides Ross and Helen, she had no idea who lived in these four rooms. Lord Robert in one, she imagined. Mayhap the steward kept the fourth, but where did the rest of the household sleep?

A rather muffled voice called for Sira to enter. Lady Helen was dressed in full, including shoes. Her kerchief laid in painfully perfect pleats over her hair. Her long braids trailed over the chair, partially obscuring the broad leather straps that formed the seat and back. She held a small book of hours between her slim fingers. She had lovely hands with healthy nails, each rubbed down to a point. There were undried tears on her cheeks.

Sira omitted any formal greeting. "Why, Helen. Have you been crying, too?"

"Too?" Helen sat up straight in surprise. "What cause have *you* to cry?"

"What cause have you?"

Helen heaved a deep sigh. "Nothing. I am completely happy. A woman would be a fool to cry when she has such a wonderful husband as Ross. If there's nothing else . . ." She opened her book again, yet Sira saw that she could not keep her hands from trembling.

Uninvited, Sira sat down in a second seat, this one shaped like a pair of hands joined at the heels. The flat seat was surprisingly comfortable. Glancing about her, Sira saw that, as Margery had said, this room was a bit more richly decorated than the one where she had passed the night. The hangings on the bed seemed newer, their intricate embroidery crisp and clear. The bed, too, was carved, not just head and foot, but the pillars that held up the canopy as well. A small alcove built out from the wall and a brazier set between the benches made a cosy room within a room to engage in winter's evening pastimes with a friend.

Sira said, "I cried because I did not realize all that being married meant. When Conn explained—"

"Oh, *he* explained. Then you are fortunate in your husband."

"Ross didn't? Oh, I see."

"I couldn't believe it when he . . . oh, what's the use in complaining!" Tossing her book aside so that it bounced on the bed, Helen pushed herself to her feet and began to storm back and forth across the carpeted stone floor. "What's done is done, and unless I suddenly take to religion, there's nothing I can do to change it."

In her agitation, Helen came very close to stepping on Sira's toes. Remembering that of the two, she was the elder and allegedly wiser, Sira said, "Conn says it doesn't always happen, not at first."

Helen snorted, sounding like Arundel. "You wouldn't know it by Ross. He took his fill last night and seemed more than eager again this morning. If I had not cried, he'd be here still."

Sira felt her brow rumple in confusion. She said, "I think we are not talking of the same thing. Conn explained about . . . about babies."

"Babies? What does he know about those? He's a knight, not a wet nurse."

"He must know more about them than I do," Sira muttered, but Helen was at the far end of the room then and did not hear her.

As she came back, her dark braids swinging like bell ropes, she said, "Maybe it isn't too late to enter a convent. If I claim to have undergone a vision in the night and fended off my wedded lord . . . No, that won't work. I'm not a virgin anymore, and the sheets prove it."

"The sheets?" That was another difference between one

chamber and the next. Her bed had no sheets, probably because there weren't enough to go on every bed.

"Of course." Impatiently, Helen stripped back the top cover. "I'm surprised Lord Robert hasn't been in already this morning to view the proof."

What Sira would have given just then for Conn to enter and explain this! Not really wanting to, yet driven by both curiosity and self-preservation, Sira stood up and shot a quick look at the sheet. At first, she had no idea what to look for. Then she saw a faint red smear or two on the dun-colored fabric.

"There, now you can testify against me."

"Helen, I'm not against you. If you want to be a virgin . . ."

The girl sank into her chair, putting her hands over her reddened eyes. "I don't. I love Ross, even if . . . And then he left so early to go ride with his brother."

"That was thoughtless of them. I shall scold Conn for that."

"Scold him?"

"Why, yes. He should have realized I would need him this morning."

"Where *are* you from? You are a wife now. You run the household, scold the servants, and bear the children. If you dare to say a word against your lord, he can do what he likes with you."

"Oh, yes. The beating you spoke of yesterday." Sira shook her head. "I told you then that Conn would never—"

"You scold him and see!" Helen's laughter was as bitter as her tears.

Sira put her head to one side and studied the girl. "You know then, about the bearing of children?"

A twitch of the shoulder was all the answer she got. "Then that is not why you are so distraught this morning?"

"Of course not. Every girl knows about that, unless she's an utter fool or not one to use her eyes. I am sure with all your gossiping with servants that you've known about that from your childhood."

"Actually, no. It came as quite a shock."

Helen laughed again. It was a pretty sound, like the tiny ice bells that Cuar the harpist played when he wanted to invoke the spirit of winter in his music. But Helen's song jangled, not yet in perfect tune. "Thank you for the joke," she said.

"I am not joking. Until Conn explained, I had no idea how you . . . how one bears children. I still have many questions about it, but you are not the one to ask."

"Why not?" Helen demanded. "I've had none myself perhaps, but I have heard the screams of women in child-bed."

"Screams?"

"And last year I myself helped when my favorite bitch whelped her pups."

"That is the same thing?"

"Of course. *Are* you a fool?"

Sira lifted her chin and turned her eyes on Helen. Though but a mortal now, she still carried within her the loftiness of spirit that she'd earned through the centuries as the Lady of the Living Lands. "I am not a fool just because I do not know everything. I may know things that you do not, yet I have not hurled hard names at you."

Helen looked slightly ashamed of herself, her eyes cast down and her mouth tucked in at the corners. Sira brushed her fingers together lightly, returning to an earlier subject. "Then you were crying because Ross did something unkind?"

"No, he wasn't unkind, just . . . abrupt."

"Abrupt? You mean—in the night?"

Helen turned her head away, as though to search intently for something on the other side of the latticework over the window. Yet at the same time, she nodded her head. "It wasn't at all the way I thought it would be. When he used to kiss me . . ." Her eyes drifted closed while a smile played about her mouth. Sira could see the circles under the girl's eyes, marring the smooth perfection of her white skin.

Then she shook herself all over as though awakening

from a beautiful dream. "So be it. With any good fortune
at all, I shall bear a son from this night's work, and that
will make it all worthwhile. For the rest . . ." She
shrugged. "I shall pray."

Sira returned to her own room with a great deal to think
about. While finding nothing to complain of in Conn's
lovemaking—she stopped in the middle of the corridor until her insides solidified again—she found herself troubled
anew by the idea of a child. "Dogs whelping?" she said
as she entered.

"My lady?" Margery looked over her shoulder, even
while she poured the water from a wooden bucket into a
stave-encircled wooden tub. While no steam arose from
the water, Sira did catch a stale floral fragrance.

"What is this?" Sira asked.

"Your bath."

"My . . ." She closed her thoughts off from every memory of a deep rock pool fed by hot springs from deep
within the earth. She made a resolution to forget the un-
guents and lotions, perfumes and attars of rose and lily,
poured in liberal amounts to create a sybarite's heaven of
hot water.

Whatever heat had been in the water when the servants
had carried it up had dissipated by the time Sira immersed
herself. The soap Margery handed her was yellow and
coarse against her skin. It repaid her rubbing with the merest scum of suds. There was nothing else, though, not even
something scented to wash her hair. Though entirely ignorant of how humans made the things they used—such
as soap—Sira felt that there had to be a better way.

"Bring up a large pot of water, Margery, and set it over
this fire. At least then there'll be a drop of hot in this ocean
of cold."

"Here, my lady? But there's no jack to hang it from."

"Then set it in the coals. And be good enough to close
the shutters. That wind is enough to flay me."

"Yes, my lady." A sniff accompanied the words.

"I'm sorry, Margery. There's so much to grow accus-
tomed to."

Then she heard a robust laugh and the sound of booted feet on the landing outside. Swiftly, Sira dunked her head in the water, washing away the soap. She pushed it off her face with both hands as Conn opened the door and strode into the room.

He threw a word over his shoulder at someone out of sight, then paused like a statue on the threshold as he caught sight of her. Sira sank down until the water lapped at her shoulders. "Did you have good hunting?" she asked.

He started to speak but had to moisten his lips before words came out. "Not until now."

A blue cloak hung around him, caught back on his right shoulder and held by a large round brooch set with white agates. The wide embroidery of gold and green that edged his cloak was echoed by his belt, pulled down on one side by the weight of his sword. His hair was rumpled by the cap that he'd just pulled off. Sira thought he had never looked more handsome, his high cheekbones reddened by hard riding and his eyes bearing that hungry look as they did whenever they fell on her. She couldn't resist that look.

Neither of them noticed Margery scuttling out behind Conn, carefully closing the door. Conn unbuckled his sword belt and cast off his cloak. Sira watched his every move, forgetting the chill of the water. She wasn't cold long.

"There's word of a tournament going to be held in Roxterby a few weeks hence," Lord Robert said enticingly. "It's a chance to show your brides off to the world."

Conn and Ross exchanged a smile over the table where they sat with their father, beakers of good ale before them. The younger man said, "Why unsettle them with a journey? Helen is happy where she is. I haven't heard a complaint in a fortnight."

"As much as that? You are fortunate. My bride dins my ears day and night with demands."

Ross chuckled. "You look as though you get little rest indeed, my brother. A mere wraith you are, with hardly the strength to lift the pitcher and refresh your brother's drink."

"Oh, I have strength enough for that." Conn let his hand shake as he raised the earthenware jug. "Or mayhap not." He let it sit again. "You'll have to go dry, Ross."

Lord Robert, ignoring their byplay, grumbled, "To think I should live to see my sons under the hen's foot! I suppose it is your wives that keep you from pursuing honors on the field."

"For whose pleasure?" Conn asked, his humor fleeting. "That witch who sits on the throne? I'll not couch a lance even in tournament while she calls herself Lady of England."

Ross said, "I must admit I am not overfond of the Angevins myself. The tales my father-in-law has heard—"

Lord Robert broke in. "It could be worse. We could be saddled with a queen like that French creature, Eleanor. A wanton, terrible creature who spends her country's money on pleasures and wickedness. The empress may not be sweet-spoken, but she at least knows which man is her husband!"

"Our true queen knows better yet, Father. Haven't you heard what Maynard's cousin wrote him last? Stephen's queen vowed for the king to relinquish all rights and titles and to separate herself for all time from him if Matilda would relent and let the king out of his confinement at Bristol."

"Then she's a fool," Robert shot back.

"I have met the lady," Conn said. "She loves her husband with all her heart. If she has sworn to give him up, it is for his good that she has done so."

"What answer has the empress sent our good queen?" Ross asked.

"Allsop had not heard, but he does not think it will be a kindly answer. The lady is haughty and her tongue betrays her."

"God save us from all such women," Ross said, piously crossing himself, then spoiling the effect by grinning. "Speaking of quarrelsome women, I'd best be going home to mine. Shall I have de Burke's clerk make a fair copy of the marriage articles? Now that this last point about scutage is clear, there should be no more delays in the payment of Helen's dowry.''

Conn said swiftly, ''I'm glad you must deal with these matters, Ross, rather than I. Come, I'll walk with you as far as the stables.''

Safe out of earshot, Ross asked, ''What's wrong with him? He has not shouted nor thrown anything in the entire time that I have been negotiating with him on de Burke's behalf. Is he ill?''

Conn didn't answer at once. ''Has it been hard on you, speaking for de Burke without destroying what Father feels for you?''

''What does Father feel for me? What does he feel for any of us? He is pleased I am married to Helen and have been named the old man's heir, that's all. He knows it matters not what concessions he makes to de Burke or de Burke makes to him. I have a manor as you do. He has two sons who will be barons, if Stephen's party prevails. That is all he cares about.''

''That may be true. But what if the king does not prevail?''

Ross stared up at his brother. ''Are you having doubts now? What next? The heavens tumble?''

Conn gazed around at the courtyard, seeing not the craftsmen at work, nor the men-at-arms practicing their archery at the far end. Rather he looked back on a memory of a bitterly cold Candlemas Day outside Lincoln Castle.

In a yet lower voice, Conn said, ''It's been six months since that she-devil locked him away. How long do men survive being manacled to a wall in a stinking chamber no bigger than a grave? Our good queen promised on his behalf that Stephen would enter a French monastery. What happens to those of us who are loyal if Stephen agrees?''

''I don't know. Yet I can answer your question with another, Conn. What if Stephen is freed or escapes and he does not accept the word his queen has given? How long will this war drag on? And what will be our place in it, if it does?''

''*Our* place?''

''Indeed!'' Ross stood proudly, facing Conn, his fists balled and resting on his hips. He looked like a bantam cock, with full as much heart as a bull. ''Do you think I'll let you gather all the plaudits while I lie snug at home? That was my part the last time you rode away to war. Next time, should there be a next time, Father won't be able to stop me from joining you.''

Conn tossed his arm about his brother's slighter shoulders and nearly pulled him off his feet with affection. ''Aye, you'll serve in place of de Burke, and I'll introduce you to the finest men in England. And the king.''

''I will hold you to that.'' Uncomfortable with so much feeling, Ross looked around aimlessly. ''I wonder where Helen has gone to?''

''In search of Sira? I'll look in the gardens.''

''Good. I'll look in the kitchens. Helen said she was planning to teach Sira how to cook, though that is a case of the blind leading the blind.''

Conn was pleased his brother had shown no embarrassment in using this common phrase. His blindness seemed like a bad dream now, and he was glad to find that others were also forgetting it.

As he promised, Conn went in search of the brides. They'd been married six weeks; it was the first week in June and everything grew tall and green under the loving eyes of the sun. The thousand shades of green struck the eyes like a miracle while the worked fields gave promise of an unparelled harvest. Birds reeled from pure joy across the wide blue sky while every bee grew drunk sipping from the masses of flowers in the hedgerows. The serf women sang at their work while the children, even while working, found time for games and sport.

Without Sira, it would have all been meaningless, not simply because she'd restored his sight.

When he found her, she was alone behind the cooling walls of the garden. She had a basket over her arm. Despite a slight breeze that made it difficult for her to control the long sleeves and dancing overmantle of her dress, she stood before a sunny wall, clipping roses. A few strands of her bright hair had come loose from the bundle at the back of her head and floated like shining ribbons in the sun. Intent on her work, she hummed a tune that Conn had never heard before. A tune of the Sudden Lands, perhaps.

Could he ever get enough of the sight of her? He loved to watch her when she was not aware of his presence, savoring like a connoisseur every nuance of her smiling face and dreaming eyes. What did she think of when alone like this? If she regretted leaving the dreamworld of the fay, would he ever know it? She claimed not to miss it, but since coming home, Conn could not help but be aware of the shortcomings of Hamdry and indeed, of the whole world he inhabited.

Though she made no complaint, was that because she had no cause or because she knew complaints would avail her nothing? Ross said Helen carped constantly, yet he seemed happy with his bride. Conn wished Sira would criticize something so he would have a clue to her thoughts.

She turned toward him, though he'd made no sound coming over the grass. "Come see!" she called.

"What are you doing?" He hated to question her on anything, hoping she'd volunteer information.

"Margery told me of an old woman who remembers your mother making rose water. She's waiting to instruct me. I hope she remembers aright."

Conn nodded, happy to see her eyes alight with this new interest. He had been aware that Sira had begun to interest herself in how Hamdry Manor was run. He had been cornered and questioned more than once by her, and his answers had not always pleased her. Nevertheless, those sessions had often ended with their making love.

Even while he listened for her plans to mix rose fragrance with sweet almond oil to add to her daily bath, Conn faced what was really troubling him. Though he himself possessed not a single doubt of the appropriateness of his marriage, he was afraid that Sira did. He'd heard tales of what happened when mortal men married women of questionable background. Take the man the late king had married his daughter to, the contentious Matilda, Empress of Germany and soi-disant Lady of England. It was widely rumored that at least two of Geoffrey Plantagent's ancestresses had been something other than human.

"Sira, have you ever heard of a lady named Melusine?"

"No, I don't think so. Why?"

"Never mind."

He helped her cut roses while running over the story in his head. They said that Melusine had been a forest maiden of mysterious origin when Count Raymond de Lusignan had married her. He promised never to bother her on Saturdays, and they had several children together before he broke his promise. They said he saw his beautiful wife sewing by herself when he peeped into her room. An innocuous activity, were it not that her lower limbs had become the tail of a great serpent—or had it been a fish tail? Conn had heard both versions around the campfires on one campaign or another.

And there'd been Geoffrey Greygown, Geoffrey Plantagent's ancestor from not so very long ago, who'd married another woman of unknown race who'd come but rarely to Mass and never stayed for the entire rite. Once her husband had tried to hold her in the church. The witch-countess had broken from him with an unearthly shriek and flown out the window, never to be seen again by mortal eyes. Everyone said she must have been a demon, but Conn had begun to wonder if she might not have been something else.

He'd never believed the tales, even scoffing, until he found himself in the same situation. Gazing at his wife, Conn felt a great heaviness in his heart. Would Sira vanish one day, leaving him alone?

"What is wrong, my love?" Sira asked. "You've given six great sighs now. Any more, and my heart will break without my even knowing why."

She put down the basket and seated herself on the grass.

Her pale violet gown puddled around her. The manor's needlewomen had been working like madwomen, trying to finish some clothing for her. Though she could never look less than beautiful, even the best of the gowns seemed as coarse as a beggar's rags when Conn remembered the fabulous attire she'd been wont to wear in her father's court. There'd been one of gleaming silk with a pattern of gold and red embroidery like a flame running about the hem.

"Another sigh?" Sira asked and patted the ground beside her in an invitation. She pulled the basket of roses onto her lap. They were the ones he'd grown before she'd taken him into her world. Though in full bloom, they looked pale and sick compared with the blossoms in the Living Lands.

Sira said, "Aren't these pretty? And smell . . . It's enough to make a woman drunk on scent alone."

"They're not what you are used to, though, are they?"

"Used to?" She lifted one rose in her tapering fingers, white and red mixing together, and held it to her nose. "Divine . . ."

"They're not like the ones you have at home."

"No, they are exactly the same. Some things cannot be improved, and one should not try. You, for example, are perfect."

"No, I'm not." Conn smiled, more because she expected him to than because he was amused. "Sira . . ."

"Hmmm?" She'd closed her eyes now and put her head back to receive the sun's blessing full on her face. Her breasts thrust out against the soft fine-spun wool of her gown. The laces that held her dress together at the bosom had parted slightly. Conn could see the corresponding opening in her shift and the slight rise of one smooth breast beneath.

Conn tried to keep hold of his yearning. He struggled to remember that making love gave him no answers. "Sira, are you happy?"

"Happy?" Her long, gold-dipped lashes lifted, and he saw puzzlement in her eyes. "Of course I am. There's not a happier woman in all the world than I."

This is why he'd put off asking that question. Even when she answered him as his wishes would have it, he was still tortured with wondering if she was telling the truth or telling him what he wanted to hear. Or perhaps it was what *she* wanted to hear.

"Battle is so much less confusing," Conn said.

"Is it? Less confusing than what?"

"Marriage. I love you, Sira. . . ."

"And I love you. What is confusing about that?"

"Nothing, I suppose." He looked down at his hands, so big compared to hers. His calluses were returning, due to the heavy schedule of training he'd undertaken. Sometimes he felt as though it were almost sacrilege to put his rough hands on her delicacy. Yet she never said a word of refusal or showed any repugnance. Only after they made love, did he sometimes feel that she was not as contented as she'd been the first few times she'd lain in his arms.

She got up on her knees to look into his face. "Conn, please tell me what you are thinking. You trouble me with these sighs and strange words. Are *you* unhappy?"

"No. No, I'm not. If you aren't."

"Why would you think I am?"

He raked his hand through his hair. "I'm not a man of poetry, Sira. I can't put into words all that I think and feel. How can anyone trap the invisible?"

She smiled with all a human woman's mystery and more. "You managed very nicely. You spread out your big arms and chased me from one corner of this garden to the other. If I had not begged for mercy—"

"I should have caught you then."

"What would you have wished for?"

"What I found eventually, anyway. A woman to love me the way you do."

"There," she said with a satisfied nod. "It's not so difficult to tell me your thoughts and feelings. Now, tell me what is troubling you. Is it your father?"

"No. Since he received your dowry, he's a happy man. Plotting and planning how he'll own this corner of Devonshire in time to pass it on to our son. I think he believes riches keep a man from dying.''

A shadow passed over her face at the mention of the future. Thinking still of vanishing witch-countesses, Conn wanted to reach out and capture her thought. But she said, ''I do like him better than I imagined I would,'' and the moment passed.

''He can be good company,'' Conn agreed. ''That brings something to mind that I meant to tell you. Father has asked me about Margery.''

''Margery? What about her? And why does he speak to you at all? She is *my* servant now.''

''Sira, she is still a serf. Her father is my father's villein. If she has lain with a man . . . if she is with child—''

''I don't want to betray her, Conn. She has been a god-send to me. She tells me the things I want to know and does not express amazement that I do not know them. Helen spends so much time exclaiming over the fact that I am ignorant of everything that she never answers my questions.''

''I know,'' he said, more in answer to her tone than to her words. He put his arm about her waist and pulled her close to his body. ''It's difficult once a servant becomes a friend. But your first loyalty is to your lord, Sira. When you married me, my father became your overlord. We have to be obedient to his wishes.''

''How obedient were you when you married me?''

''Oh, I was a rebel then, willing to be hanged rather than to lose you.'' He tipped her face up and kissed her instantly responsive lips. He realized that this was the longest time between kisses that there had been in their marriage so far. He never wanted there to be a longer interval.

When he lifted his head, she sat across his lap. Her half-abashed smiled told him she knew how her kisses had aroused him.

''About Margery?'' he said.

''Oh, yes.'' Sira settled herself with a wriggle into a more comfortable position and laughed with her eyes at his expression. Outwardly, she looked as meek as a nun. "I don't want to give her away, Conn. Please don't ask me."

"You can't protect her for long. Already she is beginning to look rounded."

"Rounded?"

Bluntly, Conn said, "Her belly is growing."

"Oh. I thought she was just getting fat. Is that where the baby grows?" She nodded when he said it was. "I had wondered about that."

She smoothed her hand over her own abdomen. "Most strange."

Conn welcomed this renewed opportunity to guess Sira's thoughts. "Sira, one day we will have a child."

"Will we?"

"I pray so. Is that what you want?"

She turned her face away. "I don't know. The idea of an infant is strange to me. I have seen some, lying in their baskets or carried in their mother's arms. They are not like people, are they?"

"No, not exactly. But every person was one, once."

She nodded. "Tell your father that I myself will pay for Margery's sin, if sin it be. She does not want the father named."

"She will have to name him. It's the law. He took what belongs to her lord. He, too, must pay."

"I—"

He said, "No. You cannot pay all the serfs' obligations. They pay us to care for them. My service to the king is part payment to them in return. Do you know what a man is charged in scutage if he does not send a soldier to the king when demanded? A huge sum, which comes from the serfs. We are all connected to each other, Sira. That is how we survive. You cannot change what is."

"Even if it is wrong?"

"How can it be wrong? It is the way." After a moment, she nodded, as though accepting the impossibility of change. "Now," Conn said, "What is the man's name?"

"He is not a serf or villein."

"He is freeborn?"

"I—I think so."

"Then you have nothing to fear for her. If a bondwoman marries a freeborn man, she, too, is free, for as long as her husband lives."

"I see. Will her child be free as well?"

"Yes. Though her husband will pay her lord for the child's blood. Since we are losing that child's labor, you see."

Sira sniffed. "Lords get paid for everything, it seems."

"Don't quarrel with feudal law. It pays for everything we have."

"I see that. But Conn, I cannot betray what Margery told me in trust. If you want to know who the man is, you must ask her."

Suddenly, Sira stared off into the distance, as though she would pierce the wall of the garden with her gaze. "Someone is there," she said in a low whisper as she moved off Conn's lap.

"Who?"

"A woman. She was listening."

Swiftly, Conn crossed the grass and pushed open the heavy gate. He looked toward the manor. Hurrying away along the path was Helen, slim in a blue gown. She glanced back, as though to be sure she went unseen. On seeing him, she stopped short.

He raised a hand in greeting. A long time seemed to pass before she answered with a half-raised arm and a flicker of her fingers. The distance was too great to be certain, yet he thought her smile was a trifle sickly.

Conn returned to his bride. Sira weighed her basket in her hands. "I hope I have enough to make what I want. Did you see her?"

"Yes. It was Helen."

"I *thought* it was a woman. I heard her skirt sweep the path."

"Well, if she was listening, she heard nothing of importance. I'll tell Ross—"

"No! Don't make trouble. As you say, she heard nothing of importance. It could be that she wasn't really listening, or perhaps she wanted to speak with me and heard you with me so decided against intruding.''

Sira thought over their conversation. They'd mentioned her one-time invisibility, but they had not been speaking loudly. Then she shrugged and dismissed the incident. "It matters not. Shall we go in? I'd like to set these petals to steeping as soon as possible. Your world is very pleasant, my husband, but your baths leave a great deal to be desired!''

Seventeen

The famous midwife who Conn had brought all the way from Exeter was not happy being summoned to the bedside of a mere villein's daughter. But Sira took no interest in the middle-aged woman's downturned mouth and rolling eyes. She held Margery's hand and whispered, "He'll be here soon. Just hold on."

"It doesn't matter," Margery said, then caught her breath as another pain struck her. "I bore the whipping without him; I can bear this child."

Sira didn't want to discuss the past. Lord Robert's insistence on whipping Margery at the cart tail in May for fornication had led to a tremendous breach between herself and Conn. It had healed now, or nearly, and she could not say Conn had not done all he could in the meantime.

Part of Margery's suffering then could be traced to the same cause as her stoic acceptance of her pains now. Sira had never in all her years met anyone as proud or as stubborn as this daughter of plain parents.

"Peasants!" the midwife muttered, as she finished her preparations. Despite her distaste for her patient, her reddened hands were gentle as she put them upon Margery's swollen belly. She nodded in satisfaction. "It shall not last long," she said. "Be of good cheer. You'll have a fine, strong child this day."

Sira gave Mistress Yalter a thankful smile. "Did you hear that, Margery?"

"I heard. For all the good it will do me."

As Margery had grown larger over the past eight months, many of her tasks had fallen to her younger sister, Adela. Silent of foot, she entered now with a flask of wine and a whispered message to Sira. Bending over her maidservant, Sira said, "Father Maynard is outside. Do you want to see him?"

"Has he come to give me the Last Rites? Thank him for me, my lady, and tell him I have no need. Mistress Yalter will see me through, right enow."

Now, though the midwife tried to purse her lips, she did not appear nearly so formidable as her narrow, bony features would suggest. Though dressed with fashionable care, her voice bore traces of an accent not unlike Margery's own. She said, "If you will take my advice, Lady Sira, you'll encourage the priest to go down amongst the men. 'Tis they who most need a word of comfort at times like these."

Margery tensed, though whether in pain or in doubt, Sira could not say. "Yes, go down, too, my lady. See if—" She bit back the words of hope she could not utter.

Margery's sister opened the door for her. "Are you afraid to stay, Adela?"

"No, my lady. Margery is strong, like our mother. She bore eight children before she died."

Though the younger girl had neither Margery's spirit nor sense of humor, she was a pretty, plump creature, with curling brown hair and clear brownish green eyes. She knew more songs than any one else at Hamdry Manor.

"Will you stay here until Margery needs me again?" Sira asked. She never could get in the habit of issuing orders rather than making requests.

Adela nodded. "It may be some little time afore anything goes forward. They do say first 'uns take the longest."

"So I have heard also." Sira had heard a thousand tales of childbed from every woman on the manor who had ever borne a child, living or dead. Some tales were enough to frighten a dragon. Few were reassuring.

She did not want to look back at the bed, yet she found it impossible to leave without a backward glance. Before long, she would be in such a position, racked by powers greater than herself yet created from her own body. The very idea terrified her as nothing else had ever done. Was this what her great love had brought her to?

Father Maynard tucked his hands in the wide sleeves of his winter robe and turned away from the open window. In the fields beyond, winter had laid its first snowfall since last year. Sira spared a thought for another storm, nearly eight months ago now. She and Conn . . . but they had not made love last night. Her increasing size had begun to make that impossible.

"My lady . . ."

"It's good of you to come, Father. But Margery is not ready yet to see you." Glancing past him out the window, she added, "You've had a long, cold walk. Come down and I shall mull you some wine. Or a taste of my new mead? Conn says it's the best I've done so far!"

To her surprise, Father Maynard's eyes did not twinkle as they rested on her. Ignorant though she was of all matters of the church, she was aware that she'd become something of a favorite with the priest. She knew that any woman who married Conn would have been, so long as she made him happy. The fact that she was going to bear Conn's child had raised her high in both Father Maynard's and Lord Robert's estimation.

"I bring news from my cousin, Lady Sira."

"Is it bad?"

"No, quite good."

"Then why so gloomy? If 'tis good, then let us toast it in my new wine."

He laid his hand on her arm to keep her a moment longer. "The king has been exchanged for Robert, Earl of Gloucester."

"May God be good to him. Has the empress retired from the war, then?"

"No. She has her brother back, and his is the cunning mind behind her soldiers."

"Ah." Now Sira understood why Father Maynard's eyes as they rested on her were both sad and wary, as though he were in sympathy with her and yet afraid she would scream or rage at this news.

With her eyes averted, Sira asked, "Is your cousin certain of his knowledge?"

"As certain as Gospel. King Stephen met his queen, she who arranged the matter, in November. Though the empress kept him manacled to the wall of his cell and short of food, his strength is such that he soon recovered his manliness. His determination to keep the throne has been, if anything, increased by his ill treatment. When our good queen tells him what humiliation she has suffered at the empress's whim, no doubt his ardor to see Matilda crushed to earth will only grow."

"No doubt," Sira said politely. Her thoughts turned to what Conn would say when he heard that his king was free, if he had not heard it already.

"By the rood, Gandy, you're being a fool!"

"No doubt, master. So Margery herself said but yesterev'n."

"Women often say things they don't mean in the heat of the moment. Why, even Sira—"

"As sweet-spoken as she is? You'll never find anyone to believe that. The gentlest lady—never shrewish. My Margery has a viperish tongue, and I have suffered stings enough."

"Well, man, you can hardly blame her."

"I don't." The young man sat on the bench outside the tavern, his head clasped in his hands. His boots were dirty, for he'd walked the five miles between Hamdry Manor and Naswith, the next village, in the early morning hours. His nails were slightly blue while his nose ran from cold, yet he did not seem to mind the chill.

He said, "I offered to be whipped in her place, but she'd

not hear of it. I even went to my Lord Robert and con-
fessed that I was the man—''

''I know; I was present,'' Conn said, but Gandy was too
sunk in misery to heed him.

''I willingly paid her fine and my own. Faced with my
confession, she still refused to make her own. 'Twas her
insistence on claiming yet another lover that sent her
through town at the cart-tail.''

''Indeed, I know it.'' Conn remembered with the ache
of an old wound awakened by cold wind how bitter the
rift had been between Sira and himself. She had accepted
so much that seemed harsh or savage in this world, yet on
this point she stuck fast. For days, there had been tears,
recriminations, and bitter silences. Yet never once had she
hurled at him the sharpest weapon; she had never declared
that she wished she had not become mortal.

Gandy had raised his head to defend himself against an
attack that came only from his own conscience. Now he
dropped it again, heavily, into his waiting hands. ''My
child will be a bastard.''

''Not if you come with me now. Make one more attempt
to wed with her.''

''She has already refused me again and again. Even after
Lord Robert's order to marry me . . .'' He sighed, a tremor
going through him. ''All the sages and all the wizards
cannot answer one man's heart-borne cry: What makes a
woman so difficult?''

''You may as well ask what makes her a woman.''

Conn dismounted and tied Arundel's bridle to a tree
branch. He sat beside Gandy on the rough-hewn bench,
resting his gloved hand on his servant's back in a comforting fashion. ''How's the ale here?''

''Excellent. Sweet and clear.''

''Landlord!'' Conn bellowed.

A bald man in a leather apron came hurrying out, sweating so that his body steamed in the cold winter air. Seeing
Conn's surcoat, embroidered with his family badge of
hound and swan, together with the dagger on his hip and

the finely caparisoned horse, he bowed clumsily. "How may I serve your honor?"

"Ale. And another for my companion." As the landlord bowed himself away, Conn added, "Heat it with the fire iron!"

He said nothing further until it came, in earthenware jugs that he hoped had been washed within the last fortnight. Being married to Sira, who tolerated none of the dirt and uncleanliness that bred in a house with no woman to look after it, had spoiled him somewhat. To do her credit, there had been no outbreaks of sickness at Hamdry since she'd begun ordering life there.

Conn raised his mug and said, "To Margery and your child. *Wassail!*"

"Wassail!" Gandy echoed listlessly.

"As always, you judge an ale a-right," Conn said, sighing with satisfaction after lowering the level by half.

"That much I can do."

"Come, man. Gladden your heart. 'Tis not every day a man's first child is born."

"Without affront, master, I will give you the same advice when your good lady offers you a child. You will not be merry then but a-feared."

"Is that why you've walked five miles on a snowy morning to drink this excellent brew? Does the fear lessen with distance?"

"Should Margery die—"

"She won't. The finest midwife in these shires is come to attend my own lady. She'll do well by yours."

Gandy did not appear to heed these words of cheer. He only shook his head slowly. "Should she die, how will I tell our child why his parents were not wed? Will he believe that it was I alone who wished for it? Does it sound sensible that Margery would refuse me? Any other woman would have leapt at an offer to be honest. Would it not appear rather that I am a good-for-naught, a seducer and rogue with neither heart nor scruple?"

"You refine too much upon it," Conn said. "All will be well. You will win Margery yet."

"But how, master?" His cry was loud enough to bring out the landlord again, bowing deeply while flapping his apron. Conn dismissed the man with a straight look and a shake of the head.

"Do as I have told you. Return with me to Hamdry. Margery is in the throws of childbirth e'en now. Come to her. Beg for her hand. Cite the words of the church, my father, her father, and your own soul. I have heard it said that oft while in the toils of the childbed a woman will agree to anything. I have one or two small matters to bring up with Sira at such a time." Conn chuckled to show that this was mere humor, but Gandy stared at him so intently that Conn began to wonder if it wasn't actually a good idea.

Though she would declare that she loved him often, he rather wished to believe it more than he did. Sometimes he surprised her with a far-off expression in her eyes that he did not think was caused by dreams of her child. Even the excitement she showed when the babe moved within her could not entirely allay Conn's worries. Was she really his? How much of her heart did he hold? How much remained behind in the land where she had been all but queen?

He himself had dreams where he walked again on the perfect velvet greensward before the great pavilion. He flew again like the eagle and plunged past human depth into the sea. The marvels of his sojourn in the Living Lands did not trouble him during the day. He went about his duties and his pleasures and was content. But at night, he returned to the glories of the king's Great Hall, to feast, to be delighted with music, and to gaze upon Sira's beauty, greater than any mortal woman's.

"Are you coming with me?" Conn asked Gandy.

"I will. Though I know my Margery. She'd not change her mind upon the rack."

Sira came out to meet him as he rode up, Gandy clinging to the saddle. In a gown of ivory wool, she stood out against the gray stone, white snow, and black earth, her hair bundled up beneath a cloth so that there was nothing to distract his eye from her face. As Conn dismounted, he could have kicked himself for thinking that her beauty had faded since their marriage.

It had only deepened. Round as a tun, with pale cheeks and slight shadows under her eyes, Sira's beauty still had the power to stop his breath. A woman now—moreover, the one who bore his child under her heart—she had a warmth and character that she had lacked as a fay. Cool and exquisite though she had been, Conn much preferred the tender and gentle woman she'd become.

Even six months ago he would have caught her hard against his body when returning after even the briefest of absences. Now he took her outstretched hands and kissed them, one after the other. "I've brought the scoundrel back."

"As I see. Go up to her, Gandy."

"Will she want me, my lady?"

"I think so. She finally agreed to see Father Maynard. They—they say it will not be long now."

Snatching off his flat cap, Gandy hastened into the manor with a hop that turned into a run.

Sira laid her husband's arm about her shoulders and walked at a more sedate pace into the manor. Conn tossed a word to the groom as the servant came out to lead Arundel back to the stable. Arundel snorted a column of warm steam into the cold winter air as he walked away.

Smiling up at him, Sira asked merrily, "And did you have a fine ride, my lord?"

"Arundel did not wish to carry Gandy as well as myself. He seemed to think enough was enough. But I promised him extra oats in his ration, so he made no further objection."

As they walked over the threshold, Sira said, "Father Maynard would like to speak with you when you have bathed."

"I'll see him now. I think I will spend an hour or two in the tilting yard, then bathe after. What does he want?"

"He brings news from London. He is closeted with your father. They've been playing chess."

"Any bloodshed?"

"Not yet." Sira kept him by her when he would have dashed up the stairs. "Conn . . ." she began and then broke off as though searching for words.

"My love?" He put his hand over hers where it rested on his arm and looked down into her face. She could not meet his eyes.

"Don't let them persuade you into anything. Choose— choose for yourself."

She tried to smile, but it was not a success. Frowning, Conn wanted to learn what she meant. She held up her hands in mock surrender. "I'm being foolish—a woman's whim. Now go. Break up their match before one outdoes the other."

Sira sat alone in her chamber, trying to sew a linen shift for her child. Though she'd learned much since coming to Hamdry—how to mull wine, how to brew fine ales and meads, how to cook some courses, and how to make excellent perfumes—she had not taken to stitchery. She had not the patience, nor did her many efforts result in anything but a tangled thread and dirty cloth. Nonetheless, she felt determined that this child would wear at least one garment of his mother's making.

Though she'd spoken of it to no one, not even to Conn, she'd hoped that this effort would make her impending child more real to her. Even if she concentrated very hard, she could not believe that in a little more than another month she would hold her own infant in her arms. It seemed like a fantasy a Sleeper might have.

With an effort that did not become easier with practice, Sira wrenched her thoughts away from the image of the Sleepers, wrapped forever in perpetual slumber. Among them, floating in peace and tranquillity, was her own mother who, unable to bear the burden of her memories, had retired to sleep the millennia away, undisturbed.

"Oh, Mother," Sira said. "How I wish you were here now."

But no. She should not wish for such a thing. Her

mother would have hated to be here among so many mortals, and the fact that her own daughter was about to bring another into the world would have appalled her.

Sira sniffed as one tear after another fell upon the hapless linen cloth. "It's so hard," she said aloud. "I try and I try, but it's so hard." Liking the sound of this, she repeated it.

She knew, of course, that she was wallowing in self-pity, yet it seemed rather enjoyable at the moment to do so. No one could see her. If necessary, she would plaster on her bright smile and fool everyone into thinking her perfectly contented.

Except she knew that she hadn't fooled Conn for a moment. He had a way of trying to look deeply into her eyes as though he knew that was where she kept her deepest secrets. Even he, however, did not know how often her thoughts turned to the Sleepers.

It sounded so wonderful: to sleep without waking, endless dreams flowing seamlessly into one another. No villeins to reward or to punish. No endless descriptions of battles and feuds, every detail of which was debated between her father-in-law and his memory. No slaughter of animals, no unwashed visitors, no husband . . .

There her thoughts paused. How could she ever want to escape him? Even now, she could feel a thrill pass over her at the thought of Conn. His big body keeping her warm all night. His dealings with his people, strength and kindness mixed. More than one whispered that he would make a far better lord than his father, who still thought a rod of iron was the only way to govern. Most of all, though, his hands on her skin.

"Farewell, Sleepers," she said quite happily. The babe thrust a small hard knob—like a knee or elbow—against her side as though applauding her decision. Then someone knocked and she called out an invitation.

Helen's dark head peeped around the door. "Are you alone? I thought I heard you talking to someone."

Sira said, "No, there's no one. Come closer to the brazier. I think it's getting colder out."

Long tapestries covered the shuttered windows and only now and then rippled in a sudden shift of wind. This made her chamber dark but snug, like a gaily decorated cave. Several fat candles on pricket holders cast a glow over her work and cast deep shadows in the space beyond her chair. When the tapestries moved, sometimes the candlelight would pick out a face split by the nose piece of a Norman helmet, a pair of praying hands, or set a flower glowing against the dark background.

Helen sat only on the edge of the padded chest. She clasped her hands uneasily, looking out beyond the circles of candlelight with troubled eyes. "It's so unsettled downstairs," she said. "No one even lit our way up the stairs."

"Did Ross come with you?"

She nodded. "He's gone to be with his father and brother. This news from London—"

"You've heard it?"

"My father has many friends, some of the queen's faction, and some with the empress." Helen rocked her upper body back and forth like a nervous child trying to comfort itself. "He says that there's no reason for the wars to begin again. There's no reason for our men to go away."

"You're worried about Ross? But he isn't a knight. He has not been trained for war."

Helen sighed impatiently. "If Ross serves instead of my father, then we save the fees we must give when we have no men to send. Ross may not be a trained fighter like Conn, but he can swing a sword and sit upon a horse's back as well as any man alive."

Her simple pride in her husband's accomplishments was a lesson to Sira. She'd never publicly rebuke Conn—though she'd come close the day Margery had been flogged—though privately they often discussed their differing views. Sira thought Conn a marvelous man, but she'd never willingly blind herself to his faults, endearing though some of them were. She wondered if Helen had gotten over her initial disappointment in Ross's lovemaking.

Sira would never ask, of course. She had also never

asked Helen about the young girl's habit of spying. The incident in the garden had been but her first attempt to overhear what did not concern her. At least four more times during the summer months had Conn and Sira believed themselves alone, only to find Helen near at hand. Conn had thought this coincidental. Sira had her doubts. She began to guard her tongue around Conn as she curbed it when with the other humans to whom she now found herself sister, friend, and superior.

At Conn's request, Sira had never taxed Helen with her spying. Yet the suspicion kept Sira from forming the attachment to Helen that she should otherwise have done. She'd forgiven and all but forgotten the girl's haughty behavior that first day, putting it down to pique at having her own wedding interrupted and then surpassed.

Sira said, "I'm certain they'll come down to us soon."

"Not they!" Helen scoffed. "They drink the king's health a few times and then move on to the queen, Prince Eustace, and the whole royal household ere they tire."

Sira recollected her duties as a hostess. "Would you care for some hot wine, Helen?"

"If you will join me."

Sira pointed to the jug and goblets behind Helen, and the girl got up to get them. Sira knew this contradicted the rules of hospitality, but they had not been devised for women who needed help to rise from any chair that offered the least bit of comfort. Sira had heard from Walter de Burke of the exemplary behavior of his wife during childbirth: how she spun flax, sang prayers, and blessed both midwife and husband as she died.

Sira intended to emulate none of these virtues. Her thoughts turned to Margery. Soon she would go to her, and if Margery had not seen sense this time about Gandy . . . well, she would do *something*.

"None for me, thank you," Sira said in answer to Helen's questioning look. "The smell is pleasant enough, but the taste makes me queasy."

"A great shame, when you mix it so well."

"I hope soon to recover my taste for it." Sira shifted

in her seat as the babe writhed within her. "I vow this child will grow up to be a jongleur! He twists and turns like an acrobat already."

Helen looked down into her goblet. "I have heard that it is possible for another to feel the child move. Is this so?"

"Yes. Conn has felt it."

"May I?"

Sira hesitated. She did not like the attitude that mortals took, that a pregnant woman's belly belonged to all. To share her child's gyrations with her husband was a tender pledge of their future. To have all and sundry wish to share in this troubled her deeply. She'd granted both Father Maynard and Lord Robert the privilege and had felt vaguely uneasy the rest of the day.

Then Sira smiled, remembering how she and Margery had compared each babe's leaps and kicks to the other's. When Margery's child had gotten hiccups for an hour after she'd eaten, Sira had laughed to feel the repetitive jerks of her servant's rounded belly. If it had not been for Margery, how lost, frightened, and perturbed she would have been.

"Very well," Sira said. "Give me your hand."

The babe had grown so strong that his movements could be felt even through cloth. Taking Helen's hand by the wrist, Sira laid it flat against her. Then they waited, the younger girl bent at the waist.

"There!" Sira said. "Do you feel that?"

"No . . . oh!" Helen snatched her hand away. "Why does it do that?"

Sira raised her shoulders. "I cannot say. I think it must be as we are in sleep. Though our minds are far away, wandering in dreams, we still move our bodies."

"But what dreams could such a one have?"

"Who knows? Dreams of me, perhaps. Or of heaven. Father Maynard says that all children come from God."

Helen walked back to refill her cup. "I have been married for months now, yet no child stirs in my womb. Other women have babies right away, even as you conceived on your wedding night."

Sira thought that she'd actually become pregnant one
night earlier than that, but it was near enough to make no
difference. "It will happen in time," she said lamely.

"The old women tell me that if a woman doesn't become pregnant in her first year, she never will."

"Old women are foolish. You should not listen to
them."

Helen went on, unheeding. "I long for a babe of my
own. So does Ross. And my father . . . I can feel the disappointment in his eyes when he looks on me. If only . . .
why do women like Margery conceive out of wedlock
when I *want* it so much?"

Sira had run out of comforting things to say. She
watched Helen pacing, her long legs taking but three
strides to cover the floor. Her skirt swept the stones between the woven mats of straw. Sira remembered a lioness
from far away, pacing back and forth before the mouth of
some cave, ready to attack without mercy any who came
between her and her young. Suddenly, Helen stopped and
knelt before Sira, her hands grasping the sides of the chair.

Before the intensity of that radiantly pale young face,
framed by night-dark hair, Sira shrank back.

"I want you to promise me," Helen said swiftly, "that
if aught happens to you after your child is born, that you
will give it to me to raise."

"What?"

"Without you, Conn will away to the wars again. Lord
Robert is no fit guardian for a child, especially should it
prove a girl. But I—I will cherish it, care for it as though
it were my own in every way. Ross, too, will care for his
brother's child with the utmost tenderness, all the more as
there will be none of his own."

"Helen . . ." Sira touched the girl's cheek. "Do not be
so passionate. Firstly, you will have children of your own
in time. This nonsense of not bearing in your first year of
marriage means never . . . ! Folly! Secondly, all will be
well with me. I have no fear of dying through my child's
birth. And even if by some mischance aught should befall

me, Conn will never leave our child. He is too wild with excitement at the prospect.''

Slowly and rather heavily, Helen stood up. ''It is but a little thing to promise.''

''It's a very—'' Sira's sharp hearing caught the sound of the men coming out from Lord Robert's chamber. ''We'll speak no more of this, if you please.''

Conn came in, his brother and his father behind him. Sira had eyes only for her husband. He looked . . . different. He moved with even greater assurance, if such a thing were possible, and his amber eyes had a glow that she'd never seen before, not even when he had first taken her in his arms. A fear struck at her heart. As though in response, the child within her stopped moving.

Eighteen

Sira was determined that Conn should never know what
effort it took to keep her voice level and calm. She choked
down the scream of hurt and betrayal that struggled to
burst free. "You cannot even wait 'til our child comes? It
will not be so very long a time to tarry."

Though his equipage of chain mail, helmet, and sword
were all in high condition due to his constant practicing,
Conn still searched over every piece with meticulous care.
A spot of rust or a dark stain on his padded leather aketon
made him click his tongue like a housewife. At this from
Sira, however, he laid aside his shield and the bag of sand
he used to polish it.

"Sira, I do not mean to ride off today. It is only that I
want to be ready should a summons come."

"But it won't, will it?"

"Why not?" He turned again to polishing the shield.
Sira looked at his averted face and wondered what he was
keeping from her.

"The king still believes you to be blind, does he not?
Doesn't he?" Her voice wanted very badly to rise into that
shriek. Again, she forced it down.

He did not meet her eyes yet. "Walter de Burke has
friends in the queen's faction."

"So Helen has said."

"He wrote an account of me, saying that I am healed.

The king is sure to send for me. He and I . . . I don't know if a simple knight can claim a king's friendship, but we stood together in more than one clash, and I stood beside him as we fought the last battle at Lincoln. The king never forgets a comrade in arms. He'll send for me."

"You knew of Walter de Burke's letter, and yet you said nothing to me."

"I did not want to worry you."

"You are too kind," she said, her voice like a fall of icicles.

As though not wanting to acknowledge her anger, Conn went on talking about the war. "I've already missed raising the siege of Winchester. Did you hear how the empress fled? It's rumored she had herself tied to a bier as though she were a corpse and then was carried away from her starving army. They say she had but one man-at-arms with her."

"She must be brave, for all her faults."

"Oh, I'll grant her that. But she is proud and arrogant withal and so headstrong that only her brother holds any sway over her. Certainly her husband has none!"

"I cannot blame her for that. Husbands are not always satisfactory."

Now he looked at her, and Sira thought it very unfair that *his* eyes should look wounded when it was she who was wronged. He said her name warmly but she hugged her anger to herself and would not melt.

"You have to understand, my love. You have given me my sight. For that, among other things, you have my whole gratitude and love."

"Your love? How much of that can I have when you are determined upon leaving me? Where is the king now?"

"At last report, he is resting in Kent until he is crowned again."

"Kent? That is far off. You may forget me."

Now he laughed as though she were a foolish child. Conn put his arms around her, ignoring her stiff back and how she turned her cheek when he would have kissed her lips. "I should forget everything ere I forgot you. But you

cannot ask me to forget my honor. I am the king's man
and will be 'til I die. Fate and you have made me fit for
battle once again. Would you have me live in your lap,
Sira?''

"Yes!" she shot back.

"You don't mean that. Unless you would have a man
who'd come to heel whenever you call? I am not such a
man.''

"No. I know it.''

"Then kiss me. And when the day comes, send me off
with pride.''

Sira wanted to weaken, to feel his arms clasping her
closely. But before her eyes was a dark picture of a trodden
field soaked in blood. Among the dead men and horses
clouds of flies swirled and danced or crawled, heavy with
feeding upon the bodies of the dead. Conn lay among
them, eyes forever sightless turned up to a brilliant sky of
blue and white.

She forced herself free of his arms. "I have come into
this world only to be with you, Conn of Hamdry. Now
you want to go leave your life upon some field of honor.
What comes to me then?''

"I—''

"Go then. Play your games of kings and queens. I will
be here if you return. I have no choice.''

She could not run out of the small armory off the stables, being too ungainly to attempt it. But she could sweep
out with considerable dignity, though tears stung her eyes.
Once outside, she still could not let them flow. Too many
idlers stood about, gossiping with all their might and main
about the news from the outside world.

She understood Conn's excitement. He was a warrior,
and though he'd not been discontented during this year,
she'd seen his restlessness. A restlessness best assuaged by
either practice with sword and shield or by making love
to her. Lately, he'd been practicing more and more. It was
the only thing that made him sleep soundly. Part of her
wanted to be understanding, to let him go off to be what
he was trained to be.

The rest of her, however, shook with terror at the thought of losing him. No one else shared her secret. To no one else could she confide her confusion at the thousand things any human-born woman would know from the cradle. When Conn left Hamdry, she would be utterly alone. Why did this not concern him more? Could it be that she was less necessary to him than he'd given her to believe?

Parrish, the steward, stepped out of the manor and searched the crowd. As soon as Sira saw him, she knew what he wanted to tell her. "Margery?" she asked.

"Yes, my lady. The midwife says it will not be long now."

"And Gandy?"

"She still refuses to see him." Parrish's forehead settled into creases. "This looks very bad, my lady. How are we to impress the young girls with the evils of such conduct if we allow Margery to flaunt her license in this way? Lord Robert says she must be sent away."

Sira sighed and raised her eyes heavenward. Though she still found religion as Father Maynard practiced it bewildering, she had more than once taken comfort from the idea of a greater being watching over her. After a second sigh, Sira said, "Tell my lord. He is within. I shall attend on Margery this instant. When you are done with your master, send the priest to the chamber."

"At once, my lady."

The stairs were exhausting. Sira did not know for how much longer she'd be able to climb them. The midwife had recommended Sira keep to her rooms for the next several weeks. She'd fought the idea at first, the idea of never getting out under the sky had utterly appalled her. Now it sounded like an unimaginable luxury.

Gandy sat on the floor outside the room where Margery lay. "She won't see me, my lady."

"She'll see me. Get up, or you'll ruin those leggings!"

Sira saw with satisfaction that sharpening her tone meant instant obedience. What a pity it would not work on Conn! But no, she did not want to rule her husband any more than she cared to be ruled by him.

She entered the chamber. The candles brought close to the bed illuminated a scene that struck Sira with terror. The sweating midwife, the squirming woman on the bed, her face distorted with pain, and a strange, sweetish smell cutting through fire smoke and the scent of hot wax seemed to whirl around Sira as though caught up in a vortex. She wanted to run out, slam the door, never to return.

Instead, she swallowed down the bile in her throat and went to kneel, clumsily, beside Margery. She called her servant's name twice, answered only with grunts. Then, whatever crisis held her in its grip, relaxed. Margery panted heavily before saying, "I did not think you were coming back."

"I said that I would. How—how are you?"

Mistress Yalter answered, as she poured herself a mug of wine. "She's a strong girl, and this child is in a hurry to come. It shan't be long now."

"So you've been saying for the last hour!" Margery let her head fall back on the sweat-stained pillow. She searched with her hand among the covers until she grasped Sira's. "It's not so bad as I had heard tell," she said. "The pain . . . comes and goes. Don't be afraid."

"I'm not," Sira lied, and her smile must have looked natural, for Margery nodded, letting her eyes close.

"Margery? Margery, Gandy is outside. He wants to see you." The maidservant's head tossed on the pillow, a motion that could be mistaken for either yes or no. "Margery, if you don't marry him, Lord Robert will force you to leave the manor. You don't want that. How could you and your child live?"

"I'd make a life for us. Mayhaps in town."

"Would you walk there? In winter? Don't be a fool. Whatever your reasons for not taking Gandy before, you must think of your child now."

"I have been thinking of it. The priest said that it is wrong to let my sins rest upon an innocent babe. I did not want to listen to him, but he is right."

"Yes, he is right. I have seen how such children are treated. How cruel this world can be!"

Margery sighed as though all the weight of the world were resting on her. "Aye. Let him come in. And the priest, too."

Before Sira could get up, another pain struck Margery. Her hand tightened on Sira's unmercifully. Sira bit her lip to keep from joining Margery in her cry of pain.

The midwife put down her mug unfinished. "Another already? Well, if you will be wed afore this child is born, my girl, you'd best to be about it!"

Conn appeared in the doorway as Father Maynard hurried through a wedding service. Gandy had taken Sira's place beside the bed. Tears were rolling down his cheeks unchecked and probably unnoticed. The vows were punctuated by Margery's groans and gasps.

Conn put his hand on Sira's shoulder. "She gave in?"

"As you see."

"Sira, please."

"What is it?"

"Don't be cold to me. I can't bear to see your eyes so distant."

"Yet you'll go off to a greater distance still. How will you see my eyes then?"

"In my memory. Let it be of my loving, laughing wife."

"You ask too much."

Sira went forward, tugging at the ring on her finger. She'd grown plump since her pregnancy, and it did not slide off so easily. Finally, it came off, leaving a red indentation under her knuckle. "Here," she said, offering the ring to Gandy. "Since you have none of your own."

"Oh, but I have, my lady. I bought it in London, long ago."

Margery panted, "For what woman did you buy it? Never me. You had never met me yet."

"No, 'tis true. Yet I saw it on a lady's hand and swore such a ring would one day be worn by my bride."

He dipped into the pouch slung on his belt, bringing out a slender fillet of silver. "I was told by the wizard who made it that should love ever die, this ring would tarnish, but so long as love burned, it would gleam bright. Of course, if he'd been any good, they wouldn't have hanged him!''

He gave the ring to the priest. Everyone watched carefully to see that the blessing did not turn the admittedly bewitched ring into anything else, like a serpent or a spider. When this part went well, Father Maynard returned the ring to Gandy. As he slipped it on Margery's finger, for a moment she looked as pretty and shy as any other bride. Then a greater pain than before hit her hard.

''All you men begone!'' Mistress Yalter said in a tone that brooked no argument.

Gandy snatched a kiss from his wife's gleaming cheek ere he left, and the priest paused a moment to sketch a second cross over the bed. Conn tightened his arm around Sira and said in a hurried whisper, ''Is it wise for you to stay?''

''I don't know, but I am staying.''

Sira said all that was proper, though she did not think the infant either beautiful nor even human in appearance. New-wet and making shocking sounds, the girl child lay on her mother's breast. Margery could not take her eyes from her child. ''Look at her,'' she said for the second time. ''Look how she holds on already. Clever, like her father.''

''Shall I go get Gandy?'' Sira said, eager to be elsewhere.

Mistress Yalter said sharply, ''Not 'til they are clean. If you want to be of help, Lady, fetch me some more clouts and another drink of this wine. For the mother,'' she added virtuously, though most of the previous carafe had gone down her own throat.

Sira sent Adela for the cloths and went herself for the wine. She was surprised to find when she looked through an arrow loop that it was still day, for it had seemed she'd been in the other chamber for hours uncounted. The candles in her room had been blown out; she supposed she must thank Helen for saving her the price of wax candles.

She reached out for the bottle of wine when something struck her amiss.

A sleeve fluttered out of a chest, caught when the lid closed. Sira felt certain *she* had not left it thus. The ivory comb that Conn had given her when she'd told him of her pregnancy was no longer on the shelf before the mirror. It lay on the floor, fortunately landing half on a mat, otherwise a tooth might have been broken. The wind might have blown off the comb, were the shutters not tight and the tapestries still hanging unruffled. Besides, how could wind open the thick lid of an oaken chest?

Sira looked inside. She'd learned to be meticulous about how her gowns were folded, for she had no fondness for wrinkles. Now, though still neat, they were not folded in *her* way. Someone had gone through all her things. Dust and fibers from the mat on a few garments told her that they'd been taken out, shaken and then thrown on the floor. Then they'd been refolded and replaced in the chest.

Sira stood up, her knees protesting that she'd been on them too long. Adela had no reason to search her room, for she'd seen everything Sira owned in her days since Margery had become too ungainly to be useful. Mistress Yalter and Margery had been otherwise engaged. The men could be dismissed from her thoughts, both low and high, for she knew full well that none of *them* ever thought of folding a thing! Sira did not want to admit that Helen was the most likely suspect.

Sira had hid her true feelings well enough when told the first time that her husband looked forward to returning to war. She'd even joined them in a toast to the king, though she'd not so much as wetted her lips in the wine. Then as soon as she could, she followed him down to the armory to talk to him. Had Helen gone with Ross? Or had she stayed behind, seizing the opportunity to do more prying?

Well, if she had, she had discovered but little. Except for the cloak of fox fur, now spread across the bed she and Conn shared, and the mirror, nothing else had come with Sira out of the Wilder World. Every stitch, from her hair nets to her shoes, came from Hamdry. Lord Robert had kindly arranged to have one of her own rubies set in a pendant for her, and this she wore on a fine golden chain about her neck.

She considered telling Conn about the condition of their room. Looking about her again, Sira noticed that his particular chest had not been mauled about. None of his things had been touched, in fact. Sira decided to keep Helen's search a secret. Conn had other things now to worry about.

As though her thought had conjured the reply, a horn call sounded loud and clear, reaching Sira even through the shuttered windows. It repeated, more loudly and therefore closer. For a moment, she stiffened, wondering if this heralded the news she dreaded. Footsteps ran past her door; Gandy, at a guess, sent by his new wife to discover what the to-do was about.

Sira followed slowly, her outstretched hand brushing the curving wall. Servants clustered about in the open hall, their chatter rising to meet her. Unnoticed, Sira reached the last step. "What's happening?" she mumbled, trying to sound like Margery or Adela.

Without looking around, a kitchen boy said, "A messenger. They do say 'e comes from the king himself!"

"Oh?" Sira felt her heart begin a long, slow slide into the pit of her stomach.

"Aye. I can't hear what they be sayin' though. Here, Parrish! What they be sayin'?"

The steward searched among the servants with a chilly gaze, intent on finding the one who'd spoken so cheekily. Instead, his sight fixed on Sira. "My lady!"

Heads turned in her direction, including that of the grubby kitchen lad. He made a sound in his throat not unlike "Urk!" Sira gave him a reassuring smile. The servants stepped aside to make an aisle for her to pass. Though Sira did not in the least want to go forward, their expectation impelled her on.

Reaching the tall steward's side, Sira asked, "What are they saying, Parrish?"

"The messenger is reading out a letter from King Stephen."

"But he was only freed—that is, the news has only just come."

"It seems that His Grace was exchanged for Robert of Gloucester in November, my lady. The letter sends his goodwill and fatherly love to Sir Conn. His Grace requests that he return in time to see him crowned anew."

Sira had wept with Conn when word of the king's harsh treatment had come to his knight. The pleadings of his queen at the feet of the enemy had awakened chords of sympathy in Sira; she could see herself in that position, willing to give up every hope of future happiness in order to secure the freedom of the man she loved.

However, she found it increasingly difficult to give even the appearance of joy at Stephen's release. For her, it would have been best if he'd remained manacled to his cell wall in Bristol. She made her way into the great hall, where the messenger, a surprisingly young man, sat with his sweaty hair spiking up around his brow while he thirstily drained a mug. He stood up when Sira entered.

She murmured words of greeting as she approached Conn. He and his father leaned together against the high table, appearing like brothers in their excitement. Lord Robert's voice was merry as he said, "This is a great day for our house, daughter! The king himself has sent for Conn—wants him present at the crowning!"

"A great honor," Sira said noncommittally as she watched her husband.

Conn said, "It *is* a great honor. He wrote that as I now have eyes, it is his wish I should see him crowned. Then he offers me a place in his personal company."

"I had not realized that there was so much love between you."

"The king is a warm man," Conn began, but his father smote him a blow between the shoulders.

"Warm! He's as good a man, as good a king, as was ever put into the crown! So he was ousted by a thrawn woman and a council of weasels in church robes! Archbishop Theobald'll crown him again, and long life to him!"

A cheer went up from the waiting servants and with it, they poured into the room. They clapped their hands as Lord Robert started an impromptu speech, fueled by wine.

Conn scowled past Sira so darkly that she turned to look over her shoulder, afraid he might be looking so at her. She saw that the messenger's cheeks had grown red and that he was studying the ceiling with more concentration than the smoke-stained beams warranted. "What is it?" she asked, while Lord Robert covered their voices with his bluster.

"He was staring at you."

"Was he? He's probably never seen a whale before."

"It wasn't in awe but in lust."

"Oh, now, come," Sira said.

"Do you think I can't tell? With child or without, you are the most beautiful woman in England. I don't know how I shall bear riding with him, the insolent hound!"

"Riding with him?"

"The king's summons must be obeyed at once. Ross and I will ride out with the messenger tomorrow." Conn's big hand covered hers. He trapped her eyes with his own. "I know you are not happy with this turn of events. Believe me, I would have stayed until spring had this message not come."

"I believe you. And I am afraid."

That night, for the first time, Sira heard the music. It wound up like smoke from the courtyard, creeping in through the seams in the shutters. Distant, yet clear, remote, yet sharp, it awakened her out of as deep a sleep as she could remember.

Conn slept on, his elbow thrown over his face, even while Sira slipped out of bed. The song was neither sad nor merry, yet it drew her as though with a promise. Simple notes followed each other, rarely varying in volume but wavering hauntingly in intensity.

Sira looped back the tapestry. Leaning out, she opened the shutters to the motionless, frigid air. The air was so crisp that, even though she had nothing but moonlight, she felt she could see for miles. The tumbled stones that crowned the hill beyond showed up with such clarity that it seemed she need only reach out her hand to touch them.

Despite her opening the window, the music did not grow any clearer, though she could now tell that it was a wind instrument; a horn or a flageolet? It stirred something in her memory, with a half-glimpsed flash and ripple, like a fish rising to the surface of a pond for a moment only to flip away.

Though a simple song that she could have repeated after but one playing, she felt that it took great skill to play it this well. She'd heard of no players wandering about the area now. Lord Robert would have hired so brilliant a performer on the spot. Therefore, it must be someone from the manor. Mentally, she reviewed who on the manor could play so beautifully. Sexburga, who spun so fine a thread, was said to pluck the strings of a lute with fingers made strong with spinning. Or Ambrose, the beekeeper, who strummed the rebec to soothe his tiny friends.

Sira glanced at Conn, hoping he'd wake to help her determine who played this night. Whoever it was deserved no more menial work but would be raised to playing for Lord Robert's family meals. This music would have soothed Saul and driven out his demons.

"Conn?" She walked over and laid her hand on his cheek. Usually, he'd wake at any sound, his senses trained by long watches when a missed noise could mean the enemy could attack with surprise.

Conn did not stir. Then Sira paused, staring at the shuttered candle by the bedside. Even on very still nights, the flame would move. Yet tonight it stood straight . . . too straight. Sira waved her hand at it, and still it did not flicker. She saw that the white wax had ceased flowing down the side, and the melted wax at the base of the wick did not pucker in the heat of the flame.

Sira knew now who played music in the courtyard, music that awakened no one but herself because it had enchanted everyone else. Even the whimpering of Margery's babe had stilled at last. No use in trying to wake anyone.

Dragging the fox cloak off the bed, Sira swirled it

around her, thanking heaven that she'd bestirred herself enough before sleep to slip on a night robe, despite making up her quarrel with Conn. She'd never enjoyed the human custom of sleeping naked.

The door made no sound as she opened it. Though nothing would wake Conn until the enchantment ended, she couldn't help glancing back to see if he'd moved. His breathing continued, deep, slow breaths.

The stairs seemed even steeper at night, with the torches out. However, a strange greenish glow seemed to emanate from walls and stones, the very steps themselves giving off a slight illumination. Sira peeped into the great hall where the house servants slept, tumbled together or off alone, lying on the strewn rushes of the floor.

Sira did not like this custom, either, though she understood it was impossible to build a separate room for each servant. She did intend, however, to see that married persons at least should be given privacy, even if it meant building outside the walls. Lord Robert did not see the sense of it; she'd persuaded Conn using a method she could not employ on his father. Conn was teachable, at least. She thought of all *she* had learned from *him,* and half-decided to return to her place beside him in their bed. But no, she wanted to find the musician.

Sira found the massive front door slightly ajar. That was sensible of someone, she thought. It will do no one any good if I break my back striving to get it opened.

The cold did not strike her to the bone but seemed friendly. Sira hurried outside, bare feet and all. "Father? Father?"

But in the time it had taken for her to work her ungainly self down the steps and outdoors, the music had stopped. Had her thoughts of Conn driven her father away?

She felt no sense of an enchantment withdrawn; everything still seemed to be *waiting.* Sira said again, "Father?"

Disappointed, Sira turned to go back into the manor. The hall loomed like a dark mouth against the luminescence of snow and moonlit stones. She drew the cloak more closely around her. Without the music, the silence of the countryside settled like a burden. There were not even owls out, searching with silent flight for a meal.

She wiped her feet free of slush as she entered. The glow that had guided her before had gone out. She heard a mutter and sigh from the hall as someone turned over in their sleep. She could wake someone to light her way.

Sira shook her head. Why disturb some hardworking manservant's sleep merely because it was dark? It wasn't as though she could lose her way.

The long staircase seemed to have grown since she'd left. It seemed as endless as a beanstalk twisting into the sky. It had certainly not been so long as this when she'd come down earlier. Struggling upward, she strove to keep her hand on the stone aisle, set into the wall. Then her foot slipped.

"It was nothing," she said to herself. "I will be more careful."

Then her foot slipped again, finding no purchase whatever on the worn stairs. With a wriggle, she managed to fall more on her side than on her front. Yet even so, she slid down the stone steps, her head hitting the edge of the last one.

Nineteen

Afterward, Sira was to torture herself with the remembrance that she'd been the one to insist that Conn go. If she had not played down her injuries, laughing off the bruise on her temple and the ache in her side, if she had wept and moaned and kept him by her, Conn might have hated her, but he should have lived.

Christmas, her first in the mortal realm, tried her high. Everyone on the manor looked forward to the days between Christmas Eve and Twelfth Night with eager anticipation. She heard much of the grand feasts that would be held in the hall, to which every man jack on the manor would be invited. There'd be white bread, two kinds of meat, apples, cheeses, and the great boar's head decorated with holly and ivy. The children were beside themselves with excitement and little was done on the manor that did not relate directly to the great day.

Lord Robert, who loved all mummers and manner of minstrelry, hired every troupe he heard tell of, even sending a messenger hot-foot to track down a particularly clever group. Margery said, "Aye, your dowry's gone to his head. It'll go quick, being spent on such foolishness."

"I don't begrudge him his joy," Sira said.

Helen sniffed. "Nor do I," she said, unexpectedly agreeing with Sira. She'd moved into Hamdry after Ross had gone off with Conn. Walter de Burke had not remained long at home. Like most men, he was eager to be away to the king's court, for that was again the center of all life and honor.

Helen added, "It's not a life I'd like, wandering about in all weathers and all conditions, searching for a warm corner to lay my head. And being run out of town more often than not because plays are the work of the devil."

"You've given it much thought," Sira said.

"Some. When I was a girl, I thought it would be wonderful to be a traveling player. I am wiser now. Fair enough in the spring and high summer, but now . . ." She gave a realistic shiver. "No indeed."

The cold had set in with a vengeance the day after Conn had gone. Snow fell, turned to ice, only to be buried by more snow. Tree limbs snapped under the weight and at least one villein's roof had fallen in. The air smelled constantly of smoke as fires burned in even the meanest hut.

Helen sat at her embroidery frame for long hours, keeping Sira company. After her fall, Mistress Yalter had recommended that Sira remain not only in her room, but abed. The first few days had been heavenly; but that had been two weeks ago. Now Sira fretted and would hop out whenever she was left alone. That happened but rarely.

Margery hovered like a mother bird. She wore little Emma slung around her neck in a broad shawl, and half the time, Sira did not even know she was there. She did not find that a baby improved on closer acquaintance. They seemed to be a great deal of trouble for little or no reward.

Helen was often in the room, having few subjects of interest in common with her father-in-law. She did have a remarkable talent for embroidery and worked constantly setting stitches in a border for a new cope for Father Maynard. The twisting pattern of grape leaves and acorns was something that Sira herself would not have been ashamed to conjure up in her former life.

Sira had not heard another note of the strange music since Conn had left.

Margery sighed as she dusted. " 'Tis hard to believe

another Yule is upon us. Seems but yesterday 'twas spring.''

"Much has happened since the spring," Sira said, echoing Margery's sigh.

They fell silent for a moment, each missing her man, away on the unfathomable business of men. Sira would never understand the fascination of war.

Then Helen said, "Tell us a tale to while the hours 'til we eat, Sira. That one about the dragons."

"No, my lady," Margery said eagerly. "The one about Princess Goldenrod and her long, long hair."

"I know!" Helen said, changing her mind. "The children and the glass mountain."

"My dears . . ." Sira said, holding up her hands and laughing. "I will tell you a story. Something new."

"Wait." Margery laid down her cloth and hurried to the door. "I'll fetch Adela. She loves your stories."

The tales Sira told were the deeds of her People and the tricks they played on humans and sometimes in aid of them. Her only difficulty came in rearranging the words so that she did not seem to be favoring The People over the mortals. She had to remember her audience's sympathies were firmly with the horrid little girls, nasty small boys, long-suffering goose girls, and selfish princes. Privately, she felt sometimes that they deserved everything they got, though she would always gift Helen, Margery, and Adela with a happy ending.

Though she knew not to expect word from Conn, she couldn't help but be disappointed as the days slipped past like pearls off a string without that word. Everyone knew the king was to be crowned again on Christmas Day, and Father Maynard said a special prayer during Mass for the deliverance of the kingdom from war.

The first Christmas feast was celebrated in high style. Sira did her best to participate, but she'd felt strange all day. Being used to leaning backward to balance her weight, she found it odd that she could straighten up without feeling like being on the point of tipping over. However, she ate well, more than she usually did.

Mistress Yalter approached her as the dancing began after the Christmas feast. "It shall not be too long now."

"The dancing? Hardly. If I know my family, it will go on until dawn."

"No, my lady. Your child. I have seen many and a-many births. It seems to me that you have lightened, which means it will not be long ere—"

"Oh, my." Sira put her hand on the smooth arc of her abdomen. To her surprise, she did notice a change. "Good. I am tired of being so ungainly."

"Yes, that's common. Send your woman to me at any hour; I shall be prepared."

"Thank you, Mistress Yalter. You have been all that is kind."

The older woman gave her a slight curtsy. "Send your friends to me, my lady."

Despite the hope this conversation gave Sira, her child showed no signs of being in a hurry to enter the world. Every twinge gave Sira pause. The thought would cross her mind that *this was it* only to have nothing further occur. Though at times she even suffered a cramp or two, which Margery said had been her first hint that little Emma was on the way, still no more progress was made.

Dozing in her room one dark afternoon a week after Twelfth Night, Sira wandered in her own land. She saw again the multicolored roofs made of lost bird feathers, trod a measure on the greenway, and beheld the face of her father, smiling at her. She smiled in answer and became slowly aware that someone called her name.

Blinking, she saw Lord Robert bending over her, rubbing her hand. With much effort, Sira sat up. "My lord? What is it?"

"I'm sorry to wake you, daughter. Especially as you were smiling in your sleep."

"Was I? I was dreaming. . . ."

Focusing more clearly, Sira saw that Lord Robert's face was gleaming most oddly. Then she realized his cheeks were wet with tears. Her hand twisted under his, a certain knowledge striking her with a physical agony.

"Father!" she cried, giving him that name for the first time. "What . . . Is it Conn?"

"Dead," Lord Robert said. "In a skirmish near Oxford. The king—the king himself has sent word."

Sira heard nothing more. She saw her father-in-law's lips moving, saw the tears flow again to mingle with his beard, but the words went by her as though she stood beside a raging cataract of floodwater. "I knew this would happen," she said.

The pain was too sharp for tears. She felt that if she cried, if she even breathed too heavily, then she would break into a thousand tiny shards. Dimly, her hearing returned. She heard people talking. She thought it might be Lord Robert and Father Maynard, but their voices weren't clear. Only a few words made sense.

"It is not wise to love a mortal man so much."

Was it Father Maynard? Somehow the voice seemed higher, more feminine.

"To fix one's heart so wholly on a fallible creature is almost a sin."

Sira wanted to speak, to protest, but still that feeling of being very carefully balanced as though upon a spear's point remained with her.

"We could have told you it would end this way."

"Who's there?" Sira whispered. "Who is it?"

"We could have told you it would end this way. You didn't listen."

Sira opened her eyes. The shadows thrown up by a single candle danced on the walls, looming over her, closing in. "Margery? Margery!"

"Yes, my lady?" She was there, quite near the bed, her child cradled against her breast.

Sira relaxed against the bolster. "I had such a strange dream. It frightened me. I dreamed . . . oh, I dreamed that Lord Robert came and told me Conn was dead. Killed near Oxford." Sira started to laugh at the absurdity of it until she looked into Margery's face. "It's true?"

The tears came then. Margery tried to comfort her with words of Conn's bravery, his nobility, and his love for her.

These failed. Sira did not tell her friend or anyone that she wept not for Conn but for herself.

Her labor began that night. The power and the pain swept through her. She was battered about by them as though she were a lifeless hulk tossed in a storm-bedeviled sea. Lost in the misery of losing Conn, she allowed herself to become that wreck and let the wind and waves do what they would. When, after untellable hours, they laid her son on her skin, she hardly looked at him. She did not want to see the brown eyes they told her were exactly like Conn's.

Her head and arms muffled in a shawl, Sira walked through the snow. Against the brick wall, the climbing stalks that had once bent beneath the weight of a thousand roses clung gray and dead to what they'd once adorned. Though it was so cold that if she closed her eyes she could feel the warmth of her lids, she seated herself upon the ground.

"It was here," she said. "This is where I first saw him."

She looked up into the sky, so pale and far-off a blue. "Father Maynard says you're up there, somewhere. Seems so strange . . . when you were buried in the earth."

Weeping might have warmed her cheeks, but she had no more tears left to cry. She felt dry and weary, her fingers a bundle of twigs, her skin but an old leather bag to carry her bones in. Rising, for she was too restless to stay anywhere for long, she wandered in the snow-shrouded garden, the white snow crunching beneath her feet.

"Two weeks . . . it takes so long to die." Her stomach had stopped rumbling at last, just as the blood had stopped flowing from when she had given birth. "They say he's a strong child, Conn. Strong like you. But you died. Or did you? Sometimes you seem like you are with me—right here." She looked around, really expecting for the moment to see him, his dark hair lit by the sun, his eyes smiling at her.

"I'm not mad," she said. "I'm not. Not yet."

She turned her face upward again to catch what weak sunshine there was. Something flickered in the corner of her eye by the wall and she tried to see, without appearing to. Was it Helen, she wondered, still spying?

"No. Helen's with the baby. She'd take her meals and sleep there if Margery allowed it. Sweet Margery . . . and Lord Robert. He guards that child as though it were a king's ransom." She chuckled to herself, cutting off the sound when she heard a mutter of voices. Sometimes clouds appeared before her eyes, dark spots and swirling lights, but her hearing remained faerie-sharp.

"Mad as a leper," Father Maynard whispered.

"Poor child," Lord Robert said and sniffed as though keeping back tears. "Ever since she struck her head. Then the shock came as too much of a blow."

"Never were two hearts more closely intertwined."

"Aye, so you've said before. What is she doing now?"

Again the smooth pate of the priest appeared above the wall. Sira almost laughed; he looked as though he feared to catch an arrow in his ear. "She's just standing there," Father Maynard said. "Hold steady, man! Do you want me to fall?"

Sira was torn between confronting them or giving the performance of a madwoman, hopping about on one foot or making noises like a chicken. She was not mad—not yet!—merely grieved to the heart with a sickness that knew only one cure. If Conn rode back, what sorrow would she know? He could go off to a war for thirty years, conquer the Holy Land or China, so long as he came back!

She remembered making him the offer, promising him everything, and he'd chosen her. Was the holding of her worth less than the anticipation? Was that why he left her?

Sira forgot about the men watching her from behind the wall. She began to wander aimlessly about the garden again. It could be that she was mad, she thought. *I've heard that music every night this week. I search for the player; I never see him. If only I could find him. . . .*

As though to tease her, she heard the flute or hautbois echoing from every corner of the garden. She spun about, trying to fix on a source. "Oh, please," she said in no begging tone, but as one who had had just about enough!

She glanced at Father Maynard, whose head still stuck up above the wall. His eyes were wide open, unblinking, one hand in the act of reaching out for a better handhold.

"My lord Father," Sira said, "please show yourself."

A sudden breeze stirred up a small whirlwind of dead leaves, fine-spun snow, and ice crystals. It spun and fell to earth, flinging the debris across an unbroken sweep of snow. Sira stared at it, frowning in concentration, until it ceased to seem a random scattering and resolved into a pattern. A face lay across the snow, drawn much larger than life size.

The thick eyebrows, the long hair lying on broad shoulders, the long, hooked nose, and a mouth with something of cruelty in its lines were as familiar to her as her own features. The face began to mold itself, developing from the bare sketch yet remaining completely monotone. White, silver, and gray, the image grew clearer from the debris and snow shadows.

Sira knelt down and said, "My lord?"

The eyelids opened as the lips took in a deep breath of air. "Sira. . . ." His voice was deep and grave, loud enough to send snow cascading from tree limbs.

"Yes, Father. I am here."

"Come back. Return to your People and the Lands of Wonder."

"I want to. Conn is dead. There is nothing for me here now."

"What of this child? This mortal child . . ."

Sira said, "There is nothing that holds me here. This is not the way my life should be. Yet how can I return to you? You said my choice would be for always."

"I have considered this for a long time. I believe there is a way."

"What way? I will do anything rather than stay in this empty world."

"Go to the fountain."

No water flowed there now. The stone was green where

the slime had dried and been blown away. A rime of snow lay in the basin, and lying on top the snow was a dagger that looked as though it had been made of ice. Sira hesitated before reaching for it. It had a deadly look with its long, undulating blade and point that was so sharp it was nearly invisible.

Sira picked it up and hissed, for the cold of it burned her hand. Nevertheless she held it and turned to show her father.

"Good. To return to us, you must destroy your human soul. Once it is done, you will be one of The People once again. You will again see the secret ways and regain your own power."

"Yes, I understand. What must I do? Suicide?" And she held the glacial blade to her breast, ready to strike at a word. The dagger seemed to twitch in her hand as though it would drink her blood rather than stab. A buzzing came into her head and she realized it was the dagger singing a song of blood. Sira could almost see the red drops falling on the snow like the rubies she'd brought to Hamdry on her wedding day.

"Stop!" The booming voice from the snow king seemed to shake the air. "That is not the way."

"Tell me. I'll do anything."

"Kill the child. Once it is dead, your human soul dies, too. You will be with your People once again."

"Kill the child?" she echoed wonderingly. Her gaze rose to the top of the manor, just visible above the garden wall. It was later in the day than she thought. Margery would be done with nursing it. Lord Robert was on the other side of the wall, frozen in time. Helen . . . hadn't she gone riding over to see if all was well at her father's manor?

"Father, shall I remember?" she asked.

"You shall forget everything. The wicked mortal who stole you away, the child, all that you have seen. You will be my own once again, and we shall be happy as we were."

"As we were. Yes. Yes, that is what I want."

As though she were dreaming, Sira passed through the garden door. Lord Robert was there, his back bent as he supported the fat priest for as long as her father's will held them there. Once inside the manor, the bustle and fuss of another day surrounded her but did not touch her. The servants had already grown used to seeing the lady Sira glide among them like a pale ghost and only the youngest remarked it anymore. If anyone saw the hand that clutched the icy dagger lost in the folds of her skirt, they shouted no warning.

Before Sira's eyes was a vision of her home. It was never too cold there or too hot. The fires did not smoke and sting your eyes so that you could hardly see for the tears. The air was always sweet with the scent of flowers or of fresh rain. All was merriment, lightness, and joy. No sorrow stained the earth. She longed for these things with a heart sore with weeping.

As she climbed the stairs, she thought of these things. Then she heard a sniveling squall and her all-but-frozen hand tightened further on the gleaming haft. One strike and she would be as she was before. Never again would she meddle with mortals. She would go her way, careless, in-different, and heartless. The rumor of her beauty would reach even the mortal world, and poets would love her in despair, knowing they'd never meet her like. All that stood between her and a return to the Wilder World was one insignificant life.

The cradle, dark wood, lay in the warmest corner of the room, muffled by hangings. The whimpering was repeated, a snuffling, aimless sound. Sira snatched back the curtains, her hand raised to strike with all her force.

A dark-eyed, dark-haired child lay in the cradle, his legs and arms splayed like a starfish thrown up from the sea. If she had not stopped to look, the moment would have gone past between one heartbeat and the next. Her arm fell to her side as her gaze went instinctively to his face, so small that it would fit in the palm of her hand.

He stared at something that only he could see. She turned to look at what held his attention so fixedly. The

white cloth that lay in the cradle with him had fallen down
from the side, revealing the dark wood. His eyes, so tiny
yet so round, moved between the dark and the light.

Sira smiled down at him. "Is that interesting? Is it?"

His eyes, so familar a brown, turned at the sound of her
voice. Both arms waved, aimlessly, endearingly. Sira
reached out in answer. The dagger in her hand hummed,
vibrating with the need to drink blood.

Her only thought to keep the danger from him, Sira
hurled the dagger across the room. It bit deep into a tapestry, sliding down under its own weight, cleaving the
weave in two. Sira shuddered to hear the dagger's scream
of frustration as it scraped over stone. It fell with a ringing
tone that abruptly ceased as the brilliant icy heart went
dark.

Sira bent and scooped her infant son into her arms. From
watching Margery, she knew just how to cup the child's
delicate head, knew just how to hold him against her
shoulder so that she might gaze and gaze into his face. He
did not cry but returned her look with innate solemnity.

"There now," she said nearly cooing. "There now. I'm
your mother, little one. You've not seen me before, but I
am going to be with you from now on."

She turned with the child in her arms as the door burst
open, rebounding against the wall into the horrified faces
of the people who pressed forward. Helen led the way,
Lord Robert directly behind her. Their faces were pale,
and everyone gabbled at once.

"Give me the child!" Helen demanded, striding forward, her fingers curved like hooks to snatch Simon away.

Sira held him more tightly, rising on her toes. "Why
should I? He is mine."

"Yours? Yours to kill, you mean? I saw you come up
here with a knife. Where is it?"

"There," Sira said with a lift of her chin. "It is un-
used." Simon whimpered, protesting the tight hold she had
on him. She relaxed it, smiling down at him again, as
Helen scrambled to search where Sira had indicated. She
blasted the clumsy feet of those who had come crowding

into the room, damning those too slow to get out of her
way.

Margery forced her way through the gawking servants
and came to stand before Sira, not even respecting Lord
Robert. "My lady, is all well?"

Sira nodded. "You were right. He is a beautiful child.
Thank you for caring for him while I could not."

" 'Twas my joy to do," Margery said. "He and my
little Emma never minded sharing, and Margery's got
plenty for all."

"Here!" Helen shouted in triumph. Forcing her way
with as many curses back to Lord Robert's side, she held
out the sharp knife. "It's as I said. She came to kill the
child! Will you let her stand there with him? The creature
may take the notion to smother him next!"

Blindly, Lord Robert put out his hand for the knife. He
gazed at Sira with wounded eyes. She said, "Be wary, my
lord. It is honed to a keen edge."

He paid more heed, taking the blade by the hilt from
Helen's hand, trembling as it was with anger. His eyebrows rose as he saw what manner of knife it was. "Is
this diamond?" he wondered, then stared at Sira anew.

"It may well be," Sira said. "It was a gift from my
father."

Suddenly, Lord Robert seemed to realize just how many
interested interlopers stood about. "Get along with you,"
he ordered. "Don't stand about with your ears flapping,
or I'll lay about you tooth and nail!"

The room cleared as quickly as it had filled, except for
Lord Robert, Helen, and Margery. Sira cuddled Simon
closer to her breast. They'd been so hard and painful the
first several days that her antagonism toward her child had
only increased. Now, holding him as he turned his head
this way and that against her, seeking for what she could
not now give, she felt a sorrow that bored through her like
a serpent. In its way, it was sharper than what she felt for
Conn's death. That she could not have helped; this was a
personal failure.

"Is he hungry?" she asked Margery.

"Aye, he shows the signs of it."

Lord Robert said coaxingly, "That's right. Give the babe to Margery to feed. She's the proper one to care for it."

"Him," Sira corrected gently. "I'll come soon, little one."

Margery looked mutinous as she took the infant from Sira's shoulder. Lord Robert had to jerk his head twice in the direction of the door before she started, slowly, toward it. Sira paid no attention to the maidservant's anxiety; she had eyes only for her child as he was carried away.

She felt as though what was left of her heart were leaving with Simon. She realized for the first time what a remarkable organ the human heart was. How quickly it changed, turning from loneliness and despair to a kind of sad joy. Though her life would be empty of Conn's love, there could be another role for her. If only she'd known before, she would not have spent the last weeks wandering, lost and alone, but here, with her child.

She meant to say something of this to Lord Robert, but he had strange glitter in his eye. It was not an expression she believed she had ever seen before.

Lord Robert said in a calm and level voice, "I knew all along you were a witch."

Margery spoke roughly to her husband. "Don't linger, Gandy. Be off with you to King Stephen's army. Find Master Ross and tell him your tale. If he'll not act, then put the matter before the king himself if you must battle every man between you and him!"

Gandy nodded decisively. "Very well, I'm away. Never fear, Margery. I'll kill a hundred horses, but I'll be there in time."

"See that you are, then!" With no more word of love than that, Gandy spurred on through the main gate into the cold dawn. Some of the eager listeners who had watched this tender marital scene raised a halfhearted cheer as he passed. But they glanced up at the manor, remembering Lord Robert, and slunk off to tend their duties.

Margery hurried to the chamber where the babies were, to give her milk to both infants. Then she wrapped her shawl about one and left the other lying in the finely carved cradle. When Adela came in, her face still marked by disbelieving tears, Margery said, "I'll be back in time for his next. Mind you pick him up when he cries."

She stopped in the kitchen for a loaf of bread and hunk of cheese. As a wet nurse to the heir, she was entitled to draw extra food whenever she chose to demand it. No one thought it worth mentioning when she carried the food away instead of eating it on the spot. Nor did anyone bring up the amount she was taking away. Never famous for her good temper, since Lady Sira's imprisonment began, Margery had been even more touchy and prone to take fire than before.

There were two entrances to the great cellar under Hamdry Manor. One was a large wooden grate in the floor of the pantry, off the kitchen. This was the commonly used route, how the cellarer and the butler went up and down a set of wooden steps, bringing out the stores. The other entrance was outside, a pair of double wooden doors set low in the wall, there for emergencies, when many people might come to be fed. Only once in Hamdry's history had there been a siege severe enough to warrant this measure, but everyone had heard the tale from the old men and women who had survived it.

Both entrances were now guarded. But in the kitchen, Margery risked running a gamut of prying eyes and wagging tongues. Outside, there was only the guard, a young man—a boy really—whom Margery had once watched over and cuffed during harvest or planting.

"Good morrow to you, Thomas."

"And to you, Mistress Margery."

"Dreary duty, this."

He nodded. Though he held a poleax with a wicked iron spike, his thin arms and trunk made him an object to be but little feared. He was also dressed like a scarecrow against the cold in every rag and twist that he owned or could borrow. Every single piece flapped as he shivered, either from the cold or from fear. Margery thought a simple *boo* would send him scrambling away.

He said, "They do be sayin' some hard things 'bout my lady."

"Oh, they are true right enow," Margery said solemnly. "Weren't I there? Didn't I see it all?"

Thomas leaned forward. "Did you? I heard tell how she attacked his lordship with a wicked spell and that he ain't right since."

"No, it weren't like that. She didn't do nothing to *him*." She moved back a trifle and he all but overbalanced. "Well, I can't stand 'bout all day gossiping with the likes of you, Thomas. Open them gates."

"Open 'em? What for?"

"What for? Ain't I still her servant? Don't she got to eat?" The babe stirred against her and she joggled it soothingly.

"The steward's been bringing her food."

Who would have guessed Thomas could be so obstinate? She'd been waiting for him to go on duty here, and now he'd turned into a doubting Thomas. Margery straightened up and fixed him with the eye of female authority. If *he* didn't remember all the times she'd clouted him, *she* certainly did. And she was willing to remind him of it in kind.

"She hasn't been eating what Parrish brung her, now has she? He thinks if I brings her food, she might. Lord Robert don't want her starving to death—not under his feet at any rate. Now you open them gates and look sharp!"

He dawdled over the task in a perfectly maddening way while Margery fretted that someone would see them. Fortunately, the cold was enough to keep most of the manor servants indoors where there was warmth and company. When one door scraped a clear spot in the snow, opening just enough to let her in, Margery said, "Good. Now leave it like that so I can see what I'm doing."

"Oh, she's got a candle. Keeps the rats away. Else they'd be nibbling on her, witch or no." His eyes narrowed. "Here, you don't want to take your babe down there. What if she tries to eat it?"

Unable to resist the force of history, Margery reached out and cuffed him across the back of his swathed head. "Ow! What's that for?"

"Teach you to mind your own ways. Now you wait here 'til I come out."

"You give call, and I'll open the door."

"You leave it open. Candle or no, I'll not go down there amongst the rats without a swift way out. I hates rats worse'n fire."

The cellar air reeked of cold-damp and must. Through it all, however, came a strong smell of cheese, mingled with the odor of beer and yes, a stink of rat. The foodstuff was piled around in sacks, barrels, and, in case of cheeses, stacked in racks, gleaming golden in the near dark.

Built out against one wall was a tiny cell with a barred door. Originally, it had held the wines for Lord Robert's table to keep behind a lock what the servants liked to steal best. The wine barrels now shared room with commoner goods. The flickering candlelight that showed through the bars told of the dangerous acquisition concealed there.

"My lady?" Margery called. She glanced over her shoulder. Thomas stood there in the doorway, casting a shadow down into the cellar. "Get away!" she called. "Do you think light can shine through you?" He shrank away, and Margery smiled. It seemed her hand had not lost its old strength.

Shifting the babe onto her shoulder and shushing it, Margery felt in her belt pouch for the key. Gandy had slipped it out of Parrish's pouch when the steward, feeling low over Lady Sira's plight, had drained a drop too much ale at midday. Unlocking the door, Margery opened it. "My lady," she said again, over the squeak of the rusty hinge. " 'Tis Margery, m'dear."

The blanketed figure in the corner moved. "Conn promised me once a bed of straw. It's more uncomfortable than he described." Sira pushed the matted and tangled hair off her face. "I'm glad to see you, Margery."

Awkwardly, because of the babe, Margery knelt on the dirt floor to spread out the cloth that carried the food. The single candle showed all too clearly the smudges on Sira's once creamy face and the bits of straw clinging to her once lustrous hair. Though still rounded from her pregnancy, she'd already lost more weight than she should have.

"Thou can't go on not eating. Here, have some of this."

Sira shook her head. "I can't. It won't go down. I seem to have this strange lump in my throat that nothing can get by."

"Course not. But I've something that'll tempt thee." Margery took the babe from her shoulder, unwrapping it enough to show the tiny face. It screwed up its eyes against the candlelight.

"Oh," Sira said on a long shaking sigh. "Is that . . . Simon?"

"Here, take him."

Sira cuddled the baby close. "I never thought I'd see him again. Lord Robert said—"

"That one! If thou ask me, 'tis himself that has the devil in him, not you. He goes stomping around, talkin' of what he'll do, thus and thus, but I can tell he's not right. It's ridin' him, the black devil. He knows he's done you wrong, and he'll do worse yet, but never get the good of it. If you ask me, he knows it full well, too."

"Margery . . ." Sira began. She was gazing down at the face of her child as though she'd never get enough of the sight. She didn't look up as she said, "I thank you for your faith in me, but I did take a knife into the room. I did intend Simon harm. If I lived forever, I could never do penance enough for that."

"Ah, but thou *didn't* do him harm, did thee? And I'd be guessin' that thee never will in all the days to come."

"No, never. Yet it's little good I'll do him, either. I can't even feed him."

"Don't let that trouble thee. With a bit of help, thou could. Didn't my own dear mother's milk dry up with my little brother? She couldn't nurse him for weeks because of a black cess in her breast. But after the cure, she started

nursing him again and before she could say Robin Good-
fellow, didn't she have as much to give him as ever?''

''Is it possible?''

''If that cow-handed midwife were still here, she'd tell
you no different. Men will tell us poor women this and so
about such things but 'tis the woman's body that knows.''

Sira smoothed Simon's tiny eyebrows with a pensive
finger. ''I won't be able to find out,'' she said. ''I won't
be here. As soon as Father Maynard comes back with the
other priest, they and Lord Robert will be certain to find
me a witch.''

''Still, they won't kill thee. They'll only drive thee out
with cross and fire.'' Margery saw Sira's apprehension.
''Oh, they say a lot of long priestly words, wave a cross
about''—she crossed herself rapidly lest she be thought to
speak lightly of sacred things—''and make thee walk over
the boundary with a couple of hooded men carrying
torches at thy back. Thou art lucky. In some places, they
hang witches . . . not that . . .'' She smiled sheepishly.

''No, I'm not.'' Sira realized she couldn't even say she
was one of The People anymore. She wasn't, not even in
her heart. The moment she'd allowed herself to love her
child, she'd become truly mortal, not just in body but in
the essence of her soul.

Sira said, ''When they drive me over the boundary, isn't
that the same as my never seeing Simon again?'' The
words were almost too painful to speak. The thought of
that separation had been keeping her from eating or sleeping or doing anything but sitting and weeping.

''Not if I'm waiting there with him and a pair of fast
horses.''

''Margery!''

''Margery can do it,'' Margery said in a hurried whisper.
''I can. Didn't I bring this babe out today and not a soul
the wiser? All babies look alike, except to their mothers,
and everyone is used to seeing me carrying my own.''

''What of Emma? You can't leave her.''

''Yes, I can. Gandy and I have it all worked out. He's
gone away to find Master Ross and, failing that, to plead

thy case before the king. He won't get very far, but I expect that. When he comes back, he'll be surprised—or act so—that his wife's gone off with you. He'll get Emma and meet us as we've arranged."

"Lord Robert won't . . . he'll never let us steal Simon."

"He won't be able to find us. Serfs disappear all the time, running off to take their year and a day elsewhere. A year and a day, my lady, means freedom. Freedom for us all."

Sira reached out to clasp her servant's work-worn hand. "Why are you doing this?"

"Gandy says it's 'cause we are servants and must choose who to serve, but I don't think that's natural. I'm doing it because it's what *he* would have wanted. He wanted you to be happy."

"Yes, Conn did want that. I will be happy, somehow." Her eyes were drawn again to the face of her sleeping son, blissfully blowing bubbles with his pursed lips.

Twenty

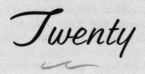

Gandy knew that his biggest difficulty would be finding the army. He asked at every stop, "Where is the king now?"

Some said Stephen had returned to the siege of Oxford where the empress was; others that he'd gone north to Yorkshire to break off a tournament between York and Richmond, such games nothing more than an excuse to gather their own army to bring against him. Still others, when questioned, claimed the king lay ill, in peril of his life, at Northampton.

At last, confused, Gandy dismounted in the midst of a wood. It was warmer here than at home. The snow had all melted away to mud but for where the shadows lived beneath the trees. Taking up a fallen stick, Gandy drew a line pointing north. He made three symbols alongside the line, repeating their meaning to himself.

"A star for Oxford, a cross for Northampton, and my mark for the last. May God guide my choice."

He tossed aside the stick. Spitting into his hand, he smacked the palm with his other fist. The spittle jumped up and Gandy watched keenly to see where it landed, for it was not like a dusty day when the wet mark would be clear.

"Oxford," he said with a decisive nod. He put away

his doubts about the accuracy of this method of divination. It was in God's hands now.

Three days later, he rode his mare into a once-pleasant field, now churned into sticky mud by the passage of many horses and other beasts of burden. He'd passed a couple of great wains, sunk to the axle in mud. A gray mist had settled down under the trees, clinging to the ground. Gandy's physical misery was acute. Water droplets made his hood and gorget heavy as chain mail and irritating drips kept creeping down his back. His boots seemed full of water.

The mist kept the smokes of the camp right down on the ground, so that he felt as though he were breathing nothing but smoke, and it didn't even smell like meat. According to the last several serfs he had questioned, this was the king's encampment. Gandy wished that the mist would lift enough for him to see a standard or some other clue that he had found what he sought.

He hailed the first figure he saw, a ghostly body emerging from nothing. "Greetings, brother. Have I found the king?"

"Nay. He's ill."

"At Northampton—I've heard."

"Then why are you asking me? But I wouldn't be going on there, if I were you."

"Be glad you are not. I must reach the king. The man I must see is with him." Gandy began to turn his horse.

"Oh!" the sentry suddenly exclaimed as though a new thought struck him an almost physical blow. "You can't go yet. I got to challenge you. If you don't know the password, I'll have to take you to the banner knight."

"But tell me first: Does the knight keep a good fire? If he does, I shan't know the password. If I don't get to a fire, I'm like to come down with an ague."

"Awright, then. Friend or foe?

"I'm Gandy of Hamdry, servant to the late knight."

"Oh, his father's dead then? You'd better tell him. He's in the third tent down. Or is it the fourth?"

"Who is?"

"Your master's son." The unseen soldier seemed to think Gandy to be rather stupid not to have gotten this clear yet.

"My master's son is a babe in arms."

"Hush! Don't let him hear you say that. He has a rare bad temper these days."

"But has he a fire?"

"The best in the camp."

The best fire in the camp made an orange glow out of the mist. Gandy could not see the tent, for its white canvas blended away into nothing. He had to dismount and approach before he saw the person who sat before the fire, his mail shirt reflecting the flames as he sharpened his sword with long strokes and cursed in a monotone. "Damn the empress, damn the earl, damn Oxford, and damn this weather!"

"Amen to that!" Gandy said from a full heart.

The knight leapt up. The firelight flickered on his youthful face and his light brown hair. "Gandy? Gandy, by all that's holy! How come you here?"

"By way of my bruised—but never mind that, Master Ross! It is in search of you that I have come."

"Of me?"

"Your father has imprisoned the Lady Sira on the charge of witchcraft. No representations from Father Maynard or any other has an effect on him. He even ordered the good father to bring another priest to Hamdry so that the judgment would not be biased in her favor."

"What, man? Do you rave?"

"If I do, my lord, it is from a sick heart."

Without apparent reason, Ross turned his head and looked into the tent behind him. In a softer tone, he asked, "But what of Helen? Surely she has some influence over my father?"

"No disrespect intended, but the Lady Helen has been the prime witness against my lady. She has stated that she has on many occasions observed the Lady Sira in commune with the"—now he shot a glance behind himself into the curtaining fog—"with the powers of darkness."

"What? Helen said that? That's impossible."

Now Gandy, too, heard a muffled sound from within the tent. Ross sighed. "He's likely trying to get up again. The leeches have told him that if he does not rest, he'll die, but he won't hear of it. I'd better go sit on his chest again. It's the only thing that keeps him quiet."

Gandy followed Ross into the tent, a wild surmise springing into full life in his head. By the light of a guttering handful of tallow dips in a lantern, a big man tossed on a cot several inches too short for him. The dark hair had been cropped so close to his skull that the gleaming skin could be seen. The ribs on his uncovered chest stood out like the joists in a church ceiling. Several wounds of new vividness stood out in puffed and seeping red stripes across his belly, the angriest stitched crudely across with coarse thread. About his thigh was bound a once-white cloth, now black with blood. Even in this cold weather, a few gore-sated flies buzzed drunkenly at the light.

Gandy sank to his knees and pushed the hood back from his head. "How is this?" he asked reverently. "Word came to us that he was dead. Killed in a skirmish of no name and little fame."

"Conn was all but dead when we found him. Not a man in this camp but believed that he was dead. Yet he lived, and lives still, though he only awakens betimes."

"The message came from the king himself," Gandy said.

Ross cursed. "Stephen is careless. He must have told a clerk to send a message. If the clerk obeyed without first ascertaining the truth . . . My God, has my father believed all this time that . . . and poor Sira."

"Poor Sira, indeed. Your father is determined to see her driven from Hamdry. Not even that she has given a son to the name means anything to him." Gandy deliberately held back the details of the crime of which Sira was accused. Margery said she was sure Lady Sira had never meant it, and he'd learned in the first few weeks of marriage the folly of arguing with Margery when she claimed to be sure.

Ross drew the coverlet over his brother, who immediately thrashed about until he was uncovered again. Every movement seemed to cause Ross nearly as much pain as it did Conn. "I try to keep him warm, but he fights me. I cannot devote myself fully to his care, and the others refuse to do such menial work."

"I do not refuse," Gandy said. "I have tended him in such case before."

Ross said, "Then I shall relinquish my command to another; de Laux is itching for the chance to grasp some glory. I shall hasten home and stop my father. As for Helen, she will have much to explain. I will persuade her to unsay what she has said."

"Again, no disrespect, my lord, but how can you stop them? Lord Robert heeds no one."

"He'll heed me. I'm not who I was, Gandy. Death has gone with me into battle, clinging to my stirrup leather. I brought my brother out of the thick of that skirmish and have my own scars to show. I have been knighted on the battlefield by the king himself."

All this was said, Gandy noticed, without pride. A plain list of accomplishments of a plain man recited as simply as a farmer mentions what crops he has planted, Ross added, "I have found that I was made for war, Gandy, perhaps more so even than Conn is. No one will be able to turn me from my purpose. My father will yield."

"Then may God speed you on."

"I shall leave at first light. But come, you have the look of a man who is echoing with hunger. If you can cook it, there's meat a-plenty at the victualer's tent."

"You are well supplied then?"

"Better than the empress, who was eating her shoes at last report," Ross said with a sharp laugh.

"Then I must make some broth for Sir Conn. He does not look as though he has eaten."

"He has eaten some, though I bear twenty bruises for each mouthful!"

Ross said later that it was worth a week at the university of Salerno, famed for medicine, just to watch Gandy go to work. First, he screened the fire outside the tent so that the

heat came in while the smoke drifted away. Secondly, he
triple-stitched Conn's blanket to the bed, pinning down his
powerful arms and preventing him from throwing off the
blanket once again. Then, by clasping Conn's nose in order
to open his mouth, he spooned enough broth down him to
sustain life's flickering ember for another day. This had
the effect of exhausting Conn, sending him into his first
peaceful slumber in three days.

When complimented, the servant said, "I'd rather hear
Sir Conn rail at me than you praise me, Sir Ross."

"So had I," Ross agreed with a smile.

"You'd best get rest if you are to ride tomorrow. As
for me, I shall do well rolled up in a blanket on the ground.
I am tired enough to sleep on a dragon's nest with the
dragon at home!" Then he added, "Never fear, I shall hear
if he needs me."

Conn awoke to the sound of stealthy footsteps. A figure,
its entire body concealed within the folds of a muffling
cloak, stood in the tent opening. Motionless, the figure
seemed to be looming like the shadow of death. Struggling, Conn found himself confined as though he were already encoffined. His gaze fell on the sleeping man beside
his cot, a face and shock of hair that he knew well. But
how had Gandy come here?

Conn called out to waken Gandy, but the man slept on,
unhearing. "Oh, it's a dream," Conn said in relief and
awoke.

He had vague memories of nightmares, horrible scenes
of Sira in deadly danger and of himself unable to stir to
help her. He still felt weak as a newborn kitten and could
not fathom why he was still unable to move though awake.
He took mental stock of his body, then wished he had not.
He knew the feeling of being bound up in his own blood;
pain was familiar to him. The tightness of not-yet-healed
wounds and the reluctant parting of blood-stiffened hair
and bandage, the sick feeling of realization to be sur-
mounted in time by the triumph of survival were known
best by the lucky, and he'd always been lucky.

He turned his head stiffly to look outside in order to judge the hour. With a gasp, he saw that the cloaked figure was still there, breathing out an atmosphere of unspeakable menace. It took one, two steps forward. As the dream feeling swept over Conn, pulling him into another nightmare, he noticed once again that Gandy lay beside him on the floor.

Then the figure put back its cowl. "It's no pleasure to me to be here. All this steel makes me nervous."

"Prince Blaic?"

The prince curled a sardonic lip. "So you do not forget quite everything?"

"Forget?" Conn repeated. His side had begun to burn fiercely, as though flicks of spark and hot ash were falling on his skin.

The prince shook water droplets from his dark gold hair. His deep green eyes glowed like a cat's in the dim light. "You've forgotten your bride entirely."

"I never shall do that. I have vowed—"

"You mortals make too many vows. You vow to your king, you vow to your wives, you vow, you vow, and then when you are tangled in a mesh of your own weaving, what to do but break the bonds! A slice with one of these weapons, and you are free."

"I'm not free," Conn said with some humor. "I can't even get out of bed. I think someone has sewn me into it."

The prince from the Westering Lands came closer still. A bright light seemed to grow from the ornately swirled cloak-brooch he wore at his throat. "So they have," he said. "Why?"

"I must have been delirious. Gandy used to . . ." He glanced down again. "He is here. How did he come here? Or am I still dreaming?"

"Ask yourself if you would be dreaming of me?" Blaic said with a derisive chuckle. With a twist of powerful fingers, he broke the threads that kept Conn motionless. Then the forest-green eyes narrowed in shock. "Never will I understand mortals. Not if I dwelt among them for a thousand years! Why do you take such trouble to get shredded like this when you could do it yourself at home in half the time?''

''We don't do it for fun.'' Conn squinted down at his flat stomach.

''What of your tournaments? Your jousts and your feats of arms?''

''That's for honor.'' Conn caught his breath on a gurgle of anguish as the prince prodded him in the stomach. ''What the devil . . . ?''

''I will undoubtedly regret this the rest of my days, but nevertheless . . .'' The prince reached into the recesses of his cloak and took out a small wooden coffer. He flipped up the lid and took out a pinch of what looked like several strands of dried grass. ''Take three hairs from a dragon's head. Bury it in the heart of a living volcano for a hundred mortal years. Then stew them well in the cup of a dead god in a measure of the finest wine the Living Lands can show.''

''What is it for?''

''Removing hangnails,'' Blaic said, rolling his eyes toward heaven. He laid one each on the most serious of Conn's wounds.

For a moment, nothing happened. Then the hairs seemed to gather themselves together and, with a squeal of joy, they dove deep into his wounds. Conn thought he'd perish just from the pain. He was aware only of the terrible agony in his vitals as those things gnawed their way deeper yet, and of Blaic standing over him with an expression of utter satisfaction. Was this the prince's revenge for Conn's marriage to Sira?

He held onto his consciousness only through the most unrelenting effort. Then, as the pain ebbed, he began to feel very peculiar. He recalled lying back in a steaming hot spring when a young man and feeling the tingle of the bubbles as they rose around his naked body. This feeling was similar, but it was as if the bubbles had gotten into his blood. Could a man be tickled from the inside?

Then he glanced down again at the planes of his abdomen. The wounds were puckering, drawing together. They itched for a moment or two, intensely. The hot red lines faded to pink, then white, then silver, hardly visible. Even the hole in his thigh, where the dragon bristles had not touched, was closing, leaving a shiny white mark. Judging by their appearance and his past, his scars appeared to be wounds five years old, if not more.

Blaic said, "If I had not done that, you would have been dead by morning, for all your devoted man here could have done."

"Then I thank you."

"It is not for thanks that I did it," Blaic said, tossing his head like a proud stallion. "But for her. Do you know what your father means by her? If you do not return to your home, Sira will be beyond your reach forever."

In few words, Blaic told Conn everything. He was not reticent when it came to placing blame. Conn, Lord Robert, even Sira came in for their share. The greatest blame, however, the prince placed on another's shoulders. "Boadach is stumbling in the world of his own grief," he said. "To lose both wife and daughter to mortals, though in different ways, is nearly more than he can stand. He has no thought now but to bring Sira back by whatever means he can use."

"Even the murder of his own grandchild by his daughter?"

"Even so. He does not think of *your* son as being his grandchild. The babe is mortal; Boadach hates your kind; therefore, he hates the babe. The strictures against contact with mortals grow ever more harsh."

"Then why do you care?" Conn sat up, feeling no more soreness in his limbs than on any other morning after a hard riding night.

The prince tightened his lips. He paused, as though judging how much to say. "I loved her with my whole heart," he said finally. "I shall never love another so much. No one believes that." He smiled as though laughing at himself. "For some reason—I believe it is my face—I am not thought to have much heart."

He sobered. "Reach Sira in time, mortal. I fear what the king may do now that he has only succeeded in making her even more of a human being. He may kill her, rather than let her be happy."

"If Gandy is here," Conn said, thinking, "he must have told Ross about all this. Ross is, in all likelihood, planning to leave for Hamdry at first light; I think I shall awaken them now."

He stood up, carefully stepping over Gandy, still soundly snoring on the ground. Conn looked Blaic straight in the eyes. "My thanks to you, Prince Blaic. My house shall not forget this."

"I already *have* immortality," Blaic began. Then an youthful grin broke out on his saturnine features, which were so at odds with his fair hair. "But I can always use a little more."

Conn waited until the prince had vanished again into the mists. Then he shook Gandy awake, put aside his cries of astonishment at his master's remarkable recovery, and said, "What's amiss at home?"

At noon, they halted outside a small village. Gandy didn't recommend entering. "Fleas and cabbage, that's all we'll get."

Conn stood with his back to the fire. "I smell snow in the air."

Ross finished patting out oaten cakes and put them in the coals to bake. "I wonder if it will delay us yet more."

"It can't. It mustn't. Even if Gandy can find the women again, if Sira is driven out of Hamdry, it will be all but impossible to bring her back." He did not speak of his fear that King Boadach might yet lure Sira out of this world. He wanted to find her now, this instant, and every moment's delay was like a lash on his shoulders.

Almost on the word, snowflakes as fat as goose feathers began falling from the sky. Gandy crossed himself as he felt the first cold touch. "There's something not right 'bout this," he muttered to Ross as he plucked a chicken. "Why so many delays? That old man said the river's never in flood at this time of the year, yet we could not cross it. One horse I've known to go lame on any journey, but three in a morning? And even in times of trouble like these, have you ever known serfs to show their teeth to mailed knights as they have to us?''

"No," Ross said. "It seems . . . unnatural." He glanced up at Conn, still standing gazing out into the forest. "What of this healing? I have but little experience of wounds. Yet I declare that my own, taken the same day, are not healed even now, and his were so much more severe."

"I have much experience, too much. It is not natural." Conn turned about abruptly. "We go on too slowly. After we eat, I shall press on tonight."

"Master . . ." Gandy began as though to remonstrate. Then he closed his lips and nodded. "I shall ride on with you. I do not need to sleep." A yawn caught him before he could finish the sentence, yet he did his best to look bright-eyed after it passed.

Ross sighed. "I wish that I had armor between the saddle and my tender regions. Yet I will ride on with you, brother."

Conn dropped into a crouch before them. "I will get on faster alone. Stay here tonight. Come on to Hamdry as fast as you can."

The two men glanced at each other. Ross prodded the fire. "Are you trying to protect us?"

Conn tried to smile reassuringly. "From what? What danger could there be?"

"You tell us, master. We are not fools. We can tell when aught is amiss."

"I know it well, Gandy. Yet there are things no man can understand until he is face-to-face with them. I feel that if I do not arrive soon in Hamdry, I might as well never made the journey."

"But you can only go as fast as Arundel can carry you."

Through the dizzying snow, Conn looked over at his great horse, his head hanging as he pawed the ground for grass. The long head lifted while thickly lashed brown eyes gazed back. There was a moment as of silent communication. "I'll go faster on foot," Conn said in a near whisper.

"Now that's plain madness!" Ross exclaimed.

"No doubt of it."

None of their protests could change his mind. He ate with good appetite. Afterward, he clasped hands with his brother and his servant, looking like snowmen with the flakes encrusting their clothing. "Go into the village," Conn said. "Even fleas are better than freezing."

Flinging his cloak about his shoulders but leaving the opening hanging over his left side so that his sword hilt protruded through the wool, he set off into the depths of the wood.

Whatever malevolent forces that had conspired to hold him back seemed to be in abeyance for the moment. Even the snow grew lighter with every step. Once sure that neither Gandy nor Ross had taken it upon themselves to follow him, Conn began to search for a doorway. He'd seen many of them while traveling in the Living Lands with Sira and Blaic. A cavern might conceal a faerie door, or a tree fallen down against another to form a rough arch. Two rocks tumbled together with a space between or, as under the sea, the ribs and backbone of a long-dead whale made as grand an entrance hall as a king might demand.

So, like a madman, he poked and probed in the woods. Every fallen branch or matted tangle of creeper might conceal the road he sought. Once through to the Living Lands, he would make his way to Sira as fast as thought. If he failed . . . but there was no room in him for failure.

He saw a red fox run across a bank, stop and look at him with strangely self-aware eyes. His mouth was open as he panted. "It's not that way, idiot!"

Conn blinked, but the fox was gone.

A moment later, he could have sworn he understood birdsong. A magpie, the white flags on its wings flirting in the air as it glided down to a tree branch, screamed its oddly melodious screech. "Wasting your time, fool!"

"Even a human ought to know better," chittered a squirrel, sticking a sleepy head out of a comfortable nest.

Conn had enough of being insulted. "Try being helpful," he said, feeling as much a fool and idiot as he'd been called. "Help me."

"Why didn't you ask before?" Blaic, still wearing his long cloak, stepped out from behind an oak. The breeze rattled through its dead brown leaves. "Here, this way, under these roots." He sighed deeply. "I'll come with you so you don't waste any more time."

Then he cast a glance at the sky. "I don't like the look of things. The king has drawn his attention away from you for a while. This means he's focusing it elsewhere. There's only one subject he's interested in now."

"Sira?"

"I fear so. Things may be moving more quickly than I thought. Through the door, man, and hurry."

Time ceased to have meaning. Conn caught glimpses of the wonders of the Lands Beyond. Yet his heart felt no yearning for the beauties and pleasures of The People. Life held no joy anywhere but at Sira's side. Let others turn to sword and fire; he would choose simpler matters. To plant a seed and watch it grow, to improve one's land for a son, to love one woman, to grow old and to die at her side was worth more than all the glories a king held in his gift. When next Stephen called for men of war, he would send whatever payment was demanded and stay at home.

"I hope you mean that," Blaic said. "I could have easily made it a condition for my help. I hope you appreciate that I did not do so."

"I do. So will Sira."

They emerged at the edge of yet another wood, one in which every stick and stone Conn knew, blind or sighted. He could just glimpse the stone walls of Hamdry across the snow-blanketed fields. "Why are we here?" Conn asked. "Are there no nearer entrances?"

"In the name of the One!" Blaic exclaimed. "You mortals are never happy. Sira is near here now. In another instant, you should see . . ."

Barefoot, she wore a thin white rag against the cold. Behind her, two men, hooded in black cloth yet shuffling along sheepishly for all their anonymity, carried torches. Between the two walked a thin, young priest that Conn did not recognize. He read prayers aloud in a ringing, righteous tone. The black smoke swirled around like a monk's calligraphy. Behind the small procession came a crowd of the manor servants and farmers. Some wept. In other faces, Conn read rebellion, while yet more seemed uncertain as to their own emotions. They had grown to love the Lady Sira, yet their lord said she was evil.

Conn had no doubt of his feelings. He rumbled, "Drive *my* wife out with cross and fire? Never in this life!"

Ignoring Blaic's clutch on his arm, Conn stepped out of hiding. He bestrode the path the solemn little processional must take and half-drew his sword. "Halt!"

Pale with cold, Sira sank down on her knees as though they'd suddenly melted away. She put up one hand as though to touch him. "I've lost my mind," she said and bent down to hide her eyes.

The priest stepped forward, his finger holding his place in his Bible. "You cannot interfere," he said readily. "This woman has been properly condemned in the correct form."

From behind him, a pair of bare, burly arms caught the young priest in a wrestling grip. "Be silent, thou puppy! He's the son of the house and just as like to skewer a pip-squeak priest as he would the best swordsman in the world. So speak small, if at all."

"Thanks, Father Maynard," Conn said. He knelt beside Sira, stripping off his glove. Cupping her chin, he forced her gently to meet his gaze. "It is indeed me, my lovely one."

"You're—you're not dead?"

"Shall a man die who has such a wife?" He gathered her in his arms and stood up. It pained him to see her icy, pale feet and to feel her all-but-frozen cheek against his own. "Come. We'll to our chamber where I'll give you hot spiced wine and warm robes until the heat returns to your blood."

"Then hold me tightly," she said against his neck. She

shook back her unbound hair and held her face up for his kiss. Her lips were cold against his, but only for an instant.

Someone set up a cheer. Even the torchbearers pushed back their hoods and gave tongue. But Conn heard the thunder of racing hooves despite the serfs' joy. He turned to Father Maynard and gave Sira into his keeping. Then he strode out, to meet his father, his four-foot sword naked in his hand.

"Do you mean to fight me?" Lord Robert asked, drawing rein fifteen feet away.

"You have done me and mine grievous wrong, Father. You have tried my wife without giving me a chance to champion her. I demand that right now."

"Trial by combat? Impossible. Sentence has already been pronounced. She is to be banished beyond my borders. There she may wander or rot as God allows. As you seem to have cheated death yet again, your marriage to this harlot and witch will be forgotten. Your son by her will be raised as your natural son and as such will be mentioned specially in my will."

"You've thought of everything. I make you my compliments." Lord Robert bowed over his horse's neck. "Except that I am alive, and therefore this woman is still mine. Banish her, and I go, too."

"Brave words, my son, but do you know what she has done?"

"Nothing." Conn looked at Sira with great tenderness. She covered her face with her hands, unable to bear the knowledge in his eyes. He said, "Who knows to what length grief may drive us? Especially when someone we trust leads us astray? Sira, I cannot wait to meet my son."

Lord Robert spoke again. "Then leave this procession to go its way, and return with me. Your son lies in the manor."

"No, he—" Sira started to say.

"Then we shall send for him and be on our way," Conn said.

"Take one step toward that child, and you lose your

head!'' Lord Robert's sword sang as he pulled it free of the leather scabbard at his waist.

But Father Maynard had had enough. He pushed Sira gently into the arms of the startled younger priest and walked with heavy purpose across to Lord Robert. With a sudden reach of his powerful arms, he jerked the baron right off the saddle.

Punctuating his words by rattling Lord Robert like a poppet, he said loudly, ''Now listen, you stubborn dog. Twice you've believed your eldest son dead; twice has God been good to you. Instead of falling on your knees rejoicing, you squabble and decree with no better sense than the foolish royalty that plunge us into war after war. There is your son. Embrace him, or by all that's holy, I'll call down such a blight on you that you'll end by envying Job!''

When the priest released Lord Robert, the baron's face was blue. As he gasped for air, he waved a hand for silence. ''But how can I be certain she will not act so again?''

Sira stepped forward, not even wincing when her bare feet touched the snow. ''I have learned so much,'' she said. Two tears rolled down her cheeks, yet her lips smiled. ''I have seen that love is not just between a man and a woman, as I believed. Nor is it a thing of shame or fear.''

She spread her arms out, encompassing not only Conn but Lord Robert, the torchbearers, the serfs and house servants, the manor, and all. ''Lord Robert, you have acted as you did through love for this manor and my child. Conn left me because he loved his king and his battles—''

''No more,'' Conn said.

She only smiled wisely and went on. ''Margery loves Gandy and her child, but she loves me and mine, too. I love Conn so much that I could think of nothing else when he was gone. I know that is wrong. I shall love Conn 'til I die, but there is more to my life now than him. There is Hamdry. There is my son. I will never do anything to hurt the ones I love. For to hurt one is to mar all.''

She cast a glance into the sky, and only Conn knew the

reason for it. She had hurt someone she loved, hurt him badly. Yet it is in the way of things for a woman to leave her father's home, even if it be a faerie kingdom.

Conn took her cold hand and kissed it. "Let us away home, Father. My bride is cold."

Lord Robert nodded, looking defeated. Sira slipped across to him and kissed his cheek. "Don't be afraid," she whispered. "Simon will grow to love and honor you his whole life long. You shall be connected through him to all the ages of man. In short, immortality."

"That is all that I want," he said. "How did you know it?"

She was about to return a light answer when a sudden wind blew up such sparkling whips of ice that no one had a thought for anything but covering their eyes. Sira found Conn beside her, struggling to remove his cloak for her. She moved against him, burrowing under the wool to find his warmth. "It's my father!" she shouted against the howling wind.

"I thought it might be. He's not going to let you go!"

"He has no more power over me, and he knows it. This is just his last word." As the wind died, she added, "I can forgive him."

On the bank above, Blaic watched with mingled pleasure and bitterness as Sira declared her everlasting love for Conn and the human world. Then a cold thrill told him that he was no longer alone. Knowing fear for the first time in his long, long life, Blaic turned his head with infinite care.

"You have betrayed me," King Boadach said. He stood there in mortal form, burly and strong. Yet his eyes were the yellow gleam of the hungry wolf, and Blaic knew himself to be prey. Beyond him stood the others of The People who were the first and the eldest. Cuar the harpist, Forgall the Wily, and Anat. Her face was wet with tears, but with no more mercy in her than in a stone statue wet with rain.

Useless to deny anything. "Yes, I have betrayed you. But I have done what was right for her."

"That was not for you to decide!" The beastlike growl
became more shrill. Then the king caught the tail end of
his control. "You betrayed not only me but your People.
For that, punishment must be meted out."

"You cannot kill me," Blaic reminded the king. "You
can banish me back to the Westering Lands—no more."

"Kill you? Nay. You will keep your immortality. Much
good may it do you."

Blaic felt it first in his feet. A heaviness, as though he
could not move them if he tried. There was no sensation
of cold, only of unbearable weight. It moved up his legs,
slowly at first but gaining speed moment to moment. Blaic
looked down, saw the gray stone spreading, and knew in
moments he'd never move again. He wrenched his head
up as his spine solidified. Let his last sight be of Sira's
happiness!

Then it was done. Within the stone, Blaic's consciousness was but a flicker, like a candle flame that burned on
despite every wind that blew. Boadach laughed cruelly
with a coldness greater than the north wind's. "There let
him stay forever!"

Behind the king, Anat spoke in a soft, soft voice. "Is it
not against the Law to condemn with magic and not to
leave a loophole?"

"What?" The king swung about on her.

Cuar stepped in front of Anat. "She is entirely right.
The Law is clear."

Boadach breathed heavily. "Very well. Forgall, cleverest of all my People. Think of a loophole. Something unlikely."

The second-eldest of The People thought, rubbing his
chin. "Very well. Speak these words, O king." He conjured a scroll, complete in every detail to the small red
tassel.

Boadach laughed as he read the words aloud. "Nevermore be flesh until a woman weeps over you as Anat
weeps. Nevermore return to your home until you betray
her as you have done your king. Nevermore be with your
People until you are wise as Forgall. Nevermore be free

until you sing like Cuar.'' The king laughed as he vanished in a great swirling wind, followed by the others.

Mayhaps it was this wind that blew the statue over. Mayhaps the ground had been softened by the alternating freezing and warming of the earth. Or, deep within, Blaic's spirit put out one last effort. At any rate, the statue began to lean forward, more and more rapidly, until it fell, tumbling head over base to land within a few yards of Sira and Conn.

The servants, who'd begun to stream back to the manor, ran back to see what had happened. Sira and Conn recognized the face, emerging from the folds of the neatly arranged hood. ''It cannot be,'' Conn said in a low voice.

''Did he help you?'' At Conn's nod, she closed her eyes in pain. ''This is my father's revenge on him. Poor Blaic. I could not love him, you know.''

''He knew that.''

Sira caught back her tears. ''I will not weep for him. He is too brave for tears. But if we could—'' She looked at Conn with hope.

''You men! Come and pick this up! Take it to my garden. There let it have a place of everlasting honor.''

The serfs would not touch it until both priests had sprinkled it with holy water.

A murmured word from Conn sent a messenger hurrying to tell Margery to bring back the baby and the horses from where they waited. Her first question was to demand of Conn, ''And what of Gandy? Where have you left my husband?''

''He'll be here in a day or two.'' Conn reached up to take the squalling bundle from Margery's arms. ''Simon . . .''

He turned to Sira. ''Look . . . he has my eyes.''

''Yes, I noticed that the first time I saw him.''

That night, they lay all three together. Simon slept on Conn's bare chest while Sira could hardly bear to take her eyes off them long enough to sleep. Though she had noth-

ing in her breasts to give her son, she was learning already
how to suckle him. In time, she hoped all would be well.

Conn held her hand, not wanting to wake Simon. Yet
soon he would put his son down in his cradle and take his
wife in his arms. When he looked into her eyes, he knew
the time had come. Yet before returning to her, he opened
the door to their room and checked the hall.

"What are you doing?" she asked. Then asked again as
he bent to look under the bed.

"Making sure Helen isn't under there. Did she truly spy
on you?"

"Yes. I can forgive her for that, but not for failing to
give the alarm when she saw I had that knife. If she had
done so, I should not have been able to come near Simon
until I was sane again. But then," she added in all fairness,
"I should not have fallen in love with him, either."

"I trust Ross will teach her to mind her nose."

Sira laughed warmly. "She will have but little time for
prying in the future. According to her maid, who is cousin
to Margery, Helen is with child. She mistook the signs for
illness and has, in truth, been pregnant since Ross went
away. That is all she wanted, you know."

"What about you?" Conn eased the coverlet back and
slid into bed beside his adored wife. "What do you want?"

She moved against him like a cat asking to be stroked.
He felt her silken warmth and bit back a moan of pleasure.
"War was never like this," he murmured.

"What?"

"Nothing." He rolled over her to take her mouth under
his own. "I estimate that I have missed about a thousand
kisses by my folly. We will have to labor hard to make
them up."

"Hmmm . . . I think it can be done. What kind would
you like first? Hard? Soft? Restrained . . . or wild?" She
suited a kiss to each word.

"I'm not sure. Could you show me again?"

As their lovemaking grew more intent, the jokes faded
until suddenly, as Conn rested poised at the moment of

completion, Sira began to laugh beneath him. He groaned.
"For the love of . . . Sira! What is it?"

"It's only . . . is this our happy-ever-after?"

"I'll tell you in a moment." When she collapsed shud-
dering around him, and he met her delight with his own,
then he whispered, "Yes. Yes, it is."

Author's Note

One of the interesting things about writing a book set so far back in the past as 1141 is that much of what we commonly think of as Medieval hadn't been created yet. The oldest order of English knights—the Order of the Garter—would not be established for two hundred years. Knighthood was still very much a practical matter, that of a man offering his service or the service of a physically able replacement to the personal service of the king. Many of the titles for nobility with which we are familiar are not formalized until the middle of the fourteenth century. Prior to this, any son of a lord was called a lord himself, though the property would pass only to the eldest unless special provision was made in a will. The chivalrous tales of King Arthur had only just begun to be written by Geoffrey of Monmouth in 1136. Even rabbits would not be introduced into England until sometime in the 1300s, when they were imported from France.

Between 1139 and 1153, England was a bone of contention between two warring parties. One was headed by the daughter of Henry I. Commonly known as Empress Matilda, she had married the German Emperor Henry V but was acknowledged as the King of England's heiress. First to proclaim her as such was her cousin, Stephen of Blois. On her father's death, however, Stephen seized the throne. No woman had ever ruled England and most of the nobles were glad to have a strong man in charge. Matilda, however, was determined on her rights. She had married for the second time and borne a son, who would be Henry II, first of the Plantagenet kings.

The factions of Matilda and Stephen warred for fourteen years, with first one victorious and then the other. The law of the land was violence. It was for good reason that these are the years the chroniclers say that Christ and His angels slept. Only when Stephen's own son Eustace died in 1153 did Stephen agree to accept Henry Plantagenet as his heir. The war was finally over. Stephen himself only survived another eleven months.

Matilda lived to see her son king though she never returned to the country she had fought to conquer for him. Until her death, she had a beneficial influence over her sometimes hot-headed son, an influence shared by his wife, Eleanor of Aquitaine.